THE STUNTMAN AND THE SWORDMASTER

Love Regency Style

ROSEMOUNT MANOR
BOOK IV

LOUISA CORNELL

Chapter One

TEDDY LEANED A SHOULDER AGAINST THE HEARTH MANTLE AND grinned at Eleanor Witherspoon, headmistress of the little *experience* director Erik Wentworth thought was absolutely necessary to the authenticity of his period film, *A Matter of Honor*.

"Teddy, you are *such* an ass!" she ended their whispered tete-a-tete and turned to go.

"Careful, Eleanor. Your American is showing. A Regency lady would never—"

"Oh, fuck you, Mr. Rousseau," the tall redhead retorted over her shoulder.

"Is that an offer?" Teddy grinned at the surreptitious hand gesture she shot him behind her ornate ivory and lace fan.

She crossed the drawing room to join the rest of the participants in her Regency boot camp, as they'd all taken to calling the last couple of months at the Duke of Turra's estate in the Highlands of Scotland.

Doing his utmost to convince the entire world he was a complete ass intent on crawling into bed with every beautiful woman he met, was all laughs and lollies when they believed him, but now, after over thirty years of wanting to believe the image he presented to the world was the real him, Teddy Rousseau wasn't quite so certain. *Bullshite!* He'd managed to convince everyone but himself.

Being stuck at this ridiculous Regency boot camp that had turned into the bloody Love Connection didn't help. Three couples, perfect strangers before this little experiment at Rosemount Manor, had married or become engaged in the past two months. This morning, news had come from the Duke of Turra's hunting lodge on the far side of the Rosemount estate that Anna Chase, author of the hottest Regency romance novel in ten years and the third woman Teddy had set his sights on, had accepted the proposal of Hadrian Cross, literary critic for the *New York Times*. Any man who could convince a woman to marry him after he'd given her book a scathing review must be packing something more powerful than a big pen.

Bella Stepford halted in her stroll across the room at the hearth near Teddy. "What do you make of our Miss Chase and Mr. Cross's engagement, Mr. Rousseau?"

Bella Stepford asked an innocent question, and Teddy would answer her in kind. She was a sweet woman, brilliant designer, and period film costumer, and as she was the best at her craft, and he was the best at his, they'd been thrown together too frequently for him to snap at her—which was exactly what he wanted to do.

"A publicity stunt?" He gave her his most sincerely inoffensive smile. "I'm beginning to think this entire experiment in Regency living has been nothing but one of Wentworth's publicity stunts to promote this film before it debuts."

"An engagement? How could something so romantic be a publicity stunt?" Dressed as a Regency-era matron of means, the feathers in Miss Stepford's updo coiffure nodded in rhythm to her always animated and dramatic speech. Teddy repressed the urge to roll his eyes.

"*Two* marriages *and* an engagement? In the space of a few weeks? A bit much, don't you think?"

"Come now, Mr. Rousseau. You and I have been in this business for more than a minute. People fall in love on movie sets all the time." She took the glass of sherry one of the footmen offered her from his silver salver of before dinner drinks.

Teddy took a glass of the whisky distilled on the estate and knocked it back in one quick swallow. "Movie sets, yes? This, whatever it is?"

He waved his empty glass around to encompass the elegant drawing room filled with people in period costume. Women in elegant Regency evening gowns and gentlemen, himself included, either in silk knee breeches or formal kilts who had all been living with no electricity, no internet or cell phones or computers, no running water, and eating period food for months now. The entire stay had been like no film he'd ever consulted on, which was saying a great deal. Teddy had instructed actors on the use of period weapons on sets all over the world.

"I take it you have not enjoyed Miss Witherspoon's Regency boot camp?"

"I fear not. Primitive living is *not* my cup of tea by any stretch of the imagination."

"Is it the primitive living, or is it that every time you have shown interest in a young lady some other gentleman has swept her away?"

"The world is full of young ladies, Miss Stepford."

"Indeed, especially now more people have joined our little band of Regency campers." She glanced around the room. "Although I don't see many of them here this evening."

Teddy took in their sumptuous surroundings. Spring in

Scotland meant lit and burning fireplaces, especially at night in this monstrous manor house. The vaulted ceilings inspired awe, particularly this one with the scenes from Greek mythology painted in large panels framed with exquisite gold filigree-work, but they also made large rooms like the duke's formal saloon hard as hell to keep warm. The thick Aubusson carpets, even at two hundred years old, managed to keep the chill of the stone floors at bay. The silk brocade upholstered furniture and the heavy mahogany pieces scattered about the room did all they could to convince the occupants they were in another era, one of genteel manners and perfect romance.

Perfect romance? What rot!

"I believe they were told they had to stay in the village if they didn't want to live Eleanor's Regency regimen. I doubt we'll see them except during the day when they're here prepping for the film. Just as well, as far as I'm concerned. Those people are day laborers at best. They have no business hobknobbing with actors and artisans like you and I."

"Such a snob, Teddy." She slapped his arm with her fan. "Oh, look! That stuntman fellow is joining us for dinner."

"Yes." He did his damnedest to sound utterly bored. "As I understand it, Eleanor insisted. I haven't the foggiest idea why. The Regency equivalent of having the lord of the manor dine with his coachman, don't you think?" He pretended a sudden interest in the Stubbs painting over the carved marble mantel of the fireplace at their end of the drawing room.

"I've never seen a coachman quite like Mr. Salazar." Good Lord, the woman had to be sixty if she was a day, and she fairly purred the man's name, and the man in question couldn't be more than…thirty-five at most.

"He's a stuntman, Bella. One is hardly an artist when all

one does is fall off horses or jump out windows. Very little skill required for that. Just muscle."

"Depends on whether you want to break your neck or not."

The British accent, with the hint of American Cajun only Teddy might discern, forced him to turn around and adopt his normal expression of amused disdain. "You would say that, Arneaux. Men like Salazar make heroic types like you look good."

The American action star, cast in the most sought-after role in the history of period films, and only God knew why, offered Teddy another glass of whisky. "Bas Salazar is the best stunt coordinator in the business. Sumbitch is the reason I'm alive, in reasonably good shape, and still looking good." He raised his glass. "*Sláinte!*"

"Sláinte." Teddy sipped the whisky this time.

With deliberate care, he ignored the group gathered around Eleanor Witherspoon and the Duke of Turra. He didn't have to look. He'd been the outsider at Eton and again at Oxford. He was the outsider on most movie sets. Teddy wouldn't lie to himself and say he preferred things that way, but neither life nor people did what you wanted them to do with any regularity.

A deep, boisterous laugh rolled across the drawing room. Instinct drew his attention to the group that, along with the overbearing Miss Witherspoon and the pompous Duke of Turra, included the actress Lily Randolph and her new husband, Lord Lachlan Innes, the duke's brother. Close by, stood Arneaux's wife and private Regency coach, Dr. Samantha Higgins, along with the duke's steward, Angus McGinty, and the boot camp's dance instructor, Sylvan Goode.

None of them, however, were responsible for the dark rumble of laughter nor the boisterous atmosphere of the pre-dinner gathering. Towering over them all and at least a few inches taller than the six feet plus heights of the duke and his brother, the stunt coordinator in a Regency shirt, neckcloth, jacket, and a formal kilt appeared to be intent on entertaining the entire party. A muscled clown. Eleanor's Regency boot camp had lacked all but that. Now, her little ensemble was complete. Perfect.

The duke's butler, Abercrombie, stepped into the drawing room and announced dinner. Teddy hung back to escort Bella into the dining room. As Eleanor usually made certain to seat him at the end of the table farthest from the duke, he had no reason to hurry to the front of the line. Unfortunately, he had no control over which side of the table he'd end up on, and he didn't fancy being seated across from just anyone.

Thank God he'd drawn Sylvan Goode and Samantha Higgins, now Samantha Arneaux. They both had the wit to make entertaining conversation and the good manners not to openly express their opinions of him when his frankness might, just *might*, deserve censure. Bella Stepford had the sort of inane chatter someone could either engage in or acknowledge with a series of noncommittal noises.

Through the lobster bisque and the fried sole courses, Teddy kept his attention on his end of the table. Difficult to do when the conversation beyond his little group had a variety of levels and a great deal of laughter. His dinner companions no doubt attributed his reticent attention to his dinner as a reaction to Anna Chase's engagement announcement. Idiots. In order for his heart to be broken, he'd have to have allowed the imaginary organ to become engaged, something that hadn't occurred since he was sixteen and an idiot himself. His heart belonged to his work, which resulted in his reputation as—

"The best swordmaster in the business, or so I've heard."

A broad, bass voice with a hint of a not-quite-Spanish accent rose over the polite volume of their normal dinner conversation.

Every head at the table turned toward Teddy. Really? *Now* they wanted a response from him? Of course they did. Their new pet celebrity had asked the question, and Eleanor indicated with her bright green eyes and butter-wouldn't-melt-in-her-mouth expression that she fully expected Teddy to participate. He wiped the corners of his mouth with his napkin and finally turned his attention to the man seated to the right of the duke. Poor Bella must have had one hell of a trial fitting this man in the shoulder-hugging jacket and silk breeches of the Regency era. The black suited him in a sort of Zorro kind of way. It matched his hair, but the paleness of his complexion and the light blue of his eyes made the white shirt and neckcloth appear all the brighter.

"I'm sorry, Mr. Salazar, have we worked on a film together before this one?" Teddy asked.

The man didn't flinch, only smiled in that supercilious way Teddy had pegged from the moment Eleanor had introduced him to their little band of Regency campers a week ago.

"We haven't had the pleasure, but your reputation precedes you, Teddy," the muscle-bound smartass replied. "I look forward to working with you."

"I hardly think our paths will cross that much. I'm in charge of weapons instruction, and you will be—"

"Falling off horses and out of windows?" The stuntman nodded at the footman's subtle offer of more wine. "Actually, Wentworth has asked me to choreograph all the battle and combat scenes, so I asked Miss Witherspoon if I can participate in your weapons classes. I anticipate your instruction will be most beneficial. Danny says he's learned a lot from you."

Bloody hell. Teddy had a hellacious time deciding which blistered his bacon more—that the man had overheard his conversation with Bella, that Eleanor had volunteered his services without asking, or that Danny Arneaux had suddenly decided to sing his praises.

"Mr. Arneaux had a great deal to learn. I doubt I can teach you anything despite Miss Witherspoon's generous offer."

Teddy shrugged against the trickle of sweat down his back. He refused to even think about the sudden flush of heat to his face. Perhaps the warmth came from the plate of roast beef, potatoes, and carrots the footman, Robbie, had this minute placed before him. He needed the calories. Working with swords and guns all day burned fat better than a pill from a diet doctor. These Regency dinners would kill most men, but not one who did the work he did and kept the secrets he kept.

"I guess we'll see in the morning." Salazar took up his knife and fork and essentially dismissed Teddy. "This food smells delicious, Your Grace."

"Mrs. Gordon will be pleased to hear it." The duke studied Teddy for a moment and then turned to speak to Abercrombie.

Time to finish his meal and get the hell upstairs. This entire misadventure had suddenly turned tedious. Teddy grew wearier by the minute. If the money wasn't so damned good and his reputation for getting the job done so important, he'd pack his bags and head back to Hampstead Heath. The glamor of working on the most important period film in a decade had lost its appeal. Or maybe he'd had his fill of pissing in a chamber pot and bathing in a copper horse trough in water that was lukewarm by the time he finished his bath.

"Care to tell us what that was all about?" Samantha asked

as she turned away from the head of the table and leaned toward Teddy.

"Not particularly, Mrs. Arneaux." He took a bite of his roast beef and glanced toward the head of the table. Dammit! Salazar met his gaze and raised his glass in salute. Teddy refused to look away first. The last thing he needed at this point was to get into a pissing match with yet another of the men involved in Eleanor's experiment. At least this time, there wasn't a woman involved. He didn't need another actor-type punching him in the nose. Although, he and Arneaux had made their peace at this point. Eleanor said something to the stuntman, and he returned his attention to her. *Wonder what the duke will make of that?*

"Teddy, you really should at least *try* to be nice to people. We're all going to be working on this film together for months on end." Samantha had grown more lovely since her marriage to her American actor. Teddy had known her a long time, and the Cajun had softened her edges. Lucky girl. She wore Regency clothes as if born to them.

"I wasn't aware I wasn't being nice."

Samantha snorted and rolled her eyes, then returned her attention to her dinner.

"You never are, poor dear." Bella patted his arm. "Aware, that is. All part of your charm, isn't it, Mr. Goode?"

"Without a doubt," the dance instructor said. "I suspect our Basque friend can take anything Teddy cares to dish out and then some. He doesn't strike me as the fragile type. Very self-assured, that one."

"One man's self-assured is another man's arrogant." Teddy's declaration met with dead silence at their end of the table.

Samantha snorted, snickered, then laughed out loud. Bella and Sylvan joined her until Teddy had no choice but to laugh with them. He owned his arrogance, wore it as a badge of honor. He'd worked his ass off to become the best at what he did. That gave him the right to be....

Why the devil did Salazar keep staring at him? *Do I owe him money?*

This time, Teddy did look away. He cocked his head toward his end of the table as if Samantha and Bella's conversation about how to make syllabub, tonight's dessert, intrigued him. He played the part so well, he ate the entire dish of the disgusting confection, and he didn't taste a bite. He *hated* syllabub. The rich, sweet cloy of the dessert's taste forced him to sit at the table with the rest of the men once the ladies retired to the drawing room to organize the night's card games. The customary glass of brandy the duke offered helped to wash the nasty taste out of Teddy's mouth.

The after-dinner conversation swirled around him. He sipped his brandy and muttered brief answers to Sylvan's questions. For some reason, the entire day piled in on him at once—the announcement of Anna and Hadrian's engagement at breakfast this morning and the appearance of Salazar and his stunt crew at the morning's weapons practice. They'd watched, talked, and joked through the entire two hours, but had not volunteered to participate. Now Salazar wanted to train with Arneaux and those of the duke's employees who had volunteered to help?

Then this evening, after a week of living and dining in the village, the stuntman had elected to move into Rosemount Manor, and Eleanor seemed determined to include the man in all her Regency activities. Everyone had a role in their group. Teddy was the arrogant jerk, and he relished his role. Despite the changeable existence his chosen profession dictated, he liked order. He didn't do well with change. His was a carefully planned out life. He needed that, for reasons he had no intention of ever revealing to a single soul.

The duke rose from his chair, the signal they were to join

the ladies at the whist tables the servants had set up in the drawing room. As the men filed out, Teddy hung back. It had been a long while since he'd had the world-on-fire sensation that came before a panic attack. This wasn't exactly the same, but close enough. His head throbbed. He broke out in a sweat. Bloody hell! A quick turn to the right once he exited the dining room, and he headed for the main staircase. Tonight someone else would have to play the jerk. He needed peace and quiet and time to think. He'd never considered eight in the morning early a day in his life. Tonight? Too damned soon by far.

He climbed to the second floor and started down the corridor to his bedroom. With luck, one of the maids would have already stoked the fire for the night. Someone else might be impressed with the big antique four-poster bed with its heavy velvet bed curtains and thick quilts and duvets, but not him. Even with the huge fireplace, the room, filled with furniture to make an auctioneer from Sotheby's weep, was never warm enough to suit Teddy. He preferred his renovated farmhouse in Hampstead Heath with its Tudor look and every mod con imaginable.

"No cards tonight, Mr. Rousseau?" Robbie approached down the corridor from the opposite direction.

"Not tonight, Robbie. I'll let them recoup their losses before I take their money this time."

Robbie grinned. "Inordinately kind of you, sir. Is there anything I can get for you?"

"No. I'm good. Shall we see the ghost tonight, do you think?"

"Nae, not likely. Weather's too fine. She prefers the storm. 'Tis her nature."

Teddy shook his head. "As you say." He didn't really believe in Rosemount's resident ghost. He hadn't seen her, but he liked to tease the servants about her.

"What ghost is that?"

Fuck! What the hell was *he* doing here?

Teddy and Robbie turned to face Bas Salazar as he joined them in the corridor. He'd wasted no time in shedding his jacket and neckcloth. Not that Teddy blamed him. *Much.*

"The Innes Witch, sir. Excuse me, sirs. Good night." Robbie, the traitor, hurried toward the staircase.

"The Innes Witch?" Salazar cocked an eyebrow and stared at Teddy expectantly.

"Local legend. Innes is the duke's family name. The first duke fell in love with the wrong girl, a midwife healer whose mother hailed from the Caribbean. His mother got rid of the girl in a particularly nasty way, drowned her as a witch."

"Nice mother."

"Well, according to the legend, she was right. The Innes Witch supposedly put a curse on all the future Dukes of Turra that they will never know happiness in marriage. Supposedly, she shows up here in the house and around the ruins of the original castle doing the haunting bit."

"Have you ever seen her, Teddy?" The man's use of Teddy's first name began to annoy Teddy. A lot.

"I don't believe in that sort of nonsense, do you?"

"In the power of love to survive even death?" The stuntman stared at him for a moment. "Absolutely."

"Well, maybe you'll see her. Everyone else has, or so they say. Screaming and running up and down the corridor in the middle of the night. You're not a screamer are you, Mr. Salazar?" What the *hell* made him ask that?

"Not unless the occasion calls for it. Ghosts don't bother me."

"What about snakes?" Oddly enough, the edges of his panic attack had subsided. Strange.

"Are there snakes in Scotland?" Salazar's voice held a tinge of amusement.

"There is one rather large one here in the manor. Miss Witherspoon has a pet python. Rumor has it, she keeps our cell phones and computers in its habitat in her room. Damned thing crawled into bed with Arneaux not long after we arrived."

"What?" The man's eyes widened. Then he grinned. Then he started to laugh, a loud, boisterous, completely unfettered laugh. He bent double, his hands braced on his thighs.

Teddy's entire body went on alert. Nerves fired. Blood heated. A shiver went down his spine. He had to get away. Now! He took the two long steps to his bedroom door and grabbed the door latch. A hand, long-fingered and strong, clamped onto his shoulder.

"I'll see you in the morning, yes?"

He refused to turn around. "Yes. Nine o' clock. Right after breakfast."

The hand tightened on his shoulder and then was gone. "Good night, Teddy." Salazar walked a few steps down the expensive Turkish carpets and went into the room next to Teddy's.

It took three tries to raise the latch before Teddy practically fell into his room and closed the door behind him. He fell back against the heavy oak slab and slid to the floor. The faint scent of some earthy cologne lingered in his nostrils. He wrestled out of his evening jacket and tossed it across the room. Didn't help. His skin still burned where Bas Salazar had touched him. His carefully crafted persona, the one that had served him well, splintered in his mind, tiny cracks only he might see.

He knew it the minute he'd first laid eyes on the big Basque stuntman. Like one of the neon signs in Piccadilly, big, bold lights flashed over and over in his mind.

Danger. Danger. Danger.

Chapter Two

THE BED WAS FAR TOO COMFORTABLE. BAS HAD SLEPT ON SO many movie set cots, RV pullouts, and hotel beds in the last ten years he'd forgotten what the caress of a truly luxurious mattress did for a man. Then why the hell had he slept so little last night? He tossed the stack of covers back and sat up on the side of the huge antique bed. One thing Robbie got right. Closing the bed curtains on the sides away from the fireplace and leaving those closest to the hearth open helped to create a nice warm cave so long as the fire burned, which it had apparently stopped doing at least an hour ago.

Bas stood and walked to the heavy oak wardrobe across from the foot of the bed. He knocked half the clothes off their hooks in search of the heavy brocade robe Eleanor had shown him yesterday when she'd introduced him to his *Regency* wardrobe. He found the robe and winced. Somewhere, a floor to ceiling window was missing its curtains. He drew the robe on and tied the belt. The costumer, Miss Stepford, had to have used yards of fabric to construct the floor length *dressing gown,* as she'd called it, big enough to fit him.

His body was built to take a pounding, *not* to look like Mr. Darcy. Teddy Rousseau had the look of a Regency romance hero, or maybe one of those Highland warriors, all lean muscle and lithe form.

And…the reason he'd gotten very little sleep came back to him. Bas had met the film's swordmaster when he'd arrived at Rosemount Manor to start mapping out the stunts for the film, *A Matter of Honor*. His reaction to Teddy Rousseau had been visceral and erotic as hell. He'd chalked it up to the man being the complete opposite of his usual type.

Mr. Rousseau wore his long hair in a period film style, tied back with a thin, black grosgrain ribbon. He was British for God's sake. An arrogant bastard to boot. He had sharp, harsh features drawn with a delicate touch. Hard gray eyes. He'd convinced everyone around him he was straight on steroids and after every attractive woman within a ten-mile radius. Checked all the boxes on the hetero hound dog checklist—which was the first red flag on Bas's horizon.

Teddy was trying too hard.

Bas had dismissed him. He wasn't so desperate for a movie set sex partner he'd crawl into the back of a closet to find one. Who the hell had time for that? His decision would have been fine if the attraction hadn't kept at him like a damned song that wouldn't stop playing in his head. Then he'd made the worse mistake of all. He and some of his stunt crew had decided to watch one of Teddy's weapons classes. The man had a right to be arrogant. His skill with swords was a thing of beauty. He went from conceited prick to ancient warrior in a matter of seconds once he had a sword in his hand.

Oh well. Time to start the day. Bas went to the hearth and began to load the fireplace with wood from the brass bucket filled for that purpose. He'd added some kindling and managed to use the tinder box to light the fire when he heard the door creak open.

"Ye keep that up, and I'll be out of a job, I will."

"Morning, Robbie," Bas said without looking over his shoulder at the footman. "Trying to get some heat on all these broken bones of mine." Bas dropped into one of the low-set leather chairs in front of the hearth. He stretched his legs out and rested his feet on the bricks as close as he could to the flames.

Robbie set a tray on the table next to Bas's chair, then went to the wardrobe to select Bas's clothes for the day. He wasn't used to being waited on, but Eleanor had assured him it was all part of the experience. So far, he wasn't impressed with the life of a Regency gentleman. The rich, dark aroma of coffee that drifted from the silver pot on the tray, however, did impress him. He filled the dainty tea cup with the brew and drank it down so fast it nearly scalded him. He filled the cup again and held it between his hands, terrified he'd crush the delicate china.

"Arneaux is right. You are a lifesaver."

"Aye, well don't be putting it about that I'm robbing the duke's coffee stores, or Mrs. Wallace will have us all three in the dungeons."

"The housekeeper? She seems so sweet." He sipped the coffee and closed his eyes.

"Let her catch ye gossiping about the guests or pilfering from Himself's larder and ye'll see how sweet she is."

Bas opened his eyes in time to see the young man shudder. "Himself?"

"The duke."

"Ah. Does the duke know you're gay, Robbie?"

"Oh, aye. He's known me all me life. Of course, he knows."

"He's never given you any trouble?"

"Has he given ye any since ye been here?"

Bas laughed. "As a matter of fact, no. Not even a raised eyebrow."

"Then there ye have it."

"But I'm not sure he even knows I'm gay."

"Trust me. Miss Eleanor's minions make certain she knows everything about every person here. And if she knows, he knows."

"Hmm. I suppose so." Bas finished his coffee and placed the cup as carefully as he could back on the tray.

"No one here will give ye any trouble, sir. Of that ye can be sure."

Bas pushed himself out of the chair and stretched his arms overhead. He cracked his neck, first one side and then the other. "Do I look like the sort of man *anyone* would give any trouble?"

"Point taken." Robbie grinned. "Let's get ye dressed for breakfast. Miss Witherspoon will have me hide if ye'r late."

"Please tell me I'm not wearing silk today."

"No, sir. Buckskin breeches, linen shirt, neckcloth, and a blue wool hunting jacket. And stockings and boots."

"Doesn't sound too bad."

He'd done his time in period films, not this period, but others so he was used to standing and letting costumers twist and turn him to get him into clothes. Something about this outfit made him feel like a combination stuffed sausage and condemned man. Robbie was an efficient valet. He had Bas completely dressed in what seemed like minutes. But when Robbie stepped back to admire his handy work, he frowned.

"I think you'd better wear the drawers," he said.

Bas pointed at the thick binder on his bedside table. "According to the handbook Eleanor gave me, gentlemen didn't wear drawers." He stepped in front of the large free-standing mirror next to the bedroom door. Eleanor had called it a cheval glass. "Why do I need the drawers?"

"Um…." Robbie dipped a quick glance at Bas's crotch.

Bas followed his gaze. "These pants don't leave much to the imagination, do they?"

"They're not pants. They're breeches and unless you want to spend the entire day thinking of England, you need to wear the drawers."

"Thinking of…. Smart ass. Fine. Give me the drawers. They'll be warmer anyway."

"Ye'll be safer too. Without them, the women will be chasing ye down to convert ye, and the men will be throwing ye in the loch with an anvil around yer neck."

"*Ixo!*" Bas shoved at the young man's head.

"Basque for 'shut yer gob'?" Robbie shook his head and let Bas use his shoulder to prop on as he stepped into the drawers and then the breeches.

"Something like that. Question. If Eleanor knows all about us, how did she miss Teddy? Or did we miss it?"

"Oh, we didn't miss it. Ye and I are the only ones who didn't. Who ye are is out there. Mr. Arneaux knew."

"We've known each other a long time."

"Aye. And ye'v never had to hide, have ye?" Robbie looked him up and down.

"Not since I was very young. What has that got to do with anything?"

"I think Mr. Rousseau's been hiding his whole life. He's wicked good at it too. The betting pool is one hundred to one against so far. He's hidden so well, he's hidden who he is from himself. Poor man."

"Betting pool?" Bas gave the footman his least intimidating glare.

Robbie ducked his head and hurried to open the door into the corridor. "Best hurry, sir. Ye'll be late for breakfast."

"I *will* find out." Bas hurried after him and closed the door. He caught up to the young man in three strides as they tread the ancient-looking rugs that covered the stone floors that led to the staircase. "What about you, Robbie? Were you ever as repressed as Rousseau?"

"Aye, sir. To the point I came close to doing meself in." He kept walking.

Bas grabbed Robbie's arm at the top of the stairs. "What the hell, Robbie?" His heart went ice cold. He'd lived through friends' suicides, either deliberate or by slow degrees. This kid was only twenty years old. "You don't feel like that anymore, do you?"

"Nae, Mr. Salazar. I told the right person." He hooked his thumbs in the waistband of his kilt and shrugged. "She saved me. Set me straight right quick."

"Good. Good." They started down the stairs together. "If it's not too personal a question, who saved you?"

"Me Gran. I tried too hard to be something I wasn't, and she saw me. Ye know, saw me."

"I do know."

"Told me a fish will nae be a bird no matter how high he jumps out of the water. She said all I needed to do was be the best fish I can be. And if that wasn't good enough for anyone, fuck 'em!"

"I like your Gran. Sounds like a wonderful woman."

"As me Gran, there's nae better. As me boss, she can be a right pain in the arse."

"Wait." Bas stopped him just before the double doors into the dining room. "Robbie Wallace. The housekeeper? Mrs. Wallace is your *amona*?"

"Me father's mam. Got me this job, she did. Taught me to

be proud of who I am." He opened the doors and stepped aside for Bas to enter. "Och, she's giving me the eye. I'm off."

He slid into the room and sidled around the walls to reach the buffet spread out on the two long sideboards. One of other footmen, Dougal, handed Robbie a large empty serving dish so he could escape through the inset door, which he'd told Bas led to the kitchens. Dougal's action reminded Bas of some of the younger guys on his stunt crew. They looked out for each other.

Bas took in the room. Talk about a bull in a china shop. Dinner last night had been bad enough. This morning, he was expected to pick up one of the duke's thin porcelain, not to mention *expensive* plates, and manage to load the damned thing with food without dropping or breaking it. Someone had already set the table with an army of silverware and half a dozen antique crystal glasses of all shapes and sizes at each seat.

Why the hell had he thought a move into the manor house and a few weeks living as a Regency gentleman was a good idea? The answer stood at the buffet deep in discussion with Lily Randolph.

"Is something amiss, Mr. Salazar?" Mrs. Wallace, dressed in the black wool dress and kind of serious frilly white cap of a period housekeeper, walked up behind him.

He turned and smiled. "Not a thing in the world, *senora*." He bent down and kissed her cheek.

The older woman gasped and clasped one hand over the spot. Flustered, she glanced around the room to see if anyone had seen. "What on earth was that for?"

"For being you." He gave her a little bow.

"Och, and who else could do the job?" She fidgeted with her skirts and tilted her head up and to the side to study him.

"Not another woman in the world. Your grandson adores

you, you know." He nodded toward the buffet where Robbie had brought out another silver serving dish.

"Silly lad." She gave the room another quick look and stood on her toes to kiss his cheek.

"And what was that for?"

"For turning him down. Thank you."

Bas's face warmed. "Thank you for teaching him the sense to accept a refusal gracefully."

"Oh, don't mistake me. If ye were ten years younger, I'd have ye handfasted to him in a minute. And if ye were twenty years older, I might make ye an offer myself. Now go on with yerself and have some breakfast before it's cold."

"Yes, ma'am."

Bas ran his finger under the neckcloth Robbie had tied, but he suspected the heat around his neck was from a good old-fashioned blush. He walked a strategic path to the second of the sideboards loaded with food and picked up one of the pretty blue and gold patterned plates. Damn, the food smelled delicious. He served himself a large spoonful of the scrambled eggs, then the fried potatoes. Next came a big hunk of steak and some bacon.

"Did I just see you *kiss* Mrs. Wallace?" Eleanor held out her plate for him to put some bacon on it.

"A gentleman never tells, Miss Witherspoon."

Bas caught movement out of the corner of his eye. Teddy had ambled, full plate in hand, to study the painting over the black marble dining room mantel. He did this a lot—separated himself from the group when the conversation got too boisterous, too happy. No, Bas and Robbie hadn't made a mistake, but what they didn't know was what it would take for Teddy to—

"You need to take that plate to the table, Mr. Salazar. I'm going to see Robbie about a bet." Eleanor gave him a weird look and glided off, elegant in her green and bronze striped gown.

Danny Arneaux stepped next to Bas as he strode to the table, as if summoned.

"Does everyone in this episode of *Regency House Party* bet on everything?" Bas asked.

Danny snorted. "Pretty much. What the hell do you know about *Regency House Party?*"

They sat down next to each other to eat their breakfast.

"After that unfortunate waterfall stunt in your film last year, I was stuck in a rehab hospital in Maui. I accidentally put it in my Netflix queue. I binge-watched the whole series. Are you in on the Teddy Rousseau betting pool?"

Danny swallowed a mouth full of eggs. "I plead the fifth."

"Do you really want to piss off the man who can make you fall off a building *and* make it look like an accident?" Bas tasted the potatoes, groaned, and took a second bigger forkful.

"Do you really want to explain that accident to my wife?" They both looked toward the head of the table where Samantha was giving McGinty, the duke's bear of a steward, a hard time. The man looked terrified.

"*Hell,* no," Bas mumbled around his food. He washed a piece of steak down with a swig from the cup of tea Dougal had poured for him. He grimaced, and Danny laughed. "I like her, Arneaux. She's perfect for you. I hope you know how lucky you are."

"Tell myself that ten times a day."

Teddy sat down next to McGinty and joined in the conversation with Samantha. From the animated hand motions the three of them used, the day's weapons lesson had to be the topic of conversation.

"Tell me," Bas said, "what's this weapons class going to be like?"

"Oh, he'll try to kill you, but you'll learn your ass off. We talk a lot of smack about him, but he's damned good and strong as an ox."

Bas dropped his fork onto his plate. The clatter made him jump. "Haven't these people ever heard of paper plates? If they charge me for the plates I'm going to end up breaking, I'll end up owing the duke my paycheck for this film."

"I'm pretty sure Knox would faint if Mrs. Wallace started having the table set with paper plates."

"Knox?"

"The duke."

"Speaking of strong as an ox. I hear you broke Teddy's nose."

"Yeah. Water under the bridge. He insulted Samantha. I punched him. Pass the jam."

Bass picked up the small crystal bowl filled with strawberry jam and set it in front of him. "And you broke his nose with one punch. Damn, Arneaux."

"Your fault." The actor slathered a corner of toast with the jam and took a big bite.

"Mine?"

"Mm-hmm. I used that punch you taught me for the fight scene in *Takedown 2? Takedown 3?*"

"Jesus! No wonder you broke his nose. How did it feel?"

"Honestly? Like winning the fucking Oscar."

They bumped fists and went back to devouring Mrs. Gordon's hearty breakfast. Bas figured he'd need his strength for the weapons lesson. For all kinds of reasons.

BAS HADN'T EXPLORED THE ENTIRE ESTATE YET. WITH thousands of acres, who the hell could? But the area around Rosemount Manor itself, the grounds, as Abercrombie, the butler, called them, had taken a while to see and map out for future scenes in Wentworth's movie. Once Bas had crossed the circular cobblestone driveway around the fountain worthy of any piazza in Rome, he crossed a little bridge to an area they called the front lawn. *Lawn?* Yeah, if you called a stretch of the greenest fields he'd ever seen as far as the eye could see a lawn.

To his surprise and amusement, the ladies of the group had assembled in little wrought iron chairs around equally diminutive tables in order to watch the morning's lesson. They all wore long, brightly colored gowns and bonnets, some gaudier than others. A few of the ladies had fancy umbrellas called parasols. The tables had tea services on them. Apparently, nothing happened at Regency boot camp without plenty of tea drinking. Bas had nothing against tea, but he'd grown up in Euskal Herria in the mountains of northern Spain. There, the people drank coffee, strong coffee. He'd been working and traveling in the film business since he was seventeen, but he still loved the heavenly taste and aroma of the rich, black elixir of life.

"Looks like we have a full house for today's lesson," Dougal said as he and Robbie joined Danny and Bas at the fence that extended parallel to the trench over which the bridge spanned. The trench was called a ha-ha, according to the handbook Eleanor had given him. And people said the Basque language was funny.

The two footmen had shed their uniform jackets and appeared in their white shirts, kilts, and boots. They actually looked more comfortable than Bas felt.

"Going kind of casual, aren't you, boys?" he asked with a tease in his voice.

"Aye. Poor Miss Stepford got tired of repairing our formal Regency uniforms after these lessons, so she told

Miss Witherspoon we needed to shed them for weapons practice."

"And how much did you two pay Miss Stepford to say that?" Arneaux asked.

"No more than you had to pay her to say you needed to practice without your jacket and neckcloth," Robbie answered for him. Only then did Bas notice the actor's jacket and neckcloth draped across the fence.

"Remind me to have a conversation with Miss Stepford," Bas said as he and the others moved to the flat, cleared area next to which some long tables held all kinds of swords. This he understood. He picked up a heavy broadsword and checked the heft and weight. Here was where Bas lived, in the world of weapons, explosions, stunts, and the idea that a man might survive anything if he learned how to control his mind and his body.

"You won't need that one for today, Mr. Salazar," a distinctly British voice called from several feet away. "Let's start with épées today. If you will?"

Bas put down the broadsword and picked up a tapered sword used for fencing. He turned slowly and followed Danny and the footmen to where McGinty and the duke's brother, of all people, stood. Apart, as always it seemed, Teddy Rousseau went through several thrusts and parries with an épée. Damned man looked like something out of a pirate movie—boots, breeches, and a white shirt with billowy sleeves and open neck. Some men might look ridiculous dressed as he was. Not Teddy. He had heavily muscled thighs and broad shoulders. His demeanor on the practice field didn't match that of the smug, suave jerk he'd been last night. Bas suspected this was as close to the real Teddy Rousseau as the man allowed people to see. Too bad.

Bas had hoped his attraction to the swordmaster was a passing whim. If it was, this whim was the most erotic and arousing he'd ever experienced, which was the very last thing he needed at this point.

"We'll go through some basic fencing forms for Mr. Salazar and Lord Lachlan as this is their first time. Robbie, you pair with Lord Lachlan. Dougal, you're with Mr. Salazar. Arneaux, you are with me."

"Oh joy," Danny muttered. "What about you, McGinty? You going to stand around and watch?"

"Aye, I am indeed. Think I'll go and keep the ladies company." The steward gave a little salute and sauntered off toward the tables. "This sport 'tis for men who are younger and lighter on their feet."

"You'd never admit that if there weren't fresh bannock and jam involved," Lord Lachlan said as he tested his épée with a few swipes.

"Ye'r a wise man, milord, and no mistaking it." McGinty settled into a chair next to Miss Witherspoon and took the plate she offered him.

"*En garde*, gentlemen." Teddy crossed épées with Arneaux but looked dead at Bas.

Well, now.

Teddy put them all through their paces. They walked through a series of fencing forms side by side, then turned and engaged with their partners using those same forms. Bas had to admit that with this particular weapon he had some catching up to do. Lord Lachlan caught on more quickly. Bas remembered McGinty telling him the duke's brother had served in the Middle East and didn't do well with guns or gunfire. If today was any example the man had no trouble with other weapons.

As for himself, Bas had no illusions about his own skills. His footwork was slow, and his reactions, while quick, weren't always quick enough to hold off Dougal, who had participated in the lessons since Teddy's arrival and was considered a favorite student. Somehow, putting Bas firmly in place had to be the swordmaster's intention,.

Clever, but not clever enough.

Bas stepped up the speed and power behind his every move. Not exactly the beauty of a fencer, but the brute strength of a swordsman out to prove a point. The point? He hadn't a fucking clue. Dougal kept up pretty well. Teddy watched. Bas sensed their instructor's eyes on him even as the man continued to spar with Danny. The scent of fresh grass, clean cool air, and sweat filled Bas's nostrils. Invigorating as a shot of whisky, but with far more bite and endurance—which was probably why he kept pushing and didn't even attempt to use the fencing skills that were the point of today's lesson.

"Enough." Silence fell at Teddy's command. As Danny said, they might talk smack about the man, but they had a measure of respect for him, for the skills he had and tried to share with them. "You're with me, Mr. Salazar. You've proven your strength. Let's try to teach you a little finesse."

The rest of the men laughed.

Dougal clapped Bas on the shoulder, and muttered, "Good luck, sir," then he joined the others who stood back to watch Teddy and Bas.

"No need to laugh, gentlemen," Teddy said as he rolled up his sleeves to reveal tautly muscled forearms. "None of you is on your mark this morning. Perhaps a little less brandy and cards in the evenings if your constitutions can't handle a little morning exercise."

"He calls this morning exercise," Arneaux stated as the others muttered in agreement.

Bas didn't have to look. He heard their heavy breathing, smelled the scent of their exertion over the past ninety minutes. He didn't know about the rest of Regency boot camp, but weapons practice pulled no punches. He suspected Teddy didn't either.

"Shall we begin, Mr. Salazar?" Teddy took a stance across from Bas and raised his épée in salute.

Well, that was a loaded question. Bas mirrored Teddy's stance and moved slowly as he followed the swordmaster's instructions. It was very much a dance, not meant to be erotic, but when Bas allowed his mind to go there, it definitely went erotic on him. As he wasn't into exhibitionism, all he had to do was glance at his fellow students or at the group of ladies seated across the way with the duke's mountain of a steward to bring the situation quickly back to that of student and instructor.

"That's better, but you are too far back on your feet. Lean in when you thrust, but not so far you leave yourself exposed to a quicker blade." Teddy slapped Bas's ribcage with the side of his épée. "Like that."

"Got it."

Bas danced back on the balls of his feet. He parried against Teddy's blade, and the man nearly knocked Bas's épée out of his hand. Their eyes met. Gray flint stared back at him. An offer he couldn't refuse. He went on the offensive. He pressed, thrust, and parried. The entire time, Teddy gave suggestions, criticisms, but never praise. They circled each other, closer and closer. They scored touches, first one of them, then the other.

Bas's heart pounded. Was he really this badly out of shape? His palm sweated around the hilt of his épée. He tightened his grip and concentrated on the pulse in Teddy's neck. The swordmaster presented a cool, efficient master aura, but Bas wasn't fooled. Bas met, parried, thrust, and focused every ounce of control on getting the upper hand. It was vitally important to him, and he had no idea why, only that it was.

Teddy's eyes widened. His mouth opened slightly. A fine sheen of sweat popped out on his face and neck. "Control, Mr. Salazar. Sword mastery is first and foremost about control. And second— What the—"

Bas, flat on his back, watched his épée fly up and nearly hit Danny and Robbie. Teddy lay sprawled on top of him, his blade pressed against Bas's chest. They should be laughing at this point. They'd both tripped over nothing and landed in the grass. However, there was nothing funny about the very prominent, physical reaction Teddy Rousseau's body pressed against Bas's thigh. Nothing funny at all.

Chapter Three

Teddy had cringed so much in the past fourteen or so odd hours he'd likely pulled a muscle. Perhaps two. Not that anyone had actually seen him cringe. Not even this morning at the end of his ill-conceived weapons class. *Bloody stupid.* He'd set the entire thing up to prove a point and to discourage Bas Salazar from further attendance. He'd failed miserably at both. Oh, he'd made a point. No doubt about that, but the last thing the stuntman had said to him as they walked back inside Rosemount Manor after the lesson was also not in doubt.

"I look forward to tomorrow's class, Teddy. Should be fun."

The bastard knew. Somehow, he knew. Well, hell, of course he *knew*. How could he not? They'd crashed to the ground after the most intense and erotic fencing bout Teddy had ever experienced. He'd lain sprawled on top of that magnificent stone-like body and done everything in his power to will away his reaction to physical contact with the man who had set off warning bells in his head the moment Eleanor had introduced the two of them. Even now, just thinking about the entire awful, wonderful moment, Teddy was rock hard and pitching a tent against his blue silk dressing gown.

He'd closed his eyes. *While everyone else broke the nervous silence with laughter and jokes, Teddy closed his eyes and took a single deep breath to draw the scent of Bas Salazar into his lungs— a dark, woodsy cologne and sweat. For a brief second, he entertained the thought of what if.*

After he'd scrambled to his feet, offered his hand, and helped the man up, after luncheon and some good-natured teasing about how clumsy they both were, after dinner where the entire event had been described in detail for the Duke of Turra's benefit…well, he'd gained control of himself. Somewhat. Enough to remind himself of all of the reasons he'd chosen his life's path. Time to get back on that path and stay out of the ditches and hedgerows.

"Bloody hell, Theodore," he muttered in his father's voice. "Don't be such a poof."

He kicked the day's clothes out of his way and settled into the tall wing-back chair he'd moved to a spot in front of the deep, wide fireplace across from his bed. Dougal would collect the clothes in the morning. He was a good lad who pouted when he had nothing to do. Thank God he'd brought a fresh pot of tea up to Teddy after dinner.

Teddy poured himself a cup and stirred in a few lumps of sugar, literal lumps as Eleanor had demanded the sugar be cut up by hand just as it would have been during the Regency. He took several sips, then returned the cup to the tea tray as he picked up the latest book on the weapons used at Waterloo. Research for tomorrow's class. Tomorrow. He'd be back on his regular routine and nothing and no one would shake him.

A half-hour later, he hadn't progressed past the paragraph he'd started. Some sort of racket had been going on in the back gardens for at least twenty of those thirty minutes. He placed his leather bookmark in his book before he closed it and dropped it into the chair as he got to his feet. His room was at the corner of the backside of the manor. The long windows on the other side of his bed overlooked the way to the ruins. The windows closest to the fireplace overlooked the back terrace and a section of the gardens.

"Odd," he murmured.

Someone had lit the series of torches mounted down the railing of the terrace. The gas lamps down the garden path, more like street lamps that could be found in the older and finer neighborhoods of London, had been lit as well. He heard the sound again, metal on metal. Two figures emerged from the shadows along the terrace. When they passed under the direct light of one of the torches, their faces became clearly visible. Danny Arneaux and Bas Salazar appeared to be practicing épée fencing up and down the terrace. A moment later, Dougal came up behind them, shouting instructions as the actor and the stuntman sparred.

"What on earth are they doing?"

Teddy glanced up at the ormolu clock on the mantel. It was nearly midnight, and the Americans were out on the terrace acting out some sort of demented *Dungeons and Dragons* scene. He snorted his disgust yet couldn't take his eyes off the scene below his window. Arneaux had already honed his skills to a respectable level. He didn't need to leave his wife's bed to practice in the dark of night. Dougal's talent for swords already put him at the head of the class.

An odd sensation swept over Teddy. The kind a person got when they fell over a cliff in the middle of a dream. Madness. Sheer and utter madness. He had no time for this, no time to think someone might go to the trouble to practice after everyone else had gone to bed. To please him? Couldn't be. To make their point at tomorrow's class? Probably. Some sort of joke they all intended to play on him. Nothing more.

A soft feminine laugh sounded somewhere behind him. Teddy turned so quickly he fell against the window but found no one there. Lavender, heather, and fresh earth. Did he smell them or was the scent simply in his head? The laughter sounded again, almost at the same time as what looked like the ivory lace train of a woman's gown disappeared through his chamber door, though the door remained firmly closed.

"What the devil did Dougal put in that tea?"

The clang of swords rose again. He studied the closed door a moment longer, then returned his attention to the three men below. They stood closer together now, the two combatants with their swords at their sides. Voices floated up to him, but he couldn't discern the words. There was some laughter and some good-natured arguing going on, that much he could tell. Dougal started down the terrace steps into the dark. The gas lamps in the gardens went out one by one.

The heady, ethereal scent he'd sworn was a hallucination only moments ago wafted through his room again. This time something soft and lacy dragged over his shoulder and against his face. He batted at thin air.

"What the bloody hell?" He turned first to the window and then to the door.

A woman's soft voice murmured out in the corridor.

"All right, you lot, this isn't funny." He snatched open his bedroom door and strode out onto the duke's Turkish carpet runners. Nothing. Not a soul in sight, though someone was coming up the stairs.

A piercing shriek sounded from the other end of the corridor where it rounded a corner.

Teddy rolled his eyes. "Oh, for pity's sake."

He turned and grabbed the saber propped just inside the doorway. By the time he reached the corner, several doors had opened behind him. Once he turned the corner, he had an unimpeded view all the way to the massive stained-glass window at the end of the hallway, except for a young maid in the long black dress, white apron, and white cap in which Eleanor had kitted all the maids. The maid stood before the window, her face as pale as her apron.

"What is it?" he asked once he reached her side. "What happened?" A pile of bed linens lay at her feet.

"I s-s-saw her. I s-saw her."

"Saw who? Who did you see?" What was the girl's name? He'd paid little attention to the maids' names since he'd been here. They were strictly off limits so far as he was concerned, something he'd decided long before the duke called him and the other male guests into his study to threaten them with bodily harm if they even *looked* at anyone in his employ. "Can you tell me what happened—"

"Hannah! Are you all right?" Samantha Arneaux, in her lacy robe and worn gray mules rushed down the hallway to join them. She put her arm around the girl and gave Teddy a furious glare.

"She said she saw someone," Teddy said, and took a step back. "I heard someone laughing and talking outside my room, and when I came out, I heard Hannah scream."

"I saw the witch, Mrs. Arneaux," the girl nearly wailed. "The Innes Witch. She c-c-came around the corner, then she flew right past me out the window, she did."

"She what?" Teddy actually went and peered out the window. "I don't see anything."

"Come on, Hannah." Eleanor stepped out of the group of guests who now crowded the hallway. Let's get you downstairs so Mrs. Wallace can make you one of her toddies." She hurried the girl away. Miss Stepford gathered up the bed linens and followed them.

"Did you see the ghost, Teddy?" Sylvan asked. He looked ridiculous in his Regency nightshirt and cap.

"I didn't *see* anything. I'm going to bed. I suggest you all do the same." He started past the group.

Heavy footsteps thundered down the main corridor toward them. Arneaux, Bas Salazar, and Dougal burst from around the bend and had to backpedal to keep from running into Teddy and the others.

"What happened?" Arneaux demanded as he hurried to his wife.

"Hannah saw the ghost," Emma, one of the maids, said.

"The ghost? Truly?"

Teddy allowed himself to focus on the person who'd spoken. Bas had changed from the evening wear he'd worn to dinner into a pair of buckskin breeches and a thin muslin shirt, open at the throat. His interest in the manor's ghost story made him look almost boyish.

"Teddy heard her," Sylvan remarked.

"I didn't say—"

"You heard her?" Danny and his wife exchanged an odd look. "She has her eye on you now, Rousseau."

"Well, unless she has a hot body or can bring me some real Cadbury's chocolate without Eleanor finding out, she needs to fix her eye on someone else. Goodnight, all." He propped the dull side of his saber blade on his shoulder and headed back toward his room.

His skin fairly hummed with awareness as the rest of the group followed. Followed at a distance except for Bas. Teddy didn't have to look back to know the stuntman was close behind. The others peeled off to their various rooms with calls of "good night" and "don't let the ghost get you." Teddy opened his door. Dougal brushed past him to fetch the tea tray and Teddy's scattered clothes. Teddy turned and leaned in the doorway. Bas stood inches from him.

"You really don't believe in ghosts?" Bas asked.

"I really don't. Do you?"

"I'm Basque. Of course, I believe."

"You also believe in practicing before your next lesson," Teddy said.

"Squealer." Bas leaned around Teddy and directed his accusation at Dougal.

"I didnae say a word." Dougal pushed past Teddy, clothes draped over one arm and the tea tray in his hands. "Maybe the witch told him." He started to whistle and strolled casually down the corridor toward the stairs.

Teddy and Bas stared at each other as the whistling drifted down the stairs and finally faded to nothing.

"Why were you practicing?" Teddy demanded.

"I didn't want another disaster tomorrow. I don't like being clumsy or unprepared. It's bad for my image."

"Your image? You don't strike me as the vain sort." Teddy's heart pounded so hard there was no way Bas didn't hear it.

"About my image as a man? Never. About my image in my profession. Always."

Teddy understood that. "You weren't so bad this morning. I've seen far worse. I suspect you'll catch on quite quickly."

"A compliment? Be still my heart. I thought you'd lumped me in with the other ordinary peasants."

Teddy rolled his eyes. "What rot. Stop listening to Arneaux. He enjoys stirring up trouble. I would never call you an *ordinary* peasant."

Bas laughed, a deep rumble that vibrated against the thin muslin of his shirt to the point Teddy imagined the sensation against his skin. "Nice to know you don't see me as ordinary."

Time to go. "Well, good night, Mr. Salazar. I expect—"

"Can I ask you a personal question?"

Absolutely not. "Certainly."

"Are you bi?" Bas's gaze never wavered. His eyes, as blue as the Mediterranean, distracted Teddy to the point he nearly forgot the question. Nearly.

"Bi?" He was buying time, and the stuntman knew it.

"Bisexual. Are you bisexual?"

Bloody fucking hell. Teddy's blood turned to water. Then the water began to boil. He curled his hand into a fist, then took a step forward with no idea why or what he intended to do. Only that he was a hairsbreadth from doing it.

"Of course not. What the hell sort of question is that? You've got some cheek asking me that."

"You said I could ask." He shrugged his big shoulders, his thumbs hooked in the waistband of his breeches. His bold expression offered a challenge, but the tight line of his jaw said something else entirely.

"How would you like it if I asked you such a personal question?" Teddy nerves sang with barely banked rage. The need to punch someone, to strike out, clawed up his throat and threatened to suffocate him.

"Ask."

"What?"

"Ask."

"Good night, Mr. Salazar." Teddy grabbed the edge of the heavy chamber door so hard his nails dug into the wood.

"Bas," he corrected. "I'm Bas." He turned to go to his room next door. "Oh, and I'm not, by the way."

"Not what?"

"Bisexual. I'm gay. But you knew that. Good night, Teddy."

Teddy stood there like a fool as Bas strolled slowly into his room. Teddy continued to stand there even after the man closed the door behind himself. Only then did Teddy step back into his room and slam his door shut with a vengeance. Probably woke the whole house. *Fuck it.*

He paced back and forth. He'd stop and pound his fists into the mattress then pace some more. A quiet rap at the door stopped him in his tracks. The clock had chimed midnight at some point during his and Salazar's conversation.

"What now?"

Teddy stomped to the door and put his hand on the latch. He waited for another knock. Silence. He raised the latch and opened the door enough to look out into the corridor. Nothing. No one. He started to close the door when he saw a white plastic shopping bag hanging on the decorative knob in the middle of the door. With a quick check to make certain no one saw, he grabbed the bag and closed the door.

He tossed the bag onto his chair in front of the fire. The logo of one of the many Edinburgh Airport shops winked up at him. For a moment, he simply stood there and studied the bag.

"It's not going to bite you, you great poof," he muttered.

Once he'd picked up the bag and dropped back into the chair, he took a deep breath. Teddy emptied the contents of the bag into his lap—two huge bars of Cadbury's Dairy Milk chocolate.

"Damn."

He snatched up the bars and cocked his hand back to toss them into the fire. No need to lose perspective completely. As much exercise he'd gotten since he'd arrived in Scotland, he could afford a little indulgence. He tucked the second bar back into the bag and opened the other. He'd have to find a place to hide the chocolate. Eleanor had a better nose for such things than Arneaux's drooling bloodhounds. He kept eating, savoring the chocolate in a way he hadn't in a long time.

The American's flea bags weren't the only creatures at Rosemount Manor capable of sniffing things out. What the hell was he going to do about it? Or rather, *him*?

◈

WHAT TEDDY LOVED MOST ABOUT THE DUKE'S ESTATE WAS access to the man's horses. The Duke of Turra had a magnificent stable with beautiful horses trained for every level of rider. Not that Teddy needed a beginner's horse. He'd been riding since he was a small child, one of the few activities at which he excelled and for which he'd received a little of his father's praise. Very little, but enough in the scheme of things.

He sneaked out after luncheon most days to ride the estate and get away from the derision he worked so hard to acquire. He could usually get in a few hours before Sylvan begged him to partner one of the ladies in dance lessons. Today, he had no intention of returning to the house until it was time to get ready for dinner. Too much on his mind, and he had no desire to be around the others in their misfit band of Regency campers. Not today.

"Let's stretch our legs, Kelpie."

He turned the big chestnut gelding toward the open fields that sprawled beyond the old castle ruins behind the manor's gardens. The horse bunched his hindquarters and leapt forward into a gallop. In seconds, Teddy leaned into the wind and reveled in the freedom only riding a horse like Kelpie afforded him. The gelding was one of the most powerful mounts in the stable, and Urquhart had expressed doubts about Teddy taking him out that first week. No more.

A bit of his tension melted away. Whatever Bas's suspicions, he hadn't shared them with the rest of the group. At least not so far as Teddy could tell. He'd long suspected

Robbie had an idea, but the boy had never voiced them to Teddy or to anyone else so far as he knew. *Dammit!* So far as he knew. As if he knew anything anymore. The solution was simple enough. He'd act as if nothing had changed and get on with it. Like riding Kelpie, that was something he could do in his sleep. Pretend, as if all was well.

The smell of grass and the air wafting down from the hills filled his lungs. Spring was slow to arrive in Scotland, even though it was May but, for the most part, the season had arrived. The bright yellow of daffodils sprang up along the outcroppings of rocks in the fields. Clumps of sheep grazed here and there, but they ignored the galloping horse. Here, for a little while, he didn't have to fight his nature or pretend to be someone else. Not that being himself did him any good, at least not when he was alone. Then again, being himself didn't do him much good when he was with others either.

He slowed Kelpie to a walk and turned back toward the loch. Maybe a little time at the water's edge would help to unscramble the bloody knots he'd tied himself into last night after he'd gone to bed. The dreams he'd had woke him up every few hours in a cold sweat, or a hot sweat, some kind of damned sweat. He hoped the noises he'd made in his sleep hadn't actually escaped his lips or he was going to have to figure out which one of the women at Rosemount Manor he'd have to insinuate he'd seduced.

"Kelpie, my friend, be glad you're gelded." He patted the chestnut's neck and turned toward the narrow lane that led to the side of the loch that met the ruins. Once the old castle came into sight, the sound of voices, arguing voices, made him pull the horse to a stop.

"Come on, Mike, we've done falls higher than this," a young male voice said. "You're getting old."

"Fuck you. Bas, tell this kid we can't do this one. I don't care what Wentworth says."

"Nothing's impossible, Mike. We need to check out the angles is all." The stuntman's slightly accented English exuded the sort of confidence Teddy lived and breathed. For him it was a necessary evil. On Bas? Just another muscle he flexed? Natural? Enticing?

Teddy urged his horse forward to the point he could watch what was going on. The stuntman crew had set up all sorts of equipment at the foot of the tower. Some checked rigging strung from the sections of the parapet that remained. A few stood at the bottom and inflated a large airbag with a noisy gas-powered air pump. One wiry guy who had to be at least fifty stood next to the airbag, arms folded across his chest, and frowned up at Bas, who stood at the very top of the castle's tallest surviving tower.

"Hey, it's the sword guy," a guy in his twenties who reminded Teddy of someone called out. He stood on the tower with Bas. Both men wore safety harnesses, the kind Teddy had seen on movie sets a couple of times. "Hey, sword guy. What's up?"

"Apparently you are," Teddy called back as he raised his hand and waved. "I don't remember this scene from the film script."

The older guy, Mike, walked over and began to pet Kelpie. "I think Wentworth added it after Bas sent him photos of this place."

"Does Miss Chase know about this?" Teddy asked as Bas shouted instructions to the group of men around the airbag.

"My guess would be no," Mike replied.

"He'd better hope Hadrian does his job on this little pre-wedding honeymoon or there'll be hell to pay," Teddy said. "Romance authors, live ones at least, don't like men changing their stories for films. That's why I usually consult on period films where the author is dead."

"Good policy. Jane Austen hasn't sued anyone yet." Mike

gave Kelpie one last pat on the neck, then went back to where the men appeared to have finished filling the airbag.

"Good morning, Teddy," Bas called from the top of the tower. "Want to come up and try this?"

"No, thanks. I'll stick to swords where the only danger is bleeding to death."

Bas gave a little salute and walked out of sight. In seconds he reappeared, stumbling backward toward the edge of the tower. He flipped over the broken wall and plummeted into the airbag. The sides of the thing billowed up around him. He flipped off the side, then headed over to stand next to Kelpie.

"Sure you don't want to try it, Teddy? It's very freeing."

"What makes you think I need to be freed?"

Bas shrugged. "Hey, Tim," he shouted toward the top of the tower, "give it a try. Lock your knees when you hit the wall or you won't get enough distance to clear the side of the tower."

"Is that one of Arneaux's stunts?" Teddy asked. "Your body type doesn't match his. Not that it's any of my business."

"Tim is Arneaux's stunt double."

Teddy glanced up in time to see Tim tumble over the wall and head for the airbag. Tall, with a lean, athletic football player's body, this Tim was the perfect double for Arneaux, except for his face, which reminded him of a young Bill Clinton.

"Then why did you do the stunt?" Teddy asked.

"I do all the stunts before I let my crew try them. That's good, guys. Finish securing everything and then head for the village. See you tomorrow around ten."

A chorus of "later dude" accompanied a lot of hurrying around and activity as Bas's crew set to work closing up shop so they could leave. According to his sources, Teddy understood their urgency. Most of the film crew in the early stages of pre-film work enjoyed short days, and apparently, they spent a lot of time in the local pub and at the nearby sports club.

"I wondered where you disappeared to the last couple of days," Bas said.

"You did better in class today. Working with Dougal helped," Teddy said.

"He's a good kid."

"Kid? He's twenty-five years old."

"Too young for me. Where are you headed?"

"The loch." Teddy started to back Kelpie away toward the narrow lane around the loch.

"Hang on. I'll walk with you. I need the exercise." Bas strode to where Mike was yelling at a couple of gaffers, then snatched up a duffle bag and turned back toward Teddy, who had already started his horse up the lane. Of course, Bas jogged to catch up to him. Teddy pulled up his horse and swung down out of the saddle. Reins in hand and with Kelpie between them, he and Bas walked down the narrow lane toward the loch.

"Anna isn't going to like Wentworth adding scenes to her story." Teddy had determined to take charge of the conversation before he ever dismounted Kelpie. The stuntman tended to steer talk in directions Teddy didn't care to go. Not that he blamed the man. Teddy knew the value of gaining the upper hand in…situations.

"You know Miss Chase well?"

"Intimately."

"Ah! One of your conquests."

"Don't tell Hadrian Cross that. He'll kill me." The lie was despicable, but Bas had him so off kilter he couldn't stop himself.

"A book critic?" Bas peered around the horse's head and

looked him up and down. "I'm pretty sure you could take him."

"Cross went to college on a football scholarship. American football."

"My money's still on you. Muscle and grace beat muscle and brute strength every time."

Teddy chose to ignore the compliment. "Speaking of grace, you make falling off a castle parapet look pretty easy. I hope Arneaux appreciates your and Tim's hard work. I've seen plenty of easy falls go wrong." Kelpie wandered around him to suss out some nice clumps of grass up the bank from the loch.

"Nothing to it. After all, *one is hardly an artist when all one does is fall off horses or jump out windows.*" Bas waited as if he expected some sort of reply.

The remark hit his intended target. Teddy inwardly winced at the slight sting to his conscience and maybe a small one somewhere in his chest. Being a right arse had its drawbacks, but not enough for him to stop.

"I suspect Arneaux's neck is worth more to Wentworth than yours, mine, *and* Tim's put together."

He kept checking the lane and the area around them. They were completely alone. The late afternoon sun warmed his skin despite the wind off the loch, which didn't account for the sudden rush of heat as Bas stepped closer. Every bite of grass Kelpie took tugged Teddy's left hand back as he clasped the horse's reins tighter and tighter.

"You never apologize, do you? Well, except for that one thing. The one you should never have to apologize for." He stepped closer.

Dressed in a kilt, white linen shirt, and leather Scots knee boots, he stood only an inch or so taller than Teddy. Teddy wasn't intimidated, but a sense of something alive and vibrant passed between them.

"What are you going on about?" Teddy tugged at Kelpie's reins to distract himself from the need to breathe or think.

"I guess when the apology for that one thing is your whole life, there's no room to apologize for anything else. And your whole life is an apologetic lie."

"I never lie. Wait. Apology for what?"

"This."

Teddy was in the middle of the kiss before he knew it. Bas never touched him except with his lips. Firm, cool, sensual lips. He didn't demand. He didn't ask. He suggested with tiny flicks of his tongue and the erotic movement of his lips against Teddy's. Teddy, whose lungs burned for air. His body refused to move. His mouth could only take in the sexy, tender allure and power of a soft, wet, almost restrained kiss. A kiss that ended long before he wanted. His vision blurred. He might have swayed a bit on his feet.

"You go ahead and tell yourself you never lie, Teddy. But the only true thing you've told me so far is that you are *not* bi. Because you are most definitely not. See you at dinner." Bas turned, his duffle bag slung over his shoulder, and walked back toward Rosemount Manor in long, confident strides.

Leaving Teddy with a raging erection, a brain thoroughly scrambled, and lips that still burned as if on fire.

See you at dinner? Teddy shook his head. "Come back here," he said too softly for Bas to hear. *For what, Teddy?*

Well, that was the question, wasn't it?

Chapter Four

BAS TUGGED AT HIS NECKCLOTH FOR THE UMPTEENTH TIME since Robbie had tied it and pronounced him fine as sixpence, which apparently translated to ready to go down for dinner. Everyone else had already gone down, or at least he assumed they had as he trekked the corridor and the staircase to the first floor. The weird evening shoes irritated him. The silk knee breeches irritated him. The white silk stockings irritated him the most because Robbie had bitched long and loud about how hard it was to tie garters around a leg built like a tree trunk. Or maybe Bas was simply irritated. With himself.

What the hell had possessed him? In broad daylight in the middle of the road? He wasn't the kind of guy who forced someone out of the closet. His own experiences had taught him how painful that could be. There was something about Teddy's hiding himself that made him want to—

"Drink?"

Bas glanced around. Somehow, he'd made it into the drawing room without noticing. Next time he'd probably walk into the lake, loch, whatever.

"Yes, Dougal. A double of whatever you're serving."

"Bring him a shot of Himself's whisky, Dougal. Looks like he might need it."

"You're a saint, Mr. McGinty." Bas meant every word. He liked the duke's burly old steward, and more important, respected the man.

Dougal sidled along to the pretty lacquered cabinet in the far corner of the room. After doing his best imitation of James Bond, he came back and slid a glass of whisky into Bas's hand. Bas downed it in one gulp, then handed the glass back to the footman.

"Better now?" McGinty asked.

"We'll see how the evening pans out."

"Now that sounds intriguing," Danny said as he sauntered up, brandy glass in hand.

"Not as intriguing as what is going on over there." McGinty nodded toward a group gathered on the far side of the main fireplace. "I think I'll join them." With a hand wave of a salute, he walked away.

"What *is* going on over there?" Bas indicated the entire group, but he fixed his gaze on Teddy and a cute young blonde woman in a purple silk Regency gown.

"The new girl?" Danny asked as they both sat on one of the silk striped sofas strategically placed around the room in group settings. "She's Wentworth's assistant. Um…Gloria. Gloria Jessup. He sent her here to take photos and report back to the boss. She's a big Jane Austen fan, so he paid for her to do the Regency boot camp thing."

"Lucky girl. Wentworth is a generous boss."

"That's right. You worked with him on one of your first stunt gigs. How long ago was that?"

"Eighteen years. Thanks, Arneaux." He punched Danny's arm. "Now I really feel old."

"Hey, watch the brandy." Danny laughed as he steadied his glass. "Sorry. Jesus, you had to have been a kid back then."

"Yeah. Don't try to make it up to me now. I was seventeen and on a temporary work visa from Spain. Wentworth helped me get jobs, then he helped me get my citizenship. I owe him." Bas continued to take in the group across the room. Teddy had turned on the charm, and Wentworth's assistant was laughing.

"You don't owe him a damned thing," Danny said. "Your stunt work has made him millions. But I'm glad you're working on this film."

"Thanks. I've only done a couple of period films since I left Spain, so I'm winging the hell out of this one. Why is it the more expensive the antique couch, the more ball-busting uncomfortable it is?"

"Try sitting on it in a kilt. You were a stuntman in Spain?" He gave a little wave to his wife who was talking to Wentworth's assistant and the others. She waved back at both Arneaux and Bas.

"I was training to be a matador when I was fifteen. I *despised* it. I went into stunt work to prove a point to my old man." He shrugged against the unseen hand that squeezed his chest. "I liked it, and there was lots of work in Spain at the time. Lots of location shoots."

"Why'd you leave?"

Bas gave him his best side-eye.

"Oh. Yeah. Forget I asked."

Bas kicked him in the shin. "I'm kidding. I've done okay since I moved to the States, so no harm done."

"I'll say. I've seen your place in Cali."

As Samantha approached, Danny slid over enough to allow her to sit between Bas and him. "Hello, beautiful. Decided to go slumming?"

"I would hardly call sitting with the two most handsome men in the room slumming."

"She's good," Bas said. "If I wasn't gay…."

"I'd have to kick your ass," Danny cut in.

"You'd have to try."

"Now, boys. Play nice." Samantha patted each of them on the knee. "What were you talking about so intently? That's why I came over."

"Bas's house in California." Danny clasped his wife's hand. "Or rather his mansion and ranch in California."

Bas rolled his eyes. "He's full of it, Samantha. Don't listen to him."

"Well," she said, drawing out the word. "You *could* invite us to visit once the film wraps. To prove him wrong, of course."

"Done and done. You two are welcome anytime."

"Lovely." Samantha squeezed his bicep with her free hand. "But we wouldn't want to intrude on a family visit or anything so—"

Danny started laughing. Loudly.

"Asshole," Bas muttered.

"What?" Samantha looked from one to the other.

"His family doesn't know where he lives and has never seen his home," Danny said, once he finally stopped laughing like a demented hyena. "Oh, they've seen a photo of where they *think* he lives, but they've never actually seen his house."

"That is *your* fault, Arneaux. That is all you."

Samantha pulled her hand from Danny's grasp and folded her arms across the bodice of her pretty bronze silk Regency gown. "*Somebody* had better explain."

Danny raised his hands in surrender and then waved them at Bas. "You do it since you want to blame it all on me. Just don't leave out the part about the tequila."

"Tequila?" Samantha pinned Bas with a surprisingly steely glare for such a petite, prim woman.

"Lots of it," Danny said.

Bas lifted a brow. "I thought I was telling this."

"Carry on, Stuntman."

"My parents and my sister *have* visited my place. They don't come very often. I'm always on a job, and they don't like to fly. My *extended* family doesn't actually know where I live or how much money I make. I don't want them to know. I have cousins who are constantly calling for money, as it is. If they really needed the money, I might be okay with it."

"I wouldn't," Danny said quietly.

"But they don't, so I see no sense in them knowing about my finances. They...weren't kind to me when we were growing up. Still aren't, unless they want something. I offend their Basque masculine sensibilities. A couple of years ago, Danny and I were on location in Arizona for one of his films, and I kept getting these calls from my cousins."

"And we were drinking."

"Arneaux, will you *please* shut up. Yes, we *were* toasted, and Mr. Action Star decides I need to send the cousins a photo of my house."

"I don't understand." Of course she didn't. Dr. Samantha Higgins was a nice girl.

Bas turned to Danny. "How did she end up married to you?"

"Fuck you, Salazar."

"You're not my type."

"Boys!"

Samantha's raised voice drew the attention of the others, but only for a moment. Teddy said something pithy, no doubt, and all eyes returned to him and Gloria What's-her-name.

"Arneaux used my phone and sent a picture of a little

bungalow in Phoenix where we shot some fight scenes. Haven't heard from the cousins since."

"It was that bad?"

"No, it was a little small and—"

"It was a dump," Danny declared. "We used it as a lowlife drug dealer's home."

Samantha tutted. "You two are terrible. I can see I cannot leave you two alone together for a minute."

"Wouldn't have been so bad if his real house hadn't appeared on the cover of some big decorator magazine three months later. Bas sent his mom a copy, and like any mother, she showed it to the entire family. Ouch, Bas. Tell a guy when you're going to punch the hell out of him." Danny rubbed the spot on his arm where Bas hit him but got no sympathy from his wife who sighed.

"The only reason it was on a magazine cover was as a favor to the decorator. He's Lily's friend, Derek. But he and his husband did an incredible job."

"Derek and Raphael did your house?" Samantha's smile dazzled him, so sincere and genuinely happy. Unlike the smile pasted on Teddy Rousseau's face at the moment. "I met them at the wedding. They're wonderful."

"They're good guys. They work out at the same gym I do when I'm in LA. And I've worked with Lily on some films. The new Lady Lachlan has good taste," Bas said. "In friends, decorators, and in men. I've spent some time with her husband scouting locations. He's quiet, but he's a good guy. Not many of those around." He gave Arneaux an overdone sneer. And received a middle-finger salute in return. "I'm telling Miss Witherspoon."

"You wouldn't dare," Arneaux replied even though he threw a nervous glance toward the woman in charge of their *boot camp.*

"And I think you wouldn't know what to do with a good

guy, Mr. Salazar," Samantha said as Abercrombie stood in the doors and announced dinner. "I think you go for bad boys."

"Take your wife in to dinner, Arneaux. She's too damned smart for me."

"Tell me something I don't know."

❧

Bas kept his attention off Teddy as they crossed the wide first floor landing to the dining room. As Teddy had attached himself to Wentworth's assistant, he ended up seated at the duke's end of the table. Eleanor, McGinty, Sylvan Goode, and Miss Stepford made up the rest of the favored few. Danny and Samantha and Lord and Lady Lachlan sat at Bas's end of the table, with him seated directly opposite the duke, which suited Bas fine. Far enough away from Teddy not to hear him seduce Gloria, the blonde bombshell assistant, but in the perfect position to watch like the masochist it appeared Bas had become.

"Mock turtle soup?" Bas looked at Dougal who grinned as he went on to serve the rest of the guests. "What the hell is mock turtle soup?"

"Trust me," Samantha said. "It is much better than the real thing. No turtles were killed in the making of this soup."

"Come on, Bas." Danny downed a spoonful of the soup and licked his lips. "It's good. You're not afraid of a little turtle soup, are you?"

"I refuse to take culinary advice from a Louisiana Cajun. You people will eat anything that doesn't fight back."

"I thought he was only half Cajun," Lord Lachlan said.

"The other half is Creole," Bas told him. "Which means he adds butter, garlic, and red beans to everything."

"This from a man who eats lamb stew and sheep's cheese," Danny muttered.

"You had your grandmother serve me rattlesnake, alligator, and nutria," Bas said. "At the same meal."

"You could have turned it down."

"She's your *grandmother*. You *knew* I wouldn't turn it down."

"Rattlesnake?" Lord Lachlan shuddered.

"One word," Lily said to her husband. "Haggis."

"Have you learned to cook it yet, Lily?" Danny asked.

"Screw you, Arneaux," she replied.

"That's okay. I prefer my limbs where they are."

"Oh, Lachlan wouldn't hurt you. Much."

"I was talking about my wife," he replied.

Their end of the table erupted into laughter. Teddy stared at Bas, who did his damnedest to ignore him.

"Well, if it comes to that," Bas said. "I can make it look like an accident, Samantha."

"I may take you up on that."

More laughter.

"Just so you know," Lily said, "apparently, you scared the hell out of the duke this afternoon."

"Me?" Bas thought back over the day. "What did I do?"

"He, Eleanor, and McGinty came to the ruins by way of the gardens to see how disruptive the film shooting is going to be, and he saw you take a header off the tower," Lily stated. "Eleanor said he went white as a sheet. She was afraid he'd swallowed his tongue."

"As if that would ever happen." This from Lord Lachlan.

Family. Bas knew all about that.

"What did he say?" Samantha asked. "What did Eleanor say?"

Lily nodded. "She said, he said the last thing he needed was a Basque ghost wandering about the place to go with the one he already had."

"I thought he didn't believe in ghosts," Bas said.

"That's the lie he tells himself," Lord Lachlan said softly.

Lily reached over and squeezed his hand.

Bas glanced up the table at Teddy. "There's a lot of that going around."

He went back to his mock turtle soup, though afterward he couldn't describe what it tasted like to save his somewhat tarnished soul—a soul that gained a little more tarnish when Bas arranged to partner with the pretty Gloria at whist after dinner. Worse, he made certain they played Lord and Lady Lachlan's team so Teddy wasn't seated anywhere near his latest target. Petty? Probably. Did Bas give a rat's ass? Not a chance.

"You're very good at this, Miss Jessup," Bas said, as he and she took their third trick in a row. "I have no clue what I'm doing, but you're making me look like a genius."

"I've attended every JASNA ball for the last ten years. I'm a terrible dancer, but they always have a card room. I've learned from some of the best whist players in the world."

"JASNA?" *Ten years? When did she start? When she was eight years old?*

"Jane Austen Society of North America. Lord Lachlan is it true you are a licensed falconer?" She played her first card of the next trick.

"Yes, I am." Lachlan Innes was one of most soft-spoken straight guys Bas had ever met. Confidence and surviving combat in the Middle East likely did that.

Miss Jessup looked a little confused by the man's to-the-point answer.

"He is more than that," Lily said as she picked over her cards before she chose one to play. "He has an aviary of some of the most amazing birds of prey you will ever see. And he trains and flies them all."

"I watched you fly some of them last week," Bas said as he contemplated his own cards. "Truly awesome stuff, sir."

He shifted in his chair and thought better of it. Damned antique chairs were pretty enough, but they weren't built for men like him or Teddy. How the hell McGinty and the other Scots dealt with them without breaking them, he couldn't fathom.

Lord Lachlan narrowed his eyes. "Lachlan. Not sir. Just Lachlan. Last week, I didn't see you."

"I was checking out some of the hills behind the barn where you keep the birds. I didn't want to disturb you. Or them."

"It's called a mews, not a barn." The duke's brother played a card. "Come by any time you like, Mr. Salazar."

"Bas. Call me Bas. And I'll take you up on that. Damn. I shouldn't have played that card." He stuck his tongue out at Lily, who whooped as she took the trick.

"Your language, Mr. Salazar," Eleanor called from the table across the drawing room where she had paired with Teddy.

"Sorry," Bas called back.

"*Your language, Mr. Salazar,*" Lily mocked quietly even as she smiled sweetly at Eleanor. "She really needs to lighten up. Your brother has her tied in knots."

"My brother has everyone tied in knots," Lachlan said. "Whose turn is it?"

"Mine." Miss Jessup tossed down a card. "I cannot believe I am sitting here with a Scottish lord, Lily Randolph, and Bas Salazar. Somebody, pinch me."

"I'm sure we can get Teddy to volunteer for that job," Lily said, and cast a glance to where Teddy and Eleanor played against Miss Stepford and Sylvan Goode.

The petite blonde rolled her eyes and made a noncommittal sound of exasperation. "No, thank you. I know his type."

"Good for you," Bas muttered. The relief that rushed

through him at what she'd said was one more thing to irritate him. "Smart girl. But I'm no big deal, Miss Jessup. I'm just your average movie stunt guy."

"Please," Lily said.

"Not according to Erik," Gloria said. "He says you're the best in the business, and he's going to need you for this film."

"He's right," Lily agreed

"Why, thank you, Lady Lachlan. Ouch!" Bas reached down to rub his shin. "Does she kick you that hard?" He addressed his question to her husband who was actually smiling, something he didn't do much.

"All the time. I wear my boots to bed. Stop calling her Lady Lachlan, and she'll stop kicking you."

"TMI!" Lily picked up an ivory fan and whacked Lachlan on the shoulder.

The man actually grinned at her. Gloria snorted, and Bas laughed so hard his chair groaned in protest.

"Speaking of needing someone for the film," Gloria said, once they'd all recovered. "Is there any way we could use *your* birds for the falconry scenes in the film, Lord Lachlan? Erik is prepared to fly birds in for Miss Randolph to work with, but I hate to put any bird through a transatlantic flight when it isn't necessary. Animals always seem so upset when they have to travel."

"Would I have to appear on camera?" he asked.

"Not if you don't want to."

"I don't. Ever. My wife is the actress." He said the words with such vehemence no one at their table doubted him. "I'll consider it."

Gloria tossed a card on the table. "Thank you. That's our trick and the game, I believe."

"What?" Lily stared at her cards then at the ones on the table. "That's impossible."

"Nicely done," Bas said to Gloria as they all stood and said their good nights. "On both counts."

"I don't know what you're talking about."

He offered her his arm, which she took as they started toward the door. "Oh, yes you do. You appealed to Lachlan's concern for the birds Erik might fly in for the film. Lachlan will let you use his birds rather than allow ones he doesn't even know be put through any stress. He's that kind of guy. I'd put money on it, thanks to you. Erik doesn't just hire the best stunt coordinator."

They walked through the door, out into the hallway, and ascended the stairs to the second floor where the bedchambers were. Teddy and Eleanor started up the stairs behind them.

When they reached the second floor, Eleanor asked, "How did you enjoy your first evening at Regency boot camp, Miss Jessup?"

"I loved it," she replied, as Bas slowed for them to catch up. "I'm looking forward to tomorrow. Can I ask you some questions about that?" She looped her arm through Eleanor's and the two women strolled away—which left Teddy standing in the middle of the old Turkish carpet runners with his mouth open from whatever Bas assumed Teddy may have intended to say to Gloria before she made her escape.

Bas didn't know whether to applaud Erik Wentworth's assistant or pat poor Teddy on the head, especially as the poor guy stood there long enough for every bedchamber door to open and close behind the other guests, leaving him alone with Bas, who was more than aware the moment Teddy realized where he was and with whom.

"Good night," the Brit muttered, and started toward his chamber door.

"I don't think so, buddy. We need to talk." Bas cupped Teddy's elbow far more gently than he wanted.

Teddy snatched his elbow free. "I'm not your *buddy*, and we have nothing to say to each other." Even as he said the words, he stepped closer to Bas. Teddy had never shown this side since Bas had known him, the side that took advantage of his height and honed muscles to try and intimidate. A lot of other men would have backed down. Bas wasn't a lot of other men.

"You're right," Bas said, as he held his ground. "I'll talk, and you listen. Back up. Or do you like being this close to me?"

Teddy backed into his bedroom door. "Fine. Hurry up. I'm tired, and I have several things to do tomorrow."

"I'm sure you do. So do I. I have another group of my stunt people arriving, and I am officially warning you to stay away from my female crew members. They'll be staying in the village, but they'll be here every day. I've seen you in action, and I've heard even more. Stay away from them."

"I don't know what the hell you're talking about, but if you've given me this speech, you've probably given another version of it to the women who work for you."

"You're a dog, Teddy. That wouldn't be so bad except your motive is self-serving and hurtful. I don't want any of my crew working with a broken heart. It's dangerous."

"You've certainly ruined my chances with Gloria. The cold shoulder I got just now is proof of that. Thank you very much." He lifted the latch on his door and pushed it slightly open.

"You ruined your own chances being your *suave* Brit self. Not to mention, she is savvier than both of us. But the next person might not be."

"You're delusional. Leave off the drinks—before and after dinner. It isn't as if it's raining women here at Eleanor's Regency boot camp."

"Yes, but how many other women have you used and

dumped just to prove you're straight? How would you like it if someone used you like that?"

Teddy's breath caught on a dark gasp. His eyes blazed with rage, but his face had turned paper white. Bas had hit a nerve, a direct hit. "If you express your little fantasies about me to anyone here, I will have my lawyers on you—"

This time it was Bas who stepped closer. Close enough that his pecs pressed into Teddy's. "I would never do that to another man, even one as far back in the closet as you. And when I *express* my fantasies about you, you'll know it, Teddy. To your very soul, you'll know it."

The swordmaster's chest rose and fell so quickly, Bas grew dizzy watching. Teddy's lips, parted slightly, tempted like original sin. *Jainkoaren Ama* he'd never wanted to kiss a man more than he did in that moment.

Bas took a half step back, turned, and went to his door without a single look toward Teddy. He managed to open the door without a hitch and slam it shut before he stumbled to the blanket chest at the foot of the bed and sat down. Hard. He drummed his fists against the scarred wood, but stopped when Teddy finally slammed his door. So, Teddy had stood there after Bas turned away. Long enough for Bas to come into the bedroom and exercise his rage on the innocent old chest.

"Should have looked," Bas said. "Why didn't you look." Because if he had, he'd have probably backed Teddy into the bedroom and not stopped backing until he hit the bed. Or a wall. Or a chair. Anything.

What the fuck was it about this snotty, British, self-loathing man? Bas had lost his mind. Worse, he'd lost control. He'd never been drawn to men who weren't interested, let alone to one who wouldn't even admit he was gay. If someone wasn't interested, he shrugged it off and moved on. Confidence wasn't a problem for Bas. Not now at least.

He'd worked too damned hard with years of bodybuilding, taking stunt jobs nobody else wanted, and avoiding drama and scandal. Working hurt, but he was the consummate professional, the toughest sonofabitch in the business.

That was why he sat on a hard-as-nails chest that crushed his balls in thin silk knee breeches that chafed and didn't get up because his legs shook like jelly. Thumps sounded from nextdoor as if someone was throwing stuff at the walls. Had to be some powerful throwing as the walls in Rosemount Manor weren't like the walls in cheap hotels or even expensive hotels. A house built hundreds of years ago didn't go cheap on the walls. What the hell was Teddy doing?

"Fuck it."

Bas snatched off his slick, damned evening shoes and tossed them toward the wardrobe. He'd actually bathed in the loch this afternoon. Years of living on the road put him in the habit of keeping a bar of soap in his duffle. Here, he had an extra bar of the sandalwood soap made in the village that Robbie had brought him. The loch was cold as hell, but after his encounter with Teddy after lunch, the cold water helped. He'd kill for a shower though.

He'd usually find Robbie waiting to help him undress after dinner and cards. Since he was capable of doing the job himself, he wrestled out of the silk jacket and vest, er…waistcoat, then wrangled his shirt over his head before he realized he hadn't untied the damned neckcloth—which was what Robbie found him cussing at when the footman finally knocked and strolled into Bas's room.

"Trouble, sir?"

"Come get this thing off me before I hang myself. I've had one helluva day."

"That bad, is it?" Robbie asked as he untied the stupid Regency hangman's knot in a few seconds.

"How much is it going to cost me for you to sneak into

the kitchen and bring me one of Mrs. Wallace's hot toddies? Make that two."

"How much ye offering?"

"Twenty dollars. American, you mercenary." Bas stepped out of the silk knee breeches and grabbed the robe from the foot of the bed.

"As bad as all that?" Robbie helped him into the robe. He took one look at Bas's face and headed for the door.

Chapter Five

I WANTED HIM TO KISS ME. TEDDY SLAPPED THE RAPIER AGAINST his thigh and flung it onto the weapons table. Again. Last night he'd wanted Bas to kiss him. Probably the most frightening moment of his life. Also the most erotic. He set to organizing the swords on the table. Some needed to be cleaned and polished. Some needed to be put back in their cases as they hadn't been used today. Not used because Bas had missed class this morning. He'd eaten breakfast in the dining room, dressed in a loose Regency shirt, no neckcloth, a kilt and boots, then he'd vanished.

Clang!

A brace of fencing foils fell off the end of the table. Probably because Teddy had spent the last several minutes shoving things around in frustration. He picked up the foils and slammed them onto the padded surface.

"Am I interrupting something?" Lily Randolph or Lady Lachlan, dependent on her mood, strolled across the grass with a small rapier in her hand. Today, she had dressed in head to toe Regency garb rather than the clothes of a nineteenth-century Highland wife. The burgundy color of her walking dress suited her.

"What are you doing with that?" Teddy had no patience today. He'd slept fitfully and spent half the night worried about the stuntman outing him. The rest of the time he'd dreamed of exactly what sort of fantasies the man might have about him.

"Bringing it back. I carried it all the way into the house after class before anyone noticed." She handed it to him by the hilt. "Are you okay?"

He placed the saber in the stack to be cleaned. "I am always okay." He turned to face her once more and leaned against the table, arms folded across his chest. "Why? Don't I look okay?"

She put her hand out palm down and wagged it side to side. "You've been acting weird for a couple of days now. What's up?"

"What's up? How very un-Regency of you."

"Very well." She slipped into her best British accent, which was to be frank, damned good. "You have been out of sorts these last days. Are you quite yourself?"

He snorted. "That is the question, isn't it? I am English. I am always weird, which means, I am always myself."

"True." She leaned against the table next to him. "But these past few days have been weird even for you. Something on your mind?"

So easy. Tell her. Tell her everything and ask for her advice. As if he'd ever done that, would ever do that. Not even with people who considered him a good friend, and there were a few. Very few. Life was a little easier for him that way. Fewer people to lie to and walk away.

"Can I ask you something, Lily?"

"Sure. I reserve the right to tell you to kiss my...reticule."

She brushed the toe of her black half-boots across the

grass. Grass so green for such a cold place. Then again, the duke had an army of gardeners and greenskeepers. For a man who was broke, he provided jobs for a great many people.

"Does your husband know we slept together?" He expected her to get angry or to look upset, or something. She scrunched up her face in what had to be complete confusion.

"What the…. It happened before I even met Lachlan. Why do you want to know?"

"Does he?"

"Yes, as a matter of fact, he does. He also knows it didn't mean a damned thing. To either of us." She maintained eye contact as if she dared him to say differently.

Teddy's entire body sagged. Internally at least. "Good. On both counts. Do me a favor."

"What?"

"Don't tell him I know he knows."

She went over his words a few times in her head, unless he read her expression wrong. "Fine? Can I ask why?"

"I like him. I don't want there to be awkwardness between us." He shrugged. "Where is he going to be today, by the by? We're doing some shooting practice with the Mantons and some other period guns. I don't want us to choose a spot where he might hear."

Lord Lachlan had severe PTSD when it came to guns. Several combat tours in the Middle East tended to produce that effect. He'd been a little better since he'd met and married Lily. Lily Randolph as a calming influence? *Bloody hell!* Speaking of which, she was staring at him as if he had three heads.

"Who are you and what have you done with Teddy Rousseau?"

"Fuck off, Lily." He went back to sorting the weapons.

"There's the Teddy we know and love. Are you sure you're okay?"

"Are you sure you don't have somewhere to be? I cannot believe Eleanor has alloted you this much free time."

"She hasn't, actually. I have letter writing lessons. Will you be in dance class this afternoon?"

"Yes, yes." He motioned with his hands and looked up to see Dougal and one of the other footmen coming their way. "Now go away so I don't have to be nice to the help." He pulled out the clean polishing cloths and containers of refined clove oil he used to clean his swords.

"I'm going. Hello, Dougal. Seamus."

"Lady Lachlan," the two men murmured as they offered her a short bow. They went to the stack of swords at the far end of the table and got to work.

"Hey, Teddy," Lily called over her shoulder.

"Yes?"

"Thanks."

"For what?"

"Lachlan will be at the mews today with some of the film people. Thanks for asking."

"Oh, do shut up." He snatched up one of the cloths and dampened it with clove oil, then grabbed McGinty's claymore and set to work.

He'd clean half a dozen swords before he sensed the dead silence and eyes on him. He'd gone bonkers. Nothing else accounted for it. He put down the cleaning supplies and walked back toward the manor without saying a word. He'd be the talk of the footmen's card games tonight. Maybe they'd assume he was upset because of Lily. She had that effect on men. Any man. Well, almost any man.

He went into the manor in search of McGinty. If anyone had an idea for a spot to fire guns on the estate where Lord Lachlan might not hear, the mountain of a Scot would be the man. Teddy's boots echoed on the marble floor. Mrs. Wallace appeared at the top of the stairs that led from the first floor to the foyer.

"Do you happen to know where Mr. McGinty is at the moment?" he asked.

"I do, Mr. Rousseau. He's in the duke's library with His Grace. They're going over some maps of the estate with some of the film people." She said *film people* as if she'd spied a speck of dust on the perfectly polished banister. To a woman like Mrs. Wallace, who had run this household for the past thirty years, this entire Regency boot camp and period film adventure was one giant speck of dirt in the life of this house—and the life of the duke.

"Good. I've a question about the estate."

He took the steps two at a time and brushed past her before she could warn him off with *"His Grace is not to be disturbed."* or *"I will see if His Grace will see you."* He strode down the corridor and pushed open one of the double doors. McGinty and the duke looked up from one of the long library tables at the far end of the room. As did the third man with them. The man whose cedar-scented cologne filled Teddy's mind before he was even close enough for it to fill his nostrils.

"Is there something you want, Mr. Rousseau?" With a British accent most Etonians would envy, the Scots duke usually set Teddy's teeth on edge—especially when the duke had dressed in a shirt, tie, and a damned kilt. He had to be baking with a fire roaring in both monstrous fireplaces. Man couldn't decide what the hell he was.

Pot, meet kettle.

"I wondered if I might ask Mr. McGinty about a location for the shooting practice this afternoon," Teddy said.

The duke might or might not have raised an eyebrow at the question. Teddy had trouble focusing on him with Bas in the room—who did everything *but* look at him.

"What is wrong with the place where you conduct your other classes?" the duke asked.

"Today, it is too close to the mews. The gunfire might carry." Teddy's skin itched. A headache threatened behind his left eye. Apparently, doing the right thing disagreed with him. Who knew?

"I see." The duke turned back to the maps on the table. He pointed to a spot on the map and McGinty bent over the table to look to where the duke pointed. "Would *Gleann Lavender* do for that as well?"

"Aye, Yer Grace. It would at that. Bas here is going over to take a look. Perhaps ye might go with him, Mr. Rousseau. If he doesn't mind."

"Suit yourself," Bas said. He picked up a piece of paper with what looked like a map sketched on it. "Might want to change into some better boots. We're walking." He folded his map and stuck it into the duffle he always carried.

"I can—" Teddy began.

"Meet me at the fountain in ten minutes," Bas cut in. "Your Grace. McGinty." He gave each of them a nod, then left the room.

The other two men looked at Teddy for a minute, then went back to their maps. Yes, Bas had been rude as hell. Yes, they saw and wondered what Teddy had done to piss Bas off. That made three of them.

"I guess I'm walking." Teddy nodded at McGinty and the duke much as Bas had, then hurried out of the room.

Once he got to his room, a quick check of the footwear assigned for boot camp meant it was Scots boots if he wanted them and Scots boots if he didn't. He wasn't sure how the soft leather boots with their crossed leather strips and period correct soles would hold up, but he had little choice. He'd be damned if he'd wear a kilt. He jammed the legs of his buckskin breeches into the boots, grabbed a heavy quarterstaff from several propped near the door, and headed for the stairs.

A rush of lavender scented wind washed over him from the corridor behind him. When he turned back, soft feminine laughter floated his way. For a split second, he could have sworn a woman in white slipped around the far corner of the hallway.

"What next? A moaning monk floating over my bed when I sleep?" he muttered to the empty corridor. Eleanor and her crew were working overtime on this ghost story thing.

He went down the stairs and waved the staff at a very confused Danny Arneaux and Sylvan Goode as he left the house.

"Planning on encountering Little John at a river crossing?" Bas asked as he pushed up from the edge of the fountain where he sat.

"One never knows." Teddy was torn between wanting to laugh and wanting to crack the man on the head. "This wasn't my idea, but we might as well make the best of it. Or you could give me the map, and I can find the place myself." He struck out toward the path to the stables.

"Not in that direction you can't."

Teddy stopped in his tracks, took a deep breath, and turned around. Bas nodded toward the steps cut into a hill at the opposite end of the house. He didn't wait for Teddy but took off in long strides toward the steps. By the time he reached the top of the hill and set off on a path that went around the side terrace, Teddy matched him stride for stride. They strode in absolute silence for over half an hour. Teddy had never been so uncomfortable, irritated, and confused in his life. He'd had enough.

"Do you intend to remain silent the entire way to this *Gleann Lavender?*"

"I didn't know you Brits required conversation in order

to hike the Scottish countryside. Should have told me. What would you like to talk about? The weather?"

"I see you've read Eleanor's boot camp manual."

"I thought Arneaux's new wife wrote the manual."

"She did, but I'm reasonably certain Eleanor has the entire thing tattooed on her body."

"And you would know that...." Bas stopped and actually looked at Teddy.

"What? Bloody hell, no! Not on your life. I have never been *that* drunk."

"So, you have to be drunk to be with women. Got it. Seems like a lot of trouble to me." Bas turned and headed back across the meadow they'd been crossing.

Dammit!

Teddy hurried to catch up to the arrogant Basque. "Is that it? You're angry because I'm attracted to women and not attracted to you. Is that why I'm getting the silent—"

In half a breath, Bas stood toe to toe with him. Bas tried to knock the quarterstaff from Teddy's hand, but Teddy gripped the wooden weapon and held fast.

"I could give two shits *who* you're attracted to, but I know, and you know it's not women. I have yet to see you look at a woman the way a straight man is supposed to look at a woman, let alone the way he looks at a woman he wants to engage in a nice, hard fuck. What makes me angry is that you insist on lying to these women over and over again. No woman deserves that. And as for you not being attracted to me"—he leaned in close so they were nose to nose—"who are you trying to convince, me or you?" Bas spun on his heel and knocked Teddy back a step as Bas started across the thick grass once more. "And that *still* isn't why I'm pissed." He didn't look back.

Teddy had never been so tired in his life. Not tired, weary. The sort of weariness where his blood turned to water. His muscles simply let go. He hadn't a clue how he remained upright nor how, after a few minutes, he started walking after Bas. Or at least in the same direction. Did he want to follow Bas? The hairs on the back of Teddy's neck stood straight up at the thought. He wanted to say something. Anything. Nothing. Because if he started talking….

By the time he found Bas, the stuntman sat against one of a group of boulders that jutted out from a grassy hillside. He drank from a bottle of water, his head thrown back, every powerful tendon outlined as he swallowed. His black hair, ruffled by the breeze held strands of silver at the temples. Teddy waited. Why wouldn't he, with a view like Bas Salazar, all sculpted muscles, harsh face, black silk hair, and, without seeing them now, light blue eyes Teddy knew would hypnotize him if he gazed into them too long.

He closed his eyes. He was well and truly lost. He wanted to do several things at once, and none were safe, wise, or worth the sacrifice. Right?

"Do you want some water?"

Teddy blinked. Bas held out a second bottle of water to him. Once Teddy got close enough, Bas tossed the bottle to him, then went back to drinking his own. If Eleanor saw them drinking from twenty-first-century water bottles, she'd have a stroke. The water was actually cold. Very.

"Some of my crew keep water frozen in their hotel rooms. They sneak it by the Regency police in coolers of ice," Bas explained as Teddy leaned against the boulder next to him.

"Regency police? Arneaux is a bad influence on you."

The water tasted good. Despite the light winds across the meadow, the heat of the sun beat down on them full force. He began to think the breeches with the boots might have been a bad idea. Bas looked comfortable in his kilt.

"Danny and I have known each other for years."

"I see." Teddy took another long swig from the water bottle. "Why *are* you pissed at me? Specifically."

"We don't have that kind of time, but most immediately? You think I'm the kind of man who would out another. *That* pisses me off."

Teddy sighed. "I'm sorry. That wasn't fair, and I apologize. What are you doing?"

Bas had set his bottle on the rock behind them, taken a pen and notebook out of his duffle, and started to write. "Marking the date. Teddy Rousseau actually apologized on this date. Tell me, Mr. Rousseau is this a first for you?"

"Fuck you."

"Is that an invitation?" Bas gave him a bitter little smile and retrieved his bottle.

Off in the distance a dog barked. Several sheep baaed in answer. The entire setting was like a Turner landscape—except for the deep, low hum of incredible sexual desire that vibrated between Bas and him.

"I can't," he finally said.

"Okay." Bas started to push off the cold, gray granite.

Teddy grabbed his arm. "Please. It's complicated."

"It really isn't, unless you let other people tell you who to be. Then it gets complicated as hell."

"Easy for you to say. You didn't grow up as the only son of a member of Parliament. A *conservative* member of Parliament."

For a minute, those harsh features froze as hard as the stones beneath Teddy's uncomfortable arse. Then Bas erupted into full, raucous laughter. The kind of laughter that bent a man double. It rather hurt. This was not something Teddy talked about with anyone, especially someone he'd just met.

"If you're just going to laugh like a bloody hyena, this

conversation is over." Teddy tried not to sound like such a prig, but not very hard.

"Don't get your breeches in a twist, Teddy. I grew up in the mountains of Spain with devout Catholic parents. Not just devout Catholic, but devout Catholic Basque parents."

The confession took Teddy's breath away. Not that he believed himself to be the only one with *father* issues, but Bas acted so…unconcerned? Normal? The right word wouldn't come to him.

"So, you understand."

"Not really. Look. My parents always suspected. My sister knew. When I decided to come out to them, I was sixteen and scared shitless. The men in my family had made it perfectly clear what they believed about men like you and me."

"Men like you and me?"

Bas rolled his eyes. "My parents were upset at first, but they love me. First couple of years were rough, especially after I left home and then left the country. Now…we're good. I think my sister helped a lot. She and her husband are amazing. The rest of the family and the town?" He gave a dry humorless laugh. "There's a reason I don't go back."

"You were lucky. My parents were in their forties when I was born. I'm their only child. They have expectations. And none of those—"

"None of those should make a damned difference to you now. How old are you?"

"What?" Teddy rubbed his hands on his buckskins. Every nerve in his body rose to the surface. They zinged just beneath his skin. He began to sweat beneath his hair, which he'd tied into a que. His lungs refused to inflate fully.

"I'm thirty-five." Bas leaned toward him. "How. Old. Are. You?" he asked, so close Teddy smelled the coffee and Regency tooth powder on Bas's breath.

"Thirty-one. What difference does that make?"

"You're not their *child* anymore. Don't you think you're old enough to start fulfilling your own expectations?"

Teddy breathed Bas in, the faintest hint of his cologne and coffee and the dark, arousing scent unique to this man. "My…expectations of what?"

"Life." The word floated across Teddy's lips. "This."

The shock jolted Teddy to the soles of his feet. He was in Bas's arms—they were in each other's arms so fast and hard his ribs creaked. Teddy opened to him, allowed Bas to pillage with full, hot lips and the invasion of a tongue determined to tease and conquer. Teddy pulsed his tongue against Bas's. When the stuntman groaned, a thrill like no other raced up Teddy's spine. He jerked Bas's shirttail from the waistband of his kilt, then Teddy ran his hands up Bas's bare ribs and around his back. So damned taut and smooth like sun-warmed marble.

Bas ran his fingers through Teddy's hair and dragged the leather tie away so the strands fell down his back. Bas cupped Teddy's head and slowly, so damned slowly, ended the long intoxicating kiss only to catch Teddy's lower lip between his teeth and pull ever so gently. Teddy made a sound low in his chest that stunned him even as an erotic shiver shot to his groin. Bas kissed him again, fast and hard, then skimmed his lips and teeth along Teddy's jawline. He reached inside the blue hunting jacket Teddy wore, unbuttoned the embroidered waistcoat, and caressed the thin muslin shirt until he found a nipple that Teddy begged to have squeezed. Teddy gasped and pushed his chest into Bas's hand.

The kisses grew more intense, faster, and harder. Bas leaned back against the rock and Teddy followed, his body half-draped over this man he had no power to resist. Rather than resist, he took Bas's mouth in the most passionate, searing kiss of Teddy's life. Every dream, every desire bubbled to the surface, and he wanted to live it all before something or someone snatched the chance away.

He nipped Bas's top lip, and when he gasped, Teddy thrust his tongue in and out of Bas's mouth in an all too familiar rhythm. He cradled Bas's face and took charge of every aspect of the kiss. He reveled in the scrape of whiskers he knew would be a shadow of a beard by sunset. Their tongues tangled. Their lips caressed. Bas continued to caress Teddy's chest over the linen shirt, to squeeze and knead, then to softly stroke. Even with the barrier of the muslin, Teddy's body fairly shook with sensation.

He didn't know who finally tore his lips from whom. They leaned together against the rock, chests heaving, and bodies shaking.

"For someone...who isn't...attracted...to me," Bas said between gasps as he stroked Teddy's back, "you just kissed the ever-loving fuck out of me. I need a cigarette. And a nap."

Teddy huffed a laugh as he rested his forehead on Bas's shoulder. "Me too. But I prefer my mattresses a little softer."

"Are you sure?" Bas arched off the rock to shove an impressive erection against Teddy's thigh.

Something cold and too damned logical came over Teddy. He ran his hands down Bas's sides and across his abs as he dragged himself away from the man sprawled across the rock outcropping like some pagan offering. Even after he stood on his feet, he allowed himself one last trace down Bas's plaid-covered, thick, muscled thigh. Bas lay there a minute longer, one arm across his eyes, then finally got up and tucked his shirt back into his kilt.

He reached out and pushed a long strand of Teddy's hair back behind his ear. "Is this where we act like none of that just happened and treat each other like a couple of guys working on a film together?"

"I...." He couldn't think, dammit. His body was on fire and his mind was a hazy mess of erotic dreams and icy realities.

"How would Regency men do it? Shake hands. Talk about the weather. Never speak of it again?" Bas picked up his duffle, grabbed the two empty water bottles, and stuffed them inside it.

"I don't know," Teddy finally said. He met Bas's gaze and held it while the Highland sun beat down on them. The air swirled around them, suddenly thick with the scent of lavender and heather, though not a sign of either was in sight. "I honestly don't know."

"I suppose that's better than *'I can't.'* Come on. We still have to check out this meadow." Bas started walking, and Teddy fell into step alongside him.

The hike to the glen took another twenty minutes. The strange-scented breeze didn't follow them. If Bas was aware of it, he didn't say. This time they talked as they walked—about Regency boot camp, about the other guests, about the joys of no showers and pissing in a chamber pot. They laughed a lot, something Teddy didn't remember doing in recent memory. In not so recent memory either.

They arrived at the glen to find it didn't actually live up to its name. Not a bloom in sight, but it was very green and rolled on forever until it rose into a grassy hill at one end.

"I'm going to check out the area around the hill," Teddy said. "Makes a perfect safety device for any stray rounds or balls that might hit one of the duke's sheep. Or his deer. Or his *coo's*, as McGinty calls them."

"Stray balls?" Bas lifted a brow. "That could get interesting. Need any help?"

How the hell could a man that looked like an extra in *Braveheart* be such a tempting flirt? Teddy gave him a dismissive wave. "Go plan your battle, Stuntman. I'll meet you back here in a bit."

"Don't say I didn't offer."

Bas strode off into the middle of the glen. He dug around in his bag and pulled out a leatherbound journal, a pen, and some sort of handheld scanning device. God help him if Eleanor saw him breaking her *no electronics* rule. Teddy stood there like a lust-struck schoolboy as Bas ambled farther across the glen.

A thought occurred to him. "Bas." He raised his voice enough to be heard at a distance.

"Yes?" Bas turned and dropped his bag at his feet.

"Don't leave without me?" Teddy wanted to cringe or kick himself. What the *hell* made him say that. "Or at least without telling me." He couldn't make out the man's expression. Probably for the best. *Such a bloody fool.*

"I won't," Bas said in that steady, slightly gruff tone of his.

Teddy turned away quickly and went to the spot he'd picked for shooting practice. The expanse of thick grass that led up to the hill ended up being perfect. The terrain was quite flat and even under the grass. There was enough area to set up targets on the large tripods he used, and if anything went through the targets, it would simply impact the hillside. Even with the echo of such an open expanse, this was far enough away not to carry to the mews where Lord Lachlan would be.

He wanted to stay on Lily's husband's good side because, whilst the man despised guns, he was beyond good with a number of swords. More important, he was an expert archer, and Teddy wanted to persuade him to put on some demonstrations for the boot camp attendees. That was the only reason he came all the way out here on foot to scout this place. Being nice to the duke's brother and the fact Bas had to come out to the same spot had nothing to do with the lack of tension in his shoulders or the liquid ease in his chest. He drank in the pleasure of simply standing in the glorious beauty of the Highland glen. He'd been here two months. How had he not noticed?

Teddy started back across the glen, breathing deeply of the fresh, clean air. Bas sat on some sort of tree stump, flipping through the pages of a book. As Teddy got closer, he heard Bas muttering.

"Problems?"

The stuntman fumbled the book and dropped it.

Teddy grabbed the book before Bas could pick it up. "*Waterloo: Four Days that Changed Europe's Destiny*, not a bad reference book."

"Wentworth sent it to me when he sent me the contracts for the job. I think he probably Googled Waterloo books and just picked the top one."

"Probably. Are you actually going to have to coordinate the entire battle?"

Bas stood and stretched his hands clasped high over his head. Even with him fully clothed, Teddy could see the muscles ripple from his calves to his neck. Maybe he just imagined. His body heated and threatened to melt into the ground.

"Just parts of it. The parts that Arneaux's character remembers. Still, a lot of horses, a lot of extras, a lot of guns, a lot of falling off horses." This last Bas said in an imitation of Teddy's accent. "I just can't get it straight in my head, and I've read through the book twice."

"Would you like some help?"

"Sure."

Teddy ended up doing a one-man reenactment of the Battle of Waterloo for an audience of one who watched his every move and even took notes. For the first time in his life, Teddy had a sense of self-consciousness. He didn't care. Bas asked pointed questions, the answers to which he wrote carefully in his journal. From time to time, he stopped Teddy and asked him to go through something again. Had anyone ever told him teaching a Basque American stuntman about the Battle of Waterloo would be the most satisfying and beautiful afternoon of his life, he'd have laughed in their face. An ordinary, borderline boring thing became everything because of who he was with.

Don't think about it. Don't think at all. He didn't want to think about it. Not just yet.

They walked back to Rosemount Manor under the noonday sun. Their conversation was comfortable. Of course it was. Neither of them said a word about the moments they'd spent in each other's arms. Teddy got the feeling Bas would wait for Teddy to say something, which was something he couldn't do.

"You do know if we're inappropriately late, Eleanor won't let us in the dining room for lunch," Teddy said in an effort to get his mind off exactly how good being in Bas's arms had been.

"You're kidding, right?"

"I never kid about food or Eleanor's rules."

Bas slapped him on the back and took off at a run toward the manor. "Then we'd better hurry," he called over his shoulder, kilt flying. "Race you!"

You will not chase the arrogant, self-assured hot guy that just rang all your bells with a kiss, okay several kisses and more. You will not—

"Bloody hell!" He broke into a run.

Chapter Six

Bas tried not to think too hard about the past few hours as he sprinted toward the corner of the manor house. The exhilaration of the run had nothing to do with the footsteps behind him. Nothing to do with Teddy admitting, if not in words, in deeds that he found Bas attractive. The cool air raced through his lungs. The sun shone so bright it caused the cobblestones of the path that melded into the circular drive around the fountain to glisten as if sprinkled with diamond dust. Kissing Teddy had turned his brain to mush. That had to be it.

Or wait.

Water.

The fountain had overflowed onto the drive. The cobblestones were slick as a movie star's agent. Bas spun to warn Teddy. Too late. The swordmaster had caught up with him He slid into Bas like a freight train. They both went down in a pile of arms and legs with Teddy sprawled on top of him like a blanket. Bas couldn't decide whether his lack of breath was due to falling on his back on some hard damned cobblestones or the sensations exploding through his body now pressed from knees to pecs against Teddy's.

"You could have warned me," Teddy gasped as he planted his hands on either side of Bas and pushed himself up slightly.

"You could have run slower. My bare ass is plastered to the driveway. Damned kilt flew up."

"You're not wearing drawers?"

"Robbie told me it's not allowed."

"He lied."

"I'll kill him. As soon as I regain feeling in my ass."

Teddy threw back his head and laughed. He was handsome as hell when he laughed, his face completely relaxed and his hair loose over his shoulders.

"This is not funny," Bas complained without a bit of ill will.

"No?" Teddy suddenly met his gaze.

Bas swallowed hard.

"I just knocked down the world's foremost stuntman. I think that's funny as hell."

"You would."

"Are we interrupting something?" Eleanor's voice had the same effect as a bucket of ice water.

Bas and Teddy swiveled their heads toward the manor's double doors, which stood wide open and were filled with most of the boot campers and a good number of the duke's servants gawking at them. Bas didn't have time to think of an answer. Teddy scrambled off him so fast it made Bas's head swim. In two seconds, the man stood next to Gloria as if he'd been there the whole time.

"We were racing," he announced. "We slipped and fell." He then proceeded to dust himself off as if he'd fallen in the dirt instead of on top of Bas.

Why was he surprised? Did he really think a few passionate minutes would drag Teddy out of hiding? Didn't mean it didn't sting a little.

"Um, Bas?" Danny had one hand kind of over his face. With the other, he pointed in Bas's general direction. "XYZ?"

"Huh?" He was still intent on Teddy's face, which had just turned a spectacular shade of red. Then Bas glanced down. *Holy shit!* He shoved his kilt down with both hands. Too fucking late. He'd had it bunched up to his waist the whole time. He didn't have to check to know everyone had gotten a great shot, the fully erect shot, before Danny warned him.

"Who won?" Lily asked, her voice full of seventeen different kinds of insinuation.

"I did," Bas and Teddy said together, which actually broke the tension as everyone cracked up.

From the look on Lily's face that was exactly what she intended. Bas vowed to send the woman a bouquet of flowers and a bottle of wine as soon as he hauled his cold, wet butt off the duke's driveway.

Danny and Robbie came to his rescue. Each of them offered him a hand and pulled him to his feet.

"Nice show, guv." Robbie grinned and clapped him on the back as everyone walked into the house.

"Screw you, Robbie," Bas muttered.

"To quote my wife," Danny said. "Play nice."

"Come along, guv, we'll kit you out for luncheon." Robbie steered him toward the stairs.

"Hey, Bas," Lily called. "You're coming to dancing class after lunch, right?"

Bas froze mid-step.

"Splendid idea, Lady Lachlan," Sylvan said. "We can always use another gentleman. Do say you'll be there, Mr. Salazar."

"Yes, do say you'll be there," Lily said.

Bas looked over his shoulder. Teddy and Gloria stood with their heads together, deep in conversation. "I'll be there."

Teddy glanced up at him, but Bas immediately headed up the stairs, Robbie close behind him.

"Remind me to kill you later," Bas said to him as they entered his room.

"Me? What'd I do?" Robbie went to the wardrobe and pulled out some clean pants of some kind, a shirt, waistcoat, and morning coat. Bas had no idea why they called it a morning coat, but okay.

"You lied to me about underwear with a kilt." Bas dropped into a chair and pulled off his boots.

"Nae, I didnae lie. A real Scot wears nothing under his kilt."

Bas dragged his shirt over his head and tossed it to the footman. "Well, it wasn't exactly nothing the entire house saw out there now, was it?"

Robbie chuckled as he handed him a clean, heavy linen shirt. "Nae. You've the right of it there. Even Miss Wither-spoon was impressed. Her eyes fair fell out of her head."

Bas groaned and pulled the shirt over his head. He took the pants and stood to step into them under his kilt. "What the hell are these?"

"They're called pantaloons. Mr. Goode prefers the gentlemen wear them for dance lessons. They're on the list of appropriate things for you to wear during the day."

"Appropriate for what? If these were any tighter, you could tell my religion." Bas twisted and turned as he tried to loosen the grip the *pantaloons* had on him. "What the hell are they made of? Some kind of Regency latex?" Bas sat back down and reached for his leather knee boots—Hessian boots or something like that.

Robbie picked up the card he'd unpinned from the instruments of torture he called *pantaloons*. "Nankeen."

"Jainkoaren Ama. I'm going to kill you right after I kill Erik Wentworth."

"As he's still in the States, I have some time. Not the boots. You need to wear these." Robbie held up a pair of the most ridiculous shoes Bas had ever seen in his life.

"*What* are those?" He pointed at the strange objects as he caught the silk stocking things Robbie tossed him.

"Gentlemen's dancing slippers. How Miss Stepford found them in yer size, I'm fair flummoxed to guess. Hurry up. Ye'll be late to luncheon, and they'll all blame me." The footman knelt down to wrestle Bas into the stockings. Robbie tied the garters, somehow fastened the buttons at the ends of the pantaloons over them, and shoved Bas's feet into the slippers.

Once Robbie finished, Bas stood, took two steps, and nearly slipped on the damned carpets. On the carpets! Robbie grabbed his arm.

"Got it?" he asked. "If ye break yer neck, they'll dock my pay."

"You can all line up and kiss my ass. All of you. Wentworth. Eleanor Witherspoon. The duke. Danny Arneaux. All of you." He walked gingerly toward the door.

"Ye'r a terrible tease is what you are."

"Get up here and help me down the stairs. If I fall, I'm taking you with me."

◈

BAS HAD ALREADY LABELED FORMAL REGENCY DINING AS A form of torture. Add the embarrassment of dining with people who had seen him with his *flag flying* less than an hour ago, and the meal achieved Marquis de Sade status. The teasing didn't bother him. He'd had far worse, and God knows he'd been caught in far more awkward positions. What irked him the most and sent him from irked to damned pissed was Teddy. With every joke and insinuating comment, Teddy grew harder, colder, and, if possible, more arrogant—as if the whole thing had been Bas's idea and simply an incredible error in judgement on Teddy's part. From the way he told the story, Bas had attacked him at the fountain, knocked him down, and pulled him down on top of him. *Bastard!*

That was why Bas dragged his feet when it came to finding the ballroom after lunch. Well, that and the fact the only thing worse than gentlemen's dance slippers on carpet was gentleman's dance slippers on the polished marble floors. He stood outside the impressive gold double doors and tried not to pull at his nankeen whatever-the-hell-they-were.

"If Eleanor finds you out here instead of in there, she's going to rip you a new one." Danny elbowed Bas in the back as he walked up behind him.

"Is that even allowed in the Regency?"

"Yes," Samantha said as she joined her husband. "But it's called tearing a strip off someone."

"Ouch! Who knew the Regency was so brutal." Bas grabbed the two door handles, then pushed the doors open wide. He stepped aside and gave Samantha a sweeping bow. "My lady."

"Thank you, kind sir." Samantha wore a blue and silver striped dress today. The woman was born to wear period clothes. She glided past Bas into the ballroom. When Danny stepped forward to follow, Bas blocked him and hurried after her.

"Don't make me hurt you, Salazar."

"As if you could."

"Mr. Salazar." Sylvan Goode greeted him like a long lost son. "I am so happy you decided to join us."

Bas turned in a circle to take in Rosemount Manor's incredible ballroom. Acres of pink, gold, and light green marble accented with giant gold and glass chandeliers and sconces with lit candles reminded him of the cathedrals in Spain.

"Don't be too excited, Mr. Goode," he said as walked into the center of the room to join the others. "You haven't seen me dance yet."

"You fell off the tower ruins without breaking your neck," Lily said. "Dancing a cotillion should be a piece of cake."

"You fell off that tower?" Gloria stared at him wide-eyed. "On purpose?"

"It's his job," Teddy, dressed head to toe as a Regency gentleman at a ball, said with his customary snide tone. "That's what a stuntman does, Gloria, dear."

The temperature in the room dropped about twenty degrees. *Fuck that!* Bas's Basque blood tended to fight ice with fire. "I guess that's how I managed to make sure Teddy fell on top of me so he wouldn't hurt himself. Wouldn't want anything to happen to our swordmaster, would we?"

"What are we learning today, Mr. Goode?" Eleanor's voice rang like an I-will-kick-your-ass bell across the ballroom. She clapped her hands like a school teacher. "Shall we, ladies and gentlemen?"

Bas was grateful to find himself paired with Lily. She was tall and, despite her reputation, the consummate professional. The actress had paid attention all these weeks and had the dance steps down pat, which helped considerably when Bas either went the wrong way, tripped over his feet, stepped on hers, or slipped on his shoes like an ice skater. A bad one.

"It would be easier to follow the steps if you didn't keep staring at Gloria's ass," Lily said softly as she turned him in the right direction for the third time. "Or is it Gloria's ass that has you so fascinated?"

"I plead the fifth," Bas said as they joined hands with the other dancers and circled to the left. "Thanks for the save this morning, by the way."

"No problem. Been there. Done that." She took his hands in hers as they danced down the line and back.

"I *so* don't want to know."

"I have an excuse. I was younger and dumber. Derek and Rafe send their best."

"Tell them I said hello if you ever get access to a phone or computer again." This time when he turned, he turned the right way and the other dancers applauded.

"I'm married to the duke's brother. I cheat when it comes to the phone thing. Don't tell Eleanor."

"Never." He glanced at the head of the line where Eleanor was paired with Sylvan.

"Then I won't tell her about your and Danny's little coffee business with Robbie."

Bas opened his mouth to say something smart back, but Gloria chose that moment to laugh and compliment Teddy's dancing. Bas clamped his mouth shut and slipped so bad on his shoes he crashed into Lily.

"Sorry."

Lily studied his face and then followed his gaze. He saw the wheels turning in her head.

"Don't, Lily. Okay? Just don't."

Suddenly, Bas wanted a nap, or maybe just a chance to fight off the sudden weariness that came over him. He hadn't been this tired in his soul in a long time. Since before he came out. He'd sworn never to allow himself to be made that tired again. Bad thing about it? That for Teddy, he was even considering the idea.

"If you will, Mrs. Wallace." Sylvan addressed Rosemount's

housekeeper who sat at the piano. "Let us start from the beginning. Assume the position, ladies and gentlemen." He waved them all into place and took his spot across from Eleanor. As the music started, Bas sensed Lily's gaze on him still.

"Jesus, Bas," she said as Mrs. Wallace played the introduction to whatever the hell dance they were doing. Lily glanced at Teddy and Gloria briefly. "I thought *I* was the worst when it came to going after unavailable men."

"I don't know what you're talking about, *Lady Lachlan*. Pay attention. I'm counting on you to keep me from falling on my ass."

"That's not the kind of falling you need to worry about, Stuntman."

They joined hands and danced down the middle of the line of dancers. Bas concentrated on the dance to keep his mind off what she'd said. He didn't miss a step this time and received shouts of encouragement from the other men. They came back down the line and moved into their places.

Lily leaned across to whisper in his ear. "Just so you know, he's not that good in bed."

BAS SAT RELAXED IN THE SADDLE. THE ENTIRE REGENCY boot camp had accompanied them from the dance class to *Gleann Lavender* for Teddy's shooting class. Some of them had decided to go on horseback because it was such a nice day. Others had climbed into the large dogcart driven by the stablemaster, Mr. Urquhart. Apparently, Teddy and some of the footmen had taken a larger wagon out earlier to set everything up.

He hadn't remembered a damned thing about the rest of dance class after Lily's announcement. Apparently, he did pretty well as he didn't have any aches, pains, or bruises from slips or falls. Then again, most of the time that sort of thing didn't register. Hazards of the job. He'd once worked two weeks with a broken wrist until an assistant director noticed his arm was black and blue. No, he'd managed to get through dance class with Lily's help despite her sharing the one bit of information he *so* didn't need to know. Come to think of it, there was no surprise there at all. Kind of sad, actually. Thank God Lily had the confidence to handle being used by a man like Teddy. He'd seen what happened when women didn't. It wasn't pretty.

"Are you excited?" Samantha rode up beside him

"Shooting guns is nothing new to Bas, *cher*," Danny said as he maneuvered his horse on the other side of Bas's.

"There is always something new to learn, Arneaux," Bas said. "You know that. I can't believe the duke is actually coming along."

"I have it on good authority that Eleanor dared him," Samantha said.

"What good authority?" Danny asked his wife.

"Robbie and Dougal."

"Those two need to go to work for the British version of the CIA." Bas shook his head. "They're dangerous."

"MI6? They'd have to stop their gambling." Samantha patted her horse's neck as they entered the glen and came to a stop.

"That's not going to happen." Danny threw his leg over his horse's head and slid to the ground. He helped Samantha down, then tied the horses to a nearby tree.

Bas followed suit and they headed for the row of felt-covered tables set up in a line some distance away but across from the targets set against the hillside.

Danny grinned. "Come on, Bas. I've got a fiver says you outshoot everyone."

"Great," Bas muttered.

He joined the others who chatted and wandered around, admiring the guns displayed on the tables. He had to admit they were beautiful pieces. Most were pistols with ornate polished wood and silver filigreed handles. Dougal and Robbie made a big show out of telling people not to touch the guns because they were all loaded. Teddy stood on the near side of the center table, arms folded across his chest, one hip resting on the table. He'd changed into a different outfit. Still Regency, but more casual.

He wore black knee boots and a deep navy-colored jacket that fit him really well, and he'd tucked his white shirt into his buckskin breeches. He looked like a character in one of those movies his sister liked so much. Definitely not Bas's type at all. Yeah. Right.

"Shall we begin, ladies and gentlemen?" Teddy announced as he straightened and waved them all together. "Robbie and Dougal have given you my instructions. I'm going to give them to you again. Stay behind the tables at all times. We have measured the distance from behind the tables to the targets and it's perfect for practice with these particular weapons. Do *not* touch a gun until I hand it to you. Do not *fire* a gun until I tell you to. You will each fire one at a time. We will never have more than one person firing at any one time. Once you have fired your gun, return it immediately to the table. I will show you how to load the pistols as a matter of interest, but you will *not* be loading the pistols. I am the only person who will load the guns. Any questions?"

A chorus of *"No's"* and *"No, sir's"* responded.

"Who wants to go first?" Teddy asked.

"Might I suggest," the duke said as he stepped forward, "the ladies be allowed to go first?"

"So the men can go after us and show us up?" Eleanor asked with a sweetness that reminded Bas of hard candy. The kind that threatened to break your teeth.

"Not at all, Miss Witherspoon." The duke bowed slightly in her direction. "So the ladies can set the bar for which we gentlemen can only hope to strive."

"He's good," Bas observed to Danny who had sidled up beside him.

"You have no idea. Those two need to get a room."

Bas laughed out loud before he could stop himself. Everyone turned his way.

"You find the idea of women outshooting men amusing, Mr. Salazar?" Eleanor asked.

Danny snorted—until Bas stepped on his foot. A couple of hundred pounds in a leather knee boot shut a laughing Cajun up real quick.

"Not at all, Miss Witherspoon. I'd call it a foregone conclusion."

"Nice try," Danny muttered, and elbowed Bas in the side.

"Mr. Salazar," Teddy said loud enough to cut through the chatter and laughter. "If you will." He motioned Bas forward imperiously.

Bas strode forward and joined Teddy at the weapons table. "I warned you about getting on Miss Witherspoon's bad side," Teddy said as he picked up an antique pistol.

"Is that what this is about, Teddy?" Bas squared up behind the table and eyeballed the target in the distance.

"What else would it be?" He held the pistol up so the others could see. "This is an 1814 dueling pistol by Joseph Manton, London's premiere gunsmith during the Regency. It is a flintlock and takes a forty-bore load."

He went on to describe the gun in detail as he loaded it and prepared it for Bas to fire. Bas listened, but he also made a study of Teddy's face. He was a born teacher. Teddy obviously loved period weapons, but even more he loved sharing what he knew with people who were really interested. There was no doubt in the man under these circumstances. No doubt at all. Sexy, fascinating, and attractive as hell all at once.

"Ready, Mr. Salazar?" Teddy moved closer to him and handed Bas the pistol.

This time, Bas didn't smell lavender or heather or earth. This time he smelled orange and ambergris. Teddy had expensive tastes in cologne. Their eyes met for a moment. This time Bas looked away first.

"As ready as I'll ever be."

This wasn't his first rodeo or even his first time shooting a gun. He sighted the target and tightened his grip on the pistol butt while he loosened his grip on the trigger. The noise and smoke when he fired elicited some jumps and a few shouts from the others. He had to admit the pistol packed a punch. Once the smoke cleared and Teddy gave the word, Dougal ran down to check the target. Bas returned the pistol to the table and took a step back.

"Just at the edge of the bullseye," Dougal shouted as he jogged back. "Good shot, sir."

The rest of the group applauded. Teddy merely stared at him. An odd flicker twisted the corner of his mouth.

"Now, Miss Witherspoon," he finally said as he picked up the next pistol. "Let's have you next."

Bas suppressed a grin at the lady's look of surprise. She stepped up to the table, and Teddy went through the entire spiel again. The pistol bucked when Eleanor fired, but she did hit the target. After that, each of the guests took several turns firing the guns. Robbie, of course, kept detailed records of every shot. A lot of good-natured kidding went on as did a number of challenges and counter challenges. Through it all, everyone listened, really listened to what Teddy had to teach them about the different pistols and even some of the fowling pieces and cavalry rifles they fired. The duke and Bas were the two best shots.

"I am astounded, Your Grace," Eleanor said after nearly two hours had passed. "I didn't peg you as a shooting man."

Danny, Sylvan, and Bas elbowed one another and grinned. Samantha tapped Danny's arm with her fan. She smacked Bas for good measure.

"One of the few things my father bothered to teach me, Miss Witherspoon. I used to be quite fond of target practice, though I never was much of a hunter." He turned to Teddy. "I appreciate the opportunity to shoot such fine weapons, Mr. Rousseau. Your collection is exquisite. Will you be using some of these in the film?"

"Very likely, Your Grace. So long as I am there to supervise their use."

Bas could well imagine Teddy's response should someone even scratch one of his weapons. The swordmaster was a meticulous man in all things. Unfortunately.

"I want to see the master at work," Lily said. "I want to see Teddy shoot against the duke and Bas."

Trust the duke's now sister-in-law to deliberately stir up trouble.

The duke glanced up at the sun. "It's a bit late in the day."

"And the wind has picked up." Eleanor gave him a sweet smile that didn't fool Bas for an instant.

Damn. This place was like a Regency soap opera.

The duke didn't look away. An odd expression crossed his face. Then he appeared to shake it off. "As much as I would like that"—he lifted a hand toward Mr. Urquhart—"I have some decidedly twenty-first-century business to conduct online, and I must return home." The words were barely out of his mouth and the stablemaster had the duke's horse at his side.

He swung into the saddle. "Please let me know how the contest goes between Mr. Rousseau and Mr. Salazar." He guided his horse away from the group, then said over his shoulder, "Robbie, put me down for five pounds on Mr. Rousseau."

"Aye, Yer Grace!"

Bas had never watched a group of people try to do so many things at once. None of them deliberately turned to see Eleanor's reaction, though from their expressions, they wanted to, badly. None of them wanted to stare after the duke, so they turned away from the direction in which he'd ridden. Danny and Bas didn't want to crack up at the whole farce, so they did their damnedest not to look at each other. Teddy got really busy wiping down his guns and returning them to their cases.

"Guess it's just you and me, Teddy. Shall we?" Bas's voice carried far more than he'd intended, but it sure as hell got everyone's attention.

Teddy stopped in the middle of closing a case. He turned his head and took his time gauging Bas's expression, or so Bas assumed. "Are you serious?"

"Always."

Bas hoped like hell the others weren't reading exactly what was going on between Teddy and him. Maybe they thought it was some kind of *High Noon* type thing. Maybe.

"Very well. Best out of five shots each?" Teddy began to place a series of pistols side by side.

"Done."

Bas stood with Danny and Samantha while Teddy loaded all ten guns. Bas ignored a quick exchange of money between the actor and Robbie. Mr. Goode and Robbie. McGinty and Robbie. *What the hell!* When Eleanor beckoned Robbie over, Bas and Danny both gawked open-mouthed. Samantha reached out to close their mouths.

Teddy stepped back from the table with a slight bow in Bas's direction.

"You'd better beat him," Danny whispered. "I've bet twenty pounds on you."

Bas was pretty sure the grunt as he walked away was the result of the Cajun's wife's elbow in his gut. He wiped his hands on his buckskin breeches. Teddy indicated the first pair of pistols. So, Bas was supposed to choose first. He picked up a pistol, another Manton according to the name on a silver plate on the butt of the gun. Dougal had run down to move all but two of the targets aside.

"Ready?" Teddy asked.

Bas simply nodded. They turned to the side and sighted down the barrels of their pistols. The smoke and noise as they fired simultaneously created a sort of vortex where only he and Teddy stood. They moved as one down the line and fired each of the five pistols in turn. Bas had seen perfect stunts less coordinated, less synchronized. Not a word passed between them. Even after they'd fired their last shots and carefully placed their pistols on the table, neither spoke. A connection ran between them made of the scent of black powder and the echo of gunfire. A strange sensation pressed against Bas's chest as if all the air beyond the smoke suddenly closed in on him. Without a bloom in sight, that air smelled of lavender and earth. Teddy turned and stared at him, a stunned expression on his face.

"I can't call it, guv," Dougal said as he jogged up with the paper targets he'd retrieved once the shooting stopped. "You take a look, Mr. Arneaux."

"Not fair," Eleanor said. "He has a wager on the results."

"Miss Stepford," Teddy said though he still looked at Bas. "A woman with your eye for detail should be the judge." The costume designer smiled brightly, pleased at Teddy's compliment. She should be. Teddy never complimented anyone so far as Bas knew.

Miss Stepford took her glasses out of the pretty drawstring bag on her wrist. She spent a lot of time on each of the targets. She measured, marked, and counted. Bas wanted to laugh at how quietly and seriously everyone waited for her verdict. He wanted to but couldn't. Every time he glanced up, Teddy's intent scrutiny sent a shiver down his spine.

"As close a thing as ever I've seen," Miss Stepford declared as she removed her glasses and tucked them back into her bag. "Every shot pierced the dead center of the target, but the closest shot was Mr. Rousseau's. I declare him the winner."

She made such a grand show of the announcement, Bas had no choice but to grin. Groans, shouts, and applause greeted her decision.

"Congratulations." He extended a hand to Teddy. "I'm not surprised you won. I'm surprised I did that well."

"I'm not." Teddy shook his hand. Bas detected something pressing again his palm in the instant before Teddy released his hand. "Dougal. Robbie. Let's pack everything up."

He and the footmen got to work wiping down the guns and putting them in their cases. Eleanor clapped her hands to get everyone's attention and asked McGinty and Mr. Urquhart to supervise everyone's return to the house on horseback or in the large pony cart.

"You owe me twenty pounds," Danny said as he and Samantha rode up next to Bas. Samantha handed him the reins to his horse.

"Nonsense," she said. "I think your efforts were admirable, Bas. You and Teddy put on quite a show for the rest of us amateurs."

"Thank you, Dr. Higgins." Bas swung into the saddle and brought his horse into line with hers and her husband's as they started across the glen toward the road.

"That's Mrs. Arneaux," Danny said.

"Not when she says something as wise and charming as that."

"Stop flirting with my wife. Ouch!" Danny rubbed his arm where his wife had struck him with her fan.

It wasn't until the two of them were deep in a light-hearted argument that Bas opened his hand and unfolded the piece of paper Teddy had pressed into his palm. The small piece of antique-looking parchment had a hand-drawn map and one word scribbled on it.

Midnight.

Chapter Seven

TEDDY DIDN'T KNOW WHETHER TO BE FURIOUS NO ONE HAD mentioned this little slice of heaven in all the time he'd been at Rosemount Manor or grateful Robbie had finally decided to have pity on him and show him the early nineteenth-century bathhouse hidden away behind the conservatory. As he settled down on the inset bench that went all the way around the circular Roman-like bath in the middle of the room, and the hot water embraced him up to his underarms, he decided not to be furious. It might involve getting out of the large circular pool of deliciously comforting water. He had no intention of doing so. For at least a week.

"How is it heated again?"

Robbie stood at the top of the steps that led down to the pool. He had a stack of Regency-era bath sheets, some flannels, and some bars of soap milled at Rosemount Manor. "The boilers that heat the water run underneath the conservatory. All I had tae do was turn a few spigots to route the water out here and light a few extra boilers. The water'll be hot for hours until the extra boilers run out. I read up on it in the history of the estate. Apparently, one of His Grace's ancestors had it installed to help with his rheumatism in about 1789 or so."

"Wise man." Teddy closed his eyes and rested his head against the lip of the pool.

"Yes, well. I also read his rheumatism had more tae do with meeting his young mistresses out here."

Teddy laughed. "I would expect no less. And you haven't told anyone else about this?"

"Haven't had the chance to test it before now. Just found the book about it a wee while back. Himself had it renovated and restored after Lord Lachlan came home from Afghanistan, but no one ever uses it. I haven't told anyone else that I actually got it working yet."

"And you'll be charging the others once you let them know?"

"Aye. Have tae be compensated for the risk I'm taking, don't I?"

"Risk?"

"Miss Witherspoon."

"She doesn't know about it?"

"Nae. Himself never told her."

"Say no more. This is well worth the price." Teddy sighed and reached for the flannel and soap Robbie had placed at the edge of the pool.

"There's more."

Robbie strode around the pool to where a heavy curtain hung from ceiling to the Roman tiled floor. Brightly lit torches were set into wrought iron fixtures at varying heights. He pulled back the curtain to reveal a raised area with stairs that led down into the pool. In the raised area sat a tall frame of some sort with a large, polished metal tub mounted on a spit-like bar with a chain attached to a wooden handle that dangled into the middle of the frame. The bottom of the frame had a skirt around it about waist high made of some sort of oilskin cloth. A door in the middle of the skirted section opened so one might step into the middle of the frame.

Teddy sat up out of the water. "What is that?"

Robbie leaned over and tugged the wooden handle at the end of the chain. A metallic slide issued from the tub, and a shower of water cascaded from the bottom of the tub very much in the same pattern as a wide shower head.

"A shower? There's been a shower here all this time, and no one said a word?"

"There are modern showers all over the manor house. Miss Witherspoon had the doors to all the bathrooms locked, except for in the duke's chambers."

Teddy stared at the Regency shower as if it were the Holy Grail. Decisions. Decisions. He wanted to soak in the pool for days, but the idea of a hot shower? Intoxicating. Then there was the other intoxicating expectation that danced around his mind. He picked up the pocket watch he'd placed on the side of the pool. Five minutes to midnight.

"I assumed the duke wasn't having to play Regency lord of the manor." He closed his eyes once more and rested his head on the folded bath sheet he'd put behind him as a pillow.

Please, take the hint, Robbie.

"If there's nothing else, I need tae get back to the house. Mrs. Wallace will miss me to be sure."

"Absolutely, Robbie." Teddy forced himself not to sag into the pool with relief. "And thank you."

"I'll leave the key in the door. Lock up when you leave, if ye will, sir?" By the sound of Robbie's voice he was already at the door at the top of the stairs.

"Aye," Teddy said.

Robbie laughed. The door closed with a heavy click. Teddy released the breath he'd held, what seemed like all day.

He'd questioned himself all his life. He'd bet his life Bas Salazar never did. He gave all the appearance of a man who lived his life the way he'd fired those pistols. No hesitation. His entire body focused on one purpose because he could. There was a certain grace in the man, a grace born of certainty at his center. Teddy would sell his soul for that certainty. Or would he?

He'd done so many things on impulse since Bas had walked into his life. None so reckless as the note he'd handed him after the shooting match. Perhaps Bas wouldn't show up. Then Teddy wouldn't have to figure out exactly *why* he'd written the note, *why* he'd given it to Bas, and the bloody hell he intended to do if the man did show up.

He slid off the bench and sank beneath the water. The stupid things a person missed about the so-called modern world. Eleanor had once commented on how easily Teddy had adapted to living the Regency life. If only she knew. The manners and restraint had come so effortlessly to him because his entire life had been one of manners, and proper, and restraint. Above all, restraint. Except for his reputation for chasing women and being a complete snob, he'd led a completely ordinary life. Some might find his career choice out of the ordinary, but as it was rooted in a deep devotion to history, it still landed him in the dull academic category.

Teddy pushed himself back onto the bench, shook his head back and forth, and ran his hands over his face to get the water out of his eyes.

"I was afraid I'd have to dive in there after you."

The dark, rich, slightly accented voice came from the top of the stairs behind him. Teddy slowly lowered his hands and took a minute to steady his breath, which had seized and then hammered at his lungs like a bird trying to escape a room with no windows. Booted footsteps sounded on the stairs. The air, already damp and filled with heat, turned warmer and heavier. Finally, he shifted in the pool toward Bas. He sit on the wooden bench where Robbie had stacked the linens and bars of soap.

"You're here." *What an utterly inane thing to say.*

"Where exactly is here? How did you find this place?"

"This is the estate's bathhouse. Built in the late eighteenth century. Miss Witherspoon doesn't know about it, but if she did, I'm certain she'd figure a way to keep us out of it."

Bas snorted. "Is that water as warm as it looks?"

"Warmer. You should try it." Teddy winced. He didn't want to sound like a flirt, did he? He was sixteen all over again and without a clue.

"Robbie, I take it?" Bas stood and walked toward the pool, his boots echoing on the tiled floor.

"Who else? And before you ask, yes, he will be charging us all for access."

"That boy needs to be working in Hollywood as an agent." Bas squatted a few feet from where Teddy sat in the pool and dangled his fingers in the water.

"Or stand for Parliament." Teddy imagined those fingers moving back and forth in the water brushing across his skin.

"Why am I here, Teddy?"

Good question. "You tell me." Yes, his flirting skills had deserted him.

Bas reached into his waistcoat pocket and pulled out a folded square of paper. "You invited me. For what?"

Teddy took a deep breath. "For me. I want...I wanted to see you. To...." He met that liquid blue gaze, and his mind blanked. Not a single word came to mind. Bas hadn't worn his jacket or his neckcloth, and he'd left his waistcoat unbuttoned.

Bas stood and shook his head. "What are we talking about? A one-night stand? I don't do those anymore. A fling for a few weeks? More? Either way, I'm not sure I can be your dirty little secret. That's not who I am at this point in my life."

Teddy could only look at Bas, watch him as if he expected something of Teddy, something he didn't know if he could give. The water was still hot, but it hardly registered. His body chilled as the truth of his unwillingness to take a chance sank into his bones.

"I understand," he heard himself say.

A lie. He didn't understand any of this. He turned his head to stare at the shower set up. He stood so abruptly he splashed water out of the pool onto the floor behind him. Bas took a step back, just the click of his boots alerting Teddy to the other man's movements.

"I'm going to take a shower. Robbie showed me how to operate the Regency shower."

Inane. Useless. Drivel.

He snatched the bath sheet from the floor where he'd dropped it, wrapped it around his waist, and walked around the far side of the pool to the steps that led to the shower. He refused to look back. Still, Bas said nothing.

Out of the pool, the temperature in the bathhouse cooled quickly. Water began to dry on Teddy's skin. He figured out how to open the half door, stepped into the middle of the shower frame, and tossed the bath sheet over the railing. He needed the cascade of water. He needed the noise and heat to block the sound of Bas as he walked away. Teddy's chest squeezed as if in a vice. He reached for the wooden handle and gently pulled it to release the water overhead slowly. Once the shower started, he dropped his head to his chest and tried to concentrate on the sensation he'd missed since he'd arrived at Rosemount Manor.

He released his breath on a long sigh and reached for the soap Robbie had left in the metal dish mounted to the side of the shower. The slow caress of rough fingertips that pushed his hair away from his neck startled him, but only for an instant. He knew that touch on a level that frightened and thrilled him to the depths of his soul. Lips, cool and firm, skimmed across the back of his neck and came to rest on the spot where his collarbone joined his neck. A gentle scrape of teeth, a sigh against his wet, hot skin, and a soft and lingering kiss accompanied that rough hand as Bas slid it around Teddy to cover an already sensitive nipple. Then he did jump and gasp.

"Tell me to go," Bas said roughly against Teddy's neck. "Tell me to leave you alone, *ene gizon ederra*."

The last phrase, growled so deeply, had Teddy's cock twitching in response. Bas brought his other hand to Teddy's abs. Now fully in Bas's embrace, Teddy realized the stuntman was naked. His perfectly toned and carved body rested against Teddy's back, the heat of him seared and caressed at the same time.

"I can't," he whispered. "I don't want you to go. Stay."

"Yes?"

"Don't stop."

"Don't stop what?" Bas pulled Teddy closer, nipped his shoulder, and ran a line of kisses down the back of Teddy's neck and the top of Teddy's spine.

"Anything. Everything. Whatever you want." Teddy's body shook.

He'd never been this aroused in his life. Nerve endings fired and sizzled to the point he was all sensation, all fire. He lolled his head back and turned to kiss Bas's jaw, the corner of his mouth. They were so close to the same height they fit together perfectly. Bas's erection pressed against the back of his hip. Bas slid his hand lower and caressed Teddy's cock

"Oh God." Teddy arched against Bas's hand in a plea for more.

Bas laughed, then wrapped his hand around Teddy's cock, and stroked one long, achingly slow stroke. *"Ona, laztana?"*

"Yes," Teddy gasped.

He didn't know what he was saying *yes* to and didn't care. He'd say anything to hold on to the glorious feeling of Bas stroking him, teasing and torturing him. He tried to turn around, to reach for Bas. The big Basque banded his free arm around Teddy's upper chest and held him in place before squeezing Teddy's pec and then his nipple.

"No, *maitea*. This is for you. All for you. Stay right there."

He latched onto Teddy's ear lobe with sharp teeth and began to suck and tug. He matched the rhythm to the now intense slide of his hand up and down Teddy's cock. Teddy arched into every stroke. He gripped Bas's forearm with one hand and one of the man's thick thighs with the other. Teddy angled his body back to allow Bas better access.

Soon, Teddy had no choice but to move his hips to meet each stroke. He dug his fingers into Bas's flesh as his orgasm began to build. He lost control. His body took over pumping into Bas's fisted hand faster and faster until his entire being exploded, and he came in one long shouted groan that echoed off the tiled walls.

He was light-headed. His knees nearly gave way. Bas held him in his arms tenderly and yet strong. He whispered in Teddy's ear, half in English and half in Basque. Teddy didn't understand any of it. He was beyond words at that point. Beyond anything. He'd never in his life experienced anything like the last…what was it? Fifteen minutes? An hour? Half the night. He didn't know. He didn't care other than to know when they might do it again.

"Are you okay?" Bas asked quietly.

He brushed Teddy's hair back off his face. Only then did Teddy realize the man had been running hands over him in long, languid strokes this entire time. This time when he tried to turn around, Bas let him.

Teddy cupped Bas's face. "What did you just do to me?"

The brush of his evening stubble tempted Teddy terribly. He kissed along Bas's jawline and across his chin before finally taking Bas's mouth in an invasive, demanding kiss. When Teddy finally stopped long enough for them to breathe, Bas laughed.

"If you have to ask, then I didn't do it right."

Teddy ran his teeth along Bas's collarbone. Bas shuddered in response, which gave Teddy the most ridiculous thrill. "Trust me," he muttered against the stuntman's hot, wet skin. "You did it right."

"Good." Bas tilted Teddy's head up to cover his lips in an open-mouthed kiss.

Before Teddy had a chance to breathe, the two of them were locked in a duel of tongues and lips as they each tried to seize control. Their groans vibrated in their chests pressed to each other impossibly close and tight.

Teddy fumbled between them, and after he found Bas's cock only half-erect, Teddy slowly withdrew from their kiss to search the other man's face.

"Did you...." He glanced down and then back up quickly.

"Oh, yeah." Bas gave a shy grin and thrust against Teddy's hip a couple of times. "You took care of that."

Teddy dropped his head to Bas's chest.

"Actually, I was ready to come the minute I saw you naked in this shower thing."

Teddy snapped his head up like a shot. The heat of what had to be his first blush in decades flooded Teddy's skin.

"Is that a blush from the unflappable Mr. Rousseau?"

"It's the hot water. Damned English pallor."

Bas stroked the back of his hand down the side of Teddy's face. "You're not pale. You're beautiful."

"Men don't say that to men." An odd sort of fissure crept across his shoulders.

Bas met Teddy's gaze and held it a long time. "That's a shame."

"What?"

"That no one has told you you're beautiful." Bas brushed Teddy's hair back, then kissed his forehead and trailed kisses down to the corner of his eye before kissing his jaw on the way to the tender spot on the side of Teddy's neck. "You are, you know," Bas whispered in Teddy's ear. "Beautiful. Powerful. Do people even know how ripped you are? How amazing your skin is?" Bas ran his hands up and down Teddy's back, which arched into Bas's touch like a housecat in search of petting.

The man's touch was seductive as sin. Teddy never wanted Bas to stop—which was exactly what needed to happen. Teddy placed his hands on Bas's chest, not to push really, but to slow things down.

"I won't be beautiful shivering with blue lips. Let's see if there's more hot water in this cistern." He pulled the handle until the warm water fell over them. "Shall we finish this shower?"

Bas didn't say much after that. He did take the soap from Teddy's hand and used it to bathe the sticky spot on Teddy's hip. Because he had no strength to resist, he let Bas bathe him. Then because Bas didn't bother to resist, Teddy did the same for him. Teddy fought against the flame of arousal that simmered inside him as he ran the soap over every cut and ripple of muscle. He memorized the scars and made a note to ask about Bas sometime. Not tonight. Tonight, Teddy was afraid to speak. The sound of the shower in the cavern of Rosemount's antique bathhouse created an enclosed chamber where only he and Bas existed and whatever this thing was that connected them closer and closer by the minute.

The water started to cool, and the cistern overhead seemed to be nearly empty. Teddy spent a lot of time rinsing the soap off Bas's butt because as shallow as it sounded, the man had a magnificent butt. Bas didn't turn around, but he grabbed Teddy's hand and pulled it around his chest until Teddy stood with his body pressed against Bas's. Teddy curled his other arm around Bas and rested his chin on Bas's shoulder as the shower stopped completely.

"Now what?" Bas covered Teddy's hands against his chest with his own.

"I'm afraid we need to find some bath sheets and dry off before we freeze. We can't stay here all night."

"We can't?"

"No." Teddy found it harder and harder to breathe, to speak.

"Shame." Bas didn't move but simply leaned back into Teddy's embrace and sighed.

"Yes." What did Bas want him to say? What did he want to say?

"Okay."

Bas pulled free of Teddy and brushed past him, then stepped out of the shower frame. He strode around the pool to the bench where Robbie had left the bath sheets. By the time Teddy reached Bas's side, Bas had wrapped one sheet around his waist and had started to dry off with another. Teddy grabbed a couple of bath sheets and did the same. Still without saying a word, Bas slipped back into his breeches, shirt, and boots. He sat on the bench, his forearms on his knees and stared off into space. Teddy shouldered his way into his heavy quilted velvet robe, tied the belt, and shoved his feet into the ornate slippers that were part of his Regency wardrobe. He ran his hand over Bas's short cropped dark hair.

"I—"

"We—"

They both laughed as Teddy sat down on the bench next to Bas.

"You know what I want," Bas said.

"Do I?"

"I want to spend time with you. You're actually good company when you're not being a British snot." He shrugged. "I want to get to know you, as corny as that sounds."

"Doesn't sound corny. Sounds lovely. And scary as hell."

"*I'm* scary as hell, or people finding out who you really are is scary as hell?"

"Both."

"Then we have a problem."

"Yes. We do." Teddy knew what was coming. He'd been through this before, not often, but often enough to know a man like Bas didn't take steps backwards for anyone.

"Jesus, Teddy, give me something. Anything."

"I…I can't. I don't know. Damn." He scrubbed his hands across his face.

Bas squeezed Teddy's knee. "I know." He stood. "Be careful going back to the house. It's cold and dark out there." He started up the stairs to the door.

"Bas?"

"I'm going to sleep on it, Teddy. That's all I can do." The sound of his boots bounced off the tile walls for a few seconds after he closed the door behind him.

Teddy listened to the steady drip of water and the groan and hiss of the pipes. By the time he finally stood and made his way out of the bathhouse, the moon had risen and lit the way back to the conservatory. He walked as quickly as he could until he reached the sanctuary of the conservatory.

The room was huge and kept warm all year round. Best of all, the floor was heated, and the hot air blew up under his floor-length robe to take the chill from his still-damp legs. Robbie, bless him, had left an oil lamp on a table next to the doors into the main house. Teddy reached for the lamp and noticed a sprig of lilac and a white rose resting beside the light. The stem had been broken not cut. He picked them up and touched them to his lips. Their melded scents, though not overwhelming, made it hard to breathe. Or perhaps something else squeezed his lungs and pressed against his chest.

"You're in the soup now, Teddy-boy," he muttered.

A soft feminine sigh issued behind him. His heart jumped and his mind worked on a story as he turned to confront the person who'd caught him sneaking about the conservatory. His mouth was half-opened to speak. No one was there. Dammit, he'd heard something. He hadn't gone that far around the twist. Yet.

"Hello?" he called softly.

The huge glass room was dark for the most part. A few gas lamps mounted in sconces along the wall of the house cast enough light to make shadows but didn't reach all the way to the doors he'd entered through.

He took a few steps into the center of the room. "Hello?"

This time, the sigh came from a stone path to his left where the duke's koi pond and fountain splashed and babbled in the silence of the massive room. Teddy followed the sound of the running water.

"Eleanor?" Teddy stopped in his tracks.

A lady dressed in white sat on the edge of the little stone wall around the koi pond. For a moment he thought she was the boot camp's steely-spined director. But her curly golden-red hair drawn over her shoulder was much longer than Eleanor's. She faced away from him, trailing her hand in the pond's water. When she finally turned toward him, he took a step back without really knowing why. This wasn't Eleanor. This wasn't—

His breath caught. A slight breeze sifted through the jungle of plants around him.

Lavender.

Heather.

Fresh earth.

The lady sighed again. The air around her shimmered. Teddy met her gaze head on and was shaken to his core. Such sadness in her eyes. For herself? For him? She rose gracefully from her seat and started toward him. He stumbled back and raised his arm to shield his eyes as the glowing figure came closer. An icy chill came over him. When he lowered his arm, he was alone.

"What the hell?"

He looked left, then right, started down the path behind the pond, then thought better of it. Teddy backed up all the way to the table where the lamp still sat. He still clutched the flowers. With his free hand, he took up the lamp and backed through the French doors into the main house. Before he knew it, he had crossed the grand foyer and was climbing the stairs as quickly as his pointy slippers and long, velvet robe would let him.

Don't look back. Don't look back. Don't look back.

He didn't—until he was halfway down the second-floor corridor and almost to his room. "What the hell!" He fell against the wall.

Robbie, a full tea tray in his hands, stood in the middle of one of Rosemount's hundreds, it seemed, of Turkish carpets, and blinked. "Are you all right, sir?"

"Define 'all right.'" Teddy straightened and went to his chamber door.

Robbie followed him inside. "I was going to ask how ye

enjoyed the shower," he said. "But I think ye need a cuppa tea first." He set the tray on the table in front of the fire and quickly filled a cup. Steam wafted up from the hot tea as he added milk and sugar.

"Bless you."

Teddy grabbed the cup as he sat in the fireside chair. He sucked down half the cup before he came up for air. He noticed Robbie had taken the lilac and rose from the table and placed them in a little porcelain vase to which he added water.

"Beg pardon, sir, but ye look like ye've seen a ghost."

"Nonsense." He didn't mean to snap, especially as Robbie was too damned clever by half.

The footman gave Teddy a long perusal and shrugged. "As ye say. I'll leave the tea." He strolled to the door.

"The shower was great, Robbie. Thanks."

Robbie turned and gave him a little bow. "Oh. I left a couple of keys on the tray for ye. The brass one is to the bathhouse." He paused with entirely too much intention.

"And the other?"

"There's a dressing room between yer room and the next room. I didn't know whether ye or Mr. Salazar might want to use the room to store equipment or luggage." He said this with a completely straight face. What was he up to?

"Does Mr. Salazar have a key?" Teddy's heart began a slow, heavy thud.

"Nae. There's only one key. If ye don't want to use the dressing room, ye can give it to him. Anything else, sir?"

"No, Robbie." Teddy did a careful scrutiny of the young man's face. The footman had suddenly become a Scots sphinx. "Good night."

Teddy finished off another cup of tea before he even looked at the keys on the tray. He grabbed them, stood, and placed the brass one inside a porcelain snuff box on the mantel. The other one was black. He turned it over and over in his hand. Finally, he sat on the edge of his bed, then rifled through the drawer of the bedside table. After a few misses, he dragged an envelope out of the drawer and dropped the black key into it. He propped the envelope against his stack of weaponry books and stared at it for what might have been five minutes, might have been an hour.

He had a decision to make, and the scent of Bas's cologne on Teddy's skin and the memory of Bas's touch under the spray of the hot shower in a Regency bathhouse of all places was the last thing he needed. What he needed was a psychiatrist. Either he was having delusions, or a ghost had visited him. A ghost who'd been murdered for love. And *she* felt sorry for *him.*

Chapter Eight

Bas lay flat on his back on the ground, unable to take even a single breath. He'd been here before, but not in a very long time. Even better, he was about to be trampled to death if the footsteps hurrying toward him indicated anything. He'd warn them to stop, but without breath in his lungs....

"Bas. Bas. Are you okay?"

Mike's voice sounded somewhere above where Bas lay. The old stuntman's face, however, was a blur. Half a dozen other voices and out of focus faces surrounded him. He raised his hands, two thumbs up. A couple of his crew cupped his elbows and helped him to his feet. He rubbed the heel of his hand across his sternum in the hope of jump-starting his lungs. Someone slapped the immortal hell out of his back. That did it.

"Wh-what the hell?" He looked over his shoulder to find Tim, grinning like an idiot. "Remind me to put you on a runaway horse later."

"You're breathing, ain'tcha?" Tim said. "No gratitude, I tell you. No gratitude at all."

Bas rubbed a spot on his side. "I think you broke a rib, asshole."

"No, that would be one of the three bounces you took off the airbag," Tim remarked.

"Or that final landing in the dirt," one of the crew said. "That shit don't give."

Nothing worse than having one of the people you've trained throw your words back at you.

"Yeah, yeah, very funny." Bas waved them all off. "How about we check everything and figure out what went wrong. Now. Please."

They all moved away, accompanied by lots of laughter, with a few *operator errors* thrown in there to make sure he knew whatever happened was likely his fault.

Bas clasped his hands over his head and stretched toward the clear blue Highland sky. He leaned from side to side and twisted left, then right. Mike didn't say a word. He stood there with his hands shoved in his jeans and his shoulders hunched and watched Bas like a hawk before he finally spoke.

"If it's any consolation, you gave everybody a nice show before you hit the ground." He glanced at Bas's kilt.

"Great." Bas ran a hand over his face. "This Regency boot camp is kicking my ass. The kilt doesn't chafe like the breeches and *pantieloons* and other shit I have to wear." He scuffed his Highlander boots in the dirt. "And they let me wear warmer socks with these instead of those damned silk stockings."

"Not like we haven't seen your bare ass before, boss," Mike said as they walked back toward the castle ruins where they'd been staging various falls and jumps. "What we haven't seen is you miss a mark like that. Wanna tell me what's going on with you?"

"Nope."

"Does it have anything to do with the film?"

"Maybe."

Mike kept his gaze straight ahead. "Somebody you're playing Regency with up at the big house?"

"Probably not."

"Would you tell me if it did?"

"Do I ever?"

Mike stopped him with a hand on his arm. "Are you headed for a fall, kid?"

Bas and the old man had been working together a long time. Mike had been Bas's mentor in the business when he came to the States. The man likely knew Bas better than just about anyone.

"I don't plan on it, Mike. I promise." He held his friend's gaze and tried to look as sure as he sounded.

"Good. Keep it that way. Last time you ended up in the hospital, we ended up outta work until you crawled your lazy ass out of bed."

"You guys could have worked while I was in rehab if you weren't so damned picky about who runs the crew," Bas said.

"Yeah, whatever."

They reached the estate Land Rover the duke had let them borrow. One of the guys had brought up Bas's fucked-up fall on the computer. One of the few Eleanor had allowed them to keep once they promised her no one from her boot camp would have p to it. The woman was relentless.

"Well, Tim, what's it look like?" Mike leaned on the Land Rover and checked out the computer set up on the hood.

"Looks like the boss man busted his ass."

Bas cuffed Tim on the back of the head. "Very funny."

It was. So long as no one figured out what he'd been thinking about when he miscalculated his fall from the ruins of the castle wall. Even as he watched the replay of him making every mistake a rookie stuntman could make, Bas replayed a very different scene in his head.

His entire body flushed from the memory of the hot water pouring over him as he kissed and caressed Teddy. The sounds Teddy made in Bas's arms, the sounds he made when he shuddered and came sent Bas's own orgasm rocketing through his body. He'd fallen asleep, finally, to those sounds. He woke up with a searing hard-on to the dreams he'd had. Now, he'd nearly broken his neck because he couldn't get any of it out of his head.

He clenched his fists so hard he dug his nails into the heels of his hands.

You don't have time for this!

"Maybe we should try the fall from the other side of the ruins," someone drawled.

Bas rolled his shoulders and punched the buttons on the computer to replay his fall. "The other side has a downhill slope. There's no way we could stabilize the bag or any of the other safety precautions. Not to mention the distance is shorter. You know how Wentworth is." His crew muttered in commiserative agreement. "Let's try it again. Without the busted ass this time."

Also without thinking about the tall, handsome conundrum who had him rethinking promises he'd made to himself long before he'd set foot in Scotland.

❦

BAS MISSED TEDDY'S WEAPONS CLASS. HAD HE MEANT TO MISS the class? It had been a busy morning. That was his story, and he was sticking to it. Lunch had been a civilized, very Regency affair as Eleanor chose this particular meal for Samantha to teach a class in proper dinner conversation. Turned out to be kind of fun because Bas, Arneaux, and the duke's brother took turns trying to insult each other in the politest terms possible while everyone else tried not to crack up. Well, everyone except Eleanor and the duke. Those two deserved each other.

For the last hour, Bas had limped through Mr. Goode's dance class in a kilt and those stupid dance slippers. Good news was he hadn't fallen down. Bad news? Class wasn't over, and his knee had decided it didn't like the way he'd landed after his fall off the safety bag this morning. Goode declared a break while he consulted with Mrs. Wallace about music for a Scottish country dance he wanted to teach them. Bas collapsed onto one of the dainty gold chairs that lined the walls of the ballroom.

Teddy sat down next to him. "You okay?" he asked even as he deliberately ogled Gloria's ass in her clingy Regency dress.

"Yeah." Bas shrugged at the irritation crawling across the back of his neck.

"You're limping."

"I'm fine. Fell wrong this morning." Bas closed his eyes, crossed his arms over his chest, and rested his head against the wall behind his chair.

"Don't you have a whole crew of stuntmen available to do that?" Teddy shifted in his chair.

Bas opened one eye. Teddy had adopted a similar pose, arms crossed and head against the wall.

"Only after I do it first."

"Makes sense," Teddy observed. "I'm the same way."

"I'll bet."

"What's that supposed to mean?"

"You're a cautious man, Teddy. I wouldn't expect you to do anything without knowing exactly what the results were going to be."

"Rather harsh," Teddy muttered over the opening bars of a new piece of music. "Especially after last night."

"If you say so. Look I—"

Teddy stood and sauntered across the room. Casual as you please if you didn't look at the stiffness in his shoulders and the tick under his jaw. As Teddy reached the group of ladies gathered around Lily, Bas closed his eyes.

"What *have* you done to upset our Mr. Rousseau?" The voice and the swish of heavy skirts told him instantly who Eleanor taken Teddy's seat.

"The usual. Doesn't take much," Bas said.

"True. But you seem to have a special gift for pushing his buttons."

"Nothing like your gift for pushing the duke's buttons."

"Touché. But my ability to push his buttons is the only reason he allowed you to crawl all over the tower ruins."

"Oh?" Bas sat up and opened his eyes to give her his full attention. "Why is that?"

She threw up a half-dismissive hand. "Who knows? He's very protective of that part of the estate. He has an office in the tower, but the rest has been off-limits for years, according to the staff. They seem to think it has something do with the ghost of the Innes Witch."

"So *that's* why I can't do any setups there at night. He's afraid the ghost might show up."

"Oh, come on, Mr. Salazar. You don't believe in ghosts, do you?" Her tone, completely casual, didn't do a lot to convince him. Her unusual blue eyes said something else entirely. Bas was pretty good at reading people who tried to fool themselves. He'd been one of them for the first fifteen or so years of his life.

"I believe there is something here. Something in this house"—he slowly looked around the room—"on this estate that isn't easily explained, and I think she can be whatever she wants because I have no intention of saying she can't." Bas brought his gaze back to her.

Eleanor laughed. "A man who knows women well enough not to want to even upset a dead one." She shook her head. "Such a pity you prefer men."

"Some days, Miss Witherspoon." He smiled a tense sort of half smile. "Some days."

"You must do me two favors," she said as Mr. Goode called them all back onto the dance floor.

"Certainly." He stood, gave her a little bow, and offered her his arm.

"You must call me Eleanor, and you must tell me if you ever find out why His Grace doesn't want anyone to go to the top chamber of the tower."

"I'm Bas, and when you put it that way, how can I resist?"

"Come along, ladies and gentlemen," Mr. Goode announced at the center of the room. "We're going to learn a Scottish reel." He began to arrange them in the formation for the dance.

"Your knee is *not* going to like this," Teddy warned him from the other side of the formation.

"I'll survive," Bas replied. "I've survived all kinds of things I don't like."

Well, that shut Teddy up, and it looked like everyone took Bas's remark as one more person who didn't like Teddy's attitude. Somehow that bothered Bas. It was unfair, even if Teddy brought people's sniping on himself. People generally liked Bas. What was it like to have to be someone people disliked to survive?

An hour later, Sylvan finally called an end to dance lessons for the day. Whether he'd intended the lessons to end or he'd finally thrown in the towel on them getting through the Scottish reel without the look of an interstate pileup, Bas and his knee heaved a sigh of relief. Once they all fled the ballroom as if released from prison, the rest of the group headed toward one of the two libraries down the corridor from the ballroom. Bas limped in the opposite direction toward the stairs that led to the floor where his room was. He had no intention of spending the rest of the day in dancing shoes and Regency spandex. He'd keep the waistcoat, jacket, and shirt with the hangman's knot of a neckcloth thingy. The *nanky pantieloons*? Not a chance. Not when there was a kilt up there with his name on it.

"I'm charging Wentworth hazard pay for this gig," he muttered as he hobbled past the dining room's closed double doors and turned the corner. "Dance lessons. Nut strangling clothes. Eel pie. What the—" Bas tried to tug his arm free. Someone strong as hell dragged him aside and shoved him into a small dark room with no windows.

Back against the door. A muscled chest pressed to his. He caught the faint whiff of a familiar cologne. Pitch dark and Bas gasped at the demanding seeking lips against his. He tried to move his hands only to find them laced with Teddy's and pressed into the heavy oak above his head. Bas kissed him back in a battle of tongues and lips, breath mingled in a panting rhythm that left Bas light-headed and aroused to the point of pain.

Teddy slowed the kiss, and Bas let him. He drew away slowly, Bas's bottom lip between Teddy's teeth. Bas dropped his head back as far as he could against the door. Teddy dragged his teeth along Bas's jawline, down his throat and then back up the side of his neck to suck the sensitive flesh behind his ear into a biting, sucking bit of torture sure to leave a mark. For a few minutes, Bas sank into the well of erotic sensation Teddy dragged him into, deeper and deeper. He wanted to surrender. Something he seldom did even with the few long-term lovers he'd had. In that, he and Teddy were alike. Control.

An illusion.

Just like whatever this was with Teddy.

"What are you doing?" Bas flexed his hands against Teddy's.

"If you have to ask, then I'm doing it wrong."

Bas gave a brief laugh. "You know what I mean. What's this about, Teddy?"

Teddy rested his forehead on Bas's shoulder. "I don't know."

Nothing like a knife to the gut to turn a raging hard-on into a lump of disappointment. Even when the reason isn't really clear. He pulled his hands free and placed them on Teddy's shoulders, then gave a gentle shove. He sidestepped from under the press of the other man's body and suppressed a shiver, instantly cold. A few fumbles behind him and he found the door latch.

"Get back with me when you do know." He didn't have to see Teddy's face. The sharp intake of breath told Bas he'd hit his mark. Self-preservation was like that, sharp and unmistakably quick.

"What if I never know, except...for when we're like this."

"I'm not going to be your dirty secret, and I'm not interested in a fuck buddy. Not at this stage in my life. I need to look for more."

Silence, especially in the dark with only the sound of their breathing slowly returning to normal, seemed so damned sad and useless. Bas lifted the latch and opened the door. He glanced outside. The hallway was empty.

"Wait." Teddy curled his fingers around the door and held it in place, open just a bit. "Here." He shoved something small and metal into Bas's hand.

"What is it?" Bas instinctively closed his hand around the object. A key of some kind?

"There is a dressing room between my room and your room. That's the key."

"I see. You're giving it to me, so I'll use it to sneak into your room?"

"I'm giving it to you, so I won't sneak into yours." Teddy pulled the door open and stepped into the hallway. "I don't know why I did this." He raised his head. His gray eyes blazed. "You were mad at me earlier. I didn't like it." He stormed down the hallway.

By the time Bas stepped out of what looked like a giant dining room supply closet, Teddy's shoes clicked on the staircase going down to the first floor. Bas opened his hand and stared at the old skeleton key.

"Great. Adam got an apple. I got a fucking key."

Worse, he kept the key. He had it in his black, embroidered waistcoat pocket all through dinner that evening. No idea why. As they'd strolled toward the larger of the two libraries Bas stuck his finger into the pocket to make certain it was still there.

"That meal was amazing," Danny said as he and his wife settled onto one of the sofas in front of the nearest fireplace.

"Tell me about it." Bas dropped into one of the high-backed leather armchairs on the other side of the hearth. "I'll take Mrs. Gordon's roast beef over eel pie any day. I'm stuffed."

"That was good," Teddy said as he took the matching chair on the opposite side of the little inlaid patterned table from Bas. "But the trifle was beyond amazing."

"I should say so," Samantha Arneaux said. "You had two helpings, Teddy."

"Your husband had three," Teddy shot back.

Everyone laughed.

"My brother has been known to eat four in one sitting." The duke had taken a seat behind the large desk away from the fireplace. He had a stack of papers at his elbow and some kind of ledger in front of him. He didn't look up as he made his remark.

"Slander." Lord Lachlan's one word response sent another ripple of laughter through the room. He and Lily sat at a large felt-covered table where someone had started an antique jigsaw puzzle a few nights ago.

Sylvan, Wentworth's assistant, Gloria, and Miss Stepford joined them.

"I'm just thankful there is no whist tonight," Bas said. "I suck at cards."

"Language, Mr. Salazar." Eleanor walked over and handed Teddy a book before she settled into the chair next to the Arneauxs' sofa. She wore a pretty, green velvet gown tonight, which highlighted the golden red of her hair.

"He meant, he's not terribly skilled at whist," Danny said in a perfect British accent.

"Thanks, man." Bas leaned across and bumped fists with the actor.

Samantha rolled her eyes at them as she handed Bas a large leather portfolio. "Thanks, Doc. Is this the latest incarnation of the script?"

"Yes." Samantha replied. "At least until Anna and Hadrian come back from their pre-wedding honeymoon."

"When *are* they getting married?" Lily smiled at her husband as she asked the question.

Lord Lachlan clasped her hand and raised it to press a kiss to her fingertips.

"No idea. Have you heard from them at all, Your Grace?" Eleanor didn't let a little thing like the man completely ignoring all of them stop her from asking the duke a question.

"I have not." Again, he didn't look up. "Ask McGinty."

Everyone in the room turned to the big Scot half asleep in

an armchair in front of the duke's desk. He stirred and opened one eye.

"Nae a word so far. Urquhart and I deliver supplies, but they've nae said a word about coming back to the manor yet. They're both writing." The steward closed his eyes once more.

"Is that what they're calling it these days?" Teddy asked as he opened his book.

Gloria giggled. Teddy, however, didn't look up. Bas glanced around the room. Everyone else seemed to be involved in their own conversations and activities. No one else noticed that Teddy had ignored Gloria. Then again, maybe Bas was the only one who was paying any attention to either of them. He gave himself a mental pimp slap and opened the script Samantha had given him. The quiet murmur of conversations bubbled around him. He studied the latest fight scene Wentworth had added to the script. This was why he was in Scotland. Not to have his life turned sideways and his heart handed to him by an arrogant British fencing instructor.

He read through the scene several times.

"Something wrong?" Teddy's quiet inquiry startled Bas.

"What?"

"Your face."

"What about it?" And why was Teddy looking at his face? The instant Bas thought about it he realized his forehead had tightened, and he'd narrowed his eyes.

"You look…confused." Teddy shifted so he faced more toward the fireplace, and more toward him.

Bas glanced at the open book in Teddy's hands. "You're reading *A Matter of Honor.*"

"Rereading it. I'm checking some of my weapon choices against what Anna's written. She's actually quite knowledge-able about Regency weapons."

"Then she's doing better than the person who made these changes to the script." He handed Teddy the leather portfolio. "Read this and tell me what you think. First impression without trying to figure it out."

Teddy's expression grew thoughtful and a little puzzled, but he started reading. Bas had no choice but to watch. Why wouldn't he? He wanted to gauge the man's reactions to the script. That was all. The fact he enjoyed looking at Teddy's sharp features, enjoyed the play of unpracticed emotions across his face had nothing to do with it at all.

"First impression?" Teddy asked without looking up from the script. "It's shite."

Eleanor cleared her throat and gave them both her best Regency police scowl.

Teddy *humphed* at her and placed the script on the table between Bas and him. He used his finger to point out several lines. "Two Regency cavalry officers would not settle a dispute, let alone a dispute over a woman, like this."

"Why not?" Bas knew when he read the scene that the scenario didn't jive with the rest of the film. He just didn't know why.

Teddy leaned toward him. An intense animation lit his features. "Two things come to mind. First, they're both gentlemen. Gentlemen don't resort to shoving and punching each other to settle an insult like that. Second, they're cavalry officers. They have a certain amount of discipline bred to the bone. They can hold off and settle a score in a more gentlemanly manner. It's part of who they are."

"A gentlemanly manner. Like a duel, right?"

"Exactly." Teddy nodded. "There are rules and a specific form for this sort of thing. Two men, officers *and* gentlemen would be hell bent on obeying the rules."

"What kind of rules?"

"Hang on." Teddy jumped up and went to a specific

section of the floor to ceiling bookcases in the duke's library. Finally, after several minutes, he returned to his chair and handed Bas a very old, beautifully bound book. "Be careful. It's a first edition."

Bas very carefully opened the book and began to turn the pages. Teddy wasn't kidding. The publication date was 1829. The book was *The Dueling Handbook* by some guy named Joseph Hamilton. The wording was old-fashioned and dense, but Bas was determined to wade through and try to understand. Several times he stopped and pointed out a passage for Teddy to explain. Once, he caught Samantha Arneaux smiling at them as Teddy went over the rules with him. Bas grinned and shook his head.

"Okay," Bas said when he finally understood. "How do we convince Wentworth that a duel can be just as exciting as a fist fight that ends up with someone falling off a castle wall?"

Teddy shrugged. "Blocking stunts is your job. Providing the right weapons is mine. Good luck."

"You have to show him," Danny said.

Bas started, and he and Teddy looked up. They'd been so deep in conversation they'd forgotten the others were there.

"What do you mean?" Bas asked.

"Block the duel scene. Film it. Send it to Wentworth."

"Arneaux's got the right of it," Teddy remarked. "Most directors are visual creatures. Show him how exciting the scene can be, and he'll go for it."

Bas picked up the script in one hand and the dueling handbook in the other. He looked from one to the other. The idea had merit. A lot of merit. He just couldn't quite—

"Read this." Teddy took the two items from Bas's hands, then handed him the book he'd been reading. "From this page right here." He flipped through the pages and held the place open with his index finger.

Bas didn't even think about it. He started reading. Most

stunt people barely read the script for a film unless the pages involved some kind of action on their part. Bas always read the entire script all the way through before he accepted a job. He'd enjoyed reading the script for *A Matter of Honor*. Great story. Intriguing characters. Lots of action. He'd let the story get under his skin, which didn't happen often.

Reading the book?

He got it. His instincts about the scene were right. He got it.

"Whoa," he said softly once he'd finished reading the scene. "No wonder Wentworth bought the book."

"Precisely." Teddy took the book back and handed Bas the script. "Which begs the question, why did he add this completely inappropriate scene?"

"Script doctors," Danny muttered. "Fuck up everything."

"Language," Eleanor, Bas, Teddy, and Samantha said together.

Everyone in the room looked up and laughed. Well, everyone except the duke, but he cracked a smile.

"Facts," Danny retorted. "So, guys. What do we do?"

Bas got up, dragged Teddy out of his chair, and went to the first of a series of long tables in the middle of the room. Library tables, Eleanor had called them. He moved a few books out of the way and grabbed a piece of old, noisy yellow paper off a stack at the end of the table. There wasn't a pen in sight. Just a bottle of ink and a feather. So not happening. Danny strolled up with a weird, flat-looking thing with what looked like a pencil lead sticking out of it.

"That'll work." Bas grabbed it and turned to Teddy. "Find that part in the book again."

Teddy flipped slowly through the pages of his book, eying Bas suspiciously the entire time. "What are we doing?"

"We're doctoring Wentworth's script, Swordmaster. Here's how I think it needs to go."

Chapter Nine

TEDDY SAT UP FROM THE SPRAWL HE'D ADOPTED WHEN HE, Danny, and Bas had come up to Bas's room to continue their discussion—after Eleanor had booted them out for being too noisy and too...modern. Translation? They'd drunk a great deal of brandy and their language had deteriorated to the point the new Lady Lachlan almost fell out of her chair laughing at them. In Bas's room, the three of them had collapsed into some low comfortable armchairs in front of the fireplace across from Bas's bed and passed the handful of pages they'd worked on in the library back and forth.

"That works," Teddy announced as he glanced at the page Bas had handed him. "I think if we use the over and under pistols, the kickback and the noise will look great on film, especially on the remains of the castle parapet."

"Then we switch to claymores?" Danny scooted to the edge of the blue and gold silk-striped chair, hands clasped between his knees. "*After* we fall of the castle walls?"

"Yeah." Bas grinned at the actor. "Pretty cool, huh? Especially in full Regency costume."

"Should be enough action for Wentworth and true enough to Regency sensibilities to suit Anna Chase."

"Easy for you to say, Teddy." Danny stood and stretched toward the ceiling until his back cracked. "All you have to do is teach me to do it. I have to actually play the scene."

"Poor thing." Bas swatted at the actor who'd tried to shove him out of his chair. "I'll make sure you don't get hurt."

"Thanks, buddy."

"He's not doing it for you." Teddy handed the page back to Bas. One strong forefinger brushed over his and sent a shock of erotic awareness down his spine. "He's afraid of your wife."

"For true." Danny gave a little salute and headed for the chamber door. "And I'm probably going to catch hell for getting thrown out of the library with you two, so thanks for that."

"Should we stop by your room in the morning and ask if you can come out and play?" Bas still sat slouched in his chair. He spoke to Arneaux, but his eyes were on Teddy.

"Good night, Teddy. Fuck you, Bas."

Danny closed the door behind him, which left the two of them trapped in Bas's room together with the actor's smart remark hovering over the antique rugs and the giant four-poster bed. For several long minutes they simply sat in a not too awkward silence. The fire crackled and spit in the fireplace. Teddy glanced around the room. Neat. Clean. Even the desk in front of the long drape-covered window was organized with papers, books, and sketchbooks in separate stacks.

"I didn't realize," Teddy said.

"Realize what?" Bas shifted forward in his chair.

"Everything that goes into blocking a scene from start to finish. I usually just teach the choreography, watch the filming, and make suggestions." He shrugged. "It was fun."

"I'm glad." Bas picked up his brandy glass and finished off the last sip or two. "Having your perspective helped. It'll help tomorrow, too, if you can spare the time. I'd like to walk Arneaux through it along with one of my guys playing opposite him."

"Of course. Besides, I want to see Arneaux's expression when he fires the pistol I have in mind."

"Knock him on his ass?" That lazy, insinuating grin of his made Teddy's stomach take a little flip.

"Definitely."

"Then you have to be there. It's a moral imperative."

Teddy snorted. "Let me know when and where."

"After weapons class and before dance class. Two things I never would have thought to be on my daily schedule. You know what else is a moral imperative?" Bas fixed his blue eyes on Teddy's face.

"What?" Gooseflesh swept up his arms. He'd taken off his jacket, waistcoat, and neckcloth once they'd all stumbled into Bas's room. He'd also rolled up his sleeves to the elbow, but the room was too warm to blame the cold.

"Fun. Fun is a moral imperative. Life's too short to live without fun."

"What makes you think I live without fun?"

Bas tilted his head to the side, but he didn't say a word. He stretched out his long, muscled legs toward the fire and winced.

"Cramp?" Teddy made no secret he was studying Bas's body.

"Yeah. Don't tell my crew, but I pulled a hamstring and God knows what else when I miscalculated a fall this afternoon." He shifted in his chair again.

"I heard about the fall. Nobody said you were injured."

"I'm not as young as I used to be, Teddy. Falling is easy. So is pulling muscles. Recovery? Not so much."

"Please. Neither of us is ready for a cane just yet."

"Tell that to my leg." He spread his hand over his kilt-clad thigh and squeezed, which only succeeded in producing a wince and a hiss of pain. "I'm getting too old for this shit."

"You're thirty-five, for God's sake, not sixty." Teddy stood, took two steps next to Bas's chair, then knelt. He shoved the stuntman's hand out of the way. "Why didn't you say something?" He didn't wait for an answer but pushed the heavy wool kilt up and started to work just above Bas's knee, kneading and massaging.

"What are you…oh. Wow. That's better. How'd you do that?"

"I was trainer for the rugby team before I actually made the team. Also, part of studying fencing is studying anatomy. The body shows cues that can indicate an opponent's next move." Teddy forced himself to view the darkly tanned flesh as simply a problem he needed to solve. He concentrated on the tightness of the muscles and the line of bruises that disappeared under the pushed-up tartan fabric. He glanced up to find Bas had closed his eyes, his head against the back of the chair.

"You're really good at that," Bas murmured, his voice dark and tempting as Mrs. Gordon's trifle. "And this is a really bad idea."

"Oh?" Teddy stopped massaging and dragged his hands away. Slowly.

"Yeah. And if you stop, I will probably kill you."

Teddy huffed and went back to work. "Make up your mind."

"I'm not the one who needs to make up my mind. I know what I want."

"Must be nice to always be so sure of oneself. Shift onto your hip."

"Huh?" Bas sat up slightly and studied Teddy for a moment.

Teddy wrapped his hands around Bas's thigh and shifted him in the chair so the side of his thigh and half his butt was accessible. "This muscle is stretched like a bow string all the way up your leg to your spine. Sit still." He shifted more of the kilt out of the way. As Teddy suspected, Bas wore his kilt like a true Scot. As Teddy had also suspected, the man had muscles everywhere, including his ass.

"You sure that's not just an excuse to fondle my— Ow! That's not a shank of lamb you're handling, you know."

"No." Teddy rose higher on his knees in order to work the muscles and tendons more deeply. "It's a beat-up piece of ass that is going to be black and blue tomorrow. Relax. I won't molest you unless you want me to. Stop tensing up."

"We people who are always sure of ourselves are always tense."

"Hmm."

Teddy used his knuckles to knead the tension out of Bas's glutes. The man's chin dropped to his chest. His body shuddered beneath Teddy's hands to the point of almost purring. Turned on his side away from Teddy, Bas's profile struck him silent for a few moments.

An ancestry of Spanish knights and Moorish warriors rested on that face. It occurred to him he'd seen that sort of ancient determination before...in his own face. Was that what attracted him in a way no one had attracted him in forever? Likely, but that was also the reason he dared not go any further emotionally with this man. Bas Salazar was too much like looking into what Teddy's life might have been. That scared the hell out of him.

He wrapped both hands around Bas's upper thigh and used his thumbs to loosen tendons drawn tight from being pulled the wrong way—which brought the fingers of one hand into proximity with a rock-hard cock of impressive size. Bas's chest rose and fell a little quicker. Teddy smiled. He brushed his knuckles deliberately against the spot where the thigh joined the groin.

"You're playing with fire, Teddy." Bas didn't open his eyes.

"Do tell."

"You're not playing fair."

"All's fair in—"

"Don't say it. All's fair in a lot of things, but not in teasing me into another casual fuck. And that's all you're after right now." He still hadn't looked at him. Just sat there, relaxed. At least his body was. His face, even in profile, betrayed too damned much for Teddy to take in willingly.

Teddy continued to massage but moved down Bas's thigh to his knee and then the back of his calf. Head down, he tried to work through what the handsome stuntman was trying to say. Of all the people to become attracted to after so damned long, he'd picked a bull-headed enigma. Typical. For him. There was nothing typical about Bas. A typical guy wouldn't turn down any offer of sex. At least any guy Teddy had hooked up with in the past. A shiver traveled down his spine. Gentle fingers lightly stroked his hair.

"What are you thinking?" Bas's voice rumbled, dark with that hint of an accent that sent Teddy's heart racing.

"What do you want?" Teddy blurted the words before he had the chance to think about it. "What do you want from me?" He raised his head to meet Bas's gaze.

He continued to stroke Teddy's hair, which was fine. Teddy didn't want him to stop. Such a simple, stupid thing to enjoy. Daft, really.

"I want to find out who you are. I haven't…." He swallowed, his Adam's apple rose and fell slowly against the front of his tanned throat. "I haven't wanted to find out everything there is to know about someone in a long time. But I do.

With you. I can find out some things by going to bed with you, but…I want more." He slid his fingers down Teddy's face and used them to lift his head higher. "I want more."

"Why?" It was the only thing Teddy could think to ask.

"Hell, if I knew that we'd probably already be in that bed going at each other until dawn." A flush of red crept beneath his golden skin. The fire's light and the glow of the candles played across his hair, drawing out shades of ebony, midnight blue, and silver.

"Is that an option?" Teddy tried to smile and failed miserably.

"Why'd you give me this?" Bas slid the antique key across the small marquetry table next to his chair.

Teddy shrugged. "To keep you safe from me? To make anything that happened between us your fault?"

"Making love to someone isn't something anyone needs to take the blame for, Teddy."

It took a few tries, but Teddy pushed to his feet. He pulled the kilt back down over Bas's arse and thigh. "I know. At least some of the time I know." He ran a hand through his hair. "Good night, Bas." The door into the corridor seemed to move farther away with every step he took.

"Teddy?"

"Yes?" He didn't allow himself to look back.

"Use the key. I know you don't want anyone to see you leaving my room…like this."

Teddy reached the door that opened to the hallway, then turned to lean against the wood, arms crossed over his chest. "Like what?"

"Like you're sneaking out after a booty call. Use the key. It'll keep the servants and the other Regency campers from talking. Robbie's the only one who knows one of us has a key?"

"Yes. You trust him?"

"I trust him. He has his reasons to keep our secrets."

"I guess he does at that." Teddy pushed off the chamber door and started across the room toward the door into the adjoining dressing room. "Bring the key."

Bas's laughter rolled across the room. "Yes, sir. Whatever you say, sir."

"I didn't mean it like—"

Teddy found himself backed into the dressing room door as if charge by a bull. Bas took Teddy's lips in a hot open-mouthed kiss so hard and quick he saw stars. A kiss that ended almost as quickly as it began.

"Come on." Bas's voice was rough with desire. "Let's see what's in this dressing room."

He fumbled with the key while Teddy slid away. The crack and creak of wood long closed startled them both. Once they pushed and pulled the door open, a whoosh of icy air rushed into the bedchamber.

"What a minute." Teddy went to the bedside table, then picked up the lit oil lamp.

"Afraid of the dark?" Bas asked as Teddy reached him and stepped into the dressing room.

"Go ahead and joke, Stuntman. This house is over seven hundred years old. You might be a pro at falling through rotting floors, but I'm not." He found a very old open travel trunk sitting in the middle of the room and put the lamp on it after he'd turned the wick up a bit higher.

"Good point." Bas stood back-to-back with him, and they did a slow circle to take in the room. "This is larger than I thought it would be. It's the size of my first apartment in Hollywood."

"If Mrs. Wallace saw all the dust and cobwebs in here, heads would roll. Look at this pier glass. Worth a fortune, unless I miss my mark." Teddy walked over to the monstrous gilt framed mirror.

"Pier glass? Oh, Regency-speak for mirror. Hey, there's another door here. Where the hell does this go?"

Teddy turned just as Bas fit the key into the keyhole of a short door set into the back wall of the dressing room. The key turned, but before Bas could open the door, a rush of lavender and heather-scented air swirled around the room. he two of them froze and stared at each other.

"You feel that?" Teddy whispered.

"Hell, yes, I felt it. I'm standing right here. Why are you whispering? Other than the fact a wind came from nowhere and smells like my *amona?*"

Teddy took a deep breath. "I saw her. The ghost. I saw her on my way back through the conservatory from the bathhouse."

"What? Wait. You saw the Innes Witch?"

"Yeah. In the conservatory."

"Please tell me she wasn't with Colonel Mustard with an axe."

Teddy slugged him in the arm as hard as he could. "Fuck you. I'm going to bed. You stay here and deal with her. Give me the key."

"I'm kidding. Come on." He turned the key, then grabbed the doorknob, and turned. The door didn't open. Bas pressed his shoulder against the wood and pushed, but the door still didn't budge. "Help me open this."

"If an angry witch comes shrieking out of this door, I *will* knock you down to keep her from catching me first," Teddy warned.

Bas found a fire poker and wedged it between the ancient iron-banded oak door and the jamb. They worked together, and eventually the door opened with a creak that would do any horror movie proud. He and Bas exchanged a look. The scent of lavender and heather billowed out of the darkness and surrounded them like a shroud. Bas actually recoiled.

"Want to get the lamp?" He leaned into the opening.

"Not really." Teddy peered over Bas's shoulder. "What do you see?"

"A whole lotta' dark. Dark as a Hollywood agent's heart."

"Fine." Teddy retrieved the lamp from the trunk and handed it to Bas. "What do you see now?"

"Steps. Stone steps going down." He moved to the side so Teddy had room to stand next to him. "Do we go down tonight?"

"I vote we don't go at all, but I certainly don't fancy going down these bloody steps in the middle of the night."

"Tomorrow then." Bas walked to the far side of the dressing room and unlocked the door into Teddy's chamber.

"Give me that key." Teddy caught the antique piece as Bas tossed it to him, then put his shoulder into the old oak door, shoved it, and locked it back up.

"Why'd you close it?"

"If you think I'd be able to sleep in my room with the portal to God knows what open in here, you're mad as a hatter."

"Afraid the witch will crawl into bed with you?" Bas stood right behind him and gave his right buttock a squeeze. He filched the key from Teddy's hand.

"Why'd you do that?" Teddy leaned back into Bas's chest.

"To keep *you* from crawling into bed with me."

He spun Teddy around and seared his lips in a long, hot meeting of mouths and tongues. When Bas tried to pull back, Teddy grabbed the back of Bas's head and held him there to plunder and suck and nip for a few minutes longer. Seemed like forever. Seemed like a mere heartbeat. This time, he was the one to pull away.

"Good night, Bas."

He took the lamp and crossed the dressing room without looking back. Once in his chamber, he closed the door and leaned against it. He flattened his hand against the cool, polished wood. The distinct *click* of the door being locked from the other side told him the night was over.

"Good night, Teddy."

He listened to Bas's footsteps as he crossed the wooden floor of the dressing room to his chamber. A quick check of his own room told Teddy that Robbie had come and gone. He'd built up the fire but had placed the guard in front of the hearth. He'd also turned down the bed and drawn the drapes on three sides, leaving the side that faced the fireplace open to take in the heat. One of the ugly flannel nightshirts Teddy had deigned to wear to keep from freezing his balls off lay across the foot of the bed.

"Thanks, Robbie," he murmured, then shucked his Regency dinner clothes, and pulled the nightshirt over his head.

He caught a glimpse of himself in the pier glass in the corner of the room. Would his father approve or see it as more evidence his only son was a *poof* git, a disgrace to the Rousseau name? A question for another day—like the thousand other questions running through his head as he crawled under the covers and turned out the oil lamp on the bedside table.

"I want to find out who you are."

There was a sure way to chase Bas Salazar out of Teddy's life forever. Feminine laughter came from behind the door into the dressing room. Teddy turned on his side away from the sound.

"Bugger off, Elsbeth. Go bother the duke. I'm bothered enough."

TEDDY SPOONED MORE EGGS ONTO HIS THIN BONE CHINA plate, then added a couple of kippers on the side. He'd sat in a chair between McGinty and Arneaux before the hairs on the back of his neck let him know everyone was staring at him. Rather than comment, he started in on the mountain of food he'd helped himself to and nodded at the footman who offered to fill his teacup.

Silence held the room hostage and, still, he ate his food and drank his tea without acknowledging any other guests at the breakfast table.

"Jesus, Teddy," Arneaux finally said.

A chuckle made the rounds of the table.

"What?" He kept his tone casual and reached for the delicate jam pot in front of him. He slathered raspberry jam onto the toast points from his loaded bread plate.

"I don't think I've seen you eat like this the entire time we've been here," Eleanor said from her seat at the foot of the table.

"I've seen truckers eat less than that." Arneaux chased a piece of sausage around his plate.

Teddy shrugged. "I'm hungry. I've a full day ahead of me."

He *was* hungry. He'd slept soundly last night for some strange reason. Deeply because his dreams had been vivid and.... A subtle check of the room startled him. Where was Bas? No way in hell he'd ask. He continued to work on the plate piled with food. Eventually, conversation picked up and moved away from his newfound appetite. He kept his head down as he ate while wondering where Wentworth's stunt director was.

Sitting so close to the head of the table, he couldn't help but hear Eleanor and the duke as they bickered back and forth with the occasional comment from McGinty. The mention of Bas's name caught Teddy's attention. He refused to be so crass as to lean closer or interject himself into the conversation. The bits and pieces he managed to hear indicated a discussion of the intact tower of the castle ruins. Someone had sent Wentworth pictures, likely from Bas's crew as they stayed in the village and still had access to computers and cell phones. He didn't know what Wentworth had requested, but he could imagine. What he couldn't understand was the duke's vehement refusal to allow anyone but himself inside the tower at all, let alone all the way to the top of it.

"Teddy? Hey, you in there?" A hand waved in front of his face. *Arneaux.*

"Yes? What is it?"

"What are we doing in weapons class this morning? Or do you need a nap and a run after what you just ate?" The actor flinched as his wife swatted him with her fan.

Sylvan, across the table from Teddy, chuckled.

Teddy glanced down to find his plate, the bread plate, and his teacup completely empty. Come to think of it, his stomach did have a sort of taut, rather surprised feeling. "I'm not the one who ate five large blood sausages, *Mr.* Arneaux." He pushed his chair back, stood, and offered a bow to the ladies at the table. "The question is, are you ready for some saber work on horseback. You *are* portraying a cavalry officer, if I recall. Mr. McGinty, are you coming?"

The big Scot erupted from his chair, swabbed a serviette across his mouth and beard, bowed to the ladies and the duke, and started toward the dining room doors. "Aye, I'm coming, but only to watch."

"Watch?" Teddy asked as he and Danny followed the duke's steward out of the dining room and down the stairs to the foyer. "I thought you were going to help me demonstrate."

"Himself won't let me." They crossed the foyer and went out the front doors, headed toward the stables. "Says I'm too old, and if I break my neck, he'll have no one to run the estate."

Teddy swallowed a laugh. "Well, I guess I can always practice on Arneaux here. I promise not to knock you off your horse more than twice."

"Fuck you, Teddy, *and* the horse you rode in on. I'll bet you—"

"Again, with the wagers." Teddy lengthened his stride to keep up with McGinty. "Is there anything you Yanks won't bet on?"

"At least I've never *wagered* a fortune on which raindrop would reach the bottom of a window first."

"Someone's been reading his Regency manual. How sweet."

"I don't have to read it. I'm sleeping with the author."

"*Haud yer wheesht!*" McGinty shouted. "Ye'r giving me a headache."

They had reached the stable yard and every working groom and the horse master, Urquhart, gawked at them.

"Sorry," Arneaux muttered.

"There's nothing to wager on." McGinty pointed toward the gate that led to the road to the loch and beyond. "There's my replacement. Says he's had plenty of experience, and he's not afraid to get knocked off a horse." He walked across the cobblestones to meet the person at the gate.

Arneaux stepped up next to Teddy, slung his arm across his shoulders, and said in a low voice, "Like hell, there's nothing to wager on. In a sword fight between you and Bas, my money's on the big Basque bastard, no matter how tall you are."

Teddy shrugged his arm away. "Longer arms and more experience, Arneaux. I'll take that wager." He strode forward and met Bas in the middle of the stable yard.

McGinty went to talk to Urquhart about horses for the lesson.

"I see McGinty's told you." Bas glanced behind Teddy, where Arneaux was no doubt making wagers with the grooms.

"Indeed. I'll try to be gentle with you," Teddy replied with a slightly insinuating grin.

"You wish. Where are we doing this little demonstration?"

"One of the fields between here and the loch. Missed you at breakfast." Teddy tried to keep his tone casual.

"I had to go into the village to check in with my crew. Wentworth is really pressing hard for the stuff he wants. Pain in the ass."

"I know. It's got His Grace's knickers in a twist. He and Eleanor were arguing about it at breakfast."

"Damn. What *is* it about that tower?"

"I have no idea. Nobody seems to know. Or if they do, they're not saying."

"Think it has to do with the ghost? The one you saw?"

Teddy started. He checked to make certain no one else stood close enough to hear. "I'd rather that didn't become common knowledge, if you don't mind. Lily knows, but no one else." He didn't know why, only that…something about his encounter with the Innes Witch was important, as if she had a message for him. He simply had to figure out what the message was.

"Lily, as in Lord Lachlan's wife?" Bas stared at him, a certain spark of sudden insight in his eyes. Mentioning Lily had been a mistake because somehow Bas was connecting the dots.

"Yes, and stop looking at me like that." Teddy had no intention of confessing that he'd slept with Lily. At least not yet. If ever.

Bas raised his hands in surrender. McGinty called to

them as he and Urquhart led a group of grooms and horses up the road toward the loch. Danny fell into step with Robbie and Dougal. Teddy and Bas followed a few strides behind them.

"Dougal brought some oil lanterns to my room this morning," Bas said as they walked up the road. "For tonight."

"Tonight?"

"The secret passage? In the dressing room? I know we said we'd do the Nancy Drew thing during the day, but when do we have time? I told Dougal I needed some lanterns to check out a location at night."

"Nancy Drew? Us?" Sounded like a recipe for a broken leg. Then again, if he had to be stuck in a secret passage with a broken leg, he couldn't think of anyone he'd want with him more.

"What? I've read the books. Sue me." Bas had adopted his *I-don't-give-a-damn* tone, but his shoulders hunched slightly, a sure sign Teddy had struck a nerve.

"I didn't mean—"

"I have a younger sister. She got me hooked on the books when we were kids, okay? Among other things." They followed Urquhart and the others through a gap in the wall of gorse hedges along the road and crossed the meadow in silence.

"What other things?" Teddy finally asked.

"What?"

"Your sister. What other things did she get you hooked on?"

Bas glanced at him, a laser-like assessment of Teddy's sincerity. "Pop Rocks and Jane Austen. And opera."

"Pop Rocks?"

"You've never had Pop Rocks?" Bas stopped in his tracks and grabbed Teddy's arm.

"Not that I recall." As much as Teddy loved the fissures of

heat radiating from Bas's hand, Teddy's instincts kicked in, and he walked on, allowing that hand to slip away.

"Hey, Arneaux," Bas called over his shoulder. "Teddy has never had Pop Rocks." He caught up to Teddy in a couple of strides as Arneaux shouted behind them.

"Sacrilege!"

"Americans," Teddy muttered as he reached the weapons table McGinty had ordered set up earlier. "I don't know about this Nancy Drew thing. God only knows what we might find down there."

"Scared?" Bas grabbed a saber, hefted it, then tossed it and caught it a few times like a circus performer. He took the reins Dougal offered him and swung into the saddle on the back of a big bay hunter.

Teddy chose a saber, mounted Kelpie, and rode past the stuntman. His body hummed with a combination of adrenaline and arousal. "Let's find out, shall we?"

Chapter Ten

Bas heard Teddy riding behind him and discovered that even an English saddle rubbed like hell against a raging hard-on. The bastard might not know what he was doing, but Bas found Teddy's combination of competence, arrogance, and assured challenge erotic as hell. Was that the attraction? The confusing, inexplicable, totally fucked up allure Wentworth's swordmaster evoked anytime Bas was anywhere near the tall, lean Brit?

No, there was a helluva lot more to this thing between them than that. Bas would have already dragged Teddy to bed otherwise. He hefted the saber as he turned to face the others participating in the lesson. In addition to him, Teddy, and Arneaux, the footmen Dougal and Robbie sat on horseback with swords in their hands, ready to practice their skills. To Bas's amazement, however, another rider sat ready to enter the fray.

The newly minted Lady Lachlan sat astride a big gray, a saber in hand. She had dressed in a simple wool gown with a plaid around one shoulder and tied at her waist. Beneath the dress, she wore what looked like buckskin breeches and a pair of top boots. Her husband, dressed like a Highlander from two hundred years ago, sat on a tall black stud, weaponless, his expression somewhere between concern and amusement.

"What the hell is that about?" Danny asked as he sidled his horse next to Bas's.

"No idea, but I intend to find out. Come on." Bas urged his horse forward, and he and the actor crossed the meadow to where Teddy, Robbie, and Dougal sat on their horses and talked to McGinty.

"Hey, Teddy-boy," Danny called which guaranteed he'd get their instructor's attention. "Care to tell us what the duke's sister-in-law is doing here? Armed."

"Exactly as she pleases," Teddy said with a quick not-so-surreptitious glance at Bas. "But as you're the only one of us she's ever actually struck in anger, the rest of us have nothing to worry about, do we?"

Nice! Wait. What? Bas turned to Danny. "She hit you? When?" Bas watched the ladies in the party—Samantha, Eleanor, Gloria, and Bella—settle onto the chairs at the edge of the meadow, frilly umbrellas over their heads like so many tropical trees.

"The day they landed in Edinburgh. In front of the now Mrs. Arneaux," Teddy said with his usual sangfroid.

"That's Dr. Arneaux to you, dickhead," Danny said. "Can we get this show on the road? The sun's pretty bright and my nuts are sweating in this kilt."

"Do we *have* to receive a weather report on the condition of your bollocks every five minutes?" Teddy rolled his eyes.

Robbie and Dougal snickered. Bas choked back a laugh.

"Just one of the many services I provide, Teddy. Shall we?" Danny turned his horse toward the middle of the meadow.

"For that, you will be sparring with Lady Lachlan first."

"Oh hell. If I hurt her, Lachlan will have my guts for

garters. Let Robbie take her on, or Dougal." Danny glanced to where Lily had started her horse toward them.

"Not us," Robbie said. "Not worth my job nor my life. Besides, she and Lord Lachlan have been sparring with swords on horseback for weeks."

"What?" Danny blurted.

"Mother—" Teddy began.

"Why on earth would he—" Bas was completely confused.

They all watched as she crossed the meadow at a canter, sword swinging through the air, taking out invisible enemy cavalry left and right. Scary as hell. They turned their attention toward Lord Lachlan, who sat on his horse, his gaze glued to his wife.

"Foreplay," the five of them said at once, followed by some raucous and rude laughter.

"I hope that donkey braying is not on my account," Lily said as she joined them.

"No, my lady," Robbie said.

"Absolutely not," Teddy said.

Danny lifted one hand, palm out. "I know better than to laugh at you, Lily."

"Never," Bas said in an even, harmless tone. "In fact, Arneaux was just telling us how much he was looking forward to sparring with you."

"Lovely," she replied. He could tell she didn't believe a word he'd said. "Show us how it's done, Teddy." She walked her horse several hundred feet to the far side of the middle of the meadow.

"I'm going to kill you," Arneaux said out of the side of his mouth, then turned his horse the opposite way and lined up across from Lily.

"Have to catch me first," Bas called to him.

Sword in one hand, Danny raised the other in a three-finger salute.

"Nicely done," Teddy said as he and Bas rode to the middle of the field.

"Thought you'd like that. How do you want to do this demo?" Bas asked.

"I want to knock you off your horse without killing you?"

"Very funny. Fine. I am yours to command, Swordmaster." Bas spun his horse around so he faced Teddy and his horse.

"If only." Teddy's wistful sigh sent a shiver down Bas's spine. "Very well, gentlemen and Lady Lachlan, let's move so there is enough space between us to swing the saber without engaging yet. We're going to go through the drills we've practiced before Mr. Salazar, and I show you the next step."

Teddy had slipped into instructor mode. The man was a chameleon, a trait Bas had never really admired before he met him. Teddy could be an arrogant prick in this mode, but with good reason. He was damned good at his job. They all began the series of sword passes and parries he'd been teaching them long before Bas joined the boot camp. No matter their opinion of Teddy, when he went to each of them adjusting grips and correcting strokes, it was obvious they respected him. Did he register their esteem? Did he know they saw him as the consummate expert in this aspect of his life, no matter what else they thought of him? Bas sure as hell hoped so.

"If you don't pay attention, Mr. Salazar, some marauding Frenchman is going to hand you your head." Teddy's voice broke into Bas's reverie right as the man brought his sword down in a dangerously close arc.

Bas parried, barely, and the connection of their swords sent a jarring rattle down his arm. This elicited a series of murmurs, mostly amused, from the other students.

"A heads-up would be nice." Bas shook his arm to loosen the still vibrating muscles.

"Marauding Frenchmen do not give a *heads-up*." Teddy indicated a spot across the meadow with the point of his saber.

"Neither do Brits who are full of themselves," Bas replied with a grin, and spurred his horse away from him.

He lined up opposite Teddy, who had ridden to the middle of the meadow and turned. At the first hint of a hand signal, Bas urged his horse into a full gallop. This time, when their swords met, his arm held rock solid. He turned and galloped back for another pass. The wind rushed past him, the Highland sunlight beat down on him—and riding toward him, Teddy, smiling with his hair flying behind him, filled Bas's heart to the point of pain.

"Well done," Teddy shouted as Bas managed to deflect his attack. "Again."

Bas laughed and rode to the end of the meadow to turn once more. This time, when they met in the middle of the field, they went through the patterns of close order saber work Teddy had spent the morning demonstrating. In the distance, as if from very far away, he heard shouts and whistles of approval. Robbie, no doubt, had already started a betting pool.

Time stood still. There was only the wind, the thunder of hooves, and the clang of metal. Neither of them held back. They were equally skilled in the avoidance of cutting each other, but their swords met strength for strength in bone-jarring clashes. Thank God he'd decided to dress in Regency Highlander gear today. With no jacket, waistcoat, or cravat, his range of motion in the billowy linen shirt helped him keep up. How the hell Teddy managed while dressed like something out of an English foxhunt painting, Bas didn't know. Swords locked, they maneuvered their horses to achieve an advantage. Bas caught a faint whiff of Teddy's cologne. Their eyes met.

"Surrender?" the swordmaster asked.

"Never in war."

"That leaves all sorts of possibilities open."

"That's up to you now, isn't it?" Bas pushed back, both hands locked on his saber.

Teddy gazed at him for a moment, his expression unreadable. He guided his horse back and slowly lowered his sword. The spectators let loose a round of applause as the two of them rode back to the group. Teddy waved them to silence.

"As dangerous as this sounds, we need to break into pairs and practice the patterns Mr. Salazar and I just demonstrated. Mr. Arneaux, you are with me. Robbie and Dougal, you two try not to injure each other or His Grace will have my head."

"What about me?" Lily asked, her chin jutted out as if she expected Teddy to tell her to join her husband who sat his horse next to where the other ladies sat in their chairs under their parasols.

"I leave you in Mr. Salazar's capable hands, Lady Lachlan." Teddy executed an overdramatic bow from the saddle, touched the hilt of his saber to his forehead in a salute to Bas, and rode off with Arneaux to an area on the other side of the open field.

"I'm going to take him down into that tunnel and leave him there," Bas muttered as he led Lily toward the complete opposite corner of the practice area.

He tried not to notice the way Lord Lachlan resembled a hawk homing in on a rabbit when the man caught his eye. Bas had the Scot when it came to weight and a little on height, but he suspected the former soldier would not go down quietly if Bas hurt his wife.

"Don't worry, Bas." Lily patted him on the shoulder as she rode past him to square off for sparring. "I won't let him hurt you."

"That Scot is *not* one of those lapdogs you used to date, sweetheart." Bas backed his horse into position. "You landed on your feet and found yourself a real man."

"Don't I know it," she said with a very unladylike leer.

"Straight sex." He mock shuddered.

His remark made her laugh, but it didn't distract her. She gave her saber a few experimental swings. He had barely settled back into the saddle and raised his saber before—

"Charge!" She rode at him like a Scottish Valkyrie.

"Shit!" Bas dug his heels into the big bay's sides. He met her less than half the distance they'd put between them. If he hadn't parried her thrust, she'd have taken his head off. "Dammit, Lily, could you try not to kill me?" He reined his horse around and they charged each other again.

With Teddy, the entire dance had been a match of strengths but measured and controlled. With Lily, it was a fight for survival or at least a fight to keep all his limbs intact.

"Scared, Mr. Salazar?" she retorted as they crossed swords with a deafening clang and then rode on.

"Terrified," he called back. "Get a better grip on your saber so your wrist doesn't snap back."

She adjusted her grip and, this time, charged a little less frantically, but not much. On the next pass, her arm held firm.

She smiled. "This is fun. Lachlan is always afraid he'll hurt me."

"He's afraid he'll hurt *you*?" He steadied the bay and prepared to make another charge.

The meadow began to sound like a battlefield with the other teams thundering at each other and the rest of the guests cheering and calling out comments. He urged his horse into a trot.

"A good hit, Arneaux," McGinty called from somewhere to Bas's left. "Nearly unseated him, ye did."

The bay broke into a canter, then a gallop. His hooves kicked up little sprays of dirt and grass. A roar of shouts from his right where the rest of the guests watched caught his attention. He only turned his head toward where Teddy and Danny sparred for a second. He raised his arm to meet Lily's sword stroke.

Clang!

Whomp!

Bas's ears rang. He saw stars. His head hurt like a mother. *What the hell?* The sounds of shouts, running feet, and horses' hooves coming and going echoed around him. He still had his saber in his hand. Where was his horse? He tried to raise his head. A feminine hand pushed him back down.

"Don't get up. Hell, Bas, I didn't mean to. Are you okay?" Lily's face faded in and out above him.

"Did you cut anything off?" For some reason it hurt to talk.

"No." She gave a watery sounding laugh. "You're all there. Just lie quietly. They're bringing the cart over."

"I've never been all there."

"Bas, what the hell? Lily, what did you do to him?" Teddy sort of skidded on his knees next to him.

Teddy started to run his hands over Bas, which would have been fine if Bas wasn't one big ache. He really wished Teddy's face would come into focus, but those gray eyes were clear as glass. Bas fought back a smile. Those eyes said Teddy cared a lot more than he wanted to admit.

"She knocked me off my damned horse. Is he okay?"

"Who?" Teddy pulled a handkerchief out of somewhere and blotted at a spot on Bas's forehead.

"My horse."

"Your horse? Of course, he's fine. You were knocked off him, not the other way around, you idiot. Where's the cart?"

"What cart?" Bas let go of his sword and flattened his hands on the grass in an attempt to sit up. "I'm getting up."

"Bugger that," Teddy actually growled. "Be still. You've likely concussed yourself." His large warm hand pressed into the middle of Bas's chest, over his heart, which had suddenly started to race.

"Your language, Mr. Rousseau." Eleanor's prim tone made Bas want to laugh.

"Fuck my language, Eleanor. Have you called an ambulance?"

Ambulance? Bas lurched up into a seated position. His entire body vibrated with pulses of white-hot pain. "I am not…going to the hospital…*shit*…because I fell off my horse." His head had begun to spin and throb like a jackhammer.

"You didn't precisely fall off your horse." Bas recognized Lord Lachlan's definitely amused voice. "My wife *knocked* you off your horse. Rather a different animal, that."

"How nice of you to remind me." He really wanted to get to his feet to prove he didn't need an ambulance or even a cart, but Teddy continued to hover next to him, his hand clamped on Bas's shoulder like a vice.

"No thanks necessary," Lachlan said. "Here's Urquhart with the cart. Come on, Rousseau, let's get him up. Robbie, Dougal, give us a hand."

"I don't need— Hey!"

Bas wasn't sure how, but he went from sitting on the ground to having four sets of hands lifting and placing him in the back of a horse-drawn cart. Better than an ambulance but a helluva lot bumpier. His head rested in Lily's lap. Teddy sat on one side of him, and Lord Lachlan sat on the other. He was vaguely aware of horses and riders following behind them.

"I left my sword," he muttered. "Sorry." He tried to look at Teddy, but his eyes refused to focus.

"Robbie and Dougal stayed to gather all the weapons. Be still." Teddy placed his hand on Bas's shoulder and left it there. "Eleanor's sent for the doctor from the village."

"Don't need a doctor. Tylenol and an ice pack." He'd started to feel a little nauseous, not that he'd tell Teddy that. The sound of water lapping told him they traveled along the loch and would reach the stables and then the house soon.

"You've a bloody wound on your forehead and a knot the size of an avocado at the back of your skull. Bloody Tylenol is not going to help," Teddy growled.

"Always has before."

"How many concussions has he had?" Lord Lachlan asked.

"Knowing him? Dozens," Lily said.

"Kiss my ass, Lily."

Teddy snorted back a laugh in unison with Lily's, "Not in front of my husband, who has custody of my sword, by the way."

"Good. Can you cut my head off please?"

"I'm not allowed to kill any more of my brother's guests. Sorry."

Bas laughed, then wished he hadn't. His vision started to curl at the edges. He took several long, deep breaths.

"All right?" Teddy's face hovered into view. "Wentworth will kill me if his stunt coordinator dies on my watch."

"Jesus, Teddy. Your bedside manner is atrocious." Lily used Teddy's handkerchief to blot at Bas's forehead.

Bas took another deep breath as the cart rocked to a stop. The sound and cool splash of the fountain told him they were in front of Rosemount Manor's main entrance. He assumed the rest of the party had stopped at the stables to leave their horses.

"This is my fourth concussion, *if* it is a concussion. You people are overreacting."

Teddy and Lord Lachlan jumped out of the cart. Lily helped Bas sit up just as the doors to the house burst open.

"What have you done to yourself now, poor lad?" Mrs. Wallace's bullhorn voice and quick, fussy walk to the back of the cart somehow made Bas feel better.

"I didn't do it." With Lily's help, Bas slid to the end of the cart and lowered his feet to the cobblestones of the driveway. "Her ladyship here did it."

"Och, and what did you do to her?" The woman was a force of nature. She ran her hands over Bas's head, which made him wince. "Get him in the house now before he falls down again. We'll need a winch to get him back on his feet, braw as he is."

"Yes, ma'am." Lord Lachlan's and Teddy's response made them sound about ten years old. They each put an arm around Bas's waist and slowly walked him into the foyer and to the grand front staircase.

"Come on, guys, I've got this." Bas succeeded in shrugging the two men off, then nearly fell on his ass. "Shit!"

"Leave off, you great *bampot*." Mrs. Wallace hurried up the stairs ahead of them. "Get him into bed, you two, before he collapses. Dr. MacPherson is on the way."

"I don't—"

"Shut. Up," Lord Lachlan whispered as he and Teddy grabbed him again and started them up the stairs. "Don't provoke her."

"Smart man." Lily hurried past them and continued up to the second floor. "Bridie, is there a fire in Mr. Salazar's room?" she called down the corridor. "I've knocked him off his horse and he needs to lie down."

Teddy snorted, and this time he did laugh. As did Lord Lachlan.

"Great," Bas muttered. "She's going to take a full-page ad out in *Variety* before this is over."

"My wife would never."

"Yes, she would," Bas and Teddy said together.

"Here we go," Lord Lachlan said as they helped Bas into his room.

They lowered him onto the bed. He sat there and tried to make the room stop spinning and moving in and out of focus. The maid, Bridie, and Lily worked to build up the fire in the big fireplace.

"Aye, and where's the patient?"

Bas slowly raised his head to see a tall, thin man of about forty dressed in a kilt and a pullover sweater stride into the room, followed by the duke and Eleanor Witherspoon, commander of Regency Boot Camp. Wonderful.

"Let's take a look." The man he assumed was Dr. MacPherson opened his black bag—he actually had a black doctor's bag—and drew out several items. Before Bas knew it, the doctor had hooked him up to a blood pressure cuff, an electronic thermometer, and had shone a bright light into each eye in rapid succession. "How do ye feel?"

"Like I got knocked off my horse."

The doctor laughed. "Aye, I heard his lordship caught a right one. If she can take out this big lad, I daresay she might be able to keep ye between the hedges, won't she, my lord?"

"She does her best, sir," Lord Lachlan said as he gazed at Lily, who stood by the hearth. His face came into sharp focus, and Bas's chest hurt at the love that passed between the two of them.

Dr. MacPherson paused in his examination of Bas to look Lily's husband up and down. "She's done well. You look good." He turned his attention back to Bas, where he poked at the knots on the front and back of his head.

Between winces of pain, Bas watched the duke actually smile at Lily. He didn't think the man capable. Didn't last long. The minute His Grace turned back to Eleanor, that smile fled faster than a fart in a wind tunnel.

"Miss Witherspoon," the duke said, "in my study if you please. Dr. MacPherson, I expect a full report." He walked out of the room with Eleanor right on his heels.

"Shite," Lord Lachlan muttered. "He'll blame her for this."

Bas slightly tilted his head in search of Teddy. He didn't have to look far. The swordmaster hovered at his side and asked questions of the doctor in rapid succession. Once Bas caught Teddy's eye, he glanced at the door through which the duke and Eleanor had just left. In a single glance, they exchanged an entire conversation. An argument, really. One Bas won as Teddy squeezed his shoulder, stopped to speak to Lily for a moment, then left the room. Lily immediately took his place at Bas's bedside.

"What did he say?" Bas asked.

"To make certain you do as the doctor says, and if you don't, I'm supposed to knock you down again."

"That's some bedside manner you two have," Bas said as the doctor continued to probe the spot on the back of Bas's head that throbbed in time with his pulse.

"Sounds like perfectly sound medical advice ta me." Dr. MacPherson dropped all his various pieces of equipment into his bag.

"What are you, a veterinarian?"

"As big as ye are, they might have done better to call auld Jenner, but I doubt ye'd appreciate where he'd put the thermometer."

Even Bridie and Mrs. Wallace laughed at that.

"Ye never lost consciousness?"

"No, Doc, not even when I wanted to."

"Aye, if a slip of a lady like this knocked me off ma horse, I'd want to black out as well."

Bas grimaced. "I've changed my mind. Call the vet."

"I don't think ye have a concussion, but to be safe, someone needs to stay with him and wake him up every few hours, at least until tomorrow morning. A couple of days bed rest, ice packs, and lots of fluids. Tylenol, not aspirin. Call me if ye cannae wake him. Inta bed with ye, lad."

"But I don't— Hey!"

Before he had a chance to fight back, Lily had removed his boots and pushed him back onto the bed. Mrs. Wallace lifted his legs and arranged him so he lay flat on his back until Lily settled an extra pillow beneath his head. She grabbed a heavy quilt from the foot of the bed and covered him.

"Come along, Bridie. I'll send her back up with the Tylenol and ice packs, yer ladyship."

"Thank you, Mrs. Wallace." Lily started to pull one of the big armchairs over to the side of the bed. Lord Lachlan picked it up and placed it where she wanted it. Once she settled into it, he kissed her and stroked her hair.

"Get a room," Bas muttered as he shifted to get comfortable. "Preferably not *my* room."

"We will." Lily took Lord Lachlan's hand as he sat on the arm of her chair. "As soon as Teddy escapes the wrath of the duke. He's volunteered to sit with you."

Bas closed his eyes. "Do you think the duke will be that bad?"

"Isn't that why you sent Teddy to defend her?" Lily asked.

"Is Lily always this…."

"Insightful?" Lord Lachlan chuckled. "All the time."

"You're both annoying as hell. I'm an injured man here. Go away."

The door burst open. Bas tried to sit up, but a sharp pain at the back of his head made him think better of it.

"Your brother is a horse's arse." Teddy announced as Bridie scurried in with a tray that held a silver pitcher, a glass goblet, a little silver bucket, and an old-fashioned looking ice pack, the kind shaped like a bag and had a lid that screwed off and on so it could be refilled as often as needed.

"Not in front of Bridie," Lily warned. She squeezed Bas's forearm for good measure. "Thank you. That'll be all."

The maid curtsied, grinned at Bas, and left the room. Teddy came to sit on the side of the bed.

"How bad was it?" Lachlan asked.

"Bad enough. He blamed Eleanor for the whole thing and threatened to call off the Regency boot camp. Said you could have been killed."

"Oh, please. Let me talk to him." Bas sat up only to have numerous hands push him back onto the bed.

"I handled it. Told him it was my fault for not training you properly. What did the doctor say?"

"Not training…that's bullshit and you know it."

"Well, His Grace bought it and actually apologized to Eleanor, so shut the hell up. What did the doctor say?"

"He said I'm fine. Just a bump on the head."

"Talk about bullshit." Lily handed Teddy a couple of Tylenol, then filled the goblet with water from the silver pitcher. "Make him take these." She tapped Lachlan on the shoulder as she headed to the door. He pushed off the arm of the chair and followed her. "Take care of him, Teddy," she ordered as she and her husband left the room and closed the door behind them.

Teddy grabbed Bas's hand and dropped the pills into his palm. "Better do as she says. I wouldn't put it past her to burst back in here to make certain we're obeying her orders. She's quite enjoying, playing *her ladyship*." He held the goblet to Bas's lips.

Bas scowled, tossed the pills into his mouth, took the goblet from Teddy, and drank the entire contents down in one long draught. Teddy plucked the goblet from his hand and placed it on the bedside table.

"You can go. I can take care of myself." Bas closed his eyes and settled back onto the pillows.

Something about the way Teddy stood there, an odd expression on his face, made Bas want to shut him out. To shut everything he wasn't saying, didn't need to say, out. Impossible to do when a sudden tender press of lips to his forehead told him Teddy did not intend to leave.

Bas kept his eyes tightly shut. "What was that for?"

"You took a bad fall." Teddy's voice was tight and strained. Bas heard the sound of him settling into the bedside chair Lily had occupied. "I'm simply glad you weren't badly hurt."

"No, just badly humiliated." Bas kept his eyes tightly closed. The light hurt his eyes.

"No need to feel humiliated. Lily has quite the reputation for ruthlessness, here and in the film business."

"According to her rep, she's a four-star bitch. She's fond of you though." This time he did open his eyes and turned his head to watch Teddy.

"Well…bitches of a feather and all that."

"I've worked with her before. Something's rubbed the sharp edges off her."

"*Someone*. I'm sure some think he deserves a bloody medal just for marrying her."

"Maybe. Who's rubbed your sharp edges off, Teddy? You're not the same jerk I met when I got here. I'm not the only one who's noticed."

Teddy's expression turned stony. "Settle down and go to sleep." He took a very old pocket watch out of his waistcoat pocket and fiddled with the tiny buttons on the side of the silver case. "I'll wake you in two hours."

No answer is sometimes the entire answer.

"Help me out of this shirt first. It's sticky and it smells." Bas sat up and began to struggle with the buttons at the neck.

Teddy swatted Bas's hands away, unbuttoned the shirt, and pulled it gently over Bas's head. Teddy headed to the washstand, poured water from a porcelain pitcher into the matching bowl, and wet a washcloth, then returned to the bed and sat on the edge of the mattress. He began to bathe Bas's chest, sides, and arms. When Teddy had finished, he pulled the covers up and returned to his chair.

"Now, sleep. Or I'll call Mrs. Wallace on you."

"Bitch. You, not her." Bas closed his eyes. He sensed Teddy standing over him. The sensation of fingers through his hair, down his neck and across his chest made him shiver.

"Molester," he mumbled.

"Tease. Sleep."

"I'd kill for a cheeseburger and a Coke for lunch."

"Shut up and go to sleep," Teddy ordered once more. He placed the ice pack on Bas's head. "I'll be right here."

The peace and warmth those words gave him disturbed the hell out of Bas—because they said so much or because they said things Teddy would never utter once this was all over.

"Teddy?" he murmured as a weary sleep began to draw him away.

"What?"

"You don't have to stay, you know."

Chapter Eleven

TEDDY'S NOSE TWITCHED. IN THE MIDDLE OF A SEARING EROTIC dream, the scent of cheeseburgers and fish and chips didn't add to the ambiance at all. He drew in a long, deep breath and decided he was well and truly awake now. Along with the distinctly *non*-Regency food scent, he found himself on the receiving end of some sharp and painful reminders he'd fallen asleep in a chair, bent like some sort of pretzel. He slowly raised his head from the pillow of his folded arms and twisted his neck from side to side.

"How the hell did you sleep like that?" Bas asked.

"I didn't." Teddy sat up so quickly he had to forcibly bite back a gasp at the twinges and aches that shot down his shoulders and spine.

"So, somebody else's snoring must have woken me up from a dead sleep." Bas, a burger in one hand and a chip in the other, grinned, then went back to eating. Bare-chested, he sat up in bed, propped by an entire army of pillows. A tray bearing a selection of foods most definitely not created in Mrs. Gordon's kitchen lay across his legs. No mean feat when Teddy considered how powerful Bas's thighs were.

Teddy stretched his arms overhead and twisted back and forth at the waist to loosen his stiff back. He'd slept in the armchair at Bas's bedside, his head rested on his folded arms on the edge of the mattress. How...weak of him.

"I take it Robbie nipped down to the village to provide you with this forbidden feast?"

"You know damned well he did. You asked him to while I slept, which is why there is an order of fish and chips wrapped in newspaper sitting on the hearth to stay warm." Bas gave him an odd sort of look and went back to his meal.

Teddy glanced at the fireplace, pushed out of the chair, and fetched his food. Bas handed him a china plate from the tray.

"Robbie said not to get any stains on the bed linens that might give us away. He's terrified Eleanor will find out."

"He's not the only one. Is this my drink?" Teddy nodded at the lidded Styrofoam cup that sat on a coaster on the nightstand.

"Yeah. Ginger ale? Really?"

"Acquired a taste for it when working on a film in Arizona a few years ago."

"Okay. Oh, and by the way, you *need* to be afraid if Eleanor finds out. Robbie and I have already decided to throw you under the bus if she does."

"Bitches." Teddy took a big bite of the golden fried fish and closed his eyes to savor the taste. "Oh, dear God, that is good."

"You're beautiful when you're happy."

Teddy nearly choked on his food. He took his time to chew and swallow the bite he'd taken before he turned his head to gaze at Bas—who sat there eating his elicit cheeseburger as if he hadn't just said the most confusing and wonderful thing in the world to him.

"What did you say?"

"You heard me. You want some ketchup for your fries?"

"They're chips, not fries. Ketchup is disgusting. And what did you mean?"

The maid and Lily had stoked the fire to perfection. The heat in the room fairly stifled him. Some part of Teddy wanted to get up from Bas's bedside and eat his food somewhere else. Across the room. Across the country. Across the world.

"I meant what I said." Bas spoke each word in a slow, clear baritone. "Eat your lunch. We have to burn the evidence in the fireplace once we're finished. You'll need your strength and another nap before we take off on our adventure tonight. You're putting vinegar on your fries?" He made a face and dipped a chip in the little plastic cup of ketchup next to his plate.

"What adventure? You're supposed to be on bed rest for the next couple of days. Or do you intend to ignore Dr. MacPherson's advice completely?"

"Not completely. We're going to explore that staircase in the dressing room tonight. I had Robbie smuggle in some flashlights from my crew in the village."

"What part of bed rest is creeping into a secret tunnel from a death trap stone staircase in the middle of the night?" Teddy slapped at the hand that reached into his newspaper wrapped lunch and filched a couple of chips. He waited for Bas to finish eating his stolen food. "Well?"

"Well, what? I'm going to finish my lunch and then I'm going to take another nap. I'll have Robbie bring my dinner up on a tray, and he can say you feel so guilty about what happened you'll look after me tonight. Once everyone else has gone to bed, we'll Nancy Drew our asses down that staircase. You know, vinegar on fries isn't so bad. Give me some more."

"When did I volunteer for this little adventure? Leave my

chips alone." Teddy handed him a packet of vinegar. "Use this. I'm supposed to feel guilty because you let Lily knock you off your horse?"

"Hurtful. You don't have to *feel* guilty. You just have to *tell* them you feel guilty." He finished off his drink with a long pull on the straw.

Teddy shifted in his chair to alleviate the sudden sensation in his groin. He had a solution for the misfiring in this brain—leave the room and send someone else to make certain Bas stayed in bed like the doctor ordered.

"Here," Bas said, and forced Teddy's attention away from his own confusion. "Throw the wrappers and cup in the fireplace and put the tray out in the hall. Is there any more Tylenol? I'm going to try to take a nap."

"Yes, sir. Whatever you say, sir." Teddy tossed everything burnable into the fire, then carefully placed the tray outside Bas's room. He grabbed the bottle of Tylenol off the marquetry table by the door and tossed it to Bas.

"Very funny," Bas said as Teddy returned to his chair to finish off his fish and chips. When Bas stared pointedly at Teddy's drink cup, Teddy handed it to him. "Ginger ale?" He tossed the pills into his mouth and washed them down with another long draw, this time on the straw in Teddy's cup. "Blech." He shuddered and handed the cup back to Teddy. "You don't have to stay. I don't have a concussion. I know how one feels, and this isn't it. Come back after dinner if you're not afraid of a little adventure."

"I'm not afraid of—" Teddy snapped his mouth shut at the sharp rap at the door.

"Come in," Bas called.

The door opened just enough for Robbie to slide in like something out of a bad spy movie. Teddy rolled his eyes and gathered all the detritus from his meal to toss into the fire.

"If that empty tray is any judge, ye enjoyed yer lunch?" Robbie took the plate Teddy had left on the bedside table.

"Very much. Thanks for taking your life in your hands to bring contraband into our little Regency prison." Bas stretched his arms toward the canopy over the bed. Every sinew surfaced under his taught skin.

Teddy swallowed as he sat back in his chair and concentrated on what Robbie was saying. Helping Bas take off his shirt turned out to be a torturously bad idea.

"Don't let him fool you," Teddy said. "I had to bribe him to defy Eleanor's orders. Robbie would no doubt charge his own mother for a trip to the village fish and chip shop."

"Aye," Robbie said. "But her I give a discount. Yer flashlights are in the dressing room, by the by." He glanced at the door into the corridor as if he expected an invasion at any moment. "I don't suppose ye'd like to tell me *why* you need the flashlights now, would ye?"

Teddy jumped in before Bas could answer. "No, we would not. Plausible deniability, Robbie. In case we get caught."

"Oh, aye. Miss Witherspoon asked Mrs. Wallace to send one of the maids up to sit with ye, sir, if need be." The footman did a quick glance from Bas to Teddy and back again.

"There's no need," Teddy said, his heart pounding so hard he couldn't feel his hands as he reached for the book and the script he'd left on the bedside table. "I have some work to do that requires quiet. I'll sit with him. There's no need to pull one of the maids away from her duties."

"Right ye are, sir. I'll be telling the ladies ye have everything under control. Is there anything else ye might be needing?" Robbie clutched the plate in one hand and Bas's dirty shirt in the other.

"As if," Bas grumbled, and began to rearrange the pillows for his nap.

"Could you ask Mrs. Gordon to send our dinner up here? Mr. Salazar needs to get as much rest as possible, if we are to believe Dr. MacPherson." He deliberately tossed Bas a censuring glare.

"Will do." Robbie gave a mock salute. "Wish me luck. I have to go down and report on Mr. Salazar's health to an entire drawing room of women. Lady Lachlan has been beside herself."

"Lily?" Bas and Teddy said together with an equal amount of disbelief.

Robbie laughed as he left the room and closed the door behind him.

Teddy finally directed his attention to Bas, who, damn him, stared back with an expectant tilt of his head.

"Go to sleep. I'll wake you in a few hours to make certain your brains aren't scrambled." He opened his book and settled back into his chair. "Or rather, more scrambled."

"I'm not the one whose brains are scrambled."

Teddy ignored Bas's remark but listened attentively as he punched his pillows into submission and rustled around on the bed until he finally settled with a deep, dark sigh. Teddy's body fairly hummed with the awareness of Bas's honed body lying under those elegant bed linens and counterpane. The sound of his breathing, the combination of his cologne, the smoke from the fire, and the laundry soap on the sheets burned itself into Teddy's memory.

He closed his eyes. The desire to draw every aspect of Bas into himself, to savor every moment, overwhelmed Teddy. Then the fullness of his senses lulled him as nothing ever had. In this room, with Bas asleep, the warmth of the fire, and the elegance of their surroundings, Teddy had to fight to stay awake. There was something hypnotic about feeling safe and secure and able to be himself, even if only for a little while.

"Teddy?"

Lovely. Now he was hearing things.

"Teddy." He fought his way to wakefulness as a hand shook his shoulder. "Get up and lock the door."

Well, that woke him up. Quick, fast, and in a hurry. "Why?" He sat up, and the book in his lap slid to the floor.

"You're going to break something if you keep trying to sleep in that chair. Lock the door and get into bed. I promise not to molest you."

"That isn't much incentive for me to lock the door now, is it?" Teddy the flirt was hard at work. Teddy the man couldn't hang on to a single coherent thought at the moment.

"Shut up. Just do it. Your snoring will wake me up in a few hours, and you can tell the ladies you checked on me just like the doctor ordered. Hurry up. My head hurts." He threw back the covers on the near side of the bed and rolled onto his side toward the other side of the room.

Teddy had a sort of out-of-body experience as he locked the door and came back to his chair to toe off his boots. He shook two more Tylenol out of the bottle and poured some water from the silver pitcher that had magically appeared refilled on the bedside table. Robbie. While Teddy and Bas had bantered back and forth, the footman had crept about doing what footmen do. The young man had great promise as a burglar. Teddy tapped Bas on his bare shoulder.

"Take these."

Bas rolled back toward him and grumbled a few phrases in Basque. Despite that, he swallowed the pills and washed them down with the water. "Get into bed, Teddy. You look tired."

"Flatterer." He did as Bas told him. Once he had settled onto his side facing away from Bas, the stuntman drew the sheets and counterpane over both of them.

"You don't need flattery," Bas said sleepily.

"What do I need?"

Silence, save for the wind against the windows and the crackle of the fire. Already late afternoon, the day had grown overcast, so the light through the mullioned panes did little to illuminate the room. Teddy settled into the bed as much as he could.

"I'll tell you what you need one day. Not today. Take a nap. We have a big night ahead of us."

"Good God." Teddy choked back a gasp as Bas curled his arm back and pulled Teddy closer to the point they lay with their backs pressed together. Bas was laughing as he did so, and the deep rumble vibrated through Teddy like the thunder that rolled across the fields of Rosemount during a storm.

"Don't worry," Bas said, his arm still resting on Teddy's hip. "I'll protect you."

Teddy snorted and relaxed against him. "You just had your arse kicked by a woman. I think I'd better be in charge of security on this mad adventure."

"Even if we run into the ghost?"

"Fuck that. If we run into Elsbeth, you're on your bloody own."

"My hero."

Teddy lay there and listened to Bas breathe while counting each breath as it pressed the stuntman's bare back against Teddy's linen clad skin. Even as he grew sleepy, he fought to stay awake. Lying in bed with Bas Salazar, he searched his muddled thoughts to try and define the strange and new sense of…what? He didn't even have a name for this. Powerful? Good? Exhilarating? He closed his eyes and sighed. He'd figure it out. Somehow. Later.

The scent of lavender and heather escorted him into a deep sleep, along with laughter. Soft, feminine laughter.

TEDDY PULLED THE HEAVY WOOL JUMPER OVER HIS HEAD AND reached for the wool socks he'd pulled out of the drawer of the highboy in his bedchamber. He played hell pulling his Regency top boots over the thick socks, but he managed. He tucked his buckskin breeches into the top of his boots in the hope of creating a sort of clothing barrier against the cold.

Nearly midnight, and the other guests had just come upstairs to check in on Bas, then toddled off to their beds. Fortunately, he and Bas had been playing cards—Bas in the bed and Teddy in the chair, when the first knock came on the door after they'd finished their dinner and sent the trays back below stairs with Robbie. Teddy shuddered to think what the others might have thought had they found him and Bas in bed together, even if all they'd done was sleep—which turned out to be one of the deepest and most restful sleeps Teddy had enjoyed in far too long to even contemplate.

"Are you coming or not?" Bas leaned in the doorway that led from Teddy's room into the dressing room dressed in a kilt, shirt open at the throat, boots, and a Regency-style wool greatcoat. Sexy as original sin, but Teddy noted the slight pallor to Bas's skin and the periodic tensing of his neck and forehead.

"That is a loaded question." Teddy stood and picked up the heavy flashlight he'd placed on his bedside table. God help them both if Eleanor saw it.

"Such a horndog. Is sex all you think of?" Bas turned and headed into the dressing room.

"Not all."

Teddy entered the dressing room and stopped. The door to the hidden staircase already stood open. The faint scent of lavender blew in on the breeze from the narrow darkness beyond the ancient doorway. "Are you certain you're up to this? If you pass out down there, I am not looking forward to dragging your heavy arse back up those stairs."

"Just try to keep up," Bas said, and started down the stairs. "Watch it. The stairs are narrow and slick."

"No…shit. Bas, these stairs are hundreds of years old."

Teddy braced a hand on the ancient rock wall and shone his flashlight at the hand-hewn stone steps. The damp was palpable, but the confined space didn't smell as closed up and musty as he would have expected. The stairs went on for what he calculated to be several floors, even lower than the kitchens and storerooms.

They reached the landing at the bottom of the stairs.

"Okay, now what?" Bas said.

From the landing, there were two corridors. One continued beneath the manor house. The other appeared to run beneath the back gardens if Teddy's sense of direction was correct.

Bas looked at Teddy. "How far down are we?"

Teddy shone the torch on the corridor to the left "Well below the main house. Dungeon level, unless I miss my guess."

Bas swept his flashlight down each corridor. The walls and the rounded ceiling, made of huge stonework, formed a narrow passageway. Wide enough for two people of smaller stature than Bas and Teddy to walk side by side, but only just. The ceiling was less than a foot over their heads. The damp became more pronounced here.

"This way," Teddy said as he started down the corridor under the gardens. "If it continues the way I think it will, we'll find ourselves in the old castle ruins."

"Really?" Bas sounded like a little kid.

"I might be wrong, but I don't think so. Either that, or it'll end in a dead end or a cave of some kind."

Their boots echoed on the stone floors as they moseyed

down the corridor, Teddy in the lead. He tried to calculate the distance they were from the house but found it difficult with Bas's heady presence behind him. His sense of time had deserted him too. Somehow, trudging through Rosemount's hidden underground made time stand still. Or perhaps, he simply hoped time stood still. Perhaps he wanted this moment to go on forever.

"Admit it." Bas nudged Teddy in the back with what he assumed was a flashlight.

"Admit what?"

"You're having fun."

"Oh yes, this is much more fun than sleeping in my nice warm bed in a room with a roaring fire in the hearth."

Bas made a rude noise. "Boring."

"If all you wanted was excitement, I could let Lily knock you off your horse again." He stopped walking. "Now this is interesting." The corridor did come to a dead end, but only because a heavy iron-banded oak door blocked the way.

"I'm never going to live that down, am I?" Bas's breath traced Teddy's ear, which produced a powerful erotic shiver down Teddy's spine.

"Not if I can help it. Here, hold this." He handed his flashlight to Bas. "Let me see if I can open this door."

Surprisingly, the door opened with quiet ease after just a few strong tugs on the iron ring that served as a door pull. They ducked their heads under the ancient oak lintel set into the stone, then tilted their heads back to follow the steep, narrow stone steps that disappeared up into the darkness. They stood crowded together in the doorway. The air that had been damp and musty now beat against Teddy's face, cold and clean. And still that hint of—

"Lavender," Bas said softly. "It's her, isn't it? The ghost?"

"Elsbeth? I don't know. Only one way to find out." Teddy took his flashlight back from Bas and started up the stairs.

"You sure you don't want me to go first?" Bas asked as he followed him up the worn, slick steps.

"No. If I slip, I'm counting on you to break my fall."

"Handsome and witty. No wonder women are attracted to you. Damn, is it just me or did ancient Scots have really small feet?"

"Says the man whose size twelves are like blocks of ice in bed. Whoa." The staircase curved sharply to the right. Teddy braced his hand against the stone wall.

Bas immediately pressed his wide hand to the small of Teddy's back. "Okay?" Bas's voice tightened and took on a dark, concerned tone.

"Yes. Wasn't expecting that. We're climbing out of the lower levels of the original keep. At least, I think that's where we are." He started up the stairs again. Bas kept his hand against Teddy's back, warm and steady. They climbed for what seemed like an hour.

The air grew fresher—the scent of night and the loch mixed with faint heather and lavender. They reached a small landing with an arrow-slit of a window. Teddy checked the view as much as he could.

"We're above ground. I think we're somewhere behind the part of the tower the duke uses as his private office." He moved over just enough for Bas to look.

"The steps keep going up," Bas said. He grabbed Teddy's shoulder and shook it. "If you're right, we can go into the tower and find out why the duke doesn't want anyone up there."

"Or we can run into a caved in staircase in the dark." Teddy shone his flashlight around the corner from the landing, and more steps appeared. "Maybe walk off a landing into nothing and land back in the dungeon?"

Suddenly, the stone walls moved in on him. Teddy had never been one for confined spaces. The constant drip of water somewhere off in the dark didn't help. The air, although cleaner, still smelled of lavender and something more. Something sad and without light.

"Teddy?" Bas angled his flashlight to illuminate Teddy's face. "You okay?"

"That's my line. How's your head?" He shook off whatever maudlin sensations invaded his thoughts.

"Compared to what?" Bas flinched when Teddy shone his flashlight into the stuntman's face. "Come on." Bas grabbed his hand and dragged him toward the steps so sloped in the center a man could nearly drink water from them.

Just like that, Teddy had Bas's fingers entwined with his. The stupid thing was, holding hands with Bas seemed the most natural thing in the world. Stupid because Teddy had never held anyone's hand, let alone another man's. Several times Bas looked back at Teddy—his face lit with childlike excitement. Teddy couldn't help himself. He grinned right back.

Eventually, they came to another iron-banded oak door, this one with a latch rather than a pull ring. Bas put his shoulder into it, and after two tries, the door creaked open like something out of a Regency gothic novel, the kind with a woman running across the moors in a white dress on the cover.

They walked into the room hand in hand. The moon shone brightly through the mullioned windows. There were only a few items of furniture—a large wooden chair with a tattered leather seat and back, a scarred table of heavy, aged wood, and a worn rug of woven rushes. The fireplace was large enough to accommodate logs of entire tree trunks, and though there was no fire now, there had been one recently.

The chair faced neither the fireplace nor the windows, which was a shame as the view of the loch was stunning. Teddy reluctantly released Bas's hand to get a better view.

The water rippled toward the shore and created a sort of trail from the reflection of the moon. Something moved across the water. Something…or someone. A figure in a white dress walked across the water. Then gazed up directly at Teddy.

"Hell!" He stumbled back directly into Bas, who stood stock still in the middle of the room.

Bas turned to catch him. "What? What is it?"

"She's out there. Walking across the bloody loch and she looked at me."

"Who?"

"Elsbeth. She's out there." To his complete embarrassment his voice shook, hell his entire being shook.

Bas peered over Teddy's shoulder. "I don't see anything."

"I saw her clear as day. She's out there."

"I'm pretty sure she's in here too." Bas grasped Teddy's shoulders and turned him toward the far wall of the room, to the spot the chair faced. With his arm draped around Teddy, Bas shone his flashlight directly in their line of vision.

"Holy hell," Teddy whispered.

The life-sized portrait hung in an ornate gold frame. The style was that of several hundred years ago. The woman who stared out at them evinced an air of command and mystery, confidence and sensuality of such power, Teddy fully expected her to speak. Blue eyes, light golden red hair, skin the golden brown of some island in the Caribbean. A mix of Scot and island ancestry that would have marked her as more than different in her time. She wore a green velvet medieval gown trimmed in simple gold ribbon. She held a small book in her hand. A gold nameplate set into the bottom of the frame left the identity of the subject in no doubt. None of that was as remarkable as her face, as who she resembled with an uncanniness that was terrifying.

"No wonder the duke has trouble dealing with Eleanor," Bas said.

"So, it's not me. She really does look like…."

"Look like?" Bas whispered. "Hell, she's her spitting image."

For several minutes they simply took in the eerie beauty of the woman murdered all those years ago, simply because she was…different. Finally, Teddy assessed the room again, this time more carefully. No cobwebs. The windows had bars on the inside, but the glass on the outside was clean. His view of the loch had been crystal clear. The floor was spotless. The chair and the table were free of dust. A small table beneath the portrait held a vase of fresh flowers—wildflowers found on the estate. Fresh wildflowers. The scent of burning wood and peat lingered ever so slightly in the air from the recently used fireplace, mixed with the persistent scent of lavender and heather. His mind turned those details over and over in search of an explanation.

"Do you think she's seen this portrait?" Bas asked, breaking the silence.

"Who?"

"Elsbeth. Who the hell do you think? Has the duke shown this portrait to Eleanor?"

"Absolutely not. He's keeping this secret to himself. I'd wager Robbie on it."

"What makes you so sure?" Bas dropped into the chair and threw a leg over one of the leather padded arms.

"This is private. This is why the duke won't let you use the tower for the film. He spends time here. Remembering."

Bas dropped his leg to the floor and turned to stare at Teddy. "Remembering what?"

"That's right, you don't know the story. I'm surprised some of your crew haven't heard the stories in town. That's where I first heard it, then Robbie confirmed the story. She was his imaginary friend when he was a child. They sent him away because of it. Now this American woman walks into his life looking just like her." Teddy shrugged. "His Grace is probably trying to figure out what it all means."

"I can't believe we're talking like this about a ghost. A ghost that hung out with this duke as a child and now is back haunting random guests. For what? Why?"

"Does there have to be a why?" Teddy went back to the window and stared across the loch, willing Elsbeth to reappear.

The creak of leather and wood and the approach of booted footsteps announced Bas's presence behind him before the warm scent of Bas's cologne teased Teddy's nose and set his body abuzz with awareness.

The stuntman braced an arm on one side of the window. "She was murdered in that loch because she loved a man others thought was out of her league. There's a why, all right. What I don't understand is why that man isn't haunting this place too."

"Maybe he's at peace. I mean, he's buried in the family mausoleum. Where is she buried? Did they find her body?"

"They? *He.* Did *he* find her body? He watched her die from this window. He probably kept this room hidden. Was this his private heaven or his private hell? To stare at someone you love and know you can never touch them, never hold them in your arms? Wherever the first duke is, I doubt he's at peace. I wouldn't be." Teddy stopped speaking with a ragged gasp. His voice had grown darker and more intense with passion at every word.

Teddy forced himself to keep his focus out the window despite the cold chills running through his body. He marveled at the cold because Bas stood behind him warm and breathing as if he'd run a marathon.

"I'm sorry," Bas murmured. "I shouldn't have made you do this. We've invaded the duke's privacy. I shouldn't—"

"Stop." Teddy turned and pressed his fingers to Bas's warm mouth. "I'm glad we did this. Whether you believe me or not, she came to me. She was trying to tell me something, and I think this is part of it." He swallowed, then allowed his hand to drop back to his side. "I can't think of anyone else I'd rather be with right now, no matter how ridiculously crazy this all seems."

Bas smiled. "Well, I do like ridiculously crazy." The words were a dark rumble deep in his chest.

He touched his lips to Teddy's. How could anything be cool and smoking hot, hard and soft as velvet at the same time? He drew Bas's kiss in like a slow sip of the duke's whisky. Bas groaned deep in his throat.

The blast of a bone-chilling wind swept through the room. The door swung open and slammed against the stone wall. The portrait rattled on the wall. The ashes stirred in the hearth, and the mullioned glass rattled in the barred windows. Teddy tensed and Bas's fingers dug into his arms. A loud click from a dark corner beyond the portrait and chair had them do a couple of double takes between each other and the location of the noise.

"What the hell—"

"Was that?" Teddy said, finishing Bas's question.

Teddy turned his flashlight on and Bas had his on in the next second. Teddy edged slowly toward the dark corner. Set into the stone wall was a tall, narrow door with an iron ring in the middle of the rough-hewn oak planks. Teddy grabbed the ring and pulled. The door barely budged. A quick check of the area showed a layer of dust and no signs anyone had disturbed this part of the room. As one, they put their flashlights down and worked to open the door enough for them to slide through.

Once opened, the door revealed an even narrower and steeper staircase than any of the others they'd encountered ascending. One exchanged look, and Teddy grabbed his flashlight and headed up the stairs, Bas right behind, pressing his hand to the small of Teddy's back. The climb headed nearly straight up. The door they came to had been set at a weird angle, tilted toward the roof of the passageway. It opened outward and Bas and Teddy had to squash together to put their shoulders into the door before it opened. They pushed so hard they practically fell through the doorway... onto the roof of the tower.

Like two adolescent boys they took turns running back and forth to peer over the battlements.

"How cool is this?" Bas asked from the near side of the tower, the section that looked out over the loch.

"No wonder Wentworth has a hard-on to shoot from here," Teddy said as he gazed out over the ruins, across the back gardens, and the huge expanse of Rosemount Manor.

"Teddy."

"I mean this is incredible in the moonlight."

"Teddy."

"Of course, His Grace will ever consent. Do you think he knows about that door? I mean—"

"Teddy, come here." Bas stood with his back to him, facing the loch.

"What is it?" Teddy crossed the parapet to him. He grabbed Bas's arm to steady himself, then swiped his free hand across his eyes—once, twice. "You see her?" he whispered.

"Woman in a white dress? Walking across the loch in the moonlight? Oh, yeah. I see her. Jesus, Teddy. What the hell was in that wine we had with dinner?"

"Hate to break it to you. We're stone, cold sober. Smell that?"

The air was redolent with the perfumes of lavender, heather, and earth.

"Yeah." Bas covered the hand Teddy had laid on his arm and squeezed. "We're in the middle of a fucking ghost story. That's a ghost. Where is she going?"

"She's a ghost, idiot. She can go wherever she— Wait. What is that?" Teddy pointed across the lock with his free hand at something suddenly illuminated by the golden glow of the full moon.

Bas looked in the direction he pointed. "Did you *know* there was an island on the other side of the loch?" he asked.

"No."

"Or that there is some kind of white structure on that island?"

"No."

"Well, your ghost just reached that structure and disappeared."

"So it would seem," Teddy murmured.

"She's there. The first duke watched her die from that window. He found her body and put her somewhere safe so he could stand here and…."

"And what?"

"Die a little more every day they were apart. She's there. And he's not. To be separated from someone you love that much, even in death? I think hell might be easier."

Bas gripped the stone battlements. He didn't look at Teddy. He didn't have to. The handsome Basque's words shot into Teddy like flaming arrows launched at an invading army.

They stood at the top of the tower and stared across the loch. The wind rushed past them, the scent of lavender and earth, and water and something intangible carried around them in sort of personal whirlwind. Hours passed. Or minutes. Teddy covered Bas's hand with his own. Bas laced their fingers together.

"We have to decide what to do," Teddy said at last.

"Yes. We do."

Chapter Twelve

BAS FOLLOWED TEDDY FROM THE TOP OF THE TOWER, through the room with the shrine to Elsbeth, and down the various medieval corridors and staircases with barely a word between them. Teddy's hand still rested in Bas's. Something that both startled and confused Bas to no end. But no more so than his reaction to walking into the spectral love story of the Innes Witch and the first duke. The sadness still washed over him like the ripples on the loch, in ever-widening circles. What a terrible thing it was to have your love for someone be the cause of that person's destruction. The idea shook Bas. That he understood. What he didn't understand was why the idea frightened him.

The strange and eerie relationship between the present duke, the witch, and reigning queen of Regency boot camp was another thing entirely. The flowers at the foot of the portrait were fresh. The flowers….

"The flowers were fresh," Bas said out loud as they climbed the steps up to the door into the dressing room, Teddy still leading the way.

"What?" Teddy stopped and turned so quickly they nearly tumbled back down the steps.

"The flowers at the witch's portrait were fresh. And the chair faces the portrait. Someone's contemplating the portrait."

Teddy squeezed his hand and tugged him toward the open doorway at the top of the stairs. "Not someone. The duke. That whole thing is so twisted. I think we'd be safer dealing with the ghost."

When they reached the dressing room, Bas started for his room. Teddy dragged him in the opposite direction into his room. He closed the door to the dressing room behind them.

"Sit down before you fall down," the Brit ordered as he released Bas's hand and strode to the small sideboard next to the door into the corridor. "You're freezing. Sit in front of the fire."

Bas bit back a smart remark about bossy Brits and took a seat in one of the armchairs in front of the hearth. Apparently, Robbie or one of the other servants had already been in to build up the fire for the night as it burned high and toasty warm.

Bas leaned forward and rubbed his hands closer to the heat. "What makes you think I'm cold? Or about to fall down?"

Teddy handed him a glass of brandy, then sat in the chair opposite him. "You're white as a sheet, and your teeth were chattering all the way up from the dungeons."

"I'm Basque. I will never be white as a sheet." Bas sipped the brandy and sighed at the nice burn as it slid down his throat and into his belly.

"I know what color you are now, and I know what color you are supposed to be. Not to mention you have furrows on your forehead. Your head is hurting again, isn't it?" Teddy drank his brandy but seemed unable to meet Bas's gaze head on.

Bas rubbed his free hand across his brow and pinched the bridge of his nose. "Maybe a little. But seeing a fucking ghost does that to a guy."

Teddy snorted. "Please. Takes more than a Scots ghost to frighten you."

Bas read Teddy's expression, knew he wanted to say more, but didn't. Good. Bas hardly understood his reaction himself, let alone with enough certainty to explain it to someone else. Then again, Teddy wasn't just someone else, was he?

"I cannot begin to imagine," Teddy remarked as he placed his empty glass on the small table next to his chair. "The first duke…watching his love die such a horrible death. What must his life have been after that?"

"A half life." Bas stared into the flames in the hearth. He slid down in his chair and crossed his booted legs at the ankle. "He had to go on. He had responsibilities. It's what men like him did. They went through the motions, did what everyone expected of them, and waited for death. Sad sort of existence, but life continues even when you don't think you'll make it through the day without that person."

"Voice of experience?"

Bas met Teddy's gaze head on and smiled. "Nope. I guess I've been in love a few times, but like that…" He stared into the fire.

"Like what?" Teddy leaned forward, elbows propped on his thighs, eyes bright with intensity.

"With the certainty that this one person is who you were meant to spend your life with without a single doubt in your mind." Bas shrugged against the sudden tilt in his balance. He'd opened his mouth and a greased slip and slide formed from his words. What the hell was he thinking?

"Do you actually believe in a love like that? That it's possible for everyone?" Teddy's question held such doubt, such absolute disbelief, Bas's eyes burned, and this throat threatened to close.

"Everyone deserves to have a love like that, Teddy. Everyone. But people sometimes miss it or fuck it up or just decide they don't want to love like that or to be loved like that. It's frightening as fuck. Or at least I think it would be."

Logs and peat shifted and sent sparks up the chimney in a mesmerizing shower of orange, yellow, and red. Bas took in the room, very much like his own, but in a more severe color scheme—hunter green and gold. The bed curtains and bed covers were velvet whereas Bas's were brocade in blue and silver. Teddy kept a tidy, almost obsessively neat desk, and a really well-stocked sideboard of liquor.

"Sounds bloody awful," Teddy murmured.

"Hmm?" Bas turned his attention back to him. Teddy had unbuttoned his shirt at the throat. The white linen clung to his body and outlined the honed muscles of his chest. His buckskin breeches fit his thighs like a second skin. He'd adopted Bas's slouched pose in the leather armchair and looked rather like a cheetah in repose. His mind had turned to mush. But his cock had turned to stone. He didn't dare look down at his kilt.

"Being someone's everything. Sounds bloody awful. The expectations. The responsibility. The guilt if you fail." Teddy's throat moved as he swallowed and shook his head. "Who would want that?"

"The glory if you succeed. If you're not afraid to risk it all." Bas fixed his gaze on Teddy. Those gray eyes, usually so hard and cynical, had gone liquid with an erotic light that had Bas ready to jump out of his skin.

"You sound like Anna Chase. She believes in the kind of love that saves you despite what the world throws at you. Bit naïve, don't you…think?" Teddy pushed himself out of the chair. He took a step closer, and Bas tilted his head to take him in, all tension and heat and something infinitely more primitive.

"Is it, Teddy? Is that what you believe?" Bas drew in a quick breath as the sexy Brit leaned over him, hands braced on the arms of the armchair, close enough to see the rapid beat of the man's pulse at the base of his throat. Bas licked his lips and tried to breathe.

"I don't know what I believe anymore, damn you." Teddy's voice was a dark growl. "I don't know—"

He seared his lips to Bas's, demanding entrance, which Bas gave with a groan that shook his ribs. He covered Teddy's hands wrapped around the leather padded chair arms so tightly the material creaked. Their tongues tangled and entwined as Bas trapped the swordmaster's hands. It was the only way Bas had any control of the kiss that threatened to burn him alive.

Teddy slowed his invasion, pulled back enough so their lips barely brushed, over and over again as Bas tried to tempt him back with flicks of his tongue. Teddy nipped Bas's bottom lip, then sucked it into his mouth to soothe and caress. He nibbled Bas's jawline and skimmed his teeth down the side of Bas's neck to bite down and suck the tender flesh until Bas shuddered in response.

Unable to resist the temptation, Bas stroked Teddy's hair, combed through the long silk, and tugged gently. Teddy lifted his lips back to Bas's and sank into a deep kiss. Bas slanted his mouth and drew Teddy's tongue inside to suck with a dark moan. Teddy fumbled to unbutton the three buttons at the top of Bas's shirt, then snatched the shirt tail out of the waistband of Bas's kilt and moved away just enough to pull the shirt over Bas's head.

"Wha— Oh. God."

Bas's head lolled back as Teddy took Bas's nipple between his teeth and tugged, all the while flicking the nerve-firing flesh with his tongue. Bas grabbed the chair arms to keep himself from stopping him. The sensations ignited by teeth and tongue skated the edge of pain, but he didn't want Teddy to stop, not even when he did. Bas gasped and searched for words. No need. Teddy set to work on the other nipple as he straddled Bas in the chair.

Every warning bell on the planet rang in Bas's head. Teddy trailed his lips up the middle of Bas's chest even as Teddy pressed his thumbs over Bas's nipples and rubbed and tweaked and tortured. Another soul searing kiss tossed all doubts from his mind. Teddy sucked Bas's tongue into his mouth and set up a suggestive rhythm that had Bas lifting his hips into Teddy's buckskin covered crotch. The Brit blazed a trail of powerful kisses across Bas's shoulders and up to the spot behind his ear that evoked shiver after shiver.

Teddy muttered such erotic, seducing things. "Your body is so damned tempting I can't stop myself. You taste...so good. You smell...sexy, dark, and I want to touch myself every time you walk into the room, damn you."

"I'd love to see that. Jesus, Teddy, don't stop." Bas reached for Teddy as he slid back onto Bas's knees, then to the floor. "What are you...."

Teddy knelt between Bas's feet and, with achingly slow hands, unfastened Bas's kilt. He spread Bas's knees wide and then pulled the sides of the kilt to drape them over the chair arms. The erection Bas had fought to quell sprang free, hard and thick and aching. Teddy ran his fingers up and down the engorged flesh, barely touching, which only made Bas's cock jerk and thrust for more.

"Teddy," Bas whispered, uncertain what else he intended to say.

His lover, because that was what he was, smiled, bent his

head, and swirled his tongue around Bas's length, sinking lower and lower with every pass.

"Oh. God. Oh…damn…."

His entire body spasmed as Teddy drew Bas's cock into his mouth and began to suck in slow, torturous pulses. He wanted to protest. He wanted to stop him. He wanted him never to stop at all. Bas rested one hand on Teddy's head and fought to cease the small, steady thrusts of his hips.

Now it was his turn to talk nonsense. "Teddy…don't. I can't. *Ederra zara… Adortzen zaitut. Ez gelditu. Ez gelditu. Mesedez. Mesedez. Nire…bihotza.*"

Pleasure roiled through him. Muscles tightened and sang. His free hand gripped the chair arm so hard he feared he'd crush it into sawdust. All the while, Teddy's head moved against Bas's other palm. And the sounds Teddy made. The noises of desire and need nearly sent Bas over the edge. He fought the orgasm that started to build as Teddy cupped Bas's balls and gently massaged while Teddy licked and sucked.

"Teddy," he gasped. "Teddy." He pushed against Teddy's shoulders, and Teddy paused to look up at him, his eyes ablaze with fiery desire. "I want…I want…."

Bas pulled the Brit to his feet and grabbed the hem of his shirt. Teddy bent so Bas could pull the shirt over Teddy's head, then Teddy wrapped his hand around Bas's sensitive cock and stroked once, twice. Bas tugged at the buckskins and slid them over Teddy's hips and down to his knees. Bas kissed the tip of the thick cock between the other man's legs.

"Off. I want these off, dammit."

Teddy laughed darkly. He toed off his boots in record time and kicked his way out of the buckskins. "Now what, lover?"

Bas wrapped his hand around Teddy's cock and dragged him back into the chair. Teddy straddled him and used his hand to bring their cocks together side by side. Bas hissed as his hot, turgid flesh met Teddy's. After a few seconds of adjustment, Teddy laced their hands together to create the needed friction. A few more seconds and Teddy's rhythmic thrusts into their joined hands sent shards of mounting pleasure through Bas. He matched Teddy, groan for groan, shudder for shudder.

Teddy rested his forehead on Bas's shoulder, then bit down on a taut sinew and thrust harder, faster. Bas raised his head and took Teddy's nipple between his teeth. Muffled sounds escaped Teddy, and his breathing thundered against Bas's skin. Sweat trickled down Bas's back. The friction of Teddy's cock as it slid against Bas's grew and swelled. Needing air, Bas threw his head back and pumped against Teddy, who braced his free hand on the back of Bas's chair. Bas clasped his free hand on Teddy's hip as he moved faster and faster.

"Oh God. Oh God. Don't stop. Don't stop. Yes. Please, Bas. Please."

"*Gehiago. Gehiago. Mesedez. Bai. Bai.*"

Bas's neck strained as he pushed his head back against the chair and shouted his way through his orgasm. Teddy covered Bas's lips with his. Shouted his own orgasm into Bas's mouth, then groaned and shuddered against him as he collapsed onto Bas's thighs and let his head drop to Bas's chest.

"Bloody...hell!"

A crack and a loud thud punctuated the last word. It took a minute for Bas to realize Teddy lay sprawled on top of him because the armchair had fallen backward. Somewhere in the farthest recesses of his mind, the knot on the back of his head sent dull shards of pain into his skull. Frankly, he didn't give a damn as the rest of his body alternated between total satiation and the sporadic shivers of pleasure still ambling from his groin to his shoulders and down his arms. He half opened his eyes. Teddy's lips moved, but Bas couldn't figure out what Teddy had said.

"Are you hurt?"

Teddy ran his hands over Bas's chest, which didn't help his hearing much. Every caress set Bas's nerve endings on fire.

"Huh?" Bas blinked.

As Teddy laughed, his naked chest vibrated against Bas's, a low and incredibly free sound from the man who kept so much of himself guarded. "We broke His Grace's chair."

Bas raised his head, his hand tangled in Teddy's hair. He took a brief inventory of where they lay. The air had begun to cool his body, at least on the outside. Inside, Bas clutched at the incredible glow of being pressed skin-to-skin with Teddy, the glow of something far more powerful than just great sex.

"I guess two-hundred year old chairs aren't built for sex," he murmured. Teddy kept laughing. "How are we going to explain this?"

"We can always blame the Innes Witch." Teddy planted his hands on either side of the downed chair and pushed himself off Bas. "Stay there. I'll be right back."

"No problem. I can't move."

"Can't or don't want to?" Teddy asked from across the room.

Water splashed. Bas closed his eyes and rested his forearm across his face. "Hmm?"

He wasn't really sure. A noncommital answer served. Suddenly he was exhausted. In too many ways to count. Teddy returned to kneel next to him, then brushed a warm washcloth up and down Bas's chest, his thighs, and gently over his cock and balls. He'd never been the type to allow someone else to take care of him like this. With Teddy, he didn't mind. More weirdness to file away for thought later, especially because it felt so damned good.

Teddy pressed a light kiss to Bas's lips and then to the cut of his jaw. "Come on. Let's get you off the floor."

"I can't just sleep right here?" Bas allowed his arm to drop to his side and gazed up at Teddy.

"I'm afraid not. Your big arse has already broken the chair. We don't want to do any further damage." Teddy pushed to his feet in one lithe, graceful move. Bas had admired that about him from the start. To be so tall and tautly muscled, Teddy Rousseau moved like a dancer. He extended his hand, and Bas grasped it, allowing himself to be hauled to his feet.

Between his relaxed, nearly boneless state and Teddy's surprising strength, Bas flew to his feet and landed square against his lover's chest. He slid his arms around Teddy instinctually, then sighed and raised one hand to cup the side of Teddy's neck. He kissed him, a slow and tender brush over his lips and then his temple.

"What are we going to do?" Teddy whispered, his brandy scented breath stirring erotically across Bas's naked shoulder.

"Do?" He struggled to hold on to the warm haze of sensation that hovered over every inch of his body. The scent of Teddy's expensive cologne, the musk of arousal and sweat, fascinated him and lured him into dangerous territory. He didn't give a damn.

Teddy raised his head. He leaned into Bas's hand but met his gaze. Didn't waver. "About this?" He brushed one hand down Bas's side.

A muscle above Bas's hip jumped. He understood what Teddy meant.

"We're going to sleep on it." He ran his fingers through Teddy's hair. "Get into bed." Bas gave Teddy a little shove toward the huge, draped four-poster. He strode to the door and turned the lock. For a moment he concentrated on the heavy polished wood. His heart thundered in his ears.

"You're going to sleep here tonight?"

Never had a question held so many unspoken emotions. Bas's chest tightened.

He turned to find Teddy sitting in bed, the covers pulled up to his waist. "If you want me to."

"Very much." The breathless catch in Teddy's voice froze the air in Bas's lungs, like breathing in icy mountain air on a cold winter's day.

"Well then." Bas caught Teddy staring at him as he moved around the room and snuffed the candles and turned out the oil lamps. He moved slowly and made a production of each task. Finally, only the light from the fire and a single oil lamp on the bedside table illuminated the room. He sat down on the edge of the mattress next to where Teddy sat up, his gray eyes soft and liquid with something far more potent than desire. "Scootch over," Bas ordered, and pulled back the heavy covers. He got into bed next to the Brit.

"You still haven't answered my question," Teddy said as he settled onto his side facing Bas. "About what we're going to do." He cupped Bas's jaw with his palm.

"About us? About what we found in the tower? About whatever is on that little island? Be more specific."

He kissed Teddy's palm and turned onto his back, pulling Teddy against his side. The cotton sheets, definitely not Egyptian but serviceable, held the warmth where his lover had lain. The quilts between them and the heavy brocade, what Eleanor had called a counterpane, helped trap that heat against his bare flesh. Delicious.

"Have it your way then, you stubborn arse." Teddy rested his head on Bas's shoulder and threw one arm and one leg over him. Bas did his best to hide the pleasure simply lying in bed in the arms of....

Whoa! What the hell was he thinking?

He sensed the tension in Teddy. Bas pulled the covers higher over the two of them and stroked the long hair that spilled over his shoulder and chest. "We're going to sleep on all of it, okay? Can we just...do that? For now?"

"Yes. For now."

Bas reached over and turned down the lamp on the bedside table. He noticed Teddy's open pocket watch. He narrowed his focus and saw the alarm had been set. A shard of something hot and pointed shot through him. Teddy began to breathe deeply and evenly. Bas couldn't tell if Teddy was faking it or had truly fallen asleep. Though exhausted, Bas was also confused, and a little afraid.

His mind returned to what they'd found in the tower. To a doomed love story and the questions he had. He closed his eyes and settled into Teddy's embrace. The scent of lavender and heather washed over him. Bas wanted to open his eyes, to see if Elsbeth was in the room. In his mind a hint of a feminine touch wisped over his forehead. An accented voice whispered so quietly he wasn't sure he heard.

"Hush. Sleep. Don't let go."

Easy for her to say.

BAS HOOKED HIS THUMBS IN THE BELT AT THE WAIST OF HIS kilt and watched as Danny, Lily, several members of his stunt crew, and a number of the duke's grooms and stablehands raced their horses down the meadow. The May sunshine glinted off the mid-morning dew, and Bas realized Wentworth had chosen this beautiful place for a reason. There wasn't a less than perfect spot in all the duke's thousands of acres. Yet, a certain amount of the dark intangible hovered just out of sight. Just beyond the hills. Just across the vast loch. In the formal gardens at dusk.

He'd watched that intangible walk toward Rosemount Manor on legs of mist and rain for the past few nights. Nights he'd spent in Teddy's bed only to climb from beneath the covers before sunrise and stand at the window to watch his lover sleep. As he did, he fought to decide which was more beautiful and which was more frightening. Then he'd allowed himself to fill with anger, resentment, and self-loathing as he crossed the dressing room and slid into his own bed alone.

Still, he'd spent the last few evenings laughing, playing whist, and talking stunts and movies by candlelight with Teddy and the others. They'd teased one another about the ghost, at least when the duke wasn't around, and he and Teddy had done their best to try and find out more about the tower and the end of the story of Elsbeth and the first duke. To no avail.

Not that he and Teddy had any intention of giving up—which was the reason why Bas gave himself permission to join the swordmaster in his chamber. To discuss the ghost. To discuss what they'd found in the tower room, and what they'd seen from the top of the tower. His reasons for ending up in bed with the man every night? Hell if he knew. Teddy was handsome. He was sexy. He was—

"Hot enough for you, boss?" Mike bumped his elbow into Bas's back and stood next to him as the horsemen formed up to make another run across the meadow.

"It's Scotland, old man. Try sleeping in a room with no electricity in the middle of a Highland night, even in May, then you can talk to me about hot. It's not even sixty degrees out here."

"Says the man in a skirt and a floofy pirate's shirt."

"Fuck you."

"My wife might object to that."

"I doubt it. She says you're lousy in bed."

M8ke grunted. "Yeah, but I keep her in credit cards with no limits."

"Am I interrupting something?"

Bas knew Teddy was there before he even spoke. His awareness of where the Brit was anytime they were in the same room apparently translated to anywhere within a hundred yards. Not that Teddy recipricated. His behavior in public the past few days had been friendly to the point of *good buddy,* as Arneaux put it, but nothing more. Behind closed doors the man couldn't keep his hands off Bas.

"Naw," Mike said. "Bas is just propositioning me. He does that all the time."

"Should I give you two some privacy?" Teddy replied with a slightly raised brow.

"You should give this old brokedown stuntman an ass-whoopin' is what you should give," Bas said as he bumped Mike with his hip.

"I don't do elder abuse unless the elder is related to me. Are we almost finished here?" Teddy's subtle change of expression, not anything Mike would notice, told Bas something was up.

"Yeah. Call 'em in, Mike. The boot campers need to get ready for lunch. Take the crew into the village. I've got to figure some things out this afternoon before we start trying those stunts we talked about." Bas cocked his head at Teddy, who gave an inperceptible nod.

"Will do. We need to practice for the darts tournament at the pub tonight, anyway."

Mike lumbered out into the meadow and waved at the riders.

Bas shook his head. "My entire crew has gone native.

They spend every minute of their down time at the pub or at the local fish and chip shop."

Teddy tilted his head toward the path that led to a narrow lane back to the manor. Dressed like a Regency gentleman about to go for a morning ride, he strolled, hands clasped behind his back, and looked so damned strikingly handsome Bas wanted to smack him. Or kiss him.

"They don't need to practice," Teddy said as he led Bas not to the manor but to the side path that went around the loch. "Your stunt people are currently the district champions."

"How is it you know that and I don't." Bas raised his face to the sun and reveled in the simple joy of a walk with someone he…. Yeah. Whatever. Dammit.

"Robbie. He's made a fortune wagering on the matches. Speaking of which…." Teddy pointed to a clump of trees and bushes at the edge of the loch.

They made their way through the brush to the water's edge where a sturdy rowboat sat, tied off to one of huge boulders that dotted the shore.

Bas looked at Teddy. "Did you tell Robbie—"

"He didn't want to know," Teddy said as they untied the boat. "Said if the duke finds out we filched the boat, he knows nothing."

Bas snorted as they got inside. They maneuvered out onto the loch and Bas began to row them across the loch.

"How much did you have to pay him? I hope you know how to steer this damned thing. I also hope this island isn't a figment of our imaginations."

"You do *not* want to know. I think the duke's footman was a highwayman in a former life. As to the other"—Teddy waved a dismissive hand as he leaned back in the boat, his other hand on the rudder—"we'll find out soon enough."

"About which? Whether you can steer or whether we've lost our minds?"

Teddy crossed his ankles and propped his booted feet on the large lidded hamper in the middle of the boat. "Of course I know how to steer a rowboat. I'm British. And as you started us on this little Nancy Drew adventure, you are most definitely out of your mind. Now, row."

"Yes, my lord. Whatever you say, my lord."

He'd said the wrong thing. Teddy's face turned instantly cold and unreadable. The Teddy he'd first met sat across from him and pretended to study the flow of the loch around them.

"Hey."

The water lapped gently at the boat. The sun stood directly overhead, and the first tiny trickles of sweat slid down Bas's spine. The continuous motion of rowing gave him something to focus on besides the heat.

"Hey, Teddy. Look at me."

Teddy faced him, that familiar sad smile in his eyes.

"I didn't mean anything by it."

"I know. No need to worry, love."

"No need to worry, love."

Bas wasn't particularly fond of endearments. They seldom registerd with him. Except now.

Teddy dropped his feet off the hamper onto the deck and turned on the bench seat in the bow. Then he propped his hands on each side of the boat and appeared to scan the horizon. When he turned back, he adjusted the rudder, and they made a sharp turn to Bas's right. Bass rowed for another twenty or so minutes when a shoreline came into view. A high sheer granite wall of a shoreline offset from the actual far edge of the loch winked in and out of view as they approached. A trick of the light and the lap of waves in the loch, but eerie as hell.

"What the fuck?" Bas muttered. "Are you seeing this?"

"The shore of an island that isn't supposed to be there? Not at all. Any idea how we're going to land?"

"You're British. You're supposed to know."

Bas used the oars to bring the boat alongside the rocks. The loch was so deep, even if they had an anchor it would be useless. He studied the top of the nearly sheer wall of rocks. A number of scraggly but sturdy-looking shrubs poked up at ground level above them, just a little over his and Teddy's heads if they stood.

Teddy locked the rudder and slowly rose to his feet. "If you'll steady the boat, I'll toss the hamper up there and try to loop the line around something so the boat doesn't drift away. Can you climb up from here?"

Bas rolled his eyes. "I grew up in the mountains of Spain. I have the climbing skills of a goat. By the way, what's in the basket?"

"Lunch. Courtesy of Mrs. Gordon."

Teddy hefted the large container over the shrubs where it landed behind the foliage with a thud. He took the bow line and whirled it over his head like a lasso. It only took him three tries to loop it around a gnarled root that stuck up on the edge of the cliff. While Bas sat in the back of the rowboat and held it steady, Teddy scrambled up the rock face.

Once he got to his feet, he tied the boat more securely. "Need some help?"

Bas shot him a bird and moved to the bow of the boat. As he stood and reached for the gaps in the rockface, the boat rocked a bit, which he expected. He waited for the back and forth to stop, then started to haul himself up to the shore. He almost made it too, but climbing in a kilt wasn't as easy as expected, and his soft Highland boots didn't give him the same traction as the thick-soled work boots he normally wore. He hung from the crevices he'd jammed his fingers into and fought to find a purchase for his feet.

"Need a hand?" Teddy knelt at the edge of the rockface and peered down at Bas.

"I've got it."

"I see that."

"Smartass." Bas gritted his teeth and pulled himself up higher, but his feet still wouldn't cooperate. "Fine. Give me your hand."

"Say the magic word."

"Screw you."

"Close enough. Here." Teddy reached down and wrapped both hands around one of Bas's wrists. "Now, climb. Come on. You weigh a— Oh shit!"

"Fuck!"

Bas hit the icy water and his heart did a double take. Water went up his nose, not to mention up his kilt. And over his head. The May sunshine didn't do a damn thing for loch water. A few quick strokes and he broke the surface. Some frantic splashes peppered with distinctly British cursing sounded nearby.

Teddy!

Bas spun. Teddy, looking like a drowned Regency rat, clung to the overturned rowboat's hull.

"Are you okay?" Bas demanded.

"Do I bloody look okay? That's the last time I try to help you."

Bas treaded water a few feet from the rowboat. Fortunately, he had had locked the oars into the oarlocks. That didn't help their current dilemma much.

"Move back. Let me turn the boat over." Bas put his shoulder into the side of the boat and managed to flip it with one shove. "How about I go first and pull you up?"

"By all means." Teddy's teeth began to chatter. "You certainly did a wonderful job before we ended up in the drink."

"Nag. Nag. Nag."

Bas crawled into the boat, balanced on the bow, then leaped straight up to grab the crevices at the top of the rock face. He locked his biceps and hoisted himself up onto the shore. When he turned and leaned over to help Teddy, the stubborn Brit had already climbed halfway up. Bas reached down, grabbed Teddy's wrists, and hauled him through the shrubbery onto the shore, where he landed sprawled on top of Bas's chest.

"That certainly went according to plan." Teddy gasped as he rolled off Bas and lay next to him on the grass and sand. "I assume you have our next move on this quest equally well thought out."

Bas turned on his side, propped his head on his hand, and met Teddy's gray gaze. "I don't know about you, but I'm going to get naked."

Chapter Thirteen

"I BEG YOUR PARDON?" TEDDY CRINGED INWARDLY AT THE British schoolboy tone of his voice. *What a bloody prat!*

Bas got to his feet and pulled the white linen shirt over his head. He strode to a broadly spread birch tree and tossed the shirt across several low-lying branches. Then he sat down on the largest of a group of boulders and pulled off his boots and thick wool stockings. Teddy sat up and watched.

"If we stay in these clothes, we'll catch pneumonia. I don't care how warm it is." Bas hung up his stockings and set his boots out on a flat rock away from the cover of the trees. "Is there a blanket or towel in that basket?" He nodded to where the hamper sat close to the edge of the bank.

"I'll check."

Teddy went down on one knee and rifled through the contents of the hamper. There was indeed a large plaid woolen blanket and a stack of cloth serviettes on top of the various food items Mrs. Gorden had packed. He tossed the blanket and serviettes over his arm, picked up the hamper, and turned toward where Bas stood with his back to him. Completely and magnificently naked.

Teddy's mouth went dry. He'd seen the gorgeous Basque naked before, but never in the glory of the Highland sunlight beneath a cerulean sky. The droplets of lock water clung to his skin and made the broad expanse of his back and the taut muscles of his arse glisten as if oiled for an erotic photo shoot. Working in film, he'd seen quite a few of those shoots. None of them held a candle to Bas in this moment.

Bas glanced over his shoulder as he straightened his kilt along a low lying tree branch. "See something you like?"

Teddy rolled his eyes. "Fishing for compliments? Yes, actually. The roast beef sandwiches Mrs. Gordon packed look particularly delicious. What shall we do first, eat or go in search of this imaginary white structure that may or may not be on this island?"

"Well,"—Bas caught the serviette Teddy tossed him and attempted to dry off his arms and chest—"as I'd rather not go crashing through the underbrush dressed in nothing but one of the duke's fancy table napkins, I'd say let's eat first. Give our clothes a chance to dry. Unless you'd like to pull thorns and stickers out of my ass."

Teddy brushed past him and headed for a patch of mossy ground in a sunlight clearing a little beyond where Bas had hung his clothing.

"There are many things I have thought of doing to your arse. Pulling thorns has not been one of them." He draped the blanket over the grass and set the hamper next to it. "See to the food while I get out of these clothes. These buckskin breeches are beginning to shrink on me like a diving suit."

He headed to the other side of the tree Bas used as a clothes line, then wrestled his way out of his clothes. A gentleman's Regency clothes were difficult enough to get out of when dry, let alone soaking wet. His hands shook. His every sense hummed. It took Teddy forever to toe off his boots. Then he was naked and barefoot and had no excuse not to join Bas at their makeshift picnic table.

"You're right about these sandwiches. You'd better snag one before I eat them all." Bas sat cross-legged at one end of the flat rock with the end of the blanket pulled strategically over his lap. Teddy settled next to him and flipped the section of the blanket hanging off the side of the rock over his own problematic lap. Hell, he'd been standing at attention since Bas had stood naked in the sunlight.

"Here." Bas handed him a sandwich, then slid a tin cup over and filled it from an earthenware jug that closed with a sort of cork thing that screwed into the top.

Teddy took a bite of the sandwich and washed it down with the contents of the cup. "Ale. Mrs. Gordon is a treasure."

"No argument here. Although, you can have the grass and butter sandwiches. There's cheese and apples too."

"Grass and butter?" Teddy checked the metal plate stacked with various items from the hamper. He laughed. "Watercress. Not grass. Try one." He held one out toward Bas, who leaned forward and took a bite, sweeping his tongue across Teddy's fingertips.

He chewed, looked thoughtful, then scooted across the blanket-clad rock to take another bite. "Not bad," he said once he'd swallowed. "Not bad at all."

"Told you." A tiny shiver went down Teddy's spine. Something had shifted between them. In the confines of his chamber, things had been easy and not so serious. Here? The difference had a singular heartbeat and rhythm, and he was lost.

"Try this." Bas held out a large strawberry dipped in clotted cream.

Teddy hesitated, then leaned across and took the tart fruit from Bas's fingers with his teeth. Bas's eyes widened and shone bright blue. *Well, what have we here?* Had Teddy caught him off guard? Or maybe Bas's reaction had been in Teddy's mind. Bas fed him another strawberry. Definintely all in his mind.

"You've got mustard…." Teddy's voice failed him as Bas tried to use his tongue to reach the spot Teddy had indicated. Some insane notion took him over and he leaned forward and lapped up the mustard with his tongue. A shudder went through Bas, and from that singular but intimate point of contact, the vibration traveled through Teddy's body.

They ate the rest of the food and most of the ale in relative silence, feeding each other bites and taking turns staring into each other's eyes. The heat crawling along Teddy's skin had nothing to do with the sun. Finally, Bas spread his arms wide and stretched, only to wince and rub his shoulder.

"You're rowing back, sailing expert. I'm out of practice."

"You practice rowing?" Teddy began to put plates, cups, and other detritus from their picnic back into the hamper.

"Yeah, on a rowing machine in my gym at home." He continued to try and massage his shoulder as he rotated his arm in a circle. "But I haven't been home in months."

"Neither have I, but I'm seldom at home as it is. Nature of the job."

"When is the last time you saw your parents?" Bas asked, still working his shoulder.

"Two, perhaps three years ago. We're…not that close."

"That's too bad."

"Not really." Teddy stood and waved Bas onto the blanket. "Let me see if I can help with your shoulder." Bas lowered himself onto the blanket and pulled Teddy down next to him. He took Teddy's mouth in a slow, sizzling kiss, curling his tongue along the roof of Teddy's mouth and sucking Teddy's lower lip between his teeth before releasing the sensitive flesh with a sharp nip.

"If you don't want to talk about it, we don't have to," Bas

said softly. He ran the backs of his fingers down Teddy's cheek and across his bare shoulder.

"Good. Lie down." He grabbed Bas's shoulders, turned him around, then pushed him forward.

"Bossy." Bas stretched out on his stomach on the thick plaid blanket and pillowed his head on his crossed arms. "Do your worst. I want to be in good shape in case we find what we saw from the tower, and the witch shows up to drag us inside for nefarious purposes."

"Nefarious purposes?" Teddy sat next to Bas's hip and began to work at the knots in his upper back and shoulder." What an imagination. You need a keeper is what you need."

"Probably, but I'll settle for a masseuse. Damn, that feels good."

"Should. How many times have you had surgery on this shoulder?" Teddy continued to massage and fought the urge to explore the raised scars with his lips.

"Only twice. Once on the other one."

"And the scars on your knee and your right thigh?"

"Are you taking inventory?"

"Maybe."

"Yeah. Right there. Yessss." Bas flexed his back, and Teddy caressed the ripple of muscles down to the small of Bas's back. "You're one to talk. Stitches across your chest, down your back, across a bicep," Bas said. "Very sexy."

"Yes, well, they didn't impress anyone except my father. He saw them as badges of honor. The scars of being a man." Teddy straddled Bas's hips and began working both shoulders at once. His cock was so damned hard he could drive nails with it. He should have pulled on his breeches, damp or not.

"Your father's an idiot. In case you didn't know."

"He's eighty years old and set in his ways. My parents were married twenty years before I came along. He thought he'd never have a son. All he ever wanted was a son to inherit...well, everything. I've been something of a disappointment."

"A straight son. All he wanted was a straight son." Bas turned his head to look at Teddy. "Straight or gay, you could never be a disappointment. If he doesn't see that, he's the one who isn't a man."

Teddy bent and kissed Bas's temple, then shoved his head back onto his crossed arms. "Change the subject, shall we?"

"To what? The witch's lair we came here to find or that impressive erection pressing into my back?" Bas's breathing grew slightly faster and he shifted slightly so that his pelvis wasn't quite flat on the ground. Teddy resisted the urge to lean over and look at what he knew had to be Bas's growing erection.

"I'm sorry." Teddy tried to scoot back and climb off the blanket.

"Don't be." Bas reached around and grabbed Teddy's thigh. He rolled onto his side, reached for Teddy's fingers, and laced them together.

Teddy had ridden numerous roller coasters in his life. Never one as frightening as this. At the top, just before the plunge, there was always that moment where all breathing ceased. Completely involuntarily—as if the air might never fill his lungs again. He tightly closed his fingers around Bas's as if the other man's strength might keep him safe. From... everything. No, not everything. From himself. He'd kept himself safe all these years from every sort of intrusion on the life he'd chosen. Every sort of intrusion but one. His true self, the person he was born to be.

His throat ached. His chest hurt. He couldn't breathe.

Bas sat up and slid his hand along Teddy's neck and beneath his hair to caress the base of his skull. He kissed Teddy's cheek, then the corner of his eye, then pressed warm lips to Teddy's, teasing the tip of his tongue along the seam until Teddy opened and let him inside. Bas's tongue was hot and slow, caressing and tickling. Teddy gripped Bas's biceps so tightly marks would form. The kiss spread a wave of hot desire down Teddy's chest. His nipples hardened. His whole life, the good and the bad, crystallized in that moment.

Bas finally raised his head just enough to pin him with an incendiary gaze. "Tell me what you want. Right now. Right here. Tell me." He breathed the words in a dark, rasped whisper across Teddy's lips.

"Everything." Teddy didn't think. No need. Bas called to Teddy's feelings, which didn't give him a chance to think. They wanted. He wanted. "With you, I want everything." He willed Bas to understand what he meant. What he needed for reasons he couldn't voice or even name.

Bas's lips parted. Then the slow release of his taut tendons, the upturn of one side of his mouth, and the light of understanding were followed by a blue-eyed blaze of hunger. No. Not hunger. More than hunger. A wanting like nothing Teddy had ever experienced from another human being. He began to tremble and doubt.

"You can have everything, Teddy. But I didn't exactly come prepared for—"

Teddy fumbled into the open hamper next to them. He did so blindly as he never wanted to stop looking at the way Bas gazed at him. Finally, he drew out a leather pouch, part of his Regency gear. With quick, jerky motions he emptied the contents onto the blanket.

"I did." He glanced at the four condoms and the bottle of body oil he'd stuffed into the pouch in a moment of madness or clarity, or both. "I know you said…I don't…. Bloody hell, I can't find the words to—"

Bas pressed a thumb to Teddy's lips. "You know what I said."

"Yes. I remember." His heart stuttered. "I want to try, Bas. I've never wanted to…be who I am…until you." His breath gave out. He shook his head.

"Well then." Bas smiled the faintest bit. "We'll figure it out, won't we?"

Teddy wrapped his arms around Bas. He lowered him to the blanket and took his mouth in a clumsy, hot kiss. The heat of the sun on his back didn't compare with the fierce heat of his chest sprawled on top of Bas's. Teddy pressed their joined hands above Bas's head as he continued to invade his mouth and nip and suck his bottom lip. He entwined his legs with Bas's as their cocks pressed together and stroked against each other in search of release from the torture of their thrusting hips. When he had no choice but to come up for air, Teddy rested his forehead on Bas's sternum, panting as if he'd come to the end of a fencing match.

Bas smoothed his hand over Teddy's hair. "You still want everything, *nire bihotza*?" His voice was the sort of growl that sent a sharp ache spreading over Teddy's groin.

Teddy raised his head. "Yes. Now."

Bas grabbed a handful of Teddy's hair and drew his head back for a short, ferocious kiss. "Then take it, lover. Now." With a palm to Teddy's chest, Bas pushed him upward. The look Bas gave him was like an erotic *en garde* and terrified Teddy. Bas snatched one of the condoms from the blanket. He reached for Teddy's cock and wrapped his fist around it to stroke once, twice.

"Damn!" Teddy gasped.

He knelt between Bas's legs as the magnificent Basque rolled the condom over Teddy's cock. With one last squeeze Bas turned onto his side, his back to Teddy. With shaky hands, Teddy unstoppered the oil and poured some into his hands. He drew his fingertips down Bas's shoulder blades, across his ribcage, and rested them on the crest of his buttocks. He retraced that path with his fingernails and Bas shivered.

Teddy poured some of the sandalwood scented oil over Bas's buttocks and rubbed it in, reaching around to caress his cock and balls in the process. The low, deep groan that vibrated through Bas's body thrilled Teddy. His mind roiled in a red haze of anticipation and desire, for the sanctuary of being joined to him completely. By the time Teddy had prepared his body and Bas's with the oil, Bas had raised himself onto his knees, his head still down while clenching the edge of the blanketed rock.

"Now, Teddy," he growled. "Now."

Teddy gripped Bas's hip and slowly entered him, a little at a time until his thighs rested against his lover's body. With a dark, animal gasp, Bas rocked against him. Teddy bent over Bas's back. He reached around to caress the other man's thick, hard cock. He pressed a kiss between Bas's shoulder blades and allowed the riot of sensory fires to rush over and through him. He didn't want to move, didn't want to breathe. He wanted only to feel, but his body was already building to take over in a blind rush of lust and need.

"Good?" he muttered against Bas's damp skin.

"God, yes. More. Don't stop." Bas rocked against him again.

Teddy drew his tongue down Bas's back and grabbed his hips, then withdrew just enough and began a slow rhythm of thrusts, head thrown back, muscles stretched to the point of snapping.

"More, *maitea*, More. I won't…break. Yes…, God, yes… like that…damn."

Bas thrust back, a string of erotic Basque and English interspersed with gasps and groans pouring from his lips.

Teddy wrapped the sound around him. He lost himself in the music of their bodies and voices coming together, higher and faster, until there was no him and him but *them*, caught in a maelstrom of pleasure and need. He fought his oncoming orgasm. He wanted this union to last forever beneath the Highland sun. He wanted…forever. With Bas.

His eyes snapped open. He tightened his grip on Bas's hips. Their voices, hoarse with passion, rose together. The orgasm hit Teddy first, a claymore of sensation so hard he nearly blacked out, then Bas shuddered as he gasped over and over before he collapsed onto the blanket, Teddy draped across his back.

Forever. With Bas.

The thought rang in Teddy's brain as they lay together, exhausted and warming themselves in each other and the Highland sun. Teddy reached up and covered Bas's hands with his own. Teddy's breath finally settled until their hearts and lungs matched rhythms and slowed, slowed to the point they dozed. Teddy struggled to stay awake, to examine the odd thought that wouldn't leave him alone. Something was terribly wrong. He'd never been so unconcerned, so certain of the moment. He was…content.

TEDDY WOKE TO THE SCENT OF LAVENDER, HEATHER, AND earth on the breeze that suddenly seemed all around him. As he struggled to open his eyes, the touch of cool, gentle lips on his bicep made him smile. Those same lips brushed against his ear.

"Do you think Elsbeth was here the whole time?" Bas whispered as he sat down next to Teddy's hip.

"If she was, she certainly got an eyeful," Teddy rolled over on the mossy ground and sat up. "Where's the blanket? Mrs. Gordon will kill us if we lose one of her good plaids." He ran his hands over his face and then stretched his arms over his head.

"It's hanging over there." Bas pointed to one of the trees they'd used to dry their clothes. He was fully dressed now.Teddy's clothes lay spread over the grass nearby. "I washed it in the loch. She might kill us if we lose it, but I hate to think what she'd do if we brought it back in the shape it was in after…." Bas kissed him and smiled a gainst his lips. "Let's just say amazing sex can be messy."

"Amazing?" Teddy kissed him back in a slow, hot meeting of lips and tongues.

Bas hummed into Teddy's mouth and ran his hands down Teddy's bare back. Bas broke the kiss and handed Teddy his shirt.

"More than amazing. Now get dressed so we can find this witch's lair." Bas started to stand, but Teddy caught his hand and held on tight. Bas gazed down at him, his head tilted to one side as if to ask what Teddy wanted.

Dear God, he wanted…. "I want this to work. Whatever this is between us. I want it to work."

"Why wouldn't it?" Bas sat back down and began to trace the lines in Teddy's palm. Teddy stared at Bas's forefinger as he moved the callous tip over and over the ridges and scars.

"Because I'm no good at this. Because I've gotten everything I've ever wanted in my career and nothing of what I've wanted in my life." He raised his head "Because I've never wanted anything more than I want this. Than I want you."

Bas put his arms around him and sighed. "What the hell am I going to do with you, Teddy?"

"Just don't give up on me. No matter what, don't ever give up on me." Teddy rested against his lover's chest. He was so damned tired of standing up to everything and everyone in his life.

"You can have whatever you want in life if you're willing to do what it takes to get it. You have to earn it. Or create it. Or take it. No one's going to give it to you. But if you really want it, no sonofabitch on earth can take it from you. Unless you let them."

"Sounds so simple when you put it that way." Teddy inhaled Bas's scent—sunwarmed linen, sweat, sex, the faintest remnant of his cologne, and water from the loch. Teddy suspected he'd never live long enough to grow tired of this man's unique perfume.

Bas kissed the top of Teddy's head and sifted his fingers through Teddy's hair to massage his scalp. "Bullshit. Gathering the things that make you you is hard as hell. Taken me thirty-five years to do it." He stood and tossed Teddy's clothes to him. "Get dressed before I pin you to this rock and jump your bones. I don't want to be on this island or the loch after dark."

Teddy pulled on his shirt and waistcoat, though he refused to button the latter. "A threat like that is hardly an incentive for me to get dressed."

"Horndog. Do you want to meet Elsbeth here after dark? How is that for an incentive?"

"Bitch. These are still damp." Teddy struggled to pull on his buckskin breeches.

"If you want to go tramping through this brush with your schlong hanging out, go right ahead. I'll just admire the view."

Teddy rolled his eyes, stepped into his top boots, and adjusted himself in the tight-fitting buckskins. "Come on, Nancy Drew. Let's find the Innes Witch." He started through the shrubs in the direction most likely to lead them to the structure they'd seen from the top of the tower.

"God help me," Bas muttered behind him.

They tromped through the overgrowth of trees, shrubs, and vines in relative silence. Only a word of warning here, a comment there. Didn't matter. There was a bubble of comfort around them. A look, a touch, and a tiny glow of rightness passed between them. Teddy wanted to say something, but he was rubbish at words. He was better communicating with a sword or at least with words about weapons and men who'd fought battles where the lines were always clear.

"Why do you think the duke— Holy hell." Bas, who had moved ahead of him, stopped in his tracks. "We found it."

"So we did." Teddy's voice fell in reverence to what sat in the clearing ahead.

Surrounded on three sides by lines of willow trees, an incredible white stone structure rose as if it had erupted from the ground fully formed. At the front, a rounded set of steps led to a columned portico. A stone dragon, at least waist high to Bas and him, stood on each side of each step.

"I can't be certain, but I think this is Elsbeth's mausoleum," Teddy said.

They stood and stared at the dazzling white structure. Modeled very much as a Grecian temple but structured from stones in the way of medieval cathedrals, there were various carved touches to denote both the witch's Scots heritage and her mother's Caribbean roots. Gothic buttresses scaled to the size of the structure were adorned with gargoyles. Visible on each side of the doorway set back from the steps by the width of the portico, stone carvings were set into the stone façade. The carvings were of large skull and crossbones flags. The detail was incredible. As was the condition of the structure.

"Pirates?" Bas started up the steps.

"Elsbeth's father was a Scots pirate."

"And her mother?"

"A healer from an island in the Caribbean."

"Look at you." Bas ran a hand over one of the flag carvings. He rested his other hand on Teddy's shoulder. "You're a regular tour guide."

"I'm a regular history geek. Another of my many failings. I prefer people and things from hundreds of years ago to the sycophants and ice queens, let alone the legal profession I'm supposed to adore. I'm a complete disgrace."

"Don't say that." Bas grabbed and shook him once. "Don't ever say that. You're brilliant, and talented, and a superb athlete. And you need to quit hiding it from everyone."

"You're only slightly biased." Teddy cupped Bas's cheek. "But you're endearing as hell when you're angry on my behalf."

Bas actually blushed, which Teddy found even more endearing.

Teddy removed his hand from Bas's cheek and Bas shifted to gaze out from the portico to the surrounding clearing. "If this has been here since Elsbeth died, then…."

"It is impossible for it to be in such good repair unless—"

"Unless the duke has someone come over here to take care of the upkeep."

"Damn," they said in unison.

They looked at each other and then at the entrance to the structure. A waft of cold, scented air came from the interior just beyond the doorway.

"Shall we?" Teddy squared his shoulders and led the way inside.

After several steps, he stopped. Bas came up quietly behind him. He brushed Teddy's hand as Bas circled one way and Teddy circled the other around the central focus of the chamber.

A magnificently carved tomb dominated the stone floor. The stone was a mottled black, something Teddy had seen in the hills around the duke's estate. An exquisite white marble weeping angel was set into each corner of the tomb and gave the appearance they supported the lid of the tomb on their outstretched wings. Also in white marble, heavily antlered stags rested as if sleeping on either side of the tomb. They all paled in comparison to the effigy lying in repose on the top of the black stone structure he assumed housed the remains of Elsbeth Dunhome, the Innes Witch. He and Bas stepped closer, one on each side, and stared at the incredible sculpture.

She lay on her right side, her cheek pillowed on her hand. Her other arm lay across her waist with her palm pressed against the black stone. Every detail of her face and hair had been exquisitely rendered, so much so it might have been the lady in the portrait lying there. Or the head of their Regency boot camp. Her gown, even carved of marble, was that of a great lady, not that of a common midwife. Teddy's vision blurred with tears and he quickly swiped the back of his hand across his face.

"Poof." He heard the word in his father's voice.

Fuck you, old man.

"Look at this," Bas whispered reverently.

Teddy came around the tomb to join him as they bent closer to the figure's right hand. Adorning her finger in delicate detail was a marble version of the signet ring the present Duke of Turra wore. Teddy reached out to trace the ring. The air in the chamber warmed and suddenly became redolent with the scent of lavender and heather.

"She's here." Teddy pressed his hand to the top of the tomb. "The first duke found her body and put her here so his mother could never find her."

"McGinty said they never found her body. He said the loch was too deep."

"That's what all of the family histories in the library say. I've read them all." Teddy started when Bas covered his hand with his own. "But if you lost someone you loved like that, would you ever stop looking for them?"

Bas gave a little huff of a laugh. "We'll make a romantic of you yet." He fell silent for several heartbeats, then said, "I'd find you if it took the rest of my life. And I'd build a shrine to keep you safe." Bas ran his thumb over the back of Teddy's hand. "I'm so sorry, my lady. I am so sorry you have to spend eternity in this lonely place." He tucked his free arm around Teddy's waist.

The chamber grew cooler and the light began to fade, though the lavender and heather remained. Teddy had no idea how long they stayed just so, keeping Elsbeth Dunhomme company as if they had no choice.

At last, Teddy released a sigh. "We have to go. We don't want to cross the loch in the dark."

Bas nodded and steered him slowly away from the tomb and out onto the portico. The sun hung low in the sky. Darkness would fall in an hour or so. They walked in silence utnil they reached the spot where they'd picnicked and made love.

Teddy gathered his jacket and the relatively dry blanket and stuffed them into the nearly empty hamper. Several of the duke's heavy silk serviettes hung on a shrub and showed evidence of having been washed and wrung out. Apparently, Bas had cleaned them up using the serviettes, then rolled Teddy off the blanket to take care of it as well, all while Teddy slept like the dead. Once he'd checked the trees, shrubs, and the grass around the flat rock that had served as both table and bed and had everything stowed in the hamper, he picked it up and started toward the sheer drop where they'd moored their boat.

Bas stood at the edge of the drop, hands on hips, and stared back at the mausoleum. Bas's expression was one of such sorrow that Teddy strode to him immediately and dropped the hamper at his feet.

"What is it?" He pressed a palm to Bas's chest.

"She isn't at peace," Bas murmured, almost as if Teddy

weren't there at all. "She keeps coming back to the house, to the gardens. Why?"

Teddy looked over his shoulder and blinked as the lowering sun glinted against the stone monument to the great love that never had a chance. A sudden shiver swept through him.

"I don't know. Let's get into the boat. Robbie will be looking for us." He half climbed and half slid down the rock face, then reached up for Bas to hand him the hamper, which he set in the middle of the rowboat before he settled onto the stern bench and unhooked the oars. For a few minutes, he feared Bas would stand there staring back at the mausoleum until nightfall.

"Bas?"

The big Basque started and turned. He ran his hand over his face and shook his head. "Hold the boat steady, sailor-man. One dunking in the loch is enough. That water's fucking cold."

"Next time, don't wear a kilt."

Bas flipped his kilt up as he scrambled down the rock face. "I thought you liked my kilt."

"I like you better out of your kilt."

Bas rolled his eyes and settled onto the bow bench. He stretched his legs across the boat and propped his feet on the hamper, intentionally giving Teddy a clear view under the kilt.

"Tease," Teddy muttered as he rowed them out into the middle of the loch and started back toward the manor.

He concentrated on pulling the oars. The air flowed cooler and the water lapped at the sides of the boat in a steady musical rhythm. Bas kept one hand lightly on the rudder, but for the most part he sprawled in his seat and stared steadily at Teddy as if trying to discover his secrets by sheer force of will.

Teddy lifted a brow. "What?"

"I'm just curious. About where we go from here?"

His shirt open at the throat, legs sprawled, and kilt above his knees, Bas was sexy as hell. He knew it too. The fact Teddy had those exact thoughts with no hint of shame or regret? *That* was the bloody kicker.

"You mean other than back to the manor for a bath and some clean clothes? Followed by telling the rest of our party what we've found?"

"You know what I mean, Teddy. Don't pretend you don't. I've come as far as I intend to alone. Whatever happens from here on out, we're either together or we're not."

"Together? I don't—"

"The fuck you don't. I'm not a demonstrative man, but if someone asks if we're together, I want to be able to say yes without you flinching. Neither of us is the sort of man people expect to be gay, but we *are*, and I'm not going to hide it or lie about it. I want to go to bed with you at night and wake up with you in the morning. I want to see where this relationship goes, and I damned sure don't want to do it in secret as if what I feel for you is something to be ashamed of.

"The woman in that tomb died for love. The man who searched for her and put her there did it for love. I want nothing less than that because, dammit, I deserve it. And so the fuck do you, Teddy. So the fuck do you." The dark baritone of his voice had turned harsh and raw.

Funny because Teddy's throat burned as if he'd gargled with carpet tacks. His eyes and nose stung as well. "You've picked a bloody fine time and place for a declaration of love, you stupid bloody Yank. How the hell am I supposed to kiss you without both of us landing in the drink. Again."

His heart hammered against his chest to the point his lungs seized up to get out of the way. This wasn't supposed to happen. Not for him. Not with someone as stubborn, and big-hearted, and loud, and rude, and amazing as Bas Salazar.

"We've got all the time in the world for you to kiss me, if that's what you—" He turned mid-sentence and looked back to where the island had disappeared from view, as if it had never been. "I know why Elsbeth can't rest."

"Excuse me? What has that got to do with—"

"Nothing. And everything. We have to tell the others. We can fix this." He fairly bounced on the wooden bench.

"Are you having a stroke? What are you talking about?"

Had the man changed his mind? Had he run mad? Both?

Bas nearly tilted the boat over as he scrambled over the hamper and knelt in front of Teddy. "She's alone out there. She wants what we want, at least what I hope you want."

The penny dropped, and Teddy understood, well at least most of it. He didn't have time to think about it. Bas kissed him with so much force, Teddy nearly fell backward out of the boat.

"Oh, and by the way," Bas said as he ended the kiss, "in case that wasn't clear, I love you. Keep rowing. We've got to talk to McGinty."

Chapter Fourteen

Bas hadn't meant to blurt it out like that. He wasn't normally that impulsive, especially when something as important as love was on the line. Somehow, the sight of the Innes Witch lying alone in her magnificent tomb seized his imagination, or more likely, his heart. Some things were too damned important to wait for in life. Love after death? Too damned painful to contemplate.

"Hello? Paging, Mr. Salazar? Well, as we actually have no way to page you, I guess I should say, 'Is Mr. Salazar receiving this afternoon?'"

"What?" Bas stopped in the middle of the lane that led to the stables and studied Teddy carefully.

"You haven't said more than two words since we turned the boat and hamper over to Robbie. Is something wrong?" Teddy's apprehension was written all over his face. The very last thing Bas wanted when it came to the strides they'd made.

"Actually, everything is about as perfect as it could be. But"—he took a deep breath—

"I'm a little...." *Hell!* This wasn't good. He was terrified of saying the wrong thing. *Him.* Who was never afraid of a damned thing.

"Stunned? Scared? Worried?" Teddy caught the corner of his bottom lip between his teeth.

"Happy. And stunned." He took Teddy's hand and waited for him to pull away. He didn't. "And hopeful?"

"Yes?"

"Absolutely. Are you okay?"

"Terrified," Teddy replied, and he looked it too.

"Oh." Bas tried to stop his stomach from dropping to his feet. Didn't work.

"Also hopeful." Teddy continued to hold Bas's hand as they neared the stableyard. "For Elsbeth. For us. But...." He shrugged.

"But what?"

"I don't know how to do this, Bas, and I don't want to bollocks it up."

"Bollocks?"

"Regency word."

"Good word. Nothing has changed. Not really. Just be yourself."

"Easy for you to say. I've been someone else for over thirty years." Teddy's hand had grown damp.

"You know who you are, Teddy. You're the man who was visited by a ghost who felt sorry for you, yet you want to help her. You're the man who stood at her tomb and wept for all the years she's been alone. Did you think I didn't see?"

"Bloody hell."

Bas laughed softly. "Hey, I'm the one who talked of nothing but reuniting Elsbeth with the first duke all the way across the loch after I delivered the worst *I love you* in history."

"It wasn't the worst. It was perfect. Now I know why you

rattled on like a magpie and then clammed up like a hermit once we left everything with Robbie."

"Oh, and why was that, Dr. Phil?"

"Fuck you," Teddy muttered.

"You already did. And hella' good too."

"You're just as terrified of all this between us as I am."

Bas snorted. "You bet your amazing ass I am."

"Robbie is a bad influence on you."

They'd managed to walk through the stable yard and to the front of Rosemount Manor without anyone seeing them—which was likely the reason Teddy still held his hand. Bas didn't want to push the Brit too hard. He dragged him over to the fountain, then sat down on the edge. When Teddy joined him, Bas gently slid their hands apart.

"So," he said, a little huff escaping his lips despite himself, "how do you want to do this?"

Teddy hadn't said *I love you too.* Bas beat that fact back to the far reaches of his mind. He'd worry about that later. After they got through the next few hours.

"As I've never done this before, what would you suggest?" Teddy sat with his elbows propped on his knees and his hands clasped tightly together. His tone alone indicated he was wound tighter than an agent at a contract negotiation.

"You have two options. March into the library and announce to the entire boot camp, *'Oh, by the way, I'm gay, and I'm sleeping with Bas.'* Or...."

Teddy narrowed his eyes on Bas. "Has anyone ever told you you're funny?"

"Lots of people."

"They lied."

Bas put his arm around Teddy's shoulders. "Or we go in there and talk to our friends about what we found on the island and let them figure things out for themselves."

"Our friends?" Teddy gave a dry, completely mirthless laugh.

"People do like you whether you want them to or not. They'll figure out we're together, and they won't care. Because that's the kind of people they are. Trust me on this, okay?"

"Do I have a choice?"

"Not if you want this to work." Bas winced inwardly. That sounded like an ultimatum. He hadn't mean it as such. Well, maybe a little.

Teddy stared at the cobblestones beneath their feet. "I do trust you," he said softly. He raised his head and met Bas's gaze head on. "I think I trust you more than any man I know."

"Well, then. There's only one other thing to decide."

"What?"

"Who do we tell about what we've found, and who do we ask about the first duke?"

Bas watched as every form of confusion flickered across Teddy's face. He was overthinking their relationship, or rather how the others would see their relationship. He wanted Teddy to think about anything but that at the moment. There was time enough for that sort of worry later. Perhaps Teddy had come to the same conclusion because he glanced at the big double doors into the manor.

"I don't know who to ask about this. We definitely don't want the duke or Eleanor involved at this point, if ever. Who do you trust in our merry little band?" Teddy asked.

"I agree about the duke and Eleanor. How about Danny and Samantha, and Lily and Lord Lachlan to start?"

"Lord Lachlan? Really?"

"He'll do what his wife tells him. Trust me."

They both grinned.

"Very well." Teddy shoved to his feet. "Let's start with

those four." He looked up at the impressive stone front of Rosemount Manor and visibly steeled himself as if about to engage in a fencing match.

"Everything will be fine," Bas murmured as he bumped Teddy's arm with his. "Trust me."

Fortunately, they didn't have to go far to gather the people they'd decided to inform about their discoveries. Danny and Samantha stood at the top of the main staircase as Bas and Teddy crossed the entrance hall.

"You two. Library. Now," Teddy ordered.

Bas rolled his eyes. "What *his highness* means is would you meet us in the library. We have something to tell you about the Innes Witch."

Danny laughed. "He's got your number, Teddy. Actually, we were headed there anyway. Hadrian and Anna are back from their pre-wedding honeymoon."

Bas and Teddy exchanged a look.

"What?" Samantha asked. "I'm dying to know what you've found out. I know they will be too."

"I know Anna," Bas said. "Can Hadrian be trusted not to go running to the duke or Eleanor?" He directed his question to Teddy.

"I think so," Teddy replied. "Hadrian will, how did you put it, *Do what his wife tells him*? They're not married yet, but close enough."

"Okay. We need to send for Lord Lachlan and Lily." Bas started up the stairs with Teddy right behind him.

"What exactly is this all about?" Samantha asked. "And why can't we tell His Grace or Eleanor?" She was asking questions but also speed-walking to the library for all she was worth.

At the top of the landing Bas saw Dougal just outside the dining room doors. "Dougal, can you do us a favor?"

The young Scot hurried toward them. Teddy intercepted

him halfway, and after a hushed conversation, Dougal jogged down the stairs and out the front door.

"This would be so much easier if we had our bloody mobile phones," Teddy muttered as he caught up to them at the doors to the main library.

Once inside, Teddy, Danny, and Samantha spent the first few minutes greeting Anna Chase, whom Bas had met when he first arrived at Rosemount Manor, and a big linebacker of a guy he assumed was Hadrian Cross. He'd heard about the first time Anna met the book critic, and Bas was impressed. She was a dainty little thing to have shoved a dish of ice cream down the linebacker's kilt.

"Bas, this is Hadrian Cross." Teddy led Bas over to introduce him. "Hadrian, this is Bas Salazar. Bas is the stunt coordinator for the film, and for some demented reason, he decided to join our boot camp."

"Good to meet you." Bas shook Hadrian's hand. "How was the duke's hunting lodge? Please tell me you at least had heat."

Hadrian laughed. "Heat, a shower with hot running water, and a sauna. It was…heaven." He gazed at Anna, who stood beside him as she spoke animatedly with Samantha.

"Ah. Then I guess there was no ice cream available." Bas winked at Teddy, who laughed.

"Actually, it was a Regency version of sorbet, smartass." The author stood on her toes and kissed Bas's cheek. "You seem none the worse for wear after your time at Eleanor's Regency boot camp." She linked her arm through Bas's as they strolled across the antique carpets to join the others as everyone settled onto one of the sofas or armchairs in front of the big main fireplace.

"Who is this?" Teddy leaned down from his chair to stroke the ears of the deerhound puppy at his feet.

"That is Elsbeth," Hadrian said as he, Bas, and Anna sat on one of the sofas. "She's mine. A gift from Anna."

Teddy and Bas exchanged another look.

"Okay, guys, what the hell is going on?" Danny asked. "This is getting weird."

"The fact we're talking about a woman who died over seven hundred years ago, one each of us has seen in this house at some point or another, that isn't weird enough?" Bas asked. "I'm assuming you've seen her too, Hadrian, or you wouldn't have named your dog after her?"

"Oh, yeah. I've seen her." Hadrian scooped up the huge, hairy puppy who had wandered over to lean against his legs. The dog was so big it took Hadrian and Anna's laps to hold her.

"Is that what this is about?" Anna asked. "The Innes Witch?"

"We found her." Teddy rose from his chair and stood, hands clasped behind his back as if he dared them to argue with him.

They all shifted in their seats, then looked from Teddy to Bas and back again.

"The hell you say?" Danny said. "You mean you actually found…."

"She's buried in one helluva mausoleum on an island in the middle of the loch," Bas said.

"There are no islands on the loch." Lord Lachlan stood inside the library doors, his wife at his side. "I grew up here. I know. What's this about, Arneaux?"

"Close the doors and come and sit down," Teddy said. "We'll show you." He came to where Bas sat and bent to whisper in his ear. "Move that long tea table in the middle of this." He waved at the seating arrangement. "I'm going to get something."

Bas stood. Once Danny saw Bas moving the table, he got

up to help. Hadrian dragged over another armchair and an ottoman. Everyone rearranged themselves to make room for Lord Lachlan and Lily, then Bas sat down in the chair Teddy had vacated. The duke's brother opened his mouth to speak but closed it when Teddy returned with a large map of the estate, which he spread over the tea table and adjusted so the loch sat at the center. He sat at Bas's feet and pointed to a spot at the far edge of the loch, close to the shore across from the manor and grounds.

He looked over his shoulder at Bas. "Is that right? Or is it farther up?"

Bas reached over him and traced a line across from where they'd put the boat into the water. "More here, I think. See that sort of shadow? As if someone painted over something on the map?" He remained that way, his hand resting on Teddy's shoulder.

"Wait a minute." Lord Lachlan leaned in, and so did Samantha, who finally knelt on the other side of the tea table.

"This map was done in watercolors," Samantha said softly. "Bas is right. Someone painted over something, just there." She gave Teddy a quick perusal. "But you knew that, didn't you? This is the map you've been looking for the past few days. I wondered why you were spending more time here than on the practice field."

"Ever since Bas and I followed the tunnels under the gardens to the secret room in the top of the tower."

Silence. Like the gathered breath before a storm.

"What?"

"You went where?"

"What tunnels?"

"When did this happen?"

"I need details, you two. Details." Hadrian shrugged when silence fell, and they all stared at him.

"He's working on a book based on the Innes Witch," Anna told them.

Danny gave a long, low whistle. "Now I understand why you didn't want to involve the duke or Eleanor."

"Oh, really?" Lachlan sat sprawled in an armchair, his arms folded across his chest. Lily, who sat on the ottoman in front of his chair, turned and patted his knee, bared by his well-worn kilt. "You went exploring *under* my brother's estate, and you don't intend to tell him about it?"

"We found the mausoleum where the first duke put Elsbeth to rest. It's…incredible. But she isn't at rest, and we think we know why. Do you really want to discuss this with your brother with everything that has gone on between the witch and him?" Teddy asked.

He still sat on the floor at the tea table. Bas counted it as win that Teddy hadn't shrugged off Bas's hand.

"How did you—" Lachlan sighed and shook his head. "McGinty." He settled back in his chair. "Perhaps you should start at the beginning and tell us everything. Then I'll decide what my brother and his event planner need to know."

BAS MARVELED THAT THEY MANAGED TO GET THROUGH DINNER and card games without alerting Eleanor, the duke, and the others that something was up.

Finally, still in their Regency evening clothes and various items of winter wear, they all descended the staircase from the dressing room and traveled through the tunnels, each of the carrying a lantern. Lachlan even brought an antique spyglass from the estate's collection. They were a noisy group, teasing and scaring each other. Until, that was, they came face to face with the portrait that looked so much like the woman who'd controlled their lives for the last three months.

"This explains a great deal," Lord Lachlan mumured, his Scot's brogue more than apparent. "I dinnae kin why he's kept it secret."

"They sent him away. They thought he was crazy." Lily made no attempt to hide her contempt for Lachlan and his brother's parents. "Can you blame him?"

They stood in silence for what felt to Bas like hours. Then Teddy pointed out the door to the parapet, and said, "You can see where she's buried from out there."

Samantha looked at Danny, and Lily said, "What the hell are we waiting for?" and they climbed the stairs, hard on Teddy's heels.

He reached the parapart and everyone rushed to the spot from which he pointed across the loch. Bas held back. Teddy slipped a little ways down the parapet and left the others alone to contemplate what the two of them had seen up close and personal.

Bas andTeddy admired the night sky and the light show above the distant hills. No thunder yet, but the sporadic lightning and the rush of the wind gave sight and sound to what the rest of the party now stared toward in disbelief.

Bas faced Teddy, and each of them rested a hip on the spaces in the crenelated wall that topped the tower.

"Do you think we did the right thing?" Teddy asked. "Telling them. Bringing them here?"

"Yes. I know you have trust issues, but they're a good group, and I think they've come to care about Elsbeth despite the fact she scares the shit out of them on a regular basis." Bas was a little surprised to see Teddy smile.

"They're not the only ones." He looked over his shoulder at the others, then back at Bas. "And I'm learning to trust people. Even if they've only come to like me because they like you."

"You're an arrogant, overbearing snob who is the best at

what he does and knows it. They like you despite that, not because of me. Get over yourself, Teddy. You're handsome, ripped, and lethal with a sword. These people aren't afraid of you. Deal with it." Bas grinned.

"Get over myself? Really?"

"Really. Besides, Lily liked you enough to sleep with you. Remember?"

"For Christ's sake, will you shut up? You're going to get me killed." Teddy gave a panicked glance over his shoulder, only to find Lily right behind him.

"Teddy knows the old Lily didn't have to like him to sleep with him, Bas." She draped an arm around Teddy's shoulders. One of the few women tall enough to do so without straining to reach. "But I do kind of like him now. He grows on you, don't you think?"

"I'd say so. Yeah. He does." Bas didn't even try to keep the warmth from his voice.

Even in the dim light of the lanterns, he didn't miss Teddy's brief moment of doubt.

Lily kissed Teddy's cheek, then leaned across to kiss Bas's. "I'm happy for you two. Lachlan will be, too, once he figures it out."

"Once who figures what out?" Danny asked as he and Samantha joined them. "Whatever it is, let's figure it out quick. It's colder than a tin top toilet in a Siberian blizzard out here."

Lily returned to where Lachlan stood gazing out over the loch, the antique spyglass he held by his side.

"I think it's amazing," Samantha said. "I cannot believe you two found all this."

"Very Hardy Boys of you and Bas, Teddy," Anna said, who had bundled up in one of Hadrian's heavy wool many-caped coats from his Regency wardrobe.

"Actually, Bas is a great fan of Nancy Drew," Teddy said with a grin.

"I *have* a sister." He punched Teddy in the shoulder.

Teddy punched him back.

"Now, boys," Samantha drawled.

Everyone laughed.

"What's yer plan, Rousseau?" Lord Lachlan's voice cut through the laughter and the whistling wind. He might have been one of his ancestors giving orders in the heat of battle as an enemy attempted to storm the castle.

They all turned toward the spot where he still stood, Lily tucked into his side, her face wreathed in concern. She truly loved this man. Bas had witnessed some of her unhappy relationships. She'd met the duke's rough and sometimes abrasive brother just in time, and Bas was glad for her.

"My plan for what?" Teddy faced the Scot.

Bas stepped up behind Teddy. Not to protect him because Teddy didn't need anyone's protection, but to let him know he was there.

"You dinnae do all of this for naught. Ye said something about knowing why Elsbeth is nae at rest despite that Scot's Taj Mahal my ancestor entrusted her body to after he pulled her from the loch. What will it take?"

Teddy tilted his head back and studied the stars in silence for a moment. Such a beautiful place to have seen so much sorrow. Bas's heart hurt for Elsbeth, but more for the first duke who'd been helpless to save her. Rosemount, this family, were cloaked in many dark and powerful things. Guilt was a heavy burden for any man to bear, especially after seven hundred years.

"She's alone out there," Bas said before Teddy could speak. "She won't rest until he rests beside her, where he belongs. You're newly married, Lord Lachlan. Have you slept even one night away from your wife since you married?"

"Nae. And I don't intend to, if I have my way."

Hadrian and Arneaux nodded agreement.

"So what do we do?" Danny asked.

"Nae we," Lachlan said. "Me. I'll be the one to speak with Knox about this. Dammit." He glared at Teddy. "Ye coudnae come up with some Sassenach religious hocus pocus to fix this?"

"Not my area of expertise, my lord. I lift weights, stab people, shoot antique weapons, and ride horses. No witch-craft involved, I'm afraid."

"I don't know about that," Hadrian said. "McGinty says you're a wizard when it comes to swords, and I have to agree. I've got the scars to prove it."

Bas gave Teddy a subtle bump to the back.

"We may need swords and sorcery if Knox agrees to let us move the first duke," Lachlan muttered. "He's buried next to his mother in the family vault." He glanced back across the loch. Lily squeezed his arm. "She's the one I would nae want haunting me." He turned back. "Ye wake her up, ye'r on yer own."

"Next to his mother, not his wife?" Bas shook his head. "That woman had issues."

"More issues than Marvel superheroes," Danny agreed.

"What about Eleanor?" Anna asked. "When do we tell her about…everything?"

The wind picked up, and the faint sound of thunder rolled across the loch. They all flinched to varying degrees. Ghosts and curses. Moving dead dukes. A seven hundred year resemblance. Yeah. They had plenty to flinch about.

"Nae until after the end of the month," Lachlan said. "She has some private party coming to stay at the hunting lodge for a few weeks. Sassenach politicians out to stalk roebucks for their amusement. Was booked before she set up your little boot camp. She'll be frantic until they're gone, and

Knox will be a right pain in the arse. He hates having to rent out any part of Rosemount, especially to the English."

"I'll try not to take that personally." Teddy sounded about as sincere as a director apologizing for a pay cut.

"As will I," Samantha remarked.

"Ye've been here long enough ye'r honorary Scots." Lachlan's gruff voice did little to hide the grudging affection there. "But if ye don't want to be wet, honorary Scots, I suggest we head back. That storm will be crossing the loch in the next few minutes."

With muttered snatches of conversation, the group gathered their lanterns and headed for the door that led into the room where Elsbeth's portrait hung. Bas and Teddy were the last to leave the parapet. Bas took a moment to follow the reflection of stars on the water to the island where his and Teddy's relationship had changed, perhaps forever. A sliver of white moved along the shore, shimmered, and took form.

"Elsbeth," Bas said on a low breath.

Teddy looked in the direction he stared. A sharp intake of breath told Bas he saw her too.

Teddy wrapped a powerful hand around Bas's wrist. "Come on. We'll figure it out. I suspect she knows that now."

By the time they got to the bottom of the stairs, the others were giving the portrait one last look as they filed out of the tower and began the trip back to the main house. There was no joking nor pretend scares this time. A few words spoken to caution each other. A few words of direction. Once they got back to the dressing room, they doused the lamps. Lachlan suggested they leave them in the dressing room for Robbie to fetch later. They agreed to wait for Lachlan to do a little reconnaisance before they gathered again and figured out what to do next.

"I guess we're all Nancy Drews now," Anna said as she and Hadrian stepped into the main hallway from Bas's room.

She studied Bas and Teddy, then smiled. "We'll see you two at breakfast?"

"Of course," Teddy replied. "I wouldn't miss Eleanor and the others planning your wedding."

"Oh, God," Hadrian groaned. "Oww! Just kidding." He waved at them with one hand while he rubbed his arm with the other.

Bas closed the door. "He's got his hands full with her. She's tougher than she looks. What?"

Teddy sat in the armchair in front of the fireplace, his expression an odd mix of several emotions. None of them particularly positive. "She knows," he said, his voice strained. "She knows, and if she does, he does. And Lily knows, which means Lord Lachlan knows."

"Knows what?"

Teddy rolled his eyes. He waved from himself to Bas and back. "About us."

"And?"

Silence.

Bas went to the bedside table. He retrieved his glasses, a piece of Regency-style paper, and a quill. He sat in the chair across from Teddy, put on his glasses and posed as if he intended to write.

"Und tell me," he declared in a really bad German accent. "How does zat make you feel?"

Teddy tossed a stray boot at him. The boot hit Bas in the leg and dropped to the floor. Teddy rubbed his hand over his face. "Honestly?"

"Always." Bas put the paper and quill down next to his chair.

"I'm still trying to suss that out. I'm not afraid. Not with them. Which is odd because I have been at odds with each of them at some point or another during this little Regency adventure. Now?" He shrugged. "I don't think I mind them knowing. I don't *think* so."

Bas's heart raced, his stomach plummeted to his feet, and his mind whirled like someone had dropped his brain in a blender on high. He wanted to believe this thing with Teddy would work. He wanted to believe Teddy was growing into who he really was. But….

Fuck it. You've had your heart broken before, mozolo.

He stood and began to strip out of his Regency evening clothes. "Let's take this one day at a time. I'm tired and cold, and I'm ready to go to bed. How about you?"

"Here? In your bed?"

"Your choice."

Bas continued to undress. He refused to allow Teddy to know how much Teddy staying meant to him. *A lot. Everything.* He wanted normal with this man. Sharing a bed all night for more than sex. Conversation without having to watch what he said or what he might do. Even the most casual gesture had become loaded with issues. He could handle these things for a while, but not forever. A real life with a real love. Was that too much to ask?

He pulled the bed curtains around three sides of the bed, leaving the fireside section open. When he heard the first evening shoe hit the floor behind him, he released the breath he'd been holding. Still, he stripped naked and went behind the screen in the corner to wash his face and brush his teeth. He snuffed the candles and turned down the oil lamps while Teddy poured fresh water into the bowl and got ready for bed. By the time Teddy finished, the room was dark except for the fire in the fireplace, and Bas had already climbed into bed.

Teddy lifted the covers and slid in next to him. "Bloody hell! When Robbie hasn't been in to warm them, these sheets are as cold as my father's heart."

Bas laughed. "Robbie didn't exactly know when we'd return from our little ghost hunting expedition." He turned onto his side away from the fire. Teddy moved over until he'd pressed his back to Bas's and rested a hand on Bas's hip.

"I'm shocked. That man knows everything that goes on, sometimes before it even happens. However, I suspect that's what makes him good at his job. And at winning all those wagers he places."

"Yeah, about those wagers. There's been one on you since the first week of boot camp."

"Oh, God. What was the bet?"

"The good news is that everyone bet against Robbie."

"Your feet are cold as blocks of ice," Teddy complained as he shifted his feet onto Bas's. "What's the bad news?"

Chapter Fifteen

Teddy caught himself humming as he shouldered into his green wool cutaway on his way down the main staircase. He'd come back to the manor after his weapons class to have a wash and change clothes. The weather had warmed considerably in the last week, and by the end of the class, they'd all looked like a group of ruffians after a Regency bender rather than the proper English gentlemen Eleanor expected them to be. Bas had missed the sweaty fun as he'd spent the morning mapping out some stunts for the Battle of Waterloo sequences Wentworth wanted to film first, once they started filming, that was. The official boot camp might be winding down, but the start date for the film had been changed and pushed back more than once.

Not that Teddy cared. These last few days had been a series of wonderful days followed by some incredible nights. With each day he grew more comfortable in his own skin—which terrified him to his marrow, but he wouldn't change a thing. In the space of a few months, these people had become a sort of family. In the space of a few weeks, Bas Salazar had become...everything.

"Teddy?" Samantha stood at the bottom of the stairs in a lovely blue silk morning dress. "I'm glad I caught you. Two things." She hooked her arm through his and started him down the passageway that went under the staircase and toward the French doors out onto the terrace. "I left the book you lent me with Bas, is that all right?"

"Absolutely. I hope it was helpful."

"It was and it wasn't."

"Oh?"

"Have you seen the swords Wentworth had made?" She kept her gaze straight ahead. "They arrived yesterday."

"I'm not going to like them, am I?"

"Perhaps it's just me."

"I doubt that, Dr. Higgans-Arneaux. I'll give them a look and then have one of McGinty's blacksmiths make them properly. And the second thing?"

She stopped just inside the French doors. Luncheon had been set up on the terrace. *Al fresco,* as their Regency queen called it.

"I'm glad you're so happy, Teddy. I knew you couldn't be such an arse. Not the way you fence."

Teddy threw his head back and laughed. The laughter shook his entire body and warmed his soul. *Bloody hell!* Who knew he might actually have a soul. Or have a friend who saw what his swords and history meant to him.

"I wasn't aware fencing was a test of *arsedom.* I shall have to remember that."

"*Arsedom?*" Danny jumped from his chair at one of the wrought iron tables formally set for luncheon and seated his wife in the chair next to him. "Is that a Regency word, and are we allowed to use it?"

"Your wife *is* the expert." Teddy took the chair next to Bas at the same table. "If she says it, it must be a word and simply has to be proper."

"I doubt you'll get that past the Regency Nazi. Oww! Who taught you how to punch? I thought romance writers were supposed to be sweet." Hadrian, seated at the next table rubbed his arm until Anna bent over and kissed the spot she'd hit.

Bella and Sylvan, who shared their table, laughed as they passed around a basket of rolls to go with the first course soup the footmen began to place in front of them.

"Makes me wonder what kind of kink you two got into up at the duke's hunting lodge," Lily said with a sly smile.

"Ha ha, Lady Lachlan. You're the one married to the Scottish version of a mountain man. Talk about kink," Hadrian remarked. She tossed a roll at him, which he caught handily. "Speaking of which, where is His Lordship?"

"Securing his birds. Those British politicians arrived last night, and they'll be out shooting sometime this afternoon. The gunfire upsets them, so he's battening down the hatches."

Teddy noticed the furrows across her brow. "Will he be all right?"

She looked startled, then nodded. "I think so. Our cottage is far enough from where they'll be hunting, so he shouldn't be bothered." Her look of gratitude did something strange to Teddy's chest.

"You know where we are if you need us," Arneaux said quietly.

The others murmured agreement.

"Thank you." Lily blinked rapidly and tucked into her soup.

"She's trying to civilize you, Cross." Bas grabbed a couple of rolls, then handed the basket to Teddy. "I understand the process is painful."

Trust the big Basque to diffuse the situation with humor. One of the many reasons Teddy...*yes, well.*

"Voice of experience?" Lily asked from her place next to the dance master.

"Hell, no. I am only barely civilized, which is as civilized as I intend to be."

"Here, here," Teddy said, and began to eat his soup.

"Exactly how uncivilized is he, Teddy?" Arneaux asked with a damnably bland face.

They'd come to a truce and even a sort of friendship in the past few weeks, but the Cajun never missed a chance to push Teddy's buttons. All in good fun, of course.

"Only as much as is necessary," Teddy said without missing a beat.

A general chuckle echoed around the terrace. Lily raised her wine glass and Teddy did the same.

Bas leaned close and whispered in his ear, "A definite hit, swordmaster. Well done."

"You can thank me properly later," Teddy murmured. "Is there a reason His Grace and Miss Witherspoon have not joined us?"

"Other than the fact they spent the entirety of breakfast glaring at each other?" Bella asked as the footmen removed the soup and served a beautifully done roast beef with potatoes and carrots.

"Indeed," Sylvan, the normally jolly and upbeat dancing master said solemnly. "I was waiting for one of them to punch the other, and they didn't utter a word."

"Knox isn't happy with the group of MPs Eleanor has booked into the hunting lodge for the next few weeks," Lily said. "He despises politicians, especially British politicians, and she has them coming to the house to meet him this afternoon. She's taking care of them, and he's holed up in his study." Lily shrugged and took a big bite of roast beef.

"Members of Parliament?" Teddy's stomach cramped.

Suddenly he wasn't hungry. "Which members of Parliament?" His entire body went cold.

"No idea," Lily said once she'd swallowed. "I only know Knox pronounced them, *'Idiotic bloody old Tory wankers.'*"

"Oh dear," Samantha said. "That doesn't bode well."

"Tory." Hadrian paused in buttering a roll. "They've been around since the Regency. Hard-line conservatives, right?"

"Extremely hard line," Teddy muttered.

"Is there any room in the duke's study for the rest of us to hole up?" Bella asked.

"I seriously doubt it." Lily shook her head. "It's where he goes when he wants to hide from Eleanor."

"Are you all right?" Bas placed a hand on Teddy's forearm.

"Of course." Teddy tried to smile. He didn't make it.

"Well, I am pretty sure shredding one of Mrs. Gordon's fresh-made rolls is a violation of the Geneva Convention."

Teddy looked down at his hands, which were covered in crumbs and pieces of bread. As was his bread plate. Fortunately, the others had latched onto the topic of the duke's animosity toward their boot camp director. Bas brushed all of the stray pieces of roll into the plate and handed Teddy another roll.

"You sure you're okay? You look kind of pale." Despite the ice running in Teddy's veins at the moment, Bas's concern warmed him from the inside out.

"I'm British. Of course I'm pale. Arneaux gave me a run for my money in class this morning, that's all."

"That's not what it felt like to me," Arneaux said from across the table. "My arm feels like spaghetti."

"That's because you're still holding your saber too tightly."

This launched the entire luncheon party into a discussion of swordplay and exercise. Teddy breathed a sigh of relief. Here, he was in his element. Here, he had the chance to push his fears about precisely which Tory politicians had come to Rosemount to the back of his mind. For now.

Once they finshed lunch, Lily went in search of Lord Lachlan. Samantha, Anna, Gloria, and Bella, went to the rooms dedicated to wardrobe creation for the film in order to work on Anna's wedding dress. Danny and Sylvan went to the stables as they and Bas intended to ride out to a more remote portion of the estate to check out some possible settings for scenes. Bas hung back and waited for Teddy.

"Are you sure you won't go with us?" Bas asked as they walked back through the house. "It's a great day for a ride, and Sylvan says he's found a spot with an incredible view." He brushed his hand down Teddy's back, and Teddy leaned into Bas's palm for a minute.

"No, I'm for the library this afternoon. There are some Regency-era records and drawings of swords made by the estate's blacksmiths. I want to pull them because I suspect I'm going to need them. Dr. Arneaux has seen some of the swords Wentworth had delivered for the film." He grimaced. "They didn't pass her inspection."

"Ouch! Then they damned sure won't pass yours." He brushed a kiss across Teddy's temple. A tendril of heat slipped down Teddy's spine. "I'll see you at—"

"Rousseau! Teddy Rousseau, is that you?"

Teddy jumped away from Bas like a guilty schoolboy. He took several steps toward the group of men who stood in the entrance hall. Bas gave him a look of such confusion, Teddy's heart threatened to crack wide open.

"Or should I say, Lord Staines?" The tall, white-haired gentleman whose voice had snatched Teddy back in time in a few simple words asked. "What on earth are you doing here?" He met Teddy in the centre of the parquet floor, his hand outstretched.

"Mr. Compton-Bowles." Teddy shook the man's hand and

forced himself not to look back. Bas was there, where Teddy had left him. Of that much, he was certain. His presence loomed, and Teddy didn't dare acknowledge him. "Consulting on a film, sir. I trust you are well."

"And your friend there?" His father's friend and political ally nodded in the direction from which Teddy had come. Teddy didn't look back.

"One of the Americans working on the film. No one really." He held his breath, half hoping Bas would speak up and half praying he wouldn't.

"Indeed. Gentlemen," he called over to the others, all decked out in hunting togs, "come and meet Chawton's heir, Viscount Staines."

Only then did Teddy see Eleanor standing behind them, her hand over her open mouth. When she dropped her hand, she mouthed *Lord Staines* at him, her perfect eyebrows raised high. The long, drawn-in breath behind him nearly brought him to his knees. He shook hands with the other men, even recognized a couple from news reports. They were all cronies of his father, the powerful Tory MP the Earl of Chawton.

"I wasn't aware *Lord Staines* was acquainted with you gentlemen," Eleanor said as she swept around them in her bright green striped day gown. "They were just on their way to the gallery to view the portraits. Would you care to join us, *Lord Staines*?" The hostility in her tone had nothing to do with the fact he'd hidden his title. As they all turned to go upstairs to the gallery, he saw the reason for her anger.

Bas hadn't moved. He stood, fists clenched at his sides, his features drawn tight with resignation, and of all things, pity. However, his skin was a pale shade of bronze. Teddy hurried to catch up to Eleanor as she led the old men of the hunting parties up the stairs.

"Please tell me you aren't doing what I think you're

doing," she muttered once Teddy reached her side. He didn't say a word. Couldn't. "You're a dick, Teddy Rousseau," she said as they reached the second floor landing.

"I know." His stomach churned. He'd walked right into a nightmare and had no idea how to get out.

⊗≉⊗

THE FUCKING NIGHTMARE CONTINUED THROUGH DINNER. THE members of the hunting party had joined them, expressing an interest in Eleanor's Regency *boot camp*. Once the evening was done, they would return to the hunting lodge in the estate Land Rovers, as they were not actually participating in the nineteenth-century experience. They'd asked the most idiotic questions, especially of the Americans at the table, which unfortunately included Bas. Once they discovered he was actually from Spain, one of the MPs, a corporate banker who had dined at Teddy's parents' home on numerous occasions, made a condescending attempt to speak Spanish with him. Fortunately the duke quickly put paid to that with a brief but pointed explanation as to the differences between Spanish and the Basque language.

Teddy had eaten an entire meal without tasting a bite or making eye contact with his lover. When the ladies left the table so the gentlemen could enjoy cigars and brandy, Bas left with them. Dressed in full Regency evening clothes, he possessed an elegance and grace the so-called *gentlemen* at the table might only dream to achieve.

Teddy hated himself.

"Aren't you gentlemen the least bit worried leaving the Basque alone with your women?" Compton-Bowles asked, which evoked suggestive laughter from the rest of the hunting party. "You know the effect those swarthy Eurotrash types have on the ladies. And that one is quite the brawny fellow."

Teddy drained his glass of brandy in one long draught. He wanted to beat his head against the table. There was a race going on between Arneaux and the duke to see whose face could achieve the appearance of stone the quickest. Hadrian opened his moutht to speak but snapped it shut when Arneaux placed a restraining hand on the book critic's forearm.

"There is nothing to be concerned about there," Sylvan said genially.

Don't say it. Don't say it.

"Mr. Salazar is gay. He is the stunt coordinator for the entire film. A very brave and accomplished gentleman is our Mr. Salazar, sir, I assure you."

Well that certainly brought the after-dinner conversation to an abrupt and uncomfortable halt. Good thing, too, as Teddy had no strength to force a single word past the lump of ice that had formed in his throat and threatened to strangle him to death.

"Shall we join the ladies?" The duke erupted from his chair and left the dining room without waiting to see if anyone followed.

Teddy found himself surrounded by his father's cronies and was swept into Rosemount's incredible Adam drawing room to be seated with them in a grouping of silk-uphol-stered armchairs and sofas near one of the marble fireplaces. The rest of the party, including the duke and Bas, had adjourned to the whist tables the servants had set up earlier.

"Have you really been living like this for months?" one of the hunting party asked. He gestured with his nearly full brandy glass at the various candlabras and oil lamps scat-tered about the room. Teddy wished Mrs. Wallace were there to see the bastard spill liquor on the duke's two-hundred-year-old Persian carpets.

"It's quite liberating once you become accustomed to it."

Teddy knew the instant someone repeated the after-dinner conversation to the ladies because they all turned to glare at the group in front of the fireplace. A group that included him. Bas continued to play cards and make Hadrian laugh. He never spared Teddy or the others a glance.

The conversation turned to politics and praise of his father's work in Parliament to save the nation from the various scourges and modernizations they all opposed. Teddy did his best to tune out their voices. Against his will, his gaze turned again and again to the whist tables, to the man who laughed and talked and pretended nothing was wrong. Pretended because, even after so short a time together, Teddy recognized the brittle edge to Bas's voice and the blankness of his eyes. Misery had a taste—bitter like a cup of tea gone cold. Sour like milk left out too long. He resisted the urge to scratch the stings of a thousand nettles that danced along his arms and around the place on his temple that Bas had last kissed.

"You've been around him all this while, Lord Staines, what do you think?" Major Something-or-Other's question snapped Teddy's attention back to his own companions.

"I'm sorry, Major. What do I think about what?"

"Well, I'm certain the ladies here have all found him attractive. I mean, look at him. What on earth would make a man built like that turn gay? Bloody curious, if you ask me."

"I…wouldn't really know, sir. I don't have much to do with any of them outside of working on the film." His throat burned, and his voice came out hoarse and thin, as if his body did not want to speak the words at all.

"What I find curious is that you've noticed how well-built our Mr. Salazar is. Major, is it?" Anna Chase delivered her observation in the most sacharine, exagerated tone Teddy had ever heard. She pinned the major with an expression of such innocence, Teddy had to cover his mouth to keep from laughing.

"What are you— How dare you insinuate that I— The bloody cheek of you. Whoever you are!" The major lurched to his feet, his face red, as he shouted across the room.

"*She*,"—Hadrian rose to his full height—"is the author of one of the bestselling novels in the world at the moment. A novel being made into a film by the top period filmmaker on the planet. *She* is also my fiancée. Who the flying fuck are you?" He would have crossed the room had Arneaux not grabbed his arm, and Bas hadn't gotten up and put himself between the critic and the group sitting with Teddy.

"Miss Witherspoon, a moment." The duke's expression never changed. In fact, he played his next card as Eleanor came to his side.

"You needn't worry, Major," Samantha said as she led her husband and Hadrian back to their seats and forced them to sit down. "You're not exactly Bas's type, is he Bas?"

The hunting party group broke into muttered conversation mixed with insults. The duke had a sudden coughing fit. Eleanor pounded him on the back while McGinty choked back a deep belly laugh. And Bas? This time he did look directly at the ridiculous men across the room. Then he turned his gaze directly on Teddy.

"No, Dr. Arneaux. Unfortunately, no one here at Rosemount Manor is my type."

Teddy closed his eyes against the icy hand that wrapped around his heart. When he opened them again, Eleanor had started across the room. Bas stopped her, and they talked for a moment. She shook her head several times, and Teddy could tell by her imperious expression she was ordering Bas to sit back down. However, Bas stood and watched as she approached Teddy's father's friends. They stood as one once she was close enough to speak to them.

"Gentlemen, it is quite late. If you will follow me, Mr. Urquhart is bringing the Land Rover around to take you to the hunting lodge."

"I beg your pardon?" Compton-Bowles said. "Young lady, by whose authority do you cast us out of this house in the middle of the night?"

"By mine." The Duke of Turra didn't deign to stand as he addressed them. "You have paid to rent the hunting lodge. Miss Witherspoon, do make certain they arrive safely. I assume everything is ready for them."

"Of course, Your Grace. Gentlemen?" Eleanor, resplendent in her blue satin Regency evening gown, glided to the drawing room doors, flung them open, and left the room without looking back to see if they followed.

Teddy stood. "I'll walk you out."

He seldom took on the arrogant personna of Viscount Staines. In fact he hated the entire idea. One glance at the group across the room, his friends, and he knew he needed to diffuse the situation. The duke still sat in his lord of the manor pose, but one more insult directed at Bas or another of the boot camp guests, and His Grace was fully capable of becoming one of his Scots ancestors—which was the last thing anyone needed.

Fortunately, the miffed MPs followed him out of the drawing room and down the stairs to the front doors. After some brief and perfunctory farewells, they climbed into the Land Rover and disappeared up the drive. Teddy wished his fears and the emptiness inside could leave with them. Abercrombie closed the doors, bowed to Teddy, and disappeared down the far corridor that led from the foyer into the service areas of the house.

"Well, that was interesting." Eleanor stood at the bottom

of the stairs, arms crossed and eyes fixed on Teddy. "Care to tell me what that was all about, *Lord Staines?*"

"My name is Teddy Rousseau, nothing more." Weariness had shortened his temper. A sense of dread sat in his stomach and threatened to rise up his throat.

"That remains to be seen." Eleanor led the way back up the staircase to the drawing room.

The whist party had continued. There was a momentary halt in the conversation once Teddy entered the room, but only until Sylvan asked Teddy to come and partner him for a hand or two. Bas was nowhere to be found. The duke had adjourned to one of a pair of chairs at the far end of the room. Eleanor crossed the blue-patterned carpets to take the chair next to his, and soon they were deep in quiet conversation.

"I certainly would not want to be privy to that discussion," Bella said quietly as she played a card.

"There are any number of conversations I would not want to be, what did you call it, *privy* to this evening." Danny cut a glance at Teddy, but went back to his cards when Samantha nudged his arm with her elbow.

The actor's anger he could take. Samantha's pity and understanding? He wanted to die. He wanted to run after Bas and try to explain.

He stayed.

In his mind, he went up those wide marble stairs and into Bas's room. His mind conjured every sort of scenario imaginable. None of them ended well. He continued to play whist, to force a pained smile at each of Sylvan's jokes, and at every accusation of cheating Hadrian tossed at Danny. His jaw ached. His temple throbbed with every beat of his heart. What the fuck had he—

"Well, I'm afraid your father's friends will not be invited back once their current stay is over," Eleanor announced as she came to stand next to Teddy's chair. "The duke has declared them, '*Ignorant Sassenach Tory bastards.*' If they hadn't already paid for their stay, they'd be on their way back to London as we speak."

"Ignorant." Danny handed his cards to Bella to put back into the Chinese lacquer box where they were kept. "Lot of that going around." He stood and offered Samantha his arm. "Shall we retire, *cher?*"

The drawing room emptied in a matter of minutes, except for Eleanor. She stood at the double doors and waited while Robbie and Dougal snuffed the candles and turned out the lamps. Teddy finally pushed out of his chair and headed for the doors. When he made to go around her, she grabbed his hand.

"Teddy, I'm sorry." The very last thing he expected the hard-nosed Miss Witherspoon to say. "If I had known...."

None of them had said a word, but they knew. Perhaps they had known for some time, but they'd never said a word —which made his behavior all the more shameful. And cowardly.

"It wasn't your fault, Eleanor. It was bound to happen sometime. I just...wasn't ready."

"Will you ever be?" There was no censure, no rancor in her question.

"That's the question now, isn't it?" He escorted her to the bottom of the stairs. "Good night, Eleanor."

"You're not coming?"

Teddy gazed up and tried to visualize what Bas might be doing at that very moment. Nothing came to mind. Perhaps because, on so many nights, Teddy didn't have to imagine at all, and the memories of those nights cut like knives now.

"No, I think I'll spend a little time in the conservatory. I'm not ready for...well...." He choked on a laugh. "Maybe I'll run into Elsbeth, and she'll put me out of my misery."

He strode down the corridor that ran toward the terrace, feeling Eleanor's gaze on him until he turned toward the conservatory's wide French doors. The glow of a hanging lamp next to a bench a few paces inside the glasshouse allowed him to find his way inside.

He'd spent a great deal of time in the duke's incredible *orangerie* to use the term Eleanor insisted upon on a daily basis. Teddy loved the quiet, the warmth and the serenity to be found in the company of the exotic plants. The view at night was breathtaking. So deep in the Highlands the stars shone in a clear black sky like diamonds on a field of velvet. A large raised koi pond at the far end of the room sent the soothing sound of rippling water into the air.

Then why the hell did he feel like he was dying?

Teddy sat on the little wall around the koi pond and had no idea how he'd walked the length of the intoxicating room without seeing a damned thing.

"I'm not going to be your dirty secret, and I'm not interested in a fuck buddy. Not at this stage in my life. I need to look for more."

He clutched his head in his hands. Tears would be nice. They burned behind his eyes like acid, but refused to fall. Why should they? The time for tears was the moment he'd denied Bas in front of people who didn't matter one damned whit. The moment Teddy had gasped at the thrust of the knife through his heart because Bas's heart was his now. The same way his heart belonged to Bas. All that bloody rot about love, the sort of love Anna Chase wrote about, was fucking true.

Not that any of that romantic rubbish could do him a bit of good now. He'd cocked it up good and proper. Just as he had at sixteen when his father caught him in bed with his best friend. Had it really been fifteen years? He'd accomplished two things in that time. He'd become England's foremost expert on swords and weaponry and hired himself out to the film industry to get even with his father, and he'd become a first-class liar and womanizer to get even with himself.

For what?

"Where are you, Elsbeth? Everyone else pities me. Add your pity, and the night will be fucking perfect."

He even raised his head and searched for her. Tried to detect the scent of lavender and heather. Apparently, even the Innes Witch had deserted him. Why wouldn't she? He'd deserted Bas. He'd deserted himself. The memory of the first duke's monument to Elsbeth flashed into his mind. Along with all the memories of that day.

"Everyone deserves to have a love like that, Teddy. Everyone."

Did Bas still believe that? Only one way to find out. Teddy stood and made his way along the winding stone path through the exotic foliage toward the doors into the house. As the pretty iron bench beneath a wisteria tree came into view, a lavender and heather scented breeze swept from behind him and rattled the French doors. Almost at the same moment, Teddy spied a battered, ancient-looking book on the bench. He picked up the fragile item, dropped onto the bench, and opened the cover. His vision swam, then adjusted to the florid quill-written script.

"Did you simply assume I can read Gaelic, Elsbeth, or...." His voice faded at the sound of faint laugher from somewhere in the conservatory. "Of course you did, you interfering old b—" He glanced around. "Banshee." A branch of wisteria slapped him gently in the face. "Sorry."

His Gaelic was rusty but serviceable. As many of the first manuals and treatises on swords and swordplay were originally written in Gaelic, the language seemed a sensible one for him to learn. Not that he'd made mention of his knowledge since his arrival at Rosemount. One overheard a great deal of helpful information when people assumed you didn't speak the language.

He labored through the first few pages before his mind settled into *Gaelic mode* as he called it. Understanding slowly dawned the further he read.

"Where did you find this, sweetheart?" he whispered. "Oh…my God."

The Duke of Turra's journal. The first duke. And a very specific journal. The entries began a week after Elsbeth had been tied to a chair and dropped into the loch on the order of the duke's mother. If she sank she was innocent. If she had floated, they'd have pulled her from the loch and burned her as a witch. Teddy understood completely the farce of a no-win situation. But the dowager duchess got what she wanted. She'd locked her son in that tower until there was no chance his love's body might be found.

Or so she thought.

Teddy read on, entry after entry, as the formidable Scots warrior grieved and ventured out onto the loch day after day no matter the weather in search of his beloved. As the entries and days continued, the duke's words grew more frantic, more disjointed. Search became obsession—as if finding her body might bring her back. Or perhaps he simply couldn't bear the thought of not knowing where she was, of not being able to be near her in any way he could.

The warmth of the conservatory, the silence, and the eerie illumination of the lamp and the stars created a place around him where time no longer existed. He sank into the mind and space where the duke searched desperately for Elsbeth during the day and mourned her absence like a wounded animal at night. Page after page, Teddy read until….

The only thing worse than searching for Elsbeth was finding Elsbeth. Still tied to a chair, her clothes in tatters and her body the source of such agony it made Teddy gasp to read the words. After that? Nothing. There were no more words to read. Then again, he didn't need the words. Everything the duke had to say after that had stood on an island in the loch for over seven hundred years.

He closed the book and dragged a hand across his face to wipe away the tears. "I'm sorry, Elsbeth. So very sorry."

A hand brushed his hair, but when he looked up, no one was there. He struggled to his feet, then strode toward the glass doors. For a split second, he saw the lady from the portrait reflected in the glass. She stared at him with such sorrow, so real and so profound.

"What do I do now? I've lost him, and I don't know what to do."

The image faded until all that was left were those luminous eyes filled with the pity of understanding. He ran up the stairs to the first floor landing and turned to head up to the next floor. A light under the door of the duke's study caught his eye. He squeezed the volume in his hand. He fought with himself—upstairs to try and speak with Bas or to the study to offer the duke…what? A chance for something Teddy had lost through his own cowardice.

He squared his shoulders and went to the study door where he knocked once and stepped inside without waiting for permission. He strode to the desk behind which a rather bemused duke sat and studied him as though he were some kind of insect.

"You need to read this." Teddy placed the journal on top of the papers scattered across the vast desk. "Then maybe you'll allow that the utterly impossible may well be possible. Do try not to cock it up as I have, Your Grace." He turned to go.

"What the hell is this? Where did you find it?"

"Elsbeth gave it to me." He opened the door and took one step into the corridor.

"Wait a bloody minute, Rousseau. You can't just walk in here and say something like that. Where are you going?"

"To bed, in the hope I will have come to my senses when I wake up in the morning."

"To your senses? What might that mean?"

"I haven't the faintest fucking notion, Your Grace. Goodnight." He closed the door behind him and didn't look back.

Once he reached his chamber, he shed his Regency evening clothes and dragged on one of the heavy velvet banyans in his boot camp wardrobe. He stood in the middle of the room as it seemed to spin around him. Every inch, every corner held memories of him and Bas.

As if he wore lead boots, he walked to the door to the dressing room between their rooms. To his surprise, the door opened easily. Light shone around the doorframe at the other side of the dressing room. He had no idea what time it was. Well after midnight at the very least. Was Bas waiting up for him? Once Teddy reached the door into Bas's room, he took a moment to decide. Knock or walk right in? The decision was made for him. He lifted the latch and pushed. The door was locked. The spot where they'd taken to hanging their keys was empty. He knocked.

"Bas? Can I come in?" He took a deep breath. "Please."

The door remained closed, but Teddy imagined Bas leaning against it, when he said, "What for?"

"For some late-night saber training. What the hell do you think for?" He had no right to be angry. Didn't stop him.

"Kind of a waste of time, don't you think? You said everything I needed to hear this afternoon." He paused so long. Perhaps....

"Good night, Teddy."

Chapter Sixteen

ROBBIE WALLACE HAD TO BE THE MOST ANNOYING PERSON BAS had ever met—which was saying *a lot*. What annoyed him the most? The footman had a supernatural ability to stare a man down and make him feel guilty without saying a word. Guilty for what? Bas had no fucking clue.

"Bas, can I come in?"

"Please."

Not his fault. He'd let Teddy in, into his heart and into his bed. No matter what Teddy had intended to say, the ending would have been the same. Bas had seen enough sad stories. He'd lived enough sad stories. This one? Not going there. He glanced up. Robbie continued to fuss over the breakfast tray he'd brought to the room. How he did it without actually looking at the tray was beyond Bas. They'd been doing this little dance for over a week now, and the footman showed no sign of giving up the silent, obedient servant routine.

Asshole.

"Miss Witherspoon asked me to tell you—"

"Wait." Bas put down his porcelain teacup filled with

strong black coffee, he'd had to bribe Robbie to acquire. "It speaks. Let me mark this down in my calendar."

Robbie rolled his eyes and refilled the cup from the silver coffee pot he'd placed on the tea table where Bas had started eating his breakfast every morning.

"If you hadn't quit her Regency experience, you might have avoided receiving messages by way of a lowly footman."

"Lowly footman my left nut. What's the message?"

Robbie grinned. "She said you are welcome to breakfast with the rest of the guests even if you no longer wish to participate in the boot camp."

"Yeah…no. No thanks. I like eating my breakfast in my room. I don't have to get dressed, and I don't have to deal with…things." He waved his hand absently and went back to his eggs and bacon.

"Not to mention having the electricity turned on in your room, no uncomfortable clothes, and you have access to the mod-cons of your electronics and indoor plumbing."

Bas laughed. "There is that."

He slathered raspberry jam on his toast. He glanced toward the now unlocked door that led to the room's private bathroom. The first day, he'd showered three times—and only fantasized about Teddy being in there with him twice.

"Which begs the question, sir." Robbie scanned the room. "Why are you still using lamps and candles instead of turning on the lights?"

Bas shrugged. "I've gotten used to it, I guess."

"But not the chamber pot."

"Hell, no!" He realized Robbie wasn't laughing any longer. Just watching him in that serious Scots way of his. "What is it, Robbie? You're not hanging around here for the pleasure of my company."

"Isn't that the damned truth." Danny leaned against the door jamb of the open door into the corridor, decked in his

Regency finest and grinning like the sarcastic Cajun pest he was. "Everyone's talking about the giant barrel of laughs you've been lately, Stuntman. I'm surprised someone hasn't paid Robbie here to smother you in your sleep."

"The offer's been made." Robbie placed a kilt and a black t-shirt on the bed. "Haven't met my price yet. Good luck, sir." This last was directed at Arneaux as the footman went out the door and closed it.

"I thought they turned your lights on when you flunked out of boot camp." Danny threw himself into the chair opposite Bas's and grabbed a handful of bacon.

"I didn't flunk out. I wasn't ever officially *in* boot camp." Bas grabbed the second teacup on the tray—interesting how it magically appeared this morning when it never had before —and filled it with coffee before he handed to his breakfast intruder. "Besides, it's over at the end of this month. That's what, a week or so from now?"

"Doesn't matter. You bailed. Ditched us for a private bathroom and electric lights you aren't even using. And coffee. Man, this is good coffee. For Scotland, at least."

"It's ambrosia compared to that stuff you had me drinking in Louisiana. I'm still missing layers of my stomach lining."

"That's not all you're missing." Danny grabbed the pot and refilled his cup.

"Don't want to talk about it." Bas stuffed his mouth with a forkful of fried potatoes.

"It or him?" Danny snatched a piece of toast from the silver toast rack and coated it in butter and jam.

Bas reached across and tucked a linen napkin into Danny's collar, taking great care to nearly strangle him. "Wouldn't want you to get a demerit in personal appearance from Miss Witherspoon. And my personal life is just that. Personal."

"'Fraid not, Mr. Salazar. Not when your personal life is making you a pain in the ass to everyone on the estate."

"What the hell are you talking about? I hardly ever see most of the people here." His neck began to itch, right at the base of his skull. Never a good sign.

"That's part of the problem. Most of us miss you, especially the ladies. Your crew wishes you'd fall off a bridge somewhere because you're as short-tempered as a gut-shot gator. And those of us in Teddy's weapons classes are tired of getting the shit beat out of us because he's even testier than you are. Oh, and that bit about boot camp being over in a few days? Not so much. Wentworth wants us to keep living Regency style until the film is done."

"He wants *you* to live Regency style. I don't have to. All I have to do is map out the stunt shots and make sure nobody breaks their neck."

"And for that you're still wearing a kilt?" Danny nodded at the clothes so carefully displayed on Bas's bed.

"I like wearing it, and it makes it easier to choreograph the stunts." He did his best to bite his tongue, but that instrument had a mind of its own. "Why is Teddy beating you up?"

"Because he's an arrogant prick? Because he's working himself into exhaustion so he'll sleep better? Because you're not speaking to him?" Danny cut his eyes away from the second piece of toast he'd filched from the rack and pinned Bas with a speculative gaze. "Pick one. Or all three."

Bas finished off his coffee and got up to change into his clothes for the day. He had to move or he'd scream. He didn't need to hear any of this. He wanted to get his job done and get the hell out of Scotland. Not that leaving would heal the big-assed hole in his heart. That would take time and distance. A lot of it. He shucked off his robe, then wrapped his kilt around his waist.

"Not my problem, Arneaux. Teddy has always been arrogant. His sleeping arrangements are none of my concern. And I do speak to him when my job calls for it. We have very civil conversations. When I see him. Which isn't too often."

Arneaux began to mumble with his mouth full. Didn't matter, as he was mumbling in Cajun. Bas still got the gist of what Danny was saying as the words *stubborn* and *idiots* and *both of you connards* made it through.

Bas dropped onto the bed to pull on his socks and soft leather Highland boots. "Say what you want. Teddy and I are being very civil and very—"

"Stupid. Being civil is overrated but do what you want. Spend all your time with your crew and in this room. He can spend all his time at that bloody forge or lurking around the conservatory waiting for the ghost to show up." Danny slurped back one last cup of coffee and grabbed one more slice of bacon. "But you two being civil is making the rest of us miserable. Just a friendly FYI." He sauntered to the door.

"What forge?"

"'Scuse me?" The damned fool stood in the open door and grinned over his shoulder at Bas.

"Where is the forge, and why is Teddy spending so much time there?" The words came out in such a rush even Bas wasn't sure of what he'd said.

"Out past Lily and Lachlan's cottage. The swords Wentworth had made didn't meet Teddy's specifications. He's helping the estate's blacksmith forge new ones. Want me to ride out there with you?"

"Who said anything about me going out there?" He grabbed his computer bag, strode to the door, then shoved Arneaux out into the hallway and closed the bedroom door.

"Whatever, man. It's your life." They walked all the way down to the entrance hall together. Danny went toward the front door but stopped when Bas started toward the back of the house. "Where are you going, Salazar?"

"To meet my crew and get to work. Later, Regency Boy."

Bas put one foot deliberately in front of the other until he crossed the formal gardens and headed down the path to the castle ruins. He couldn't resist a glance up at the top of the tower but quickly turned his attention to the Land Rovers and various equipment tables set up on the other side of what was left of the first duke's fortress. Too bad the poor guy didn't realize his most dangerous enemy was inside the walls.

"But if you lost someone you loved like that, would you ever stop looking for them?"

Those words rolled around in his head for hours, all while he instructed his crew and walked them through the various stunt action sequences and tried his best to keep his tone upbeat and even. He didn't snap at them once, not even when they screwed something up royally, which meant he overcompensated because they still stared at him when they thought he wasn't looking.

Filming would go on for months, and as he'd stepped away from the actual boot camp, maybe he needed to move into the hotel in the village with the rest of his stunt unit. However, being on site was more convenient. That was what he told himself. Better for his work. Yeah. Right.

"What do you think, boss?" Mike studied him expectantly.

Once Bas pulled out of his head, he saw that the entire crew stared at him as if he was about to say something vitally important, which meant only one thing.

"I think you poor flowers are wilting in this heat and want to run to the pub for some lunch and a beer or six. Have your asses back here in a couple of hours. We've still got plentyof daylight to work with."

A noisy collection of whoops and smart remarks ensued, but the crew wasted little time securing everything and piling into the Land Rovers.

"Coming with, boss?" Mike asked.

Bas shook his head. "I've got to check on one more thing and then I'll go up to the house for lunch."

"Yeah. I hear they bring your meals to your room on a tray like you're some kind of big shot."

"Well, at least somebody recognizes my place in the world." Bas punched the older man's shoulder, waved at the departing vehicles, and started to walk away.

"Hey, Bas? You okay?"

Bas fixed a smile on his face and turned to face his friend. "Yeah, Mike, I'm fine. See you after lunch. Don't let them get into any trouble."

He nearly turned back several times as he left the main path and cut across to where a narrow lane led to Laclan and Lily's cottage and beyond. When she was at the main house, Lily dressed in her Regency gear and did everything according to Eleanor's rules. He'd visited the newly married couple in their simple country home, and there Lily dressed in the clothes of a Scotswoman of two hundred years ago. But she had access to all of Lachlan's electronic devices too. That was what happened when you married a duke's brother.

And Teddy was an earl's son.

You sure as hell know how to pick 'em, Bas.

Once he passed the cottage, he had to walk a good distance around a curve in the narrow cobblestone lane and up a hill before the steady clang of a hammer on metal echoed in the Highland stillness. A long, low, stone building stood at the top of the hill. A wide chimney belched smoked into the blue Highland sky. For some reason, he felt the need to creep silently along the back of the building to the far end of the forge. In addition to the sound of the roaring fire, the bellows, and the ring of a hammer on metal, several voices mixed in conversation and instruction. So intense was the concentration of the men at the ancient art, Bas walked quietly into a spot where he had a view of the entire scene—which revealed a couple of startling pieces of information.

The first? Teddy in a kilt and boots and nothing else but the glisten of sweat on his chest and arms had the power to pretty much short-circuit Bas's brain no matter how mad he was at the man. Every inch of muscle in Teddy's torso, biceps, and forearms rippled like fine silk as he swung the hefty hammer over and over against the blade across the anvil. His hair fell around his shoulders and covered his face. Bas nearly swallowed his tongue. He adjusted the sporan Robbie had brought him a few days ago because he said the kilt looked naked without one. His body hurt. His lungs squeezed against breathing. His heart couldn't find a rhythm to beat.

The next surprise caught him gawking. McGinty, the duke's steward, stood in his shirtsleeves and kilt and worked the bellows as he pointed out flaws for Teddy to beat out as he worked.

McGinty spotted Bas and nodded in acknowledgement without saying a word. Bas recognized one of the guys from the stables, and the footman, Dougal, who, out of uniform and dressed like McGinty in *Scots casual*, or at least what Bas assumed was Scots casual, tended the fire and watched everything McGinty and Teddy did. When Dougal glanced up and saw Bas, he gave a little wave.

Teddy straightened and slowly faced Bas before he put down the hammer and caught the piece of toweling McGinty tossed him. "I didn't know you knew where the forge was. Is there something we can help you with?"

Well, fuck! Professional Teddy was back and in top form. Just as well. Bas tightened every muscle to keep from rubbing the spot on his solar plexus where every regret he'd ever had had just taken up residence.

"Yeah. I need to ask you about the swords you're making.

My guys have been training with yours and now Wentworth's. I need to ask you a few things about these new ones."

He inwardly winced at the bullshit he'd just spewed and headed to where a massive ash tree stood at the crest of the hill. The heavy leaves and first flower blossoms would give them a little privacy. By the time Teddy caught up, he'd toweled off and dragged his shirt on, though it still clung to his body in places.

"The swords Wentworth sent are rubbish," Teddy began. "They won't last the whole film shoot and they'll look like shit onscreen. Not to mention, they'll handle so badly someone will get hurt." Teddy crossed his arms over his chest. "We'll have them ready in a week or so, and I'll work with your people to—"

"The swords will be perfect." Bas swallowed his impatience and his pride. "I know that. That isn't what I wanted to talk about."

"I see."

The man was a master at looking as if he could give two fucks. Years of practice probably—which struck Bas as really sad. Teddy obviously wanted this over with, and suddenly so did Bas.

"I shouldn't have pushed you. You weren't ready, and I had no right. I'm sorry. Whatever happened between us, there's blame on both sides."

"Oh, really?"

"Yes. I'm owning mine. You don't have to own yours if you don't want to." He ran his hand over his head and tried hard to breathe evenly.

"This truly isn't necessary, Bas. I can't—" Teddy took a step closer. "I can't explain why I did what I did. And I want to promise you it won't ever happen again, but...."

"You can't. I get that." He shook his head. "Well, no, I don't, but I don't have to get it. It's okay. No harm, no foul."

"I don't think that's true. For either of us." He reached out and squeezed Bas's forearm. "I wish…."

"What is it you told me? *If wishes were horses…*" Bas smiled despite himself.

"*Then beggars would ride.*"

"Yeah. I'm going back to the house. If I sneak into the kitchen, maybe Mrs. Gordon will whip up a burger and fries for my lunch."

"Don't let Eleanor catch her doing that."

"For real." He drew in the scent of the flowering ash tree. A warm breeze stirred Teddy's hair away from his face. Bas wanted to touch him. He didn't dare. "See you."

He turned and took in the view of green fields and blue sky like something out of a painting. When he looked back at Teddy in his Highland clothes, feet planted apart and thick arms crossed, something inside Bas began to tear like stitches nearly healed and now broken.

"I meant every word I ever said to you, Teddy Rousseau. Remember that. I hope you find someone. Someone who will make you never want to lie about who you are again. I do."

He faced forward again, then hiked down the hill and kept walking until Rosemount Manor came into view. When he slipped into the back door of the house's massive kitchen, Mrs. Gordon took one look at him and shoved him onto a wooden bench at one of the long work tables. She retrieved a bottle of Tennet's from a bucket of ice and took off the top with an old-fashioned bottle opener.

"Burger and fries?" she asked in her thick Scottish brogue as she handed him the bottle, then wiped her hands on her apron.

"Aye." Bas blinked a few times, then took a long swig of the beer.

WELL AFTER MIDNIGHT, AND TEDDY STILL HAD NO DESIRE TO climb the stairs to his nice comfortable, albeit primitive by most standards, bedchamber. Dinner had been pleasant enough, and he'd won handily at whist with Lily as his partner. He'd abandoned the conservatory after an hour or so. The damned iron benches, while pretty and appropriate for the vast glasshouse, didn't help his aching body. Working in the forge kept his mind off other things and usually tired him out enough that he wanted to crawl into bed and fall fast asleep. Not tonight. Not after he'd so utterly botched his latest encounter with Bas.

The moment Teddy saw him standing outside the forge, Teddy's heart had nearly jumped out of his chest. For a single moment, he'd hoped Bas had forgiven him and wanted to start over. That wasn't the case, at least, not once Teddy wrapped himself in his stodgy Brit cloak and gone all defensive on the man. Bas didn't deal well with defensive. He shut down. Teddy knew that, and yet he'd persisted. The big Basque didn't pick fights. He walked away—which really pissed Teddy off sometimes. He'd wanted Bas to fight for them. Despite Bas's promise, he'd decided Teddy wasn't worth the fight.

Apparently, even Elsbeth had given up on him. He'd waited in the duke's orangerie every night since his father's friends had headed off to the hunting lodge. Since that first night when she'd left the first duke's journal for him, he'd neither seen nor sensed her presence. He had, however, endured some rather pointed glances from the present duke. Had he read his ancestor's diary? Damned if Teddy could tell.

He leaned forward in the comfortable armchair in front of one of the library fireplaces and poked at the fire to stir life into the embers. May or not, the nights tended to be cold in the Highlands. The room was so large and the ceilings so high, he imagined the cold remained at night well into summer.

"Hadrian said I would find you here. Teddy, do you have any idea what time it is?"

He leaped to his feet to face Anna Chase. She was wrapped in a full length heavy men's banyan, strolled across the library, her felt mules shushing on the antique carpets. The hem of what was likely a plain cotton nightgown peeked out from beneath her the robe.

"Do you, soon-to-be Mrs. Cross? Come and sit by the fire before you catch your death. Wait. How did Hadrian know I'd be here?"

She settled into the chair and fussed with her robe so it covered her feet. "It's what he does. He watches people."

"I see. Does he know you're down here with me?"

He pulled the glass stopper on the decanter of the duke's best brandy he'd filched from the sideboard in the dining room and refilled the glass on the marquetry table next to his chair. He picked up a second glass, filled it, and offered it to Anna.

She took the glass in both hands and, after a long, dainty sip, fixed him with that all too discerning gaze of hers. "What happened, Teddy?"

"Beg pardon?"

She rolled her eyes and made a rude derisive noise. "Between you and Bas. What happened?"

"Bloody hell." He set his now empty glass on the hearth so hard he was surprised he didn't break it. "Is nothing private here?"

"You're attending a long Regency house party, Mr. Rousseau. You're lucky it isn't on the front page of the *Times*. Or being sold on a scandal sheet in the streets of London for a penny."

"Very funny. You want the short answer?"

"By all means."

"I fucked it up."

"Well." She took another sip of the brandy. "That *is* short. Care to elaborate?"

"I figured the others would have told you by now."

"Oh, we saw most of it. I guess what I'm asking is why. Why did you do it, Teddy? I'm an expert on the subject, and not for nothing, but Bas truly cares for you. And I think you care for him."

"My feelings for him are…complicated. His for me? After today, I'd say I am definitely on his *cut direct* list."

"You didn't see him peek in the door tonight after dinner. He watched you play cards for half an hour."

"Please. I can assure you Bas Salazar doesn't give a damn about me. He was likely bored or trying to signal Arneaux to join him for a beer."

"If he didn't give a damn, he'd have come busting up in here in his jeans and t-shirt just to see the look on Eleanor's face."

Teddy had to laugh. Everything came at him in a rush. Eleanor. The duke. Elsbeth lying all alone in that beautiful monument—the last gift he could give her, a place to spend eternity. Bas saying he loved Teddy in such an offhand way as if it wasn't news. As if it was as normal and common as a remark on the weather. Was that love? As ordinary and easy as a spring day or a row across a loch?

"Are you okay?" Her voice drifted to him on a wave of silence with the faintest noise of the crackling fire as counterpoint. In the vastness of the dimly lit library, he might not have heard her if he hadn't been listening so attentively for something, anything to take his mind off Bas and the idea of an eternity without him.

"I didn't mean it. I didn't. I…reacted. Like the coward I

am, and now I've lost him. So fucking stupid." He held his head in his hands and wished she'd leave so he could wallow in his misery alone.

"Do you love him?"

"Yes, dammit, and it's a bloody nuisance."

"Would you do anything to prove it to him?"

When Teddy raised his head to check her expression, he froze. Her raised eyebrows denoted speculation. Her smile, however, bore an uncanny resemblance to the one Elsbeth gave him every time she popped in to haunt him. That sad sort of, *you-poor-bumbling-fool* smile.

"What?" He tried to sound confused rather than hopeful, but had no idea whether he'd pulled it off or not.

"What would you do to win him back, Teddy? Or is that sort of thing beneath you?"

He stared at her. Even when she got up, put her brandy glass on the little table, and started to turn, he stared at her.

"Maybe it's better this way. Bas needs someone who isn't going to bail on him at the first sign of trouble. Good night, Teddy."

"Wait." He leaped to his feet, and spun to face him. "Anna, wait. What...I mean, is there anything I *can* do? I mean—Whoa!"

Suddenly the petite author shoved him back into his chair. She strode into the darkened recesses of the library behind him. This was madness. He was desperate and drunk and...mad as a damned hatter.

"Anna?" He twisted in the chair and craned his neck to try and see what she was doing. "This is silly. Why don't you...."

She reappeared out of the darkness with a stack of paperback books in her arms, which she unceremoniously dumped in his lap. She pulled a leather ottoman close to his chair and plucked one of the books from the stack. With no trouble at all, she flipped to a passage toward the end of the book.

"Read," she ordered.

Discretion being the better part of valor, he did as he was told. He'd no sooner finished that passage than she snatched the book away and handed him another, also opened to a specific passage. Even without having read what came before, he realized these were romance novels, and the guy in the novel had fucked up in a big way. When she went to hand him the third one, he flipped it over to see the cover.

"You wrote this." He pawed through the other books. "You wrote all of these."

"Guilty as charged. You want to know how to apologize to Bas? How to convince him that you love him enough to fight for what you might have together?"

Teddy refrained from rolling his eyes. "Now you sound like a romance writer."

"I *am* a romance writer, smart ass. I am also the only hope in hell you have of becoming the hero of your own romance."

"Good God." He closed the book he'd just read. "I can't do this. Whatever this is. Real life is not a romance novel." The little bit of hope he'd felt vanished like Highland mist.

"This"—she slapped another open book into his hands—"is called *the grand gesture*, and it has worked for romance heroes since Anthony handed Egypt to Cleopatra. The only reason life isn't like a romance novel is because most people don't think they deserve that kind of happiness. So they aren't willing to work for it. What about you, Teddy? Are you willing to work for it? Or have you decided you don't deserve it?"

Damn, Anna Chase sounded like Dirty Harry when she talked about romance. No wonder Cross was crazy about her.

"Well?" She lifted a brow.

"I don't deserve it, dammit," he blurted. "I proved that when I insulted Bas in front of my father's friends."

He wanted to go to bed for at least six weeks. He wanted never to have come to Wentworth's little Regency boot camp. He'd landed in a damned romance novel and couldn't get out.

"What about Bas? What does he deserve?"

Teddy hesitated. "Someone better than me."

"Careful, Teddy. Your self-pity is showing. I guess I'm wasting my time." She started to get up, then halted when he picked up one of the books in his lap. "He loves you, Teddy, and you need to give him the chance to decide what he deserves."

All the ways this might end badly, painfully badly for him, went through his mind. Without really thinking, he handed the book to her. "The grand gesture." He met her smiling, triumphant gaze. "This is going to be really embarrassing, isn't it?"

"All the best grand gestures always are." She opened the book and handed it back to him. "Keep reading."

Chapter Seventeen

BAS HAD BEEN SO BUSY WITH HIS STUNT CREW THE PAST TWO
days he hadn't had a moment to think about his last
encounter with Teddy. *Bullshit.* Every single word from that
last conversation on the hill beyond the forge pounded at his
brain each time he let down his guard—which was at least
ten times a day and even more often the last two nights. He
didn't need the distraction. Not with the stunts they were
working on tomorrow. That was why he sat in the middle of
the maze at the center of the duke's back gardens. Hiding.
From what? Who the hell knew. He damned sure couldn't sit
here forever. The stone bench, in addition to being cold as
one of the blocks of ice in Mrs. Gordon's ice house, was hard
as a damned rock. Talk about a ball buster.

"That's Lady Ballbuster to you, Mister Stuntmaster." Lily
dropped down onto the bench next to him. "And yes, you did
say that out loud."

"I was talking about the bench."

"I see. And to whom were you talking?"

"Myself."

"Always said you *jump-out-of-moving-car* types were

missing a few screws. Talking to yourself is never a good sign."

"A good sign of what?" Bas braced his hands on the back of the bench and tilted his head to catch the last warm rays of the setting sun. The sensation evoked a memory of him and Teddy lying in the sun in the clearing before Elsbeth's mausoleum. A soft breeze ruffled the leaves of the hedges of the maze, and Bas pulled the air into his lungs and impossibly caught the scent of Teddy's skin that day, the scent of sweat and cologne and sex. But there was more. The sensation of hands on his body, and the glow of passion and something he'd thought was love in Teddy's eyes.

"A good sign you're not over him," Lily said. "That you might not ever be."

"Thank God you're a great actress because you *suck* at being a psychiatrist."

She patted him on the leg. "Do you need a psychiatrist?"

"I need to have my head examined. Yes. I managed to fall in love with the most unavailable, confused gay man on the planet. Then, when he pretty much told me to go to hell, I went there."

"To hell?"

"That's where I am now, sweetheart. And I'm stuck here until this film is over."

"Poor Bas." She slung her arm around his shoulders.

The sky had gone purple and gold in the distance. *Boom!* They jumped in unison. The sound had come from somewhere in the hills beyond the front of the main house. *Boom!*

"What the hell is that?" Bas stood and turned from side to side to get a bead on where the noise came from.

"Gunfire. The damned Sassenach politicians are at it again. They aren't supposed to be this close, dammit." Lily stood and started toward the back terrace.

"Where's your husband?" Bas followed her up the steps and through the French doors into the back of the manor.

"I don't know." Lily clutched the skirts of her Regency gown in one hand and clasped her other fist to the middle of her chest. "Eleanor. Eleanor where's Lachlan?"

Eleanor had just burst out of the downstairs drawing room, followed by Samantha, Anna, and Bella. "I don't know. He isn't with you?"

"Does it look like he's with me? Would I be this upset if he was with me? You should have tossed those Brits out on their asses when Knox said so. They've caused nothing but trouble since they arrived."

"Language, Lady Lachlan."

"Fuck my language." Lily started up the stairs.

Bas held a halting hand out to Eleanor and caught Lily in two steps. "Hey, Lily. Calm down. He's probably already back at home waiting for you. I'll walk you there to check on him." He took her hand and squeezed.

"Thank you, Salazar." The duke's voice drifted down from the first floor balustrade. "That is an excellent idea. Lachlan was here earlier, Lily, but he left over an hour ago to stop by the mews and then he was for home. Miss Witherspoon?"

Bas crossed the entrance hall and mouthed *Good luck* to Eleanor as he did.

"They're leaving in the morning, Your Grace," the boot camp director snapped. "I am not coming up there for you to dress me down this time. We're planning Hadrian and Anna's wedding."

Bas and Lily made it to the corner of the house before they cracked up.

"I cannot *believe* she said that to him," Bas said once they'd stopped laughing.

"It's about time. Eleanor is a pain, but he is awful to her. I thought reading the first duke's journal would soften him, but—"

"What journal? When did this happen?" He offered her his arm as they cut through the stableyard and headed up the cobblestone lane toward her and Lachlan's cottage. The insects began to sing, and the first stars winked their way past the darkening sky. The air held a slight chill.

"Teddy didn't tell you?"

It wasn't so dark yet that she could possibly miss the *really, bitch* look her gave her.

"Apparently, Elsbeth left it in the conservatory for Teddy. He read it, then took it to Knox and told him to read it."

"Did Teddy tell him the rest of it? About the mausoleum and the island and the painting in the tower?"

"No. We're all waiting for those Brits to leave before we do that. By *we*, I mean you and Teddy. You found the painting and the mausoleum so...."

"There's no me and Teddy. Remember?" One day he'd be able to say that without his throat tightening.

They didn't talk much the rest of the way to the cottage. Lachlan and his scrap of a dog greeted them at the gate. Lily invited him in, but Bas saw the shadow of PTSD on the duke's brother's face. The man needed time alone with his wife. Besides, a walk in the night air along the banks of the loch sounded like a great idea. Anything to avoid running into the boot camp guests as they got dressed for dinner. He wasn't all that hungry, but he'd stop by the kitchens and snag a sandwich and maybe a dish of cranachan when Mrs. Gordon wasn't looking. He didn't feel like dealing with Robbie or Dougal if they had to bring him a tray. He always found it easier to narrow his focus and clear his mind when he didn't have to deal with other people.

That was probably why he took the long way back to

Rosemount Manor. The steady lap of the water against the shore drew his attention to the loch. The view stopped him in his tracks. Night had fallen, and the loch's surface was a mirror of black that undulated with the water's back and forth flow under the conduction of the wind. The entire expanse glittered with the stars reflected in the water, and when he rounded the corner, the light from the moon appeared to lay a carpet of white through the field of stars.

"Ederra," he murmured as he moved off the path and closer to the edge of the shore.

For a second he contemplated the possibility of stepping onto the silver path and walking across the lake. Boy, the last few weeks had turned him into a real ball of romantic mush. Not a good look on someone like him. The faint music of feminine laughter drifted toward him from across the lock, followed by the sweet scent of lavender, heather, and fresh earth. Bas propped his ass against one of the huge boulders at the water's edge.

"Go ahead and laugh, Elsbeth. I live to entertain." His bitter tone bothered him. Talking to a ghost, when he didn't really believe in ghosts, didn't bother him as much as the idea he'd hurt her feelings. *I am losing my mind.* "You can laugh if you want to. You've earned the right after what they put your through."

A sultry, soft, lavender blanket of wind wrapped around him. The breeze ruffled his hair. At least he thought the breeze did it. Admitting to the existence of ghosts was one thing. Having one touch him? Something else entirely. He searched across the expanse of darkness and tried to bring the hidden island into view. He'd broken so many of his rules on that island. Rules he'd set to keep himself safe because, dammit, life owed him that much. Rules he'd swept aside. For Teddy.

What did we learn, nire semea?

After a rough childhood and some rocky teenaged years, Bas and his father had made peace with each other. His father's love had overcome the macho attitudes of his ancestors. Hearing *his aita's* voice in his head set up an ache in his heart. For his family. For what he thought he'd found. For the man he'd thought—

"What the hell?" He blinked several times.

Farther up the shore she stood, dressed in white so ethereal he saw the exquisite beauty of her golden brown skin and the fiery glow of her red hair as plain as if she stood in daylight. He pushed off the rock and started toward her, his steps slow, then hesitant. Her expression stopped him once he was almost close enough to touch her. Such sadness. And pity. For him? Why?

She shook her head.

You know why, mozolo.

"You're right, Elsbeth. But there is nothing I can do about it anymore."

The air around him grew bitter cold. So cold he had trouble catching his breath. As cold as…the grave. A wave of such loneliness swept over him his thoughts went dark and blank. The spectre of the Innes Witch gave him one last look, then started across the loch. The train of her dress floated across the waves as she walked on the water as if it were the parquet floor of Rosemount Manor's entrance hall. She never turned back. A mist had risen on the water. He hadn't noticed it before but did now because the beautiful woman, tortured to death seven hundred years ago, disappeared into the gray-white clouds stretched over the star-touched loch. Did she return to her lonely resting place?

He shivered and returned to the path. Suddenly, he had a real urge to get to the house and sit in front of the fire in his room. Electric heat might be more efficient, but Bas was pretty sure he needed a real roaring fire to pull the chill from his bones right then. He lengthened his stride and told himself over and over again not to look back. Elsbeth had a message for him. He wished she'd been a little clearer on exactly what that message was.

The back of Rosemount Manor showed not a single light in the windows thanks to Eleanor's boot camp rules, except for one. The glow of an oil lamp shone in one bedchamber window and illuminated the figure who gazed directly at him. He should be getting ready for dinner, not tracking Bas's progress up the cobblestone lane that led to the stables. Bas fixed his gaze on Teddy's bedroom window until he passed far enough down the lane his view was of the side of the manor, not the back. How long had Teddy watched for him? And why?

Figure that out when you get to your room.

He'd ask Robbie to bring him a tray after all. He didn't want to chance running into anyone. Not tonight. He hurried up to the front door and stepped into the foyer.

"Hello, Bas." Teddy's voices echoed in the foyer where the ceiling was at the very top of the however many floors the house had. He stood at the top of the landing, Bas in the middle of the elegant entrance hall. They might as well have been on different continents.

"Teddy. Shouldn't you be getting ready for dinner?" He slowly curled his fingers into his palm to stop the weird rhythm of his heart.

"Not really hungry. Are you going to dinner tonight?"

"No. I'll have Robbie or Dougal bring me something. I've got some work to do before tomorrow."

"You're doing sword fights and falls from the old ruins tomorrow, aren't you? Arneaux mentioned it."

"Yeah. I've got to make him look heroic without breaking his neck."

Teddy smiled. "Good luck with that."

Silence. Long and painful and a real pain in the ass. That type of silence made people blurt out things they didn't always want to say.

"Did you see her? When you were looking out your window. Did you see Elsbeth?"

"Yes." Teddy glanced around as if he expected the duke to pop out of the woodwork. Or maybe Elsbeth herself. "Did she say anything to you?"

"No. I think she felt sorry for me. But she didn't speak."

Teddy laughed a short little laugh with no real happiness. "Eleanor told me you walked Lily home. I was… worried."

Dear God, his gray eyes shone like polished marble. What was he thinking? What was he trying to say?

"I came around the loch. Took longer than I thought."

"Yes. Well." Teddy appeared to give himself a sort of shake. "You're here now. Enjoy your dinner. Good night."

"Teddy."

Too late. The swordmaster practically ran up the stairs and disappeared from sight.

Bas dropped his head and studied the black and white pattern of the floor. He'd move to the village tomorrow. This shit was too damned hard to deal with, and he needed to be able to focus before someone got hurt.

"Ye'll be wanting a tray in yer room?" Robbie had an uncanny ability to walk down the marble floors from the kitchens without making a sound.

Bas had an urge to punch him for making him jump. "Yes, if it's not too much trouble. I'm going to put a bell on your ass if you scare the hell out of me again."

"Bollocks. Ye've seen the witch and didn't run screaming. Not much scares ye, I think."

"You'd be surprised," Bas muttered as he started up the stairs.

"Sir?" Well, that was new. Robbie had left off calling him sir a while ago.

"Yeah, Robbie?"

"Are ye the forgiving sort?"

Bas turned around and stared at the young footman. "What kind of question is that?"

"An easy enough one, I should think. Are ye the sort to forgive a man for making a horrible mistake?"

"You drop my dinner tray, and you're going to find out." It was his day for weird conversations. Something in Robbie's face made Bas answer differently. "I try to be forgiving, Robbie. I really do. Why?"

"Good. I'll go fetch yer dinner."

Bas continued on to his room and vowed not to go anywhere near the door between his room and Teddy's. There was so much going on his mind. If he knocked on that door he'd be too damned weak to resist whatever Teddy offered him. Even if all Teddy offered was scraps. Bas couldn't settle for that. He wouldn't. Not again.

For some reason, after he'd picked over his dinner, read some of Anna Chase's book, the latest script from Wentworth, and actually crawled into bed, Bas had slept like a rock. Well, once Teddy stopped moving around in the room next door and talking and arguing with someone. Eventually, the noise stopped, and Bas finally fell asleep. Good thing too. If he hadn't, he'd have spent the entire night wondering what was going on on the other side of the dressing room. More important, with whom it was going on.

He stood at the base of the ruined walls of the old castle and assessed the angle of the airbag directly ahead. He shoved on his sunglasses against the glare of the sunlight in the clear Highland sky. They'd been at it all morning. After a brief break for lunch, they were back at the castle trying to get things right. Still. He didn't get it. His crew kept making the same mistakes over and over again. These were his best guys. Even in period kilts and boots, they didn't screw up. Until today.

"Is it just me or is everyone and his brother out here?" Bas asked Danny, who was getting wired up to do a practice fall from the top of the castle walls.

"Maybe." The actor raised his arms for Mike to check the harness.

"Maybe? That's all I get from Mr. Big Mouth Action Star? Maybe?"

"Yep." The bastard, decked out in his breeches and boots, grinned at him.

"Don't let Eleanor hear you say *yep*. She'll have a, what do you call it? A fit of the vapors?" Hadrian jotted down notes in a journal with a stubby antique pencil. These people had taken their Regency experience to a whole new level.

"Why would Eleanor hear him?" Bas walked with Danny and Hadrian toward the staging area. "She never—" *What the fuck?* "Okay, you two. Care to explain why Eleanor *and* the duke are here along with the rest of you inmates from the Regency asylum?"

"Likely to defend you from those ruffians." Arneaux's British accent was spot on.

Hadrian just snorted and rolled his eyes.

"Who invited the asshole party?"Bas muttered.

Teddy's snotty friends, in full British regalia, stood next to the duke and Eleanor and pointed at various spots on the ruined castle walls.

"Who the hell wears tweed jackets in May?" Bas asked. Then he looked at Danny and Hadrian in their buckskin breeches, top boots, coats, vests, and white shirts with cravats up to their chins. "Forget I asked. Do I look like I need protection from them?" He flexed his chest and arms under his black t-shirt. "I may be wearing a skirt, but I'm not afraid of that bunch of Brits."

"I dare ye to call it a skirt in front of McGinty," a familiar voice said from behind him. "And I suspect my brother is looking for an excuse to punch at least one of them." Lord Lachlan stopped next to him and crossed his arms over his chest.

"I'm going to join the other ladies." Lily patted her husband's bicep and swished away in a way Bas suspected no Regency woman had ever walked, even in a dress as elegant as hers.

"She just wants a good view if the Brits piss off the duke," Danny said.

"Probably," Lachlan said in agreement.

Bas tried to shake off the feeling something was up. The hair on the back of his neck stood at attention. He scanned the area and did all he could to keep his expression neutral. Either he'd slipped into complete paranoia, or everyone—his crew, the boot campers, a number of the duke's staff—was sneaking little looks at him. He checked his kilt, front and back.

Well, it was a nice day, and Arneaux was going to be trying some cool stunts. Maybe that was the reason everyone had turned out. *Wait.* Everyone except…. A painful breath sighed through him. At least he wouldn't have to hear Teddy deny Bas's very existence in front of Teddy's father's friends. His father, the earl.

"What's so funny, boss?" Mike asked.

"Funny?"

"You just laughed. What's so funny?"

"Me, Mike. Me and this whole Scotland adventure. Let's commence torturing Arneaux."

The older man rubbed his hands together. "You're too good to me, boss."

"I hate all of you," Arneaux muttered as Mike led him away. "Next movie, I'm playing a Regency king so I can have you all beheaded."

The crew dispersed. Bas began his pre-stunt checks. The spectators moved back to gather beside an ancient knee-high remainder of wall along the cart path around the ruins. The crane dragged Danny off his feet and slowly raised him toward the free-standing castle parapet on the side of the ruins nearest the cart path. Once he was up there, a couple of Bas's guys unhooked him from the crane. They walked through the choreography while Bas went over his notes and barked out orders at the key members of the crew. He was busy as hell and tried not to pay much attention to the Rosemount contingent. He deliberately ignored the British hunting party.

An odd sensation tickled along the back of his neck. A lavender breeze swept by him, then died in an instant. He raised his head. Everyone's attention was on the castle ruins behind him. Sure they were. Danny always made a big show of doing his own stunts. His crew had gone silent.

"Okay, guys, what the hell is—"

He turned and his notes slipped from his fingers as he took in the remains of the first duke's home. Not the wall where Danny and Bas's crew members sat straddling the gaps in the crenellations, but beyond that where the intact tower stood. Standing at the top of the tower, hands braced on the ramparts in skin-tight Regency breeches, white shirt, and vest and jacket in a deep hunter green, stood Teddy. He had left his hair loose around his shoulders. Bas's mind went blank. He forgot everything and everyone around him.

"How did you get up there?" he shouted.

He could see the eyeroll from where he stood. "How do you think?"

"What are you doing up there? Does the duke know you've invaded his tower?" Bas glanced back at the duke. A sort of shock went through Bas when he remembered *everyone* who was observing him at the moment.

"I asked permission." Teddy's answer drew Bas's attention back to the tower.

"Why?"

"For this." Teddy pushed at something on the wall around the top of the tower. A white banner unfurled several feet. It took Bas a minute to realize there was writing on it in a beautiful florid script of letters at least a foot tall.

Bas's heart stuttered. Did that banner actually say—

"What—what—what is this?" He jabbed a finger at the banner.

Teddy propped one booted foot up aganst the stone barrier. "If the spelling is off, blame your sister," he shouted. "She helped me with it after I talked to your father."

"You talked to my— How the hell did you talk to my family?"

"I borrowed Lachlan's phone. God knows what Eleanor will have me doing to work off my boot camp demerits."

Bas stepped closer. He had to see Teddy's face as clearly as possible.

"Well?" Teddy propped his hands on his hips.

"Well what?"

"Is it spelled correctly?"

Bas forced his eyes back to the banner. His eyes hadn't lied. It said what he thought it said.

Maite zaitut.

Mesedez, eskondu nirekin.

I love you. Please, marry me.

Bas jerked his gaze onto Teddy. "Have you lost your mind?"

"Very likely. But withstanding that, will you?"

"Will I what?" Bas had never felt so dumb in his entire life.

"Will. You. Marry. Me?" Teddy shouted. "Oh. And by they way, I love you."

A loud murmer shot through the snotty Brits behind him.

"Why are you doing this, Teddy? This is just…insane."

"You're ruining my bloody grand gesture. You know that, right?"

Grand gesture? Bas wanted to laugh. Teddy sounded so pissed. Bas wanted to cry too, because God help him, Teddy sounded so sincere. Dangerously sincere.

"What the hell is a grand gesture?"

Teddy waved his arms around. "All of this, you great looby. Anna, is this supposed to go like this?"

Anna?

Bas whipped his head around. Anna was trying not to laugh. The rest of them? His crew? The other participants in the Regency boot camp? The servants? They were all in on it. Every last one of them, dammit. They stared at him expectantly. He turned back. He met Teddy's eyes. Every instant, good and bad, of the past few weeks played over in his head. What was it his *amona* always said? *When the gods want to punish you, they give you what you want.*

"How do I know you won't regret this?" Bas swallowed hard. "I would never want to become the one thing you wished you'd never done."

Somebody snickered. Teddy shook his head, but he was smiling.

"Bas, you're the one thing in life I will never regret. Even if you say no today. I will never regret you. It's also a little late for me to take this back. I mean, I just proposed to you

"Did you mean what *you* said?" Bas clasped Teddy's forearms and stared into his eyes as if by doing so he could detect the slightest doubt.

"Every word." Teddy appeared to hold his breath.

"Then you're damned right I'll marry you."

"What the bloody hell is going on here, Lord Staines? Does your father know about this?" Compton-Bowles, the arse, demanded.

The entire audience crowded around the side of the airbag, led by Teddy's father's friends.

"*This,*" Teddy said as he took Bas's hand, "is Bas Salazar, my fiancé. Bas, these are… no one. No one at all. And they were just leaving, I believe. Weren't they, Your Grace?"

The duke stepped through the crowd and stared down the members of the hunting party. "Indeed. Immediately, in fact. Urquhart?"

"Aye, Yer Grace?"

"Load them up and get them off the estate, if you please."

"Aye, Yer Grace.

"Do feel free to tell my father and all of London the news. It will save me the expense of announcing it in the *Times,*" Teddy called as Urquhart and a couple of the grooms dragged the Brits toward a waiting Land Rover.

A sudden silence fell.

"Bloody hell, Teddy," Arneaux finally said. "When you burn a bridge, you burn that bastard to ashes."

Laughter rippled through the crowd.

Teddy took Bas's hand and led him past their friends. "You burn a bridge because you never intend to cross it again. Everything I want and need is on this side. Why would I ever need that bridge again?"

Bas pulled him close. "Everything?"

"You. Always. Forever."

"If you don't kiss him, Bas, I will," Lily said.

"No, you won't, Lady Lachlan." Teddy grabbed the back of Bas's head and sealed their lips in one of those knee-shaking kisses Teddy did so well. Bas's heart stuttered and started with joy and fears and anticipation. This marriage wasn't going to be easy, but God, it would be worth it.

When they finally came up for air, the shouts and applause around them finally registered. Bas touched his forehead to Teddy's and grinned. They were both blushing like teenagers.

"I daresay champagne is in order," the duke said as he led them back to Rosemount Manor. "You will, of course, have the wedding here. I am certain there is at least one date in June Miss Witherspoon has not yet scheduled."

"Here?" Teddy sounded more than a little astonished. He didn't understand that these people had become family. Bas could help him with that.

"I insist." When they reached the house, the butler already had the doors open. "Ah, Abercrombie. Champagne, please, in the library." The duke offered Eleanor his arm. "Miss Witherspoon?"

Eleanor took the man's arm but made no attempt to hide her shock. Neither did everyone else. Robbie gave Bas and Teddy a thumbs up as he followed the duke up the stairs. Then he went back to collecting money from guests and fellow servants alike. Bas didn't want to think what the subject of this bet was. He turned back to Teddy, who stared, not at the crowd headed up to the library, but at the landing one floor up. Bas followed his gaze. A shadowy wisp of a figure stood gazing down at them.

"Thank you, Elsbeth," Bas whispered. Had his heart ever been as full as it was now?

"No," Teddy said as he put his arm around Bas's waist. "Thank *you*."

"For what, *nire bihotza?*"

"For not giving up on me." Teddy gave him a soft lingering kiss.

"I never will." Bas kissed him back.

"Get a room," Danny called from the landing. "But get your asses up here and drink this champagne first. Abercrombie uncorked the good stuff."

"The good stuff?" Teddy blinked as their kiss ended.

Bas smiled. "For the rest of our lives. Nothing but the good stuff."

SNEAK PEEK AT THE DUKE, THE WITCH, AND THE PARTY PLANNER

The Duke, the Witch, and the Party Planner

Talking the director of the hottest period film in a decade into shooting his movie at a Highland estate was a stroke of genius. Running the circus Eleanor Witherspoon calls a Regency boot camp intended to prepare the movie stars for filming might be just as brilliant an idea—if the duke of the estate wasn't such an arrogant, overbearing, cold-hearted ass...with the sexiest eyes, the hottest kiss, and hidden passion hot enough to thaw a Highland winter.

When Knox Innes's father dies, he sacrifices his life in London and accepts the title of Duke of Turra. That means returning to his father's bankrupt estate and facing the ghosts of his past. Literally. When his ghost comes to life in the sexy, red-haired Caribbean queen he hires to make Rosemount Manor solvent again, Knox fears everyone is right, and he truly is mad.

Surrounded by a troop of high-strung actors, temperamental Scots, the servants' betting pool, an ancient curse, and the Innes Witch, Knox and Eleanor fight their incendiary passion for each other. When dark secrets come to light, it seems history is doomed to repeat itself and Rosemount Manor is about to become another Innis heir's worst nightmare.

Chapter One

Rosemount Manor, Scotland

Twelve-year-old Knox let the expensive sheaf of stationary slip from his fingers. The letter fluttered to the library carpet as he drew his feet up onto the thick window seat cushion where he sat. He folded his arms on his raised knees, then rested his cheek there and gazed out the tall, mullioned windows that overlooked the back gardens. Lightning flashed in the gloaming sky and illuminated the hedges, flower beds, and statuary, then the garden plunged back into the fading grey of evening. Thunder shook the house. No mean feat with a place as large as Rosemount Manor. His chest tightened. *My home.* Nae. Not any longer.

"What's this? To Lord Knox Alexander Wallace Innes, Marquess of—"

"Bloody hell!" Knox nearly jumped out of his skin.

His brother, Lachlan, always moved so quietly as to frighten everyone in the house. Which was why he was always the one to steal treats from Mrs. Gordon's kitchens whilst Knox played lookout.

"It's a letter," Knox muttered without turning away from the view out the rainswept windows. "Father gave it to me when he called me on the carpet after supper."

The power flickered off, then back on again. Somewhere down the corridor a television blared to life. His mother hated the monstrous big screen his father had installed in the drawing room. But at least it kept Father occupied most of the time, and away from the rest of the family.

Lachlan bounced onto the window, the letter in hand. "What'd ye do this time?"

"Nothing." Knox continued to stare at the rain.

The thunder rolled closer and closer with each flash of lightning. A blur of white in the gardens below disappeared around the entrance to the maze. His heart did a little flip, but he refused to acknowledge a thing. He was done with Elsbeth and done with all the trouble she'd caused him.

At twelve, Knox was supposed to look and sound like an adult. His father told him so at least a dozen times a day. He was too old to speak Gaelic. He was too old to spend time with his old pony. He was too old to steal biscuits from the kitchens. He was too old to have an imaginary friend.

"Ye saw her again, didn't ye?" Lachlan always sounded far older than a mere eight years.

"Who?" He finally looked at his brother.

Lachlan chewed on his bottom lip and swiped at his nose with the back of his hand.

"Ye shouldn't talk about her. It only makes Father angry, and makes Mother cry."

"Father makes Mother cry, nae me. Nae Elsbeth."

Lightning lit the sky and a boom of thunder followed immediately.

Lachlan's eyes widened. He pulled his legs up into the window seat and wrapped his arms tight around his knees. "Don't s-say her name."

"She won't come, silly. She never does when I want her. When other people are around."

"That's because she's *yer* friend. That's why no one else can see her." Lachlan became the solemn little soldier again. The one who stood there perfectly still whilst their father raged at them for the slightest misdeed, real or imagined.

"No one will be seeing her anymore. I'm going away." Knox pried the letter from his brother's grip and smoothed it out against his raised knees. "That's what this letter says. They're sending me away to school in England."

"Why?" Lachlan snatched the letter back and started to read, his lips moving as he did.

"Because they think I'm mad and school will cure me." Knox shrugged. "Maybe it will."

"But yer not mad, are ye? Ye see her, the Innes Witch. She talks to ye."

"It doesn't matter. I'm leaving Rosemount in the morning."

"But I don't want ye to go away, Knox. Where is Eton? Is it very far away?"

"Yes. Very far. And I don't know when Father will let me return. I want ye to promise me something." Knox blinked hard against the sting of repressed tears.

"No. I won't." Lachlan's bottom lip trembled. "I don't want ye to go."

"We don't have a choice. Maybe in a few years they'll send ye to Eton too."

"I don't want to go to Eton. I want to stay in Scotland. I want to stay home, and I want ye to stay home too." Lachlan's voice grew tighter and higher. He was ready to cry and Knox didn't want him to cry because if Lachlan cried so would he. Sons of the Duke of Turra dinnae cry. Ever.

"Well, yer not in charge and neither am I. We don't have a choice, and I want ye to promise me something right now.

Father won't let ye see me off. He's already said so. Promise me."

"I don't want to." Lachlan raised his chin and poked out his bottom lip.

"I'll let ye have my longbow." His brother continued to glare at him like one of the sheep in the high meadows, refusing to come down for the winter. "And all of the sweets in the trunk under my bed."

"All of them?" Lachlan's face brightened.

"Yes."

"What do ye want me to promise?"

"Promise me ye'll look after Gaisgeach." Knox's throat went dry. Even the thought of leaving the pony on which he'd learned to ride made him want to cry. "He likes Mrs. Gordon's oat cakes and lemon biscuits. Promise me ye'll visit him every day, and ye'll nae let Father sell him." Knox extended a hand.

Lachlan clasped his hand and shook it hard. "I promise. What about Nero?" Trust Lachlan to ask after Knox's hunter, the horse he was currently riding.

Knox still gripped his brother's hand. "Urquhart says Father has already arranged for him to be sent to Eton in a few weeks. Ye look after Geechy and the dogs. Agreed?"

Lachlan shook his hand again. "Agreed."

Knox released him and they both returned their attention to the storm. Knox spotted the figure in white at the edge of the maze. She moved in the direction of the terrace steps to the main house. He forced himself not to react. Lachlan was afraid of Elsbeth. Knox was afraid of her as well, but for completely different reasons. The French doors at the far end of the library rattled.

Lachlan gasped and grabbed Knox's hand. "She's here, isn't she?" he whispered, eyes wide and his face pale.

"Go to bed, Lachlan. I'll come up in a bit."

"Ye won't go without saying goodbye, right?"

"Right. Leave yer lamp on."

"On yer honor?"

Knox snorted at their old vow, the one they'd used when they played Knights of the Round Table in the fields beyond the stables. "On my honor. Go on now."

Lachlan scrambled off the window seat and, eyes on the French doors, padded quickly out of the library. Knox sighed and turned back to the show the Highland storm provided as it rolled across the estate. He wanted to cry. Badly.

Rosemount was all he'd ever known. And when his parents weren't in residence, he and Lachlan were happy. They had the run of the estate. Everyone from Mrs. Wallace, the housekeeper, to Abercrombie, the butler, to McGinty, the estate steward, had a hand in raising him and his brother. They'd been indulged but not spoiled. A series of tutors and governesses had come and gone. Their educations had been haphazard, but good. Why couldn't they go on like that forever?

Money. His father spent too much of the estate's earnings on his women and parties.

Revenge. His mother was determined to take her anger at Father out on all of them.

Elsbeth. Which meant this was all his own fault.

"You're too old for this nonsense. I'll not have people thinking my son is a mad boy who talks to ghosts," his father had railed earlier that day. *"I never should have allowed this to go on for so long. A few years in a good English boarding school will knock this notion of imaginary friends and Highland witches right out of your head."*

Father paced back and forth across his study rug, and as he did spittle gathered like foam at the corner of his mouth. His face went bright red.

Still Knox persisted. "I cannae help it if she appears to me.

I dinnae ask to see her. I dinnae want to go to England. I want to stay here."

His father's slap came so fast Knox didn't register the attack until he fell to the carpet. The hot sting across his cheek and the painful brush of the carpet across both knees, bared by his kilt blurred his vision.

"You will go to Eton, and you will not embarrass me with this talk of ghosts. You will stay in England until the English drive every bit of this Highland superstition from your head."

Knox raised his head and met his father's furious gaze. "And if they don't?"

"Then you won't be coming home until I'm dead and you're the duke."

Knox rose. "Done." He stuck out his hand, his head raised in defiance, and his knees knocking beneath his kilt.

Knox still couldn't believe he'd defied his father in such a way. The old bastard shook his hand and sent him out of the study like any other servant. That's what he was, a servant. He'd been born to two people who hated each other but had to carry on a name and a lineage he'd grown to hate. So, he'd go to England. He'd become English. He'd study architecture like he'd always dreamed and he'd never come back to the Highlands. Lachlan loved Scotland. He could be the duke. He could run the estate and carry on the family name. Knox was never coming back as long as he lived. Ghosts haunted places, not people. He'd leave his parents, Scotland, and the bloody Innes Witch behind and live the life *he* wanted. They'd see. He'd show them all. He would never—

"*Mo thighearna.*"

The French doors blew open and brought the icy wind and rain into the library.

"Go away." Knox continued to study the gardens. He tightened his arms around his knees.

"I am here to say farewell."

"Farewell. Now go away."

"Look at me, mo thighearna. Or are ye afraid?"

Knox unfolded himself from the window seat and turned slowly to face the spectral figure who glided toward him not quite touching the antique carpets. Her red hair shimmered in tight curls across her shoulders and down to her waist. Her skin appeared a golden brown in spite of her pallor. Elsbeth Dunhomme, the Innes Witch, had been his friend and companion for as long as he could remember. He'd never let the fact she'd been dead for hundreds of years stand in the way of their friendship. Until now.

"I'm leaving, Elsbeth, and I'm nae coming back." He stood as straight and tall as possible.

"Are ye now?" She smiled and shook her head.

"I am, and I want yer word on something."

"Oh?"

"Stay away from Lachlan. He's afraid of ye, and he'll nae understand why yer here. Yer word on it?"

"On my honor," she said, and her eerie laughter floated around the room.

"I mean it, dammit. Leave him alone." He had to be mad, arguing with a ghost.

"Yer the one leaving him alone with yer parents. And I meant what I said. I'll nae bother the lad."

"Good."

Knox clasped his hands behind his back and rocked on his heels a few times. For the first time since she'd shown up in his bedchamber to comfort him during a storm very like the one hammering Rosemount Manor now, Knox didn't know what to say.

"'Tis well, mo thighearna, I'll wait. I've waited this long." She came closer and the air around him grew bone-chilling cold.

"Wait for what? I mean it, Elsbeth. I'll nae return. I'll nae see ye again."

"As ye say. I can wait." With that she faded away into the darkness at the far end of the library. The French doors closed quietly behind her.

"For what?" he murmured as he gathered the stack of books he'd pulled from the library shelves to take with him.

"For ye, mo thighearna. For ye." Her voice came out of the darkness.

Knox shivered and hurried out of the library and up the stairs. He had to talk to Lachlan and then he had to pack to leave Rosemount Manor and Elsbeth forever.

Chapter Two

Rosemount Manor, Scotland
Mid-January, twenty years later

KNOX INNES, DUKE OF TURRA, FISHED AROUND IN THE POCKET of his heavy wool coat and pulled out yet another of the apples he'd filched from Mrs. Gordon's pantry. He offered it on his flattened palm to the old Shetland who'd been nudging his pocket for the last ten minutes. Urquhart, Rosemount's horse master, tutted at him and turned to give one of the lads some instructions about the horse in the next stall.

"Ye spoil that worthless old blighter, Yer Grace. He's gone ta fat, he has," Urquhart said without turning back to him.

"Leave be, Urquhart." Angus McGinty lumbered into the stables and kicked the snow off his boots before he came to stand next to Knox. "That old pony has earned a bit of spoiling. Teaching this hard-headed lout to ride."

"True enough," Urquhart muttered as he turned, touched his cap, and shuffled deeper into Rosemount's massive stable block.

"Is that any way to speak about a duke?" Knox asked.

"'Tis, when ye've changed the duke's nappies." McGinty's grin faded almost the moment it arrived on the bear of a man's wrinkled face. "She's here."

"Who?"

McGinty rolled his eyes. "Ye know who. The American woman. Miss…Witherspoon."

"Ms. Witherspoon."

McGinty loosed a particularly vile Gaelic curse. "Whoever she is, she's here with enough bags for an invading army, some *mòr* of a glass cage, and she wants to speak with *His Grace* before she starts preparing the house for whatever Sassenach nonsense that rich American director is paying for."

"Dear God." Knox ran a hand through his hair, gave the pony a last pat, then walked slowly out of the stable block. "Can't you deal with her, McGinty? You're my steward. I agreed to whore out my house and estate for this abomination. Do I really need to talk to these people?"

"Yer not whoring Rosemount out. You're repairing the harm yer father did the best way ye know how. There's hardly a laird in England or Scotland who has nae done something like this ta bring a bit of money in to keep his people in the black." McGinty clapped his bear paw of a hand onto Knox's shoulder and held him in place. "You've done well these last years since the Lord took yer father. Ye've saved our home and the jobs of most of the people in two counties."

Knox tried to look away.

"Ye've nothing to be ashamed of and ye know it. Even if no one else knows, I know what ye gave up ta come back here and save Rosemount." The old Scot gave his shoulder a last squeeze and they continued across the cobblestoned stable yard.

"The Lord wouldn't touch my father with a tabor. The devil took the old bastard and I hope he's roasting in hell. I didn't have much of a choice about coming back now, did I?" He shoved his hands into his coat pockets and hunched his shoulders as they walked into the bitter Highland wind that whipped up the path to the manor.

"Ye could have left it ta your brother."

McGinty didn't mean a word of what he'd just suggested. They both knew it too.

"No, I couldn't."

His brother had returned from the battlefields of the Middle East and gone to ground in the wilds of the estate like one of the foxes their father used to hunt. Knox's choice had been to stay in London and run his successful architecture firm or to return to Scotland and save an estate on the brink of complete financial destruction, thanks to his father.

"But I still don't want to talk to this…party planner, is it? I can think of a great many things to call this little money-making scheme, but a bloody party isn't one of them. You talk to her." They reached the corner of the manor and headed across the main drive to the front of the house.

"You'll have to talk to her eventually. Ye cannae avoid the woman for an entire year or more."

Knox stopped in his tracks. The wind had to be playing with his hearing. He clapped the heel of his hand against his ear a few times. McGinty looked at him as if he'd run mad.

"A year? A year!" His voice echoed across the circular drive, in front of the manor's monstrous front doors. "This is supposed to be a three-month Jane Austen house party, or some such utter nonsense. Who said anything about having Americans running loose in my home for a fucking year?"

"Actually, you did, Your Grace," a distinctly feminine voice, accompanied by the crunch of footsteps, announced her presence behind him. "When you signed the contracts I sent you after your conversation with Mr. Wentworth?"

Knox turned smartly on his heel to face the person who approached him from around the fountain in the middle of the drive. "Have you lost your bloody—"

His throat closed tight around his words. His blood drained to his feet so quickly he strained to hear the splash of water in the fountain. His heart thundered in his ears like the Edinburgh Tattoo. The world in his vision faded to a narrow strip of cobblestones between him and the apparition walking toward him. She appeared as if down a dark corridor of memory.

The woman was tall, though not as tall as him. She was slender with long elegant limbs. Her skin was a golden bronze color and her hair, caught up in a neon flowered cloth band that matched the floral pink, orange, and yellow pattern of her ankle-length frilly skirt, curled in a mass of ringlets of several shades of red and gold past her shoulders. She wore a bright pink entirely-too-thin-for-the-Highlands sweater. A large leather satchel that matched the material of her butterscotch boots hung over her shoulder. None of that mattered. Although somewhere in the far reaches of his scrambled brains the image of a 1960's flower child came to mind.

Knox closed his eyes tightly, counted to ten, and opened them again. He hadn't done that since he was a very young lad. Didn't help. Her face and hair remained the same. Each and every delicate line was a combination of Caribbean beauty and Highland strength. Her hair was a tumbled mass of taut curls in the golden red he'd thought unbelievably magical as a child. They were the face and hair, the woman, of his childhood memories. Now even he believed he had finally run mad. There was no other plausible explanation.

She stopped a few steps away and executed a very formal curtsy. McGinty elbowed him, though Knox hardly felt it. She extended a hand and glanced at his steward expectantly.

"Yer Grace," MacGinty's voice fairly boomed. "May I present *Ms.—*"

Knox reached out before the move even registered. "Els—"

"Eleanor Witherspoon," McGinty finished. He gave Knox a nudge and a stern look.

She took his hand. Knox started as if struck by lightning. Once her dainty fingers wrapped around his, he couldn't let go.

"I'm very pleased to finally meet you, Your Grace. I'm so looking forward to us working together." She smiled and his heart stuttered to a stop.

This had to be a dream or a nightmare or some wicked combination of both.

Knox dropped her hand, gave her a curt nod and, with no thought to the shame he was doing his Highland ancestors, spun, and walked one degree below a run into the house and straight up the stairs to his study. He was sure the shocked expression he'd glimpsed on her face in the instant before he'd turned followed hard on his heels. The memory kept him up half the night. He finally gave up just before first light and sat up on the side of the massive ducal bed. The wind howled like a scorned woman against the long windows next to his nightstand. He said the name he'd not even thought of since he'd left Rosemount as a child.

"Elsbeth?"

The wind only shrieked all the louder.

ELEANOR GLANCED OVER HER SHOULDER ONCE MORE AS SHE ascended the grand staircase behind Mrs. Wallace, the duke's housekeeper. The duke in question had disappeared like a date who'd been presented the check at a high-end restaurant after she'd told said date he wasn't getting any that night. Was it something she'd said? He hadn't given her the chance to say much. She gave her armpit a surreptitious sniff as she reached the first-floor landing and turned up the next staircase.

Her deodorant was still holding. Check.

She was decently dressed. Check.

She hadn't said anything rude or condescending or nosy. Check.

Then what the hell was the Duke of Turra's problem? He'd looked at her so strangely. Then he'd grasped her hand, held tightly for several seconds, then dropped it like a lit firecracker. Why had he done that?

Another staircase and a long corridor later, the poker-faced housekeeper finally stopped in front of a set of double doors. She pushed the doors open and strode into the room like a drill sergeant.

"Your rooms, Miss Witherspoon. I hope you will be comfortable." Mrs. Wallace paced to the huge fireplace and flicked a long piece of brocade with a tassel at the end. The bell pull if Eleanor remembered right. "If you need anything pull this and one of the maids or footmen will be up in a few minutes." She folded her hands at the waist of the stiff white apron she wore over an even more stiff black dress. "Is there anything you require?"

"Uhm," Eleanor stared as she turned in a slow circle and took in the gorgeous antique furniture in the room. "The bed? Where would the bed be?"

"This is your private sitting room." Mrs. Wallace pointed to another set of doors to the right. "Your bedchamber is in there. Robbie and Dougal have brought up your luggage and your…pet." Most people had to suck down a whole basket of lemons to muster up a pucker like the one the duke's house-keeper was wearing. Then again, Persephone, who went with Eleanor wherever she traveled, wasn't everyone's idea of a normal pet.

"Good. Thank you. I can't think of anything I need right now."

Mrs. Wallace inclined her head and turned to go.

"Mrs. Wallace?"

The older woman turned back. "Yes, Miss Witherspoon?"

"Has the duke told you what will be going on here for the next months and then the rest of the year? I mean, about the boot camp and the movie being filmed?"

"His Grace does not discuss his business with me outside of my running the house. Why do you ask?"

"He just seems kind of pissed I'm here to be perfectly honest. Make that very pissed."

A series of emotions flickered across the stoic woman's face. "I'm sure I wouldn't know." She nodded again and walked to the still open doors. "But you may be assured if Himself *is* pissed, as you say, you'll have no cause to doubt it." She stood with a hand on each of the two doors' handles and smiled. "No cause at all."

"Well, that's not scary as fuck," Eleanor muttered once the housekeeper was gone. She went to check out her bedroom next door. "Oh, hello." She stepped into the bedroom to find two young men in kilts, white shirts and black vests eying Persephone's specially designed travel crate as if they expected her to pop out and chase them down the stairs.

"Miss Witherspoon?" the dark-haired one asked.

"Of course she's Miss Witherspoon," the red-haired one said. "Who else would she be?" The two of them elbowed each other.

The travel-crate rattled and they took a step back. Eleanor tried not to laugh. Then she got a look at the room.

"Damn. Is there any room in this house that isn't fabulous?"

Everything from the four-poster bed-curtained bed to the antique carpets covering the floor to the wardrobe and highboy and other furnishings screamed "My family has been rich for generations." She couldn't believe she'd be spending the next year or so here.

The Innes clan has lived here for over five hundred years," the dark-haired one said. "Plenty of time to decorate. I'm Robbie, by the way."

"And I'm Dougal," the other one said as he blushed bright red.

"I'm Eleanor Witherspoon." She shook each of their hands in turn. "I see the guy from Edinburgh has Persephone's home all set up." She inspected the spacious floor to ceiling glass case very carefully. The temperature gauges indicated the perfect levels of heat and humidity. The various branches and platforms were in the exact right positions. Of course, she had sent the man carefully worded instructions on how to put the habitat together correctly.

"Oh, aye," Robbie said. "He left his card and asked that you call him. He wants to know who designed this…habitat." The footman pulled the card from his vest and handed it to Eleanor. She tucked the card into her bag and tossed the bag onto the huge bed.

"Come on, sweetie," she said as she opened the travel crate. "Let's get you settled." She pulled an undulating section of her albino python out and handed the thick coils to Dougal who didn't step back quickly enough. "Here, Robbie, take this." She turned around to find the poor guy frozen in place, save for the frantic shaking of his head. "She won't hurt you. I can't lift all of her myself. See, Dougal's doing it." She glanced at the other footman whose face had gone white as a sheet. "Oh, for God's sake, boys, don't tell me you've never seen a snake before." She gave them a wicked grin.

Robbie snickered. Dougal looked ready to faint. She pulled the rest of her pet from the crate and took control of the snake's head as she walked over to open the glass case. She fed Persephone onto the first climbing branch and the snake immediately crawled into the habitat in search of the platform in front of one of the heat lamps. Eleanor and Dougal supported her body until she fully slithered inside the habitat.

Dougal swayed on his feet. Eleanor guided him into a beautiful brocade upholstered chair. "Put your head between your knees. You'll be fine."

"She's orange," Robbie observed as he stepped close to the glass enclosure. "How much does she weigh?"

"She's an albino, a mutation, that's why she's orange. She weighed in at 120 pounds at the airport."

"Does Himself know about the snake?" Dougal asked when he finally raised his head and took on a better color.

"In theory? Yes."

The two footmen looked at each other and grinned.

"What?" Eleanor narrowed her eyes and tried to figure out what was so damned funny. "Is Persephone going to piss him off? Apparently, my presence here has already pissed him off, if the way he ran away after our introduction as if his kilt was on fire is any indication."

"Why? What did he say?" Robbie asked as he pulled Dougal to his feet and headed toward the door.

"He didn't say anything. He shook my hand, dropped it like I had leprosy, and ran." Eleanor tried not to sound insulted or hurt. She was actually shocked at how much his behavior stung.

"Trust me, miss," Dougal said. "If Himself were angry with you, you'd know it."

Robbie nodded so vigorously she half expected him to cross himself. They nodded to her and promptly left the room.

"What the hell have I gotten myself into?" Eleanor toed off her boots and started toward the fireplace to warm her feet. As she crossed the thick carpet, she spotted movement from one of the tall windows along the far wall of the bedroom. The duke. She recognized the walk, especially as he was walking away from the house just like he'd walked away from her. She went to the window and settled onto the cushioned window seat.

There was something familiar about his walk, something familiar about him, as if she'd met him before. She hadn't. She knew that. Still, his reaction to her was odd and she wished like hell she knew why. He wasn't a willing participant in her regency boot camp idea, nor in the idea of a period film taking up residence on his estate for at least a year. Tough shit. He was broke, and he needed the money. Himself's title was useless without money. Which was why he'd hired her, an event planner with no major event planning experience, to come up with a scheme to save Rosemount Manor.

She might be dependent on his grumpy grace's goodwill for her first big job as an independent event planner, but he needed her too. Eleanor watched as he strode out of the gardens below her window and into the fields beyond. Like something out of the period film that was about to be filmed at Rosemount Manor, he strode away head up, shoulders back. Which was why when he stopped and looked back at the house, she nearly fell out of the window seat. He was looking directly at the window where she sat. For a minute she wanted to duck down out of sight.

The hell with that.

She stood and braced her hands on either side of the window and stared back at him in the distance. He didn't look away.

She'd say it again. "What the hell have I gotten myself into?"

www.scarsdalepublishing.com

Rosemount Manor
LOVE REGENCY STYLE

Cajun in a Kilt

Sassenach in Stilettos

Critic with a Claymore

The Stuntman and the Swordmaster

The Duke the Witch and the Party Planner

Stay tuned for the next Rosemount Manor series THE PRICE
OF LOVE

To keep up on all the Rosemount Manor romances and all our other
great books join our Newsletter

Stay tuned for the next Rosemount Manor series

THE PRICE OF LOVE

Trademark Acknowledgements

Love Connection
Dungeons and Dragons
Cadbury's Chocolate
Braveheart
Waterloo: Four Days that Changed Europe's Destiny by Tim
Clayton
Google
High Noon
Land Rover
Pop Rocks
Tylenol
Marvel